PRAISE FOR THE NOVELS
OF LORELEI JAMES

"Her sexy cowboys are to die for!"
—*New York Times* Bestselling Author Maya Banks

"Lorelei James knows how to write one hot, sexy cowboy." —*New York Times* Bestselling Author Jaci Burton

"The down-and-dirty, rough-and-tumble Blacktop Cowboys kept me up long past my bedtime. Scorchingly hot, wickedly naughty."
—Lacey Alexander, author of *Give In to Me*

"She's the queen of cowboy romance."
—Happily Ever After-Reads

"Hang on to your cowboy hats because this book is scorching hot!" —Romance Junkies

"Lorelei James knows how to write fun, sexy, and hot stories." —Joyfully Reviewed

continued . . .

SADDLED AND SPURRED

A BLACKTOP COWBOYS® NOVEL

LORELEI JAMES

A SIGNET BOOK

SIGNET
Published by the Penguin Group
Penguin Group (USA) LLC, 375 Hudson Street,
New York, New York 10014

USA | Canada | UK | Ireland | Australia | New Zealand | India | South Africa | China
penguin.com
A Penguin Random House Company

Published by Signet, an imprint of New American Library, a division of Penguin
Group (USA) LLC. Previously published in a Signet Eclipse edition.

First Signet Printing, June 2014

 REGISTERED TRADEMARK—MARCA REGISTRADA

ISBN 978-0-451-46812-3

Printed in the United States of America
10 9 8 7 6 5 4 3 2 1

PUBLISHER'S NOTE
This is a work of fiction. Names, characters, places, and incidents either are the
product of the author's imagination or are used fictitiously, and any resemblance
to actual persons, living or dead, business establishments, events, or locales is
entirely coincidental.

Chapter One

∽

"**You**'re firing me?" Harper Masterson stared at her boss.

Alice Samuels, owner of the Tan Your Hide beauty emporium, jammed a darkly tanned hand through her salt-and-pepper curls. "Harper, honey, it ain't nothin' personal. People ain't spending money on luxuries, like maintaining a year-round tan and buying customized facial products, when the economy is in the toilet. I gotta close up shop. Truth is, I should've done this a few months ago, but I knew . . ."

That you needed the job.

Harper bit the inside of her cheek, hard, to keep from crying—a trick she'd learned from her older sister, Liberty. "I appreciate all you've done for me, Alice."

"I know you do. You've still got your job at Get Nailed, right?"

She nodded absentmindedly. She'd taken the job at Tan Your Hide last year because working part-time as a nail technician wasn't paying the bills after the Tumbleweed Motel had closed for the season and she'd lost her job cleaning rooms. For the hundredth time Harper cursed her mother for taking off. She cursed this town for its limited opportunities. She cursed herself for the lack of schooling that would've given her a wider range of choices.

"Harper? You okay? You're awful quiet."

Harper glanced at Alice, but she couldn't muster even a small smile. "I'll be fine. What are you going to do now?"

"Roger is coming tomorrow to load the tanning beds. I got a line on a place in Casper that wants them. I'll keep my inventory of beauty products and sell 'em outta my house."

"Does the landlord have another renter lined up?" But it was probably too much for Harper to hope that another business would move into Muddy Gap, which boasted less than a dozen businesses—total.

Alice shook her head. "I'm afraid we'll have another empty storefront. Sad, how this town is dyin'."

Dying? This town had been dead since the day Harper's mother had dragged them here. Problem was, Harper was stuck, at least for another few months, until her younger sister, Bailey, graduated from high school. Then Bailey could realize her dream of attending college. Since Bailey had been through so much in the last year and a half, Harper didn't want to add more stress by admitting that she'd lost yet another low-paying job.

Three months. Harper needed to find work for just a little over three months. Then they both could shake the Wyoming sage off their shoes and move on with their lives.

She gave the space one last, wistful look. "I'll miss this place." She glanced at her boss, even more misty-eyed. "Mostly I'll miss you, Alice." Harper removed the front door key from her key ring, set it on the glass-topped counter, and snagged her winter coat from the closet.

As Harper untangled the fringe at the end of her fuchsia scarf, Alice said, "Wait. I have something for you," and handed her a slip of paper.

Harper squinted at the paycheck, written out in Alice's flowery scrawl. The amount was a hundred dollars off. She passed it back. "You made a mistake. This is too much."

Alice squeezed Harper's hand. "Consider it severance pay."

She waffled, hating to take charity in any form, but the reality was . . . she needed the cash.

"Please," Alice said.

Pride wouldn't pay the bills. "Okay. Thanks."

"You're welcome." Alice leaned in to hug Harper, enveloping her in the scent of Emeraude perfume. "Take care of yourself, Miss Harper. We'll see each other again. Muddy Gap ain't that big."

And that was the biggest problem.

∾

The bitter January wind stung Harper's cheeks as she trudged to the small rented cottage she called home. Numb, not only from the weather but with dismay, she went on autopilot and fixed herself a cup of tea. Donning her robe and slippers, she curled into the couch and gazed out the window as she mentally listed the businesses in Muddy Gap.

Buckeye Joe's, the only bar in town.

The Horseshoe Diner, the lone restaurant in town.

Dunlap's, the only feed store and gas station in town.

C-Mart, the sole convenience/grocery store in town.

Danke Law Office.

The Tumbleweed Motel, the only motel in town.

Bernice's Beauty Barn, the lone hair salon, which also housed Get Nailed, the only nail salon in town.

McMasters Farmers Union Insurance, the only insurance agency in town.

Wyoming First Credit Union, the only bank in town.

The Methodist Church.

The Lutheran Church.

The Baptist Church.

The Catholic Church.

Yeah, Harper's options were limited. Severely limited.

Susan Williams, owner of Buckeye Joe's, would never hire her, since Harper's mother, Dawn, the former cocktail waitress at Buckeye Joe's, had run off to Mexico with Susan's husband, Mac, eighteen months ago.

Genie Lewdonsky, owner of the Horseshoe Diner, would never hire her, since Harper beat out Genie's only daughter, Mariah, for the title of Miss Carbon County. And homecoming queen. And prom queen. Harper's last-minute entry in the Miss Sweet Grass contest irked Mariah—and her mother—especially after Harper won the crown.

Bruce Dunlap, owner of Dunlap's Feed, would never hire her, since Harper's mother snuck off with Mac when she was supposedly "in love" and involved with Bruce.

Ralph Doughtery, manager of the C-Mart, would hire her only if she dated him—aka bedded him. Since the man covered his bald head with a cheap toupee and his teeth resembled those fake "Billy Bob" kind found around Halloween, that wasn't happening. Oh, and he'd run around with her skanky ho of a mother too.

Danke Law Office was open only one day a week.

McMasters Farmers Union Insurance was a family-run operation. Unless she married Jimbo McMasters, the fortysomething only son everyone in town suspected was gay, she couldn't even fetch coffee for them.

According to local gossip, Wyoming First Credit Union hadn't hired a single new employee in the last twenty years.

The Tumbleweed wouldn't reopen until June.

And she already worked for Bernice.

Harper doubted any of the churches in town would let her heathen hands even scrub their toilets.

Her head fell back onto the couch cushions. She stared at the dingy, rust-stained ceiling tiles. No doubt she'd have to drive to Rawlins to find work. Which could be problematic, with Bailey's school schedule and the fact that they had only one car. Luckily Bailey was staying overnight with her friend Amy—Harper was glad Bailey wasn't around to see her panic and distress.

Sad that her life had always run parallel to one of those down-on-her-luck country songs.

Her cell phone jangled, startling her out of her morose musings, and she dug in her purse until she found it. "Hello?"

"Do you have any idea how fucking boring it is driving across Texas? My God. And people think there's nothin' to see in Wyoming? Dude. This stretch of road is like the highway to hell. Seriously."

Her friend Celia Lawson seemed to have a sixth sense, knowing when Harper needed to talk. "Texas, huh? Isn't that out of your circuit?"

"Yep. I'm heading to Tanna Barker's for a few days. Her vet is gonna look at Mickey's leg before we hit the next event."

After sneaking around for a few years on the local rodeo circuit, Celia finally had her brothers' blessing to chase her dream of becoming a world champion barrel racer. The new rodeo season commenced in January, and Celia was determined that this year she'd make it to the American Finals Rodeo in Las Vegas. "It's still giving him problems?"

"Some. It hasn't affected my performance yet, but I wanna make sure it's nothin' serious. And it'll be a while before I get back up there so Eli can take a look at it."

"How long is a while?"

"At least a month. Why? Do ya miss me?"

"No."

Celia laughed. "Liar. So what's up with you?"

That's when Harper completely broke down. Her words were an incoherent jumble as she sobbed. Through a bout of hiccups, she mumbled, "Sorry. I didn't mean to unload."

"Now you've really got me worried because you never cry."

"It's different this time, Cele. I've used up every bit of grant money I had left over. I wasn't making much at the tanning salon, but some was better than none. And we both know why no one in town will hire me."

Celia was quiet on the other end of the line—a rarity for her.

"So because our rent is so cheap here and we're close to Bailey's school, I'll have to find a job in Rawlins. Probably in a bar or supper club so the nighttime hours won't interfere with Bailey's schedule."

Again Celia didn't respond.

Maybe she was put off by your babbling.

"Celia? You still there?"

"Yeah. Just thinkin'. Tossing a couple of things around." Another pause. "You ain't opposed to workin' outside, are you?"

Harper bit her lip to keep from bawling. Good-hearted Celia would call her brothers and line up work on their ranch. While that was above and beyond, Harper had enough problems holding her head up in this town. "Look, Celia—"

"Can that tone, Harper. Jeez. I'm not gonna ask Abe

and Hank to hire you, but there might be another option. So do you have a problem with ranch work?"

Should she admit she had no idea what "ranch work" entailed? No. She'd hear Celia's proposal first. "No problem with it. Why?"

"Sit tight. I've got a call to make and then I'll call you right back."

The line went dead, and Harper wondered what Celia was up to. It wasn't like she had anything else to do but wait and find out.

∞

Bran Turner ignored his cell phone the first time it rang. And the second. At the third attempt, he just picked the fucking thing up and snarled, "What?"

"Jesus, Bran. You always this grumpy first thing in the morning?"

"I am when I just fell into bed two hours ago."

"Up late partyin', were you?"

"Fuck off. I was up late calving."

She laughed. "Oh, I see. That's why you're in such a pissy mood. You fell into bed all by your lonesome."

"Like that's news. Is there a point to this call, little girl? Or you just bored and needin' someone to harass?"

"'Little girl,'" Celia snorted. "For the record, I'm twenty-three. And the raunchy things I've seen against the pickups, in the horse trailers, and behind the chutes, traveling the circuit? Dude. They'd even make *you* blush."

"Doubtful." Bran rolled flat on his back. His buddy Hank's little sister, Celia, suffered from loneliness on the road to rodeo glory and phoned him from time to time just to shoot the shit. But this didn't feel like one of those calls. "Is this your way of asking me for advice on how to spice up your sex life? Or do you want a personal demonstration?" He grinned. That oughta get the hellcat's back up.

"No. Like I'd ask you for advice, you fuckin' pervert," she retorted. "Hank'd castrate you if you laid a hand on me."

"True. It'd feel incestuous, bein's I've known you since you were toddling around in diapers."

"Story of my life. I'm trying to make up for lost booty time, since all the hot, hunky cowboys I grew up around refuse to see me as a woman. But I'm changin' that. Just you watch."

Bran frowned. Sounded like Celia had a specific cowboy in mind.

Before he could demand names or remind her to be careful, she said, "Look, here's the deal. I know you're busting ass, doin' everything yourself since Les's accident."

"And?"

"And I know from talking to Hank that no one's applied for the job as your temporary hired hand."

A freak accident with an ornery bull had left Bran's hired man, Les, with a busted hip and out of commission during the busiest part of the year in the cattle business. It sucked on a number of levels. Not only did he feel guilty about Les's injury, but he couldn't permanently replace the guy while he was healing up. Which meant whoever Bran hired would have the job only until Les was back on his feet.

Muddy Gap wasn't exactly a hotbed of job prospects— even when the job paid well. Word of mouth among his friends and other ranchers hadn't yielded any applicants. Putting an ad in the *Muddy Gap Gazette*, which reached four other communities? That was pointless too. Not a single man had applied. Bran had resigned himself to doing everything alone and just dealing with the exhaustion.

"Bran? Did you fall asleep?" Celia demanded.

"No. Just trying to figure out what you're up to."

"Why are you so suspicious when I'm just bein' a good neighbor?"

He snorted. "Because I know you, Celia. You lie."

"I do not! Name one time."

"How about all those times you kept the fact you were competitively barrel racing a secret from your brothers? For over three years?"

"Which only means I'm good at keeping secrets from people I love for their own good," she replied sweetly.

"You are very manipulative, especially if you get something out of it."

"I am not! Name one time I've manipulated you."

"How about right now?"

She sighed dramatically. "Fine. I totally understand that you don't trust me. I'm a little hurt that you think I'd take advantage of you to somehow benefit myself."

"Oh, I've no doubt you'll get over that sting of hurt," he drawled. "I've no doubt whatever scheme you're up to will have some added benefit for you. So why don't you quit playing the part of the insulted maiden and tell me what's what."

"You know . . . I don't think I *will* tell you that I found you a hired hand, Mr. Smart-ass."

That made him sit up and take notice. "No joke?"

"No joke. I swear. That's why I called you."

"Where'd you find him?"

"Don't you worry about that. Drop your cock and grab your socks, Bran. Your new hired hand will be on your front stoop within the hour." The phone went dead.

Bran glared at his cell phone. "Son of a bitch. When I get my hands on that girl, I'll . . ."

You ain't gonna do jack shit, hoss. You're gonna get your ass in the shower, brew a pot of coffee, and wake the hell up.

Still cursing, Bran threw back the covers and stumbled down the hallway to his bathroom.

∞

Harper pounced on the phone the second it rang. "Celia?"

"Good news! I found you a job, right outside of Muddy Gap. It might have funky hours the first few weeks, but after that it should level off. It pays well."

"Okay," she said slowly. "What's the catch?"

"No catch. You'll be workin' on a ranch."

"What will I be doing?"

"Whatever Bran tells you to do."

Harper froze. Her mouth went bone-dry. "Bran. As in Bran Turner?"

"Yep. He's a longtime family friend, his hired hand got injured, and he's needing temporary help."

Skeptically, Harper asked, "How'd the guy get injured?"

"I dunno. Between us, Les is not that bright. I think he tripped over his own two feet. Anyway, he's out of commission until the end of May, which fits into your time frame perfectly."

"Too perfectly. You sure this isn't some kind of romantic fix-up?"

Celia laughed. "You and Bran? Please. You are *so* not his type. And vice versa. This is just me helping out two friends who need something from each other."

Harper stopped pacing. "Bran's okay with this?" She couldn't bring herself to ask the real question: *Does Bran know I have zero experience with livestock and anything else related to ranching?*

"I just got off the phone with him. He's expecting you in about forty-five minutes." Pause. "You know where he lives?"

"No clue."

"Three miles past the turnoff to my house, there's a

fish-shaped mailbox. Turn right at the cattle guard and go a quarter mile until you see his trailer. He keeps the road plowed. That's how you'll know you're in the right place."

"Got it." Harper closed her eyes. "Thanks, Celia. Even if this doesn't work out, you have no idea how much it means that you've gone out of your way to try to help me. Everyone else . . ." *Has made me pay for my mother's mistakes.*

"That's what friends do, dumb ass. And you're welcome. Now get crackin' out to Bran's place. Let me know next week how it goes."

"Next week? Why can't I call you later tonight?"

"Because Tanna's folks' ranch is out in the middle of freakin' nowhere. I don't know when I'll have cell service, so it'll be best if I call you. Later. Good luck."

"What does luck . . ." And Harper was speaking to the dial tone.

No matter. It'd take a solid thirty minutes to drive out to the Turner place, so she'd better get a move on. She changed into her "lucky" interview outfit—a pin-striped pencil miniskirt, a white silk blouse, a Western-cut bolero jacket embroidered with tiny gold guns, and her black patent stiletto boots, which came up just over her knees.

The Dodge Neon didn't warm up until ten minutes into the drive. January in Wyoming was always cold, but this year seemed colder than years past.

She shivered. She'd never had a job working outdoors. She'd worked in food service, either as a waitress or as a cocktail waitress, and during her last semester of college she'd scored a part-time job in a Western retail store.

Harper's thoughts drifted to the summer before her senior year in high school, right after she moved to Wyoming from Montana. She'd befriended Celia Lawson and they'd clicked immediately, which was odd because Harper was a girly girl, Celia a self-professed tomboy. They spent most of their time at Harper's cramped rental house in town rather than at the Lawson ranch because Harper's mother didn't care if they were out all night at the local "field" parties, whereas Celia's brothers, who had been raising her after their parents had died, had been very strict.

But once in a while they'd crash at Celia's house. Harper loved that Celia's older brother, Abe, got up and cooked a big breakfast. She loved time spent outdoors in the sun, staring at the big sky and the endless horizon. She loved the normalcy of their family. Of their life.

Over the course of the summer, when Hank and Abe learned that Harper had never been fishing, they organized a fishing party with all their buddies at the closest lake. It'd been an ideal day. Frolicking in the sun. Splashing in the water. Floating on inner tubes. Surrounded by hot, shirtless cowboys. Good tunes on the radio.

One by one, all the guys—Hank, Abe, Kyle, Eli, Devin, Ike, and Max—tried to show her how to cast a line. Harper was hopeless, constantly snagging the hook in the tree above her, or the grass behind her, or, once, in Devin's skin. They ribbed her endlessly about how a Montana girl didn't know how to fly-fish.

Before the journey to the lake, Harper had braced herself for lewd comments and sexual innuendos, because in her past experience, that was what guys did when faced with a woman wearing a bikini. But these men's actions never veered from gentlemanly conduct, although she'd been aware of the appreciative glances sent her way from time to time. Any teasing had been done in good humor, until Kyle suggested that Bran, the fishing "expert," take a crack at showing her how to fish.

Harper still remembered Bran's leisurely perusal as

she'd stood before him. Those dark eyes were shadowed beneath his cowboy hat as his gaze started at her toenails. It inched up her bare legs, taking in every curve of her thighs and hips. Flickering across her belly and the long line of her torso, resting briefly on her ample chest, stopping at her mouth. Bran never looked into her eyes. He scowled and chugged half his beer and said, "She surely don't need to know how to fish. That body of hers is already quite the hook."

The guys had pelted Bran with empty beer cans for the comment, calling him an asshole, knocking his hat off his head. Celia even slapped his sunburn. But he hadn't apologized.

Yet Harper knew he'd watched her closely the rest of the night. While they'd roasted marshmallows and made s'mores. While she sprawled on a blanket next to Celia, laughing and studying the stars. While Devin McClain sang cowboy tunes by the bonfire. While Hank and Kyle talked about life in the rodeo arena. While Abe and Max yammered about local politics. But Bran never said a word.

So maybe Celia's comment about her not being Bran's type was dead-on. Harper was fully aware that she embodied society's idea of a dumb blonde. Fluffy hair, big chest, curves from her lips to her calves—plus she would never turn the academic world on its ear with her intellect. From the time she was ten years old, her mother called her "the pretty one." Competing in local beauty contests reinforced the stereotype of her being attractive packaging and no substance, even when the only reason she entered the pageants was for the prize money.

"Former beauty queen" on a résumé only got her first in line for a job at a T & A sports bar. The lower the cut of her bra, the higher her tips. Truthfully, Harper didn't know how long she would've lasted at that gig. She'd hated dressing in the skimpy uniform the first night. By the end of her two-month mark of jiggling her butt and her boobs for cash, her mother had taken off, forcing Harper to quit both jobs—and community college—to return to Muddy Gap to become Bailey's legal guardian.

Over the years, after the fishing hole incident, she'd occasionally run into Bran. He'd never said a whole lot. He just studied her from beneath the brim of his Stetson, looking like the rugged, one hundred percent Wyoming cattleman that he was. They'd both danced at Buckeye Joe's, but never together. They'd both gone out drinking at Cactus Jack's in Rawlins, but never together.

Harper passed the turnoff to the Lawson place and watched the odometer. As soon as the green and orange fish-shaped mailbox appeared, she turned. Although the road was plowed, it was still slick, so she slowed to a crawl.

The buildings came into view over the next rise. A traditional wooden barn. Alongside it were four metal structures of varying sizes and an old farmhouse that appeared to be abandoned. Off to the left a trailer and two pickups were parked in front of an enormous detached garage.

Her heart beat faster. This was a real working ranch. This was way out of the realm of her job experience. Out of her comfort zone. What if she couldn't do it?

You can do it. You have to. Just a few months and then you're outta here.

She parked behind the older pickup and gazed across the yard to the metal structures and the enclosed pens. Did Bran have chickens as well as cattle? Would taking care of those critters be part of her chores?

Only one way to find out.

Harper climbed out of the car and scaled the steps of the deck attached to the front of the trailer. Standing on the mud-covered mat, she gathered her courage and knocked.

The door didn't immediately open. Just as she was about to knock louder, the handle turned and the door swung inward.

The stunned expression on Bran Turner's face might've been comical if it hadn't filled Harper with dread.

His mouth tightened. His dismissive gaze swept over her as if she'd coated herself in skunk oil. "You've got to be fuckin' kiddin' me. *You're* my new hired hand?"

Chapter Two

⚮

*B*ran glared at Harper Masterson, wondering if he'd become the butt of some joke. He said as much to her, steeling himself against the tears he imagined would fill her eyes.

But her golden brown eyes narrowed. A bit haughtily, in fact. "Celia didn't tell you I was coming?"

"Celia told me she'd found me a hired hand. She didn't say a damn thing about it bein' *you*."

Harper's chin shot up. "You don't have to sound so disappointed."

"I am." *Shit. Not the right thing to say.* "Look, I don't know what Celia told you about this job—"

"She didn't tell me anything except to drive out here and talk to you. So here I am." She pierced him with another lofty look. "Are you conducting the job interview on the porch?"

He scowled, biting back, "Ain't gonna be a job interview." Instead, he stepped away from the doorframe and said, "Might as well come in instead of standing out there freezin'."

"Thank you." Harper wiped the soles of her domina-trix boots and peeled off her pink leopard-print gloves. When she pushed the cowl of her wool coat back, her golden hair stuck up in a million directions, making her seem approachable, not like a goddamn beauty queen.

A beauty queen. As his hired hand.

She smoothed her hands over her head, taming the wild strands. Then she jammed them in the front pockets of her fancy velvet suit jacket, with its gold embroidery, and ignored his pointed stare.

Jesus, she was stunning. A wide face composed of such sharp angles and strong lines shouldn't look so startlingly feminine, but it worked perfectly on her. Add in a gener-ous mouth with a tiny beauty mark above the curve of her full lips and those brandy-colored eyes, and Bran was nearly struck stupid by her magnificence.

Get a grip, man.

He gestured to the couch. "Have a seat. Coffee?"

"Yes. Please. Black."

Bran poured two cups, handed one to her, and parked himself in the easy chair across from her. They both took a sip. He waited for her to speak. When she didn't, he said, "Why would you even be interested in this job? Don't seem like your kind of thing."

She wouldn't meet his eyes, instead focusing on the dark liquid in her mug.

"Harper?"

Finally she glanced up. "With all due respect, Mr. Turner, you don't know anything about me. So how would you know if this was my kind of thing?"

Damn. She did have a little fire. "I'll give you that. And that answers the last part of my question, but not the first. Why do you wanna work as a hired hand?"

"Honestly? Because I'm out of options." Harper set her mug on the table and rubbed her hands across her skirt. Her tight skirt that'd inched halfway up her thighs the instant she'd primly perched on the edge of his lumpy sofa.

Good Lord. The woman had worn a miniskirt, a silky shirt, and hooker boots to apply for a job . . . as a ranch hand. Didn't she realize that most days she'd be covered in cow shit, mud, and hay?

Probably not. This would be the shortest "interview" in history. Pity, really. He'd almost like to see what outfit she'd wear to the branding. Images of her rockin' a red thong, topped with metallic chaps and a teeny bra with strategically placed silver stars and blue fringe popped into his head.

"I went to work this morning at Tan Your Hide and Alice informed me she's shutting it down."

"Is that your only job?"

"No, I also work part-time at Get Nailed, which is part of Bernice's Beauty Barn, but that hardly pays the grocery bill. So when Celia called me and heard my tale of woe, she lined this up." She locked her troubled gaze on his. "Believe me, I had no clue she hadn't told you that I was the one applying for the job."

"Have you ever worked on a ranch?"

She shook her head. "That's why I was suspicious when Celia suggested it. She knows I'm not a ranch kid."

Silence.

They both said, "Look," at the same time.

Bran smiled. "Ladies first."

"I may not have cleaned barns or spread hay, but I have been working since I was twelve years old. I've babysat, served fast food, cleaned motel rooms, waitressed, sold clothes in a retail store. I have a great work ethic. I'm not afraid to try new things, nor am I set in my ways on how ranch work should be done, as I suspect other hired hands with experience might be. So if you're wanting a reliable worker you can train to do things the way you want them done, that would be me."

"Nice pitch," he murmured.

Harper blushed.

Oh, hell, no. Not a blusher. The pretty pink tinge on her cheekbones made him wonder if her whole body flushed that color.

"I don't want permanent employment," she said, forcing his thoughts away from the image of her rosy naked body rolling around in his flannel sheets.

"Why's that?"

Harper gave him a sardonic look. "No offense, but I can't wait to get out of Muddy Gap."

"Remind me again how you ended up in our part of Wyoming?"

"My mother hooked up with some trucker from here when we lived in Montana, so she followed him, once again believing it was true love, which once again lasted, oh, about four months before she kicked him to the curb."

Bran was tempted to chuckle, but he didn't think Harper saw the humor in the retelling even now, so he kept quiet.

"Moving again was the dead last thing I needed, since I'd just started my final year of high school. But Mom never cared what any of us wanted. However, she couldn't force the issue because I'd won a couple of pageant titles that required me to live in the area for the duration of the reigning year."

"How many titles did you win?"

"Six. Sounds like a lot, but Wyoming can't boast a big pool of candidates to choose from, so some I won by default."

That was . . . humble. And unexpected. He'd figured with the knockout way she looked, she'd be cocky as hell.

Hasn't she already pointed out once that you've prejudged or maybe misjudged her?

"How long have you lived here?" he asked, as if the rumor mill hadn't churned the instant the "hot jailbait blonde" rolled into this sleepy Wyoming town.

"Six years. Longest we've stayed anywhere." She frowned. "Although Mom didn't make it that long. Anyway, as soon as Bailey graduates from high school, we're gone. Celia made it sound like your hired man would be back on his feet by then?"

Bran nodded.

"How did he get hurt?"

"A freak accident. A bull stomped on Les's foot and when he fell, he twisted his body, breaking his hip when he hit the dirt. Never had that happen before."

"Ouch." Harper sipped her coffee.

He sent her a challenging look. "But be aware. Accidents happen with the livestock and the equipment all the time. I've been kicked damn near every place on my body. I've practically ripped my hand off fixin' fence. Almost lost my arm getting tangled up in a rope with a runaway horse. I've nearly been struck by lightning. I've been tossed on my ass by a horse. Knocked on my ass by cows and by bulls. Flipped over my ATV. Got my rig stuck in the mud. And in the snow. I've been chased by bulls. Chased by cows. Been stung by bees, wasps, and hornets. Almost burned up in a wildfire a time or twenty."

"You trying to scare me off?"

"No, I'm sharin' the cold hard facts so you know what you're up against."

"So you're considering me for the job?"

Say no. "Possibly. Can you work seven days a week?"

Harper paled a little. "Ah. Sure."

"It's only until we're through the worst of calving. Then it'll be more normal."

"Normal being . . . what?"

"Six in the morning until four in the afternoon."

"What's the pay?"

Bran shrugged. "Negotiable."

"That isn't a dollar amount. I need a solid number."

He tossed out a number, but he honestly wasn't sure what Les made. "One hundred dollars a day."

Her eyes widened. "For how many hours a day?"

Harper wasn't the pushover he'd imagined. Not that he would take advantage of her, but it was encouraging that she paid attention to details. Maybe she'd be detail-oriented on the job too. "A ten-hour day. Obviously any hours you logged over forty in a seven-day period you'd get paid time and a half. Paychecks are cut every other week by my accountant." He drained his coffee. "Is that more or less money than you expected?"

"More."

Well, well. Miss Half A Dozen Beauty Titles didn't hedge either. "I ain't gonna lie. It's damn hard work."

"I know." Harper's forehead crinkled and he was as fascinated by her coy demeanor as the long, sooty eyelashes that brushed her cheek. Those had to be fake, didn't they?

Bran's cell phone rang, breaking his contemplation of other parts of Harper that might be fake. "Hello."

"Thought I'd catch ya nappin'."

He snorted. "I'm nappin' just about as much as you are these days, Hank. What's up?"

"Same old, same old. Lainie wants to know if you're free for supper tonight."

"Sure. I've always got time for supper with a pretty woman."

He felt Harper's curious gaze.

"You *are* aware I'll be there too," Hank said dryly.

"A man can hope against that." When Hank made a snarling noise, Bran laughed. "What time?"

"Six-ish?"

"I'll be there. Tell her thanks." He hung up and looked at Harper.

She set her empty coffee cup on the table and met his gaze. "So, where do we stand on this? Are you gonna give me a shot?"

Bran gave her a head-to-toe inspection, frowning at her attire. "Be here tomorrow. Six a.m. And for God's sake, leave the pearls, beauty sash, silk shirt, fuck-me stiletto boots, and tiaras at home. Come dressed ready to get down and dirty with me."

∞

Six hours later Bran shifted from boot to boot as he waited on the Lawsons' front porch. He knocked again.

The door swung open and Hank grinned at him. "Ah. Sorry we didn't hear you knock. But you are early."

The top two buttons on Hank's shirt were undone and his shirttail was untucked. Guilt kicked Bran in the ass at seeing his friend's state of undress. Since Hank and Lainie lived with Hank's brother, Abe, alone time was rare for them. Hank had been busting ass building a house a quarter mile away from this, the Lawson homeplace. Weather, work, and finances kept the sprawling ranch house from getting finished as fast as Hank and Lainie would've liked. But they weren't willing to sacrifice any amenities, and that meant waiting.

Hank said, "Wanna beer?"

"Sure." Bran followed Hank into the kitchen. The delicious scents of roasted meat and a chocolaty dessert filled his nostrils. His mouth watered—Lainie was a helluva cook. Hank handed over a bottle of Moose Drool.

"You broke out the good beer. We celebrating something?"

"It's a step up from Bud Light, but it ain't exactly high end." Hank twisted the cap off his bottle. "The only thing we're celebrating is bein' at the ass end of calving season."

"How many you got left?"

"Forty. As soon as we're done, I'm hitting house construction hard. I've lined up a couple of guys to help out."

"Anything I can do to speed stuff up?"

"I'll let you know."

Lainie waltzed into the kitchen, and Bran couldn't help but notice how Hank's face lit up. She wrapped her arms around him and stood on tiptoe to whisper in his ear. Hank chuckled and whispered back before planting a kiss square on her smirking mouth. She turned around. "Bran. I'm glad you could make it."

"Thanks for the invite."

"No, thank you. I'm afraid Hank's gotten tired of my company."

"Never." Hank kissed the top of her head. "You want a beer?"

"No. I'd rather have a glass of wine."

Bran wondered if Harper drank wine. She didn't seem like the beer-drinking type. Actually, she didn't seem like the type who drank at all.

What does it matter? Ain't like you're gonna be swilling beers with her after the workday ends.

"Tell us what's new in your world," Hank said.

"Well, I'm not as far along calving as you guys are. I've got another solid month before it'll taper off. Oh, and I hired a new hand today."

Hank's eyebrows lifted. "Really? Where'd you find one?"

"Actually Celia's the one who hooked me up."

Lainie and Hank exchanged a look.

Oh, hell, no. They hadn't been in on it too? "Did you know who Celia sent to my front door?"

"No. It's just ... we haven't heard from Celia since the new rodeo season started," Lainie said.

"Why's that?"

Hank shrugged. "Who knows with that girl? But me'n Lainie suspect it has something to do with Nancy, Abe's girlfriend. They didn't exactly hit it off over Christmas. She mention anything about it to you?"

Even if Celia had complained, Bran wouldn't have broken her confidence. Plus, he didn't like Abe's new girlfriend either. "Nope."

"So who's your new hired hand?"

Bran took a long swallow of his beer. "Harper Masterson."

Both Lainie's and Bran's mouths fell open in shock. "Harper? You've gotta be kiddin'."

"'Fraid not. Of course, Celia didn't tell me Harper was the 'perfect' hired hand when she called. Nor did she tell Harper that I had no clue Celia had sent her my way."

"But Harper is so ..."

Beautiful? Built? Sexy?

Annoyed at the direction of his thoughts, Bran said, "She's so what?"

"'Inexperienced' comes to mind," Hank said cautiously.

Lainie shook her head. "She's probably that too, but the truth is Harper keeps to herself after that nasty business with her mother. She's kind of shy—that's probably why Celia stepped in. Why was Harper looking for work?"

Bran didn't feel comfortable blabbing Harper's problems to his friends. "All I know is Harper showed up on Celia's recommendation." He knocked back another swig of beer. "I've decided to give her a chance."

Lainie and Hank exchanged another look.

"Jesus. Would you guys stop doin' that married couple silent communication crap? It's fuckin' annoying. Just come right out and ask me the goddamn question."

Hank flashed his teeth. "Fine. Did you hire Harper because of the way she looks?"

Bran grinned back at his nosy friend. "No. Although I'll admit that's a plus. A big plus. But the real reason is Harper's only gonna be around Muddy Gap about as long as Les is laid up, so it seemed like a sign."

"Then where's she goin'?"

"No clue. She told me as soon as her little sister graduates from high school they're both outta here."

"Did you tell her that staying overnight at your place was part of the job?"

Hank had known Bran long enough to understand that Harper was exactly the type of woman Bran was attracted to. But women that hot and gorgeous never reciprocated the attraction, so he'd always shied away from them.

"Let it go, Hank," Lainie warned.

Surprisingly, Hank did. He passed out another round of beers.

"Where's Abe tonight?" Bran asked.

"At Nancy's."

"Thank God she ain't here again," Hank muttered. "I never thought my brother would find a woman I liked less than Janie, but I'll be goddamned if he didn't."

"I never understood your beef with Janie. If I'd had to put up with Abe's 'master of the house' bullshit, I'da left him too."

Hank scowled at Bran.

"Master of the house?" Lainie repeated, swirling the wine in her glass. "Do tell. All I've ever heard about the ex-wife is how she left poor Abe high and dry."

Bran shrugged. "In my opinion, Abe married Janie wanting her to be just like his mom. A happy home-maker whose only purpose was to service this ranch and the Lawson family's needs. When Janie turned out not to be that type . . . Abe tried to force her into becoming that type. Janie's biggest issue was the living situation. She didn't want to live with Hank and Celia indefinitely. She wanted them to have their own place. Instead of keeping his wife's confidence, Abe told you and Celia and you both hated her. Abe chose his family over his wife. That's why Janie left. And who could blame her? Not me."

Hank wore a look of shock, as if he'd never considered that Janie needed alone time with her husband. A feeling Bran knew Lainie understood, and now Hank did too—hence they were building their own house.

Lainie ran her hand up Hank's arm. "There was no way you could've known. And it wasn't your problem to solve. It was Abe's."

"How is it that you know so much about my brother's ex-wife?" Hank asked suspiciously.

"She adored my grandma and she missed her after she passed on, so she kept coming around since I was the closest neighbor. Besides, wasn't like she had anyone else to talk to after you and Celia shut her out."

"Why didn't Abe know any of this?"

"Because he didn't ask her. It wasn't my place to tell him—you know how he gets."

Lainie nodded in total understanding.

"But I'm really goddamned happy you two ain't makin' the same mistake. No one said because you run the ranch together that you had to live together forever like the fuckin' Waltons. And why would you want to?"

Silence.

Then Lainie laughed.

Hank clapped Bran on the shoulder. "Remind me again why you're still single?"

"Fuck off."

During the meal, they caught up on their friends' lives. Gauging Kyle Gilchrist's chances of winning the CRA world championship bull riding title. Talking about Devin McClain's newest CD and world tour. Speculating if Eli Whirling Cloud's plans to rehabilitate injured horses—racing and rodeo—with the help of their pal, veterinarian August Fletcher, would be a successful venture. Discussing Celia's minuscule chances of beating out Lainie's buddy, world championship barrel racer Tanna Barker, for the title this year.

As Hank cleared the plates, Lainie brooded into her half-empty wineglass.

"Something goin' on in that pretty head of yours, Missus Lawson?"

She smiled. "Flatterer. Talking about life on the road and such . . . I'm just worried about Celia."

"That makes two of us," Hank said. "How often does my little sister call you, Bran?"

"Occasionally."

"And how was she? I mean, did she act different?"

"No. She seemed fine when I talked to her. Why?"

"Probably nothin'. We're pretty sure Celia is seein' a guy on the circuit, but she won't fess up to who it is. Makes us wonder if she's embarrassed or something."

Bran drained his beer. "You want me to point out the obvious? She's an adult, entitled to a life that don't got nothin' to do with you guys."

Hank glowered at him.

So Bran decided to poke him, just for fun. "You know, I wish I could see Celia as the gorgeous, sexy woman she is and not as the pesky little tomboy sister that she was. It'd make all our lives easier if we got hitched. She's aware of what it takes to run a ranch, we could have tons of babies and horses, and she'd live close enough to annoy the hell out of you and Abe forever."

Instead of snarling, Hank shot Bran a sly look. "Tell you what. If you propose to her and she accepts? As a dowry I'll give you those fifty acres down by the creek that you love."

"Hank! That is not even funny," Lainie said, swatting at him.

Bran grinned. "If I thought I had a snowball's chance in hell that Celia would go for it, I'd suggest it. But I've seen that girl castrate calves. I shudder to think what she'd do to me if I offered to marry her on her brother's behalf."

The front door opened. Voices echoed from the entryway and Hank threaded his fingers through Lainie's when she tensed.

Abe and Nancy came into the kitchen. Abe clapped Bran on the back. "Hey. How's calving been so far?"

"Slow. Not quite to where you guys are, as I've barely started."

"There's a lesson for you," Nancy said. "Maybe you should get Abe's advice before you turn the bulls out with the herd so your calving doesn't lag so far behind everyone else's."

Bran froze. Had this woman actually just told him how to better manage his cattle operation? What the hell did she know? She worked as a secretary in an auto repair shop.

Abe looked embarrassed. "Nancy, Bran runs one of the most successful cattle businesses in the county. Me'n Hank should be takin' his advice, not the other way around."

But Nancy had tuned Abe out. She frowned at the

dishes piled by the sink and the food scattered across the countertop. "Why in the world didn't you clean up after you finished eating? I hate coming home to a dirty kitchen." With a dramatic sigh, she headed to the sink.

Lainie said, "Leave them. I planned to do them after our company left."

Nancy ignored Lainie. How the woman could be oblivious to the tension in the room—tension she'd caused—boggled Bran's mind.

Water ran. Dishes clanked. Hank glared at Abe. Abe merely shrugged.

Lainie pushed to her feet. "I said I'd do them, Nancy."

"It's fine."

"No, it's not fine." Lainie reached over and shut off the water. "I don't do things on your timetable. And I'm not going to let you run roughshod over me in my own damn kitchen and continue to embarrass me in front of our friend. Now please leave."

Nancy's head whipped around and she gave Abe a hangdog look, as if she expected him to intervene on her behalf.

Abe didn't.

She snagged a towel, dried her hands, and stomped away. Abe trailed behind her. Ten seconds later Abe's bedroom door slammed shut with enough force that the dishes in the china hutch rattled.

This Nancy woman was trouble. She'd already driven a wedge between Abe and his siblings. Sadly, Bran had seen it happen many times with families whose working lives were tied to the family ranch. Hatred and resentment ripped families clean apart simply because of a sibling's unfortunate marital choice. It'd kill Bran to see the Lawsons so divided, but it would happen if Abe didn't pull his head out of his ass and rid himself of Nasty Nancy.

Bran donned his coat and hat and said his good-byes. For the first time ever, he was damn glad to be an only child.

Chapter Three

⚮

The following morning, Bran said, "Let's take a ride in the truck and I'll show you around the ranch. That'll give you a better breakdown of what I need in a worker. Sound fair?"

"I suppose so."

They dressed in winter gear—hers appropriate today except for the bright purple zebra-striped scarf and matching gloves. Bran led her to his Dodge Diesel quad cab. When Harper started to put her seat belt on, Bran shook his head. "Not that I ain't about safety first, but you're gonna be hopping in and out of the truck, opening gates. Top speed in this rig as we're checkin' stuff out is never more than twenty miles per hour."

"I remember the gate thing from helping Celia."

"So you ain't completely green?"

Harper smiled brazenly. "Oh, I'm completely green."

At the first barbed wire gate, he gave her the run-down. "This one is the old loop kind. Lift the loop off the fence post and pull the gate inward. I'll drive through and you close it behind us."

She hopped out and followed his directions to the letter. For some perverted reason, that caused him to wonder whether she would follow directions in the bedroom that easily too.

Her voice startled him out of his mental porn starring the former Miss Sweet Grass. "You work all by yourself? No other family members?"

When phrased that way, it sounded awful damn lonely. *It is, isn't it?*

"I've been doin' everything since my grandparents died. But truthfully, they were getting on in years as I was growing up, so I've been running this place by myself since I was seventeen. I'm an only child of an only child, so it ain't like I've got a lot of choice." *Don't give her your life story, dumb ass, especially when it's so damn boring.* He paused at the next gate. "This one's got a hook on the top."

She slid from the cab. It took two tries, but she managed to open the gate. After she climbed back inside, she said, "This gate opening and shutting thing takes twice as long when you're by yourself?"

"Yes, ma'am." Bran focused on the cattle huddled by the windbreak. One was lying down, away from the herd. "You ever seen a live birth?"

Harper faced him, her eyes wary. "Umm, no. Not human or dog or cat or cow."

"Well, that's about to change." He pointed to the prone cow. "Stick close and watch." Bran threw the truck in park, facing away from the laboring animal. "Let's go."

The snow crust was hard enough that he didn't break through as he started downhill. Harper stayed plenty close; he practically felt her breath on the back of his neck. He kept himself in the mother cow's direct line of vision so she wouldn't bolt.

"Looks like you're almost there." Bran ran a gloved

hand down her heaving side. "Lemme check and see where we're at." He motioned for Harper to kneel next to him. "See the hooves coming out pointing down? That means it's coming out the right way. The rest of the body slides out."

"Is it always like this? Calves just plop out?"

"I wish. Sometimes the calf is breach and I gotta either stick my arms up there and turn it around or put the chains on it and pull it out."

Her eyes went comically wide.

"There it comes." The upper half of the calf's body was showing, the membrane protecting it still intact.

Harper leaned over to take a closer look.

The mama made a huffing noise. Her belly muscles rippled and disgorged the calf. It slipped out in a wet gush as the sac broke. Immediately the mother stood, mooed, and sniffed the calf's face. The baby twitched and the mother kept sniffing, right through the afterbirth.

Bran glanced at Harper, half expecting to see disgust, but her face wore an expression of awe. Her eyes were shining. High color dotted her cheeks. And her mouth had curved into a soft smile. "Harper? You all right?"

She met his gaze. "That was amazing. Now what happens?"

"She'll clean the baby up and then it'll nurse. But it'll have to get up on its feet awful damn fast because she'll need to eat. Nursing mothers require a lot of feed. Calves gain up to ten pounds a day."

"And they say milk won't make you fat," she said dryly.

He grinned. "I ain't touching that one. Tomorrow we'll come out here and ear-tag the little bugger. I'm guessing we'll have quite a few others to do too."

"If you're talking about tomorrow with me, does that mean I'm hired?"

"You sure this is what you want? I've only shown you one thing—there's lots more."

Harper studied him. "Will you just cut me loose right away and have me checking the herd? Because I'm nowhere near ready for that."

"No. It'll be both of us doin' this stuff. It's too much work for one person with a herd this size."

"How big is your herd?"

"Around seven hundred cows, which means I'll end up with roughly seven hundred calves. About fifty bulls. We keep them in separate pastures until it's time to breed."

"So in addition to watching for calves, you've gotta feed the cows and the bulls every day?"

"And a half dozen horses. Plus I've got goats."

"Goats? I must've missed those when I drove in."

"They're caged because they eat damn near anything you set in front of them, and even stuff you don't want them to eat. You should also know—"

His cell phone rang. He said, "Just a sec."

Harper turned toward the window.

After Bran listened to Les ramble on about nothing for a good two minutes, he ended the call. He stopped at the next gate, and Harper hopped right out without prompting.

She didn't say much as they made the trek back to the house.

"Any questions?"

"I'm sure I'll have fifty million the second I start down the drive."

He pointed at her car. "Is that the only vehicle you own?"

Color bloomed on her cheeks. "Yes. Why?"

"Because, no offense, but that ain't gonna cut it. The wind blows really hard out here and the entrance to the road can drift shut in a matter of hours. Since Les won't be needing the ranch truck, you should drive it."

"Really?"

"Yep. I'll need you out here every day, no matter what the weather does in town. The only exception is if the highway patrol closes the road. That truck might look rough, but it runs great and gets around in the snow like a champ."

"Okay. But I can't leave my car here. Bailey uses it after school most days."

"What do you do when she's got your car?"

"Walk."

The life he'd attributed to Harper the beauty queen seemed a far cry from her reality. "Tell you what. I'll follow you into town. You can park your car and drive me back out here. That way I'll be with you to see if you've got any problems driving it."

"Thanks." Her sweet, unsure smile loosened something inside him and he found himself smiling back.

He switched vehicles and followed her Dodge Neon into Muddy Gap. Harper parked in front of a small house set back from the street. She left the keys in the ignition and got out so she could drive.

Once they were back on the highway, Harper said, "It's been a long time since I've driven a truck. I forgot how much higher up you sit."

"I can't remember the last time I drove a car."

Silence stretched between them.

Bran wasn't one to run off at the mouth, but in his experience most women were. They'd fill dead air with mindless chatter. Maybe it surprised him that Harper wasn't like that. She hadn't turned on the radio either.

So it was really strange, his desire to linger after she pulled up to his trailer. To find out everything about her. To discover what else he'd gotten wrong.

Jesus, you're pathetic. She's working for you. Would you have these same thoughts if you'd hired a male hand?

No. Goddamn it. He started to bail out of the truck, but she placed her hand on his arm, stopping him.

"Thank you for giving me a chance. I appreciate it more than you'll ever know, Bran. You won't regret hiring me."

As Bran looked at her beautiful, earnest face, he couldn't tell her he already had regrets. Because chances were very high that he wouldn't be able to keep his hands off his sexy new ranch hand.

⚭

The front door slammed.

"Whose truck is parked out front?"

Harper stopped sorting through the pile of bills and glanced up at her younger sister.

With her square glasses, glossy brown ponytail, checkered school uniform, and enormous backpack, Bailey looked like the brainiac she was.

"It's mine. For a while anyway." Harper pointed to the plate of Rice Krispie treats on the coffee table. "There's your snack."

"God. Let me get out of this stupid uniform. I hate uniforms." She stripped as she headed to her room and returned thirty seconds later wearing baggy gray sweatpants and a Death Cab for Cutie T-shirt. Bailey threw herself on the couch and grabbed a treat. "So tell me about the redneck wheels." She shoved the entire square bar in her mouth.

"Alice fired me yesterday."

Bailey choked.

Harper was right there, helping her sit up and handing her a glass of water. Bailey sputtered and swallowed.

When she got control, she said, "Warn me next time. God, Harper. You got fired? Are you okay?"

"It's been bizarre. But hours after I lost the job, Celia told me that Bran Turner needed a temporary hired hand. Today he gave me the ranching lowdown, and I watched a calf being born—coolest thing ever, by the way—and he hired me. The truck comes with the job."

Bailey's green eyes widened. "You're working for Bran Turner?"

"How do you know Bran?"

"Jeez, Harper. Everyone knows Bran. He's a real cowboy, not a wannabe like some of the losers around here who put on shitkickers, a cheap cowboy hat, and a fake rodeo buckle. Dude. He's got that mean, squinty Clint Eastwood stare that's scary as shit."

Bailey had hit it dead-on. Bran was the real deal. That was partially why he made her so nervous. She felt like an absolute idiot around him—even more stupid than she usually did.

"I wish you'd stop saying shit like that, Harper. You're not stupid," Bailey said.

She was unaware that she'd spoken out loud. "I'll be working for him during the day. But he mentioned there'd be some late nights too."

Bailey waggled her eyebrows. "Can I just say how jealous I am of those late nights? You and studly cattleman Bran. All alone. Cold. Sweaty. Dirty. Tired. Who knows what might happen."

"I'm sure Bran will be a perfect gentleman while I'm his employee."

"For your sake, I sure as hell hope not."

Before Harper could rebuke her sister, Bailey's cell phone buzzed. Immediately after digging it out of her backpack, Bailey glued the phone to her ear, walked to her bedroom, and closed the door.

Although Harper was used to Bailey's tendency to drop everything when her cell rang, she wished for more

time to talk. Yawning, Harper stretched out on the couch.
Maybe she'd just close her eyes for a bit and relax before
starting supper.

∞

Harper arrived at the Turner ranch at six the next morning and parked the truck where she'd seen it the day before. But there was no sign of Bran's vehicle. Huh. Where
could he be? Out in the field?

*Maybe he's not home yet from his late-night sexca-
pades.*

With his rugged features and the sexy, laid-back way
Bran carried himself, no doubt the cowboy had his pick of
women to share his bed. Would she face that situation in
the coming months—a woman rolling out of Bran's bed
before they started morning chores?

That thought didn't sit well with her. Neither did sitting
around in the truck in the cold and waiting for him.

Maybe she should explore, get the lay of the land, so
to speak. She'd dressed warmly enough to be outside. No
reason she had to stay in the pickup with her hands
primly folded.

Harper checked out the farthest barn first, wondering
if Bran had parked to load up supplies for the still mys-
terious "ranch work." No sign of him. The next metal
building, filled with unrecognizable machine parts, had
that same eerie emptiness. She wandered back via the
driveway, deciding to check the old-fashioned wooden
barn. As soon as she cleared the far side, something
moved.

What the heck?

She waited. Sure enough, she saw that blur of white
again and chanced a peek at an enclosed pen. Looked
like she'd found the goats. Amused by their antics, she
watched them, staying out of sight. A big one climbed
onto the highest point of the metal shed, which was en-

closed inside the pen. Another one, smaller than the first, scrambled up on top too, as they played a game of king of the mountain.

Goats perched on the edge of the shed, peering over the side? Priceless. What a killer photo op. Harper slid her cell phone from her pocket and clicked the camera option. Keeping the lens trained on the curious animals, she stepped into their line of sight and said, "Say goat cheese."

Almost in slow motion, the goats tumbled off the edge of the shed. They hit the ground with a muffled thud and then stayed still.

Horrified, Harper opened the gate and raced into the pen. She froze in front of the motionless white forms. Had they broken their necks? No blood spilled on the ground, but it looked like total carnage.

Carnage she'd caused by taking a Kodak moment.

Omigod. She'd killed Bran's goats. On her second day on the job. Not only would he fire her for sure, but how could she live with the ugly truth that she'd accidentally led two innocent animals to their deaths?

Maybe if she gave them CPR . . . She leaned over the closest one and poked it in the ribs. No movement.

That's because they're dead. Don't bother putting your mouth on goat lips. Nothing's gonna happen but getting a firsthand taste of dead goat breath.

So what should she do?

Hide the evidence. Throw the bodies in the shed and shut the door.

No! That would be wrong.

You need this job. Maybe Bran will think the goats died of natural causes.

Huh-uh. Bran knew everything about his livestock.

Shove them in the shed for now. Take them out later, pitch them in the back of the truck, and cover them with a tarp. Before you take off for the day, leave the pen gate open. Then tomorrow morning Bran will think his goats ran away.

Due to her total panic, that was the option Harper chose, even when she was aware it was the worst option.

She dragged the goats by the back legs and laid them in the metal shed. She shut the shed door and latched it. When she heard the rumble of Bran's rig in the drive, she sprinted out of the pen and headed straight for the truck.

Inside the cab, she rested her forehead on the steering wheel, attempting to level her breathing, trying to act normal. Trying not to act like she'd just entombed Bran's goat family.

When Bran rapped on the window, she screamed.

Naturally Bran jumped back. His eyes narrowed on her and he opened the truck door in a panic. "Harper? What happened? You all right?"

No! I'm a goat-murdering cover-up artist!

She blinked at him. Opened her mouth, but she could not force the confession out. Could not.

Chicken.

Good thing Bran didn't have chickens or else she might've killed them too.

He aimed that squinty-eyed Eastwood gaze at her and she almost cracked.

Almost.

"You been sitting in the truck long enough that the exhaust fumes have turned you loopy?"

She laughed, a bit hysterically. "Where were you? I thought maybe I was late and you'd started chores without me."

"Nope. I was out of coffee and made a store run. Lemme take this in the house, and then there's a couple of things we need to talk about before we get started."

Harper's heart dropped to her toes as Bran momentarily disappeared inside the trailer. What if he'd seen the whole goat episode and was waiting for her to confess to gauge her honesty?

Mired in guilt, she didn't hear him come up behind her. She must've jumped a foot in the air when he said, "We'll do a livestock check first."

She froze. Livestock. Did that mean the horses and goats? Her stomach lurched. She wrestled with the right way to break it to him.

His boots crunched across the driveway.

No time to waste. She had to tell him. Now. She chased him down, because the man was scarily fast. "Look, Bran. There's something I need—"

He whirled around, putting his gloved finger to his lips. "Hear that?"

Harper lifted the band of her wool cap off her ears and listened. Sure enough, she heard something solid hitting metal. Over and over.

"What the hell?" Bran put his hands on his hips, cocking his head in the direction of the sound. After he heard it again, he hustled toward the old barn, which housed the great goat catastrophe.

"Bran. Wait."

He ignored her and kept walking. Running, actually.

Harper shuffled along behind him, dread dogging her every footstep as the noise got louder. Hey, maybe the sound was her guilty heartbeat, like in that Edgar Allan Poe tale. She rounded the corner of the barn beside the pen just as Bran unlatched the door to the metal shed.

I can explain. Really. I didn't mean to kill them.

But as soon as the shed door opened, two shaggy white forms bounded out. *Bounded* out, doing a little happy goat jig.

Harper gasped.

Bran spun toward her. "Do you know why my goats

were locked up in this shed? Jesus. They kicked the living shit out of it." His gloved hand traced the bumps in the metal, dents that'd been made from the inside out. From something trying to get out.

She gaped at the goats, flashing back to *The X-Files* Chupacabra episode that dealt with a Mexican blood-sucking goat. Were these goats somehow ... possessed? Able to come back to life?

"Harper?"

"Omigod! I thought they were dead!"

"Run that by me one more time?"

She couldn't tear her gaze away from the two frisky goats that were jumping—*jumping!*—on top of the metal shed, once again playing follow-the-leader.

Hey. Was one of them *smirking* at her?

Bran grabbed her sleeve, forcing her to look at him. "What in the hell is goin' on with you?"

"What is wrong with *me*? What is wrong with your goats? They're evil! And they're laughing at me! Look at their smug little goat faces! Go on. Look at them!"

"Harper. Take a deep breath. You're babbling."

"You'd be babbling too if you'd killed two goats this morning and they miraculously came back to life!"

Those steely gray eyes narrowed. "What do you mean you killed them?"

Harper briefly closed her eyes. "When I arrived here you weren't around, so I went looking for you. I ended up by the goat pen and I saw them standing on the shed. I thought it'd make a cute picture. Before I could snap off a single shot, they fell off the roof onto the ground! I ran in, hoping I could save them, but they weren't moving, so I dragged them into the shed and shut the door, thinking I'd come up with a way to explain to you how I killed your goats on my second day as a ranch hand."

Something unreadable flitted through his eyes.

Oh, God. Did Bran think she was totally bonkers? "I swear—"

"Lemme ask you something. Did the goats see you before you took their picture?"

Harper frowned. "I don't think so. I was watching them from the side of the barn."

"So you could've startled them?"

"Well, I did jump out and yell, 'Say goat cheese!' So I suppose that might've startled them."

Bran started to laugh. He laughed so hard he had to bend over to catch his breath. Just when she thought he'd stop, he'd look up at her, tears swimming in his silvery eyes, and then look over at the goats and start laughing all over again.

Although he was busting a serious gut, she didn't find any humor in this situation at all.

Finally, he said, "Goddamn. I'm sorry, Harper. It's just . . ."

"What? I'm not crazy. Those goats were dead to the world."

"I believe you." He grinned like he had a huge secret. "But it'll be easiest to show you." He faced the pen and yelled, "Boo!" while leaping against the chicken wire covering the cage.

Just like before, both the goats fell off the metal shed and lay on the ground, completely still.

Harper moved beside Bran, hooking her gloved fingers through the holes in the chicken wire. "What are they, possessed?"

"No. This kind of goat is called a Kentucky stiff leg. The odd thing is, they faint whenever they're startled. And it starts a chain reaction among the other goats around them. They just faint dead away—pardon the pun."

"How long do they stay like that?"

"Anywhere from one minute to five minutes. These two seem to stay out of it longer than others I've seen."

"What are their names?"

"Pox and Hex. Pox is the smaller one. She's pregnant."

That made Harper feel worse. Didn't it hurt the kid when the mama goat plummeted to her fake death? "Wait. Pox and Hex? Strange names."

"Charlie gave them to me as a surprise."

"Does he hate you or something?"

Bran snorted. "Or something. You must've moved pretty fast if you got 'em in the shed before they came to."

Harper hung her head and stared at her feet. "I'm such an idiot about this stuff. I'm sorry."

"Hey." Soft leather brushed her chin and Bran lifted her face up to meet his eyes. "Not your fault. I should've warned you. Since I've been around ranch work my whole life, this stuff comes natural to me and I don't even think about it."

"Bran. There is nothing natural about fainting goats."

He smiled, but his gaze seemed stuck on her mouth. "I may forget to teach you some things. But I'd never do it intentionally to make you feel stupid, Harper. I ain't that kind of man."

A warm feeling flowed through her. "Thanks. And I promise if I make another mistake, I won't try to hide the evidence."

"Workin' with you ain't gonna ever be boring—that's for damn sure." His smile faded and he stepped back. "Come on. Chores are waitin'."

∞

Hours later Harper stumbled in the door and headed directly for the shower. She'd managed to act blasé around Bran, as if being covered in birth gunk and cow poop hadn't bothered her in the least.

But it had. Oh, man, had it ever.

She flipped on the shower to warm it up while she stripped. Once the hot water hit her cold skin, she didn't even mind the stinging sensation. She lathered up with her favorite peach soap and let the steaming water flow over her. Sometimes a hot shower was better than an orgasm.

Probably not better than the orgasms Bran could give you.

She shuddered, wondering what it'd feel like having Bran's strong, rough-skinned hands all over her.

Heavenly. Bran could probably do sexual things she'd only read about.

Not that it would be difficult, since Harper had limited sexual experience. Due to her mother's reputation of spreading her legs for any man, of any age, size, race, or creed, Harper had gone in the opposite direction and remained chaste. She'd lost her virginity simply out of curiosity, choosing a college guy with more brains than brawn. They'd dated a while. Sex between them hadn't driven her to the pinnacle of ecstasy her girlfriends raved about. Then her mom had uprooted them from Montana, ending her brief stab at a romance.

After she'd started winning pageants, the coordinators constantly warned her to be discreet in her dealings with the opposite sex. Apparently many men considered bagging a beauty queen a sign of masculine prowess, entitling them to bragging rights. So Harper decided to deal with that issue by staying abstinent, never expecting that it would last four years.

Within a week of passing off her final crown and title, she accepted a date with a man older than the college guys who'd been sniffing around. She learned firsthand there was no substitute for a sexually experienced male who took pride in pleasing a woman in bed. A mere month into the relationship, Harper learned her mother had bailed on poor Bailey. Since she'd moved back to Muddy Gap, no man had captured her interest.

Until Bran.

Too bad you're not his type.

No, too bad he was her boss.

Harper toweled off and applied minimal makeup—foundation, mascara, and pale pink lip gloss. After tossing her dirty clothes into the tiny laundry room, she pawed through her dresser. She couldn't wait to wear something besides jeans and boots for her short shift at Get Nailed. Bran was paying her enough that she could give notice to Bernice, but spending time chatting with her customers allowed her to feel part of the community. None of the women who patronized Bernice's Beauty Barn ever uttered snarky comments about Harper's mother or her mother's irresponsible actions. Those wonderful ladies accepted her. Period. Which was worth way more than the pittance she earned.

Standing in front of her jam-packed closet, she chose a long tan moleskin skirt, a Western-cut shirt with black and tan checks mixed with strips of solid black and brown paisley, and black beaded moccasins. She adored clothes, jewelry, shoes—anything related to fashion. Chances were slim that she could carve out her dream career in fashion merchandising without a degree, but she still took time to look stylish. Even if the only people who saw her and appreciated her quirky style were the sixty-, seventy-, and eightysomething patrons of Get Nailed.

The wind practically blew her inside the building. Get Nailed was located in the back of Bernice's Beauty Barn. In a small community there wasn't a need for a full-time, full-service hair salon, to say nothing of a full-time nail salon, so Bernice scheduled nail appointments at the end of the day on the days she was open.

She hung up her coat on the coat tree, an oddly endearing monstrosity that Bernice's husband, Bob, had fashioned out of elk antlers. When she turned around, all five women in the shop were gawking at her. "What?"

"Oh, nothin', dear. We're just surprised to see you."

Harper's eyes zipped to Bernice. "Why? You planning on firing me too?"

Bernice clucked her tongue and resumed snipping a section of Tilda O'Toole's snow-white hair. "No. I figured with you bein' Bran Turner's new hired hand and all, you might be giving *me* the boot."

"Heaven knows I wouldn't kick Bran Turner out of bed," Tilda piped up.

"Unless he wanted to do it on the floor," Garnet Evans added with a snicker.

"Garnet!"

She shrugged. "Just sayin'. I'm old. I ain't dead."

"How did you guys hear about me going to work for Bran?" Harper demanded. "It's only my second day."

Tilda's eyes flicked to Harper's in the mirror. "Honey, do you really need us to remind you how small this town is?"

"Plus," Bernice added, "Bran's hired hand's truck has been parked at your place since yesterday. Given the state of Les Daaugard's hip, we know you weren't makin' time with him."

A chorus of female titters erupted.

"Now, don't get sore at us, Harper. We were just funnin' with you," Garnet said.

"I know." She rubbed her hands together. "So who's my first victim—I mean client—today?"

Maybelle Linberg pushed to her feet. "That would be me."

"Come on back. It'll take me a second to get ready."

"No rush. It's not like I've got anywhere else to be or anyone waiting on me."

Harper's heart ached for Miz Maybelle, who'd lost her husband of fifty years six months back. None of her children or grandchildren lived close by, and Harper thought it'd only be a matter of time before Maybelle moved on if she didn't find something to occupy herself.

She slipped an apron on and set up the nail station, draping towels across the hand board. She filled a pan with disinfecting solution and added hot water. "Have a seat." After Maybelle was situated, she removed the old nail polish on Maybelle's short fingernails. The majority of Harper's clients were older women who didn't want the fuss of acrylic nails and preferred an old-fashioned manicure with their gossip.

"You know, I heard a rumor that Bootsie Mitchell is looking for a new society reporter for the *Muddy Gap Gazette*," Harper said.

"Now, you know I'm not one for rumors and such, but where on earth did you hear that?"

Harper fought a smile. Maybelle always pooh-poohed the evil rumor mill, but immediately perked up with interest at the word *gossip*. "Evidently Bootsie mentioned it to Bernice last week during her perm. Seems Lila Aldean is hanging up her reporter's pen for the society column."

"As well she should." Maybelle tsk-tsked. "Lord, Lila is almost ninety-five years old."

"I think you'd be the perfect person to fill the position, Miz Maybelle. You've lived here your whole life and you're about the only person I know who doesn't consistently use the word *ain't*, so your language skills are better than most."

A thoughtful pause followed. Then Maybelle said, "Why didn't you apply, dear? I know you're looking for work."

"Because it's a volunteer position. And I won't be around much longer."

Maybelle dunked her slightly gnarled hands into the solution and sighed. "Why is it that with all the years I spent up to my elbows in soapy water washing dishes, it never once felt like this? I feel so guilty."

"Don't feel guilty about pampering yourself. After all the years you cooked and cleaned for your husband and your family? You deserve it."

"I suppose that's true." Maybelle squinted at the rows of polish. "I'm thinking I'd like a bright color this time. Something daring."

"How about scarlet?" Harper plucked the color from the rainbow-hued lineup. "This one even has tiny specks of glitter."

"That'd give 'em something to talk about after bridge club, wouldn't it?"

"Yes, ma'am. They'll be so busy gawking at your nails they won't pay attention to the cards and you'll whip 'em good."

"Scarlet it is."

Harper dried Maybelle's hands and rubbed oil on her cuticles, giving her a hand massage.

"So is there any more news on Bailey's college applications?" Maybelle prompted.

"She's been accepted to Montana State, Colorado State, University of Nebraska, Idaho State, University of Northern Colorado/Boulder, and University of Wyoming. The only scholarship offer she's gotten is from UW and it's a full ride, for four years, including room and board."

"And she hasn't taken it because she thinks there's something better out there?"

Harper frowned. She didn't know why Bailey hadn't

jumped at the chance for free college. Whenever Harper brought it up, all Bailey would say was she was considering it. "Isn't that human nature? Always thinking there's something better out there?"

"What about you, Harper?"

"I'll go wherever Bailey goes. She'll need my support." *Even when she thinks she doesn't need it.*

Maybelle turned her hand and squeezed Harper's fingers. "That's not what I meant."

Confused, she looked up.

"Sometimes what we need is right in front of our faces and we can't see it."

Okay. That was vague. Harper smiled. "Let's get those nails buffed up and ready for that hoochie mama polish."

Maybelle tittered like a schoolgirl.

After she finished with Maybelle, Chrissy Baker raced in for a repair job because she'd broken two nails changing a flat tire on her pickup and she had a late date. Then Garnet requested a quick color change, which morphed into a full manicure and another round of whether a man was sexier wearing boxers or briefs.

Knowing she'd need the caffeine for later, Harper poured a cup of coffee and sipped, waiting for her next client.

"So you ended up working for Bran Turner, huh?" Bernice said.

"Yep. Luckily I don't have to drive to Rawlins every day and serve up fries or make beds to earn a living."

Bernice lit a cigarette. "That's all you feel you're qualified to do?"

Harper nodded.

"What were you studyin' at that community college in Casper?"

"Fashion merchandising and marketing."

"Really?" Bernice inhaled and blew out a stream of

smoke. "That seems the perfect fit for you. Do you plan on finishing your degree once you leave Muddy Gap?"

Harper was too embarrassed to admit that if she hadn't come home to take care of Bailey, she might've ended up coming home anyway because she hadn't been doing so hot with some of the college courses. "Depends on where Bailey and I end up."

Bernice studied her through the blue haze.

"What?"

"You gonna be okay when Bailey ain't your responsibility anymore?"

She'll always be my responsibility.

The doorbell clanged and all three hundred pounds of Mimi Julanski thundered in, saving Harper from having to answer Bernice's question out loud.

Chapter Four

❧

One week later . . .

*D*ue to a partial snowmelt Bran suggested they
check cattle with the ATVs instead of the truck.
It'd been a month since he'd double-checked a couple of
problem areas that he couldn't get to in his pickup. After
he'd loaded up wire cutters and other supplies, he wondered how Harper would fare helping with the most mo-
notonous aspect of ranching—fixing fence. But he didn't
doubt her ability. She'd done remarkably well with every
mundane task he'd set in front of her the last week.

So when Harper breezily assured him that she had
experience driving an ATV, he'd sped off ahead of her,
expecting that she would keep up.

She hadn't.

Not even fucking close.

Jesus. The woman drove like a ninety-year-old retire-
ment home escapee. At the rate she was meandering
along, it'd take them all damn day to reach the freakin'

fence, let alone have time to fix the damn thing once they actually got there.

Bran waited impatiently by the gate—the gate *he'd* had to open because his gate opener was a quarter mile behind him.

And when she'd finally puttered up alongside him, her cheeks pinkened by the wind, strands of blond hair sticking to her face and poking out of her hood, looking so goddamn cute and yet breathtakingly beautiful, he got instantly hard. And he got instantly mad about getting hard. He snarled, "Damn it, Harper. Is it too much to ask you to keep up with me?"

She peered at him over the top of her sunglasses. Dark, movie-star-type sunglasses bejeweled with pink and purple rhinestones in the corners above her eyes, for chrissake. "I didn't know we were racing."

"We're not. But—"

"This is a dangerous job. I'm not about to pitch myself off this thing headfirst into a snowbank because you want to prove you can outmaneuver me. You can. You win."

"The only danger you're in, sweetheart, is from falling asleep at the wheel because you're goin' too goddamn slow."

Harper smiled slyly. "Is that what you said to Les before his hip got broken? 'Hurry up'?"

He growled. "Just keep up."

"You go on ahead. I'll close the gate, boss."

Boss. Bran growled again. He zipped through the gate and across the field. All the way across the flattest part he didn't hear the rumble of her ATV close behind him, and since there wasn't a side mirror, he couldn't just glance in it to see where the hell she was.

Don't turn around and look for her.

He resisted the temptation for, oh, about . . . forty-five seconds. He slowed and spun around.

Fury bloomed when she raised her arm, from two hundred yards away, and waved at him like a goddamn . . . beauty queen atop a parade float.

She is a beauty queen, dumb ass.

Like he needed that reminder—it was obvious every time he looked at her. Regardless if she wore filthy, ripped, oversize coveralls, she carried as herself as regally as royalty. Bran waited. And fumed. When she got within ten feet of his machine, he thought about spinning a cookie and coating her with snow, just to be ornery.

But he didn't. He clenched his teeth.

"Is there a problem?" she shouted.

Yes. You are my problem. You've gotten under my skin like a burr and I can't stop thinking about you. All the damn time. Further incensed by his crushlike behavior, he snapped, "Do you have to work at the nail salon later this afternoon?"

"Yes. Why?"

"You'd better get a move on, then, because a section of fence needs to be fixed. Today."

"You're telling me I'm not leaving until it's done?"

"That's exactly what I'm telling you." He bumped along the trail to the broken fence line and noticed she'd managed to keep up after his pointed reminder.

Probably made him an asshole, but he slowed down. Way down.

Harper zoomed up, flanking him. "What's wrong?"

"Nothin'. Just makin' sure we're safe." He flashed his teeth at her.

She hit the gas, sped ahead, and sprayed him with snow.

Damn woman did have a little sass. And that was more appealing than seeing her in a swimsuit.

Okay. That was a total fucking lie. He'd give his left nut to see her in a skimpy bikini again. The last time he'd laid eyes upon the glory of her nearly nude body? She'd practically been jailbait and he shouldn't have been gawking at her, but he couldn't help it—she'd looked damn fine. The years had been good to her. Very good to her.

He was so lost in visions of Harper in a string bikini that he almost plowed over a fence post. He skidded sideways and killed the engine, acting as if he'd intended to get close enough to get splinters in his teeth and his tires.

He tossed the roll of barbed wire on the ground and grabbed his pliers. "See that sixth fence post in?" He pointed. "Take this end"—he unwound a section of wire—"and walk down there with it. Keep it straight and keep a tight hold on it."

"How tight?"

"Tight as you can. I like it tight and hard and I'm gonna be jerkin' on it harder than you'd expect."

Harper's mouth opened, then closed with a bashful smile.

When Bran realized how he'd phrased it, he actually blushed. He almost snapped at her to get her mind out of the gutter, when she inquired sweetly, "Wouldn't it be easier to put a metal clamp on it and then try to fix it?"

He loomed over her. "Excuse me, Miss Sweet Ass, but how many miles of fence have you fixed?"

"It's Miss Sweet *Grass*, Mr. Rude Behavior, and I was just offering a suggestion."

Fuck. He couldn't believe he'd called her Miss Sweet Ass. "I don't need your suggestions, Harper. I need you to do what you're told."

She gave him her back and sauntered away. And were his eyes deceiving him? Or had Harper saluted?

Unreal.

Sexy as hell, though, that little bit of sass.

Luckily, she held on to the wire tight enough so by the time he reached her it was a quick tie-off and then he could go to the next post. She walked to the broken section of fence line without being told.

Everything would've been fine and dandy if the woman hadn't felt the need to hum all the damn time. If he'd wanted to listen to tunes, he would've worn his iPod. But Harper wasn't whining, complaining, or, God forbid, chattering like a squirrel, so he let it go.

By the time they finished repairing the fence, a cold front had moved in and fine snow drifted down like powdered sugar, cutting visibility.

"Let's head back before it gets worse out here."

Harper helped him pick up his tools without him asking her, which he appreciated. As she headed to her ATV, she lost her footing. Bran snagged the back of her coat, keeping her upright. "Be careful."

She skidded sideways and latched onto the straps of his overalls to retain her balance. "Sorry. I'm not especially graceful."

"Not a problem." Her brown eyes were nearly gold in this light. Bran couldn't look away. But he knew if he didn't force himself to step back, he'd be tempted to brush the tiny flakes of snow from her pink cheeks. Or press his mouth to hers to see if he could warm up her cold-looking lips.

Her gaze dropped to his throat and she released him first, backing up. Way up. "Ah. Yeah. I'd better get a head start since I'm so slow."

Bran signaled for her to follow him. They cut across the sloped field to the cattle shelter. She stayed on her ATV while he took a quick count of how many cows he had in labor. Four. It'd be an easy night. But an easy night was always followed by a hard night.

The frigid air bit through his layers of clothes and he sped toward home. He was busy thinking about things he had yet to finish, when he heard a whining crunch behind him. He cranked his head and watched in shock as Harper was ejected off the ATV. She landed hard, her body crumpling, and the machine abruptly quit.

He jerked the steering wheel and raced back to her, panic flooding his chest. He'd barely gotten his ATV stopped before he skidded on his knees beside her on the frozen ground.

She was sprawled flat on her back. She wasn't fucking moving. Mouth dry, heart racing, fear ripping at his insides, Bran tried to remember what to do.

Check her pulse. Check her breathing. Check for injuries.

After tearing off his gloves with his teeth, he unzipped her jacket to the middle of her chest. He placed his shaking fingers on the pulse point of her neck.

Thump. Thump. Thump.

Beating heart. Thank God.

Harper's neck wasn't twisted at a weird, broken angle. But she'd been knocked out cold. Probably had the wind knocked out of her too. He lightly laid his head on her chest to hear her breathing.

Her chest lifted beneath his ear. Her lungs appeared to be working fine. He mapped the planes of her cold face and loosened her hood, running his hands over her scalp to see if she'd sustained a head injury.

No blood. No bumps.

"Harper? Sweetheart, can you hear me?"

Was it his imagination or did her nose wrinkle?

When he leaned near enough to feel her exhalations on his upper lip, her eyes opened.

Being a hairsbreadth away from Harper sent a shot of adrenaline straight to his groin. Holy hell, the woman was even more beautiful up close. He found his voice, although it didn't sound like his voice. "You okay?"

"I think so. What happened?"

"I don't know. I heard a noise and then saw you hit the ground. What's the last thing you remember?"

She stared at him. A look of comprehension entered her eyes. "The ATV got stuck in a lower gear. I glanced down at the RPMs and tried to shift, but it wouldn't budge. When I looked back up . . . I . . . umm . . ."

"What?"

"A bunny jumped in front of me and I swerved to miss it. Then I went sailing through the air. Guess I must've smacked into the ground pretty hard, huh?"

Bran rested on his haunches. "A bunny. You took a chance with your own life and your own safety to save . . . a fucking bunny?"

"Yes. You don't have to be such a jerk about it."

"I had visions of you . . ." *Hurt and it being my fault for pushing you.* He got to his feet angrily. "Never mind." He offered a hand to help her up and she batted it away.

"Where are my sunglasses?"

This woman was an absolute piece of work. She almost killed herself for a goddamn rabbit and now the only thing she gave a shit about was her sunglasses?

He spun around away from her, knowing if he stayed there another second, he'd chew her ass.

Crunch.

Looked like he'd found her stupid sunglasses. He closed his eyes and counted to twenty.

As he bent over to pick up the crushed plastic, he heard her gasp behind him. He whirled around and saw Harper crawling to her ATV.

Crawling. She'd rather crawl than accept help from him?

Can you blame her? You're being an ass and she prob-

ably is injured. She just has too much pride to admit it to you.

Screw that.

"What in the hell do you think you're doin'?" *Real compassionate, Bran.*

"I'm basting a turkey," she snapped. "What does it look like I'm doing?"

Jesus. Sweet Harper was snapping at him? Maybe she had smacked her head on a rock. Bran stepped in front of her, wrapped his fingers around her biceps, and hauled her to her feet.

Shit. Her eyes held that vacant look. "Harper? Sweetheart?"

"I'm not your sweetheart, but I am dizzy. Really dizzy." Her head fell forward into his chest. "I'm tired. Just let me sleep, you big meanie."

She called him a big meanie?

He could deal with being called an asshole, a douche bag, or a dumb fuck. But her calling him a big meanie . . . that made him feel ten times worse. No way in hell was she driving back to the ranch.

Resigning himself to having her tempting curves pressed against him, Bran lifted her into his arms. She was solid, but he managed to deposit her on the jump seat of his ATV with little trouble. He scooted in front of her, shoving her hands in his jacket pockets. He knew she was somewhat aware of what was going on when her arms tightened around him and she nestled her head into the middle of his back.

After what'd happened with Les, Bran didn't relish carting Harper to town to get her checked out, but he didn't want to take chances with an undiagnosed injury becoming serious either. It'd be better if he could get a medical opinion out here. Quickly.

An idea occurred to him. He dug out his cell phone and dialed Fletch, giving Fletch a vague rundown of her injuries and his location. Luckily Fletch was in his truck not far away and promised to swing by the ranch immediately.

Bran dug a thermal blanket out of the rear compartment, tucking it around Harper as best as he could, and waited.

Finally Fletch's big rig bumped into the pasture. Then Fletch hopped out, carrying a plastic-coated sheet and a duffel bag. The man was still built like the linebacker he'd been in college, so his gentle nature shocked most people.

But Fletch wasn't wearing his usual easy grin. He stopped in front of Bran's ATV and scowled. "Where is she?"

"Now, don't be getting mad, Fletch, but I didn't know who else to call."

Fletch nudged his cowboy hat up, training his gaze on Harper's form slumped behind Bran. "Jesus Christ, Turner, please tell me she isn't the injured heifer you were referring to when you called?"

Naturally, Harper chose that exact moment to become coherent. "What injured heifer? Where?"

Don't say it.

"He was referring to you, sugar," Fletch pointed out.

Shit. Bran felt her entire body stiffen behind him.

"Bran called me a . . . heifer?"

"Yes." Fletch snapped at Bran. "She's clearly not in need of *my* medical expertise."

Then Bran did something rare—he babbled. "She got pitched off the ATV. I thought she was fine. I did the basic checks for head and body injuries and then, wham! It was as if she clocked out. Vacant eyes. Listlessness. She couldn't even stand. She just . . . crashed."

"You didn't drive her to town . . . why?"

He didn't answer because really, what could he say?

"Because you knew I'd come running out here and save you the trouble, that's why," Fletch finished for him.

Harper peered around Bran's shoulder. "Excuse me. Who are you and why are you here?"

All Fletch's surliness vanished. He dropped his duffel and the sheet and smiled that cocky grin that made women swoon.

Maybe this hadn't been the best idea. Bran sure as hell didn't want Harper swooning over his buddy.

"I'm August Fletcher and I'm here because my lame-brain friend called me to check out your injury."

"Are you a doctor?"

"Of sorts."

Harper waited.

"I'm a veterinarian."

Silence.

Shit. Shit. Shit. This wasn't good.

Harper bailed off the back of the ATV like it was about to explode. Or maybe she was about to explode.

"A *veterinarian*, Bran Turner? Really? You called a *veterinarian* to look me over?"

Before Bran could formulate a reasonable argument, Fletch stood in front of Harper, probably to block the blows she intended to inflict upon Bran's neck and head.

"Now, look, sugar, I know you're mad at him. With good reason. But I am here. There are a couple of basic checks I can do to see if there's need for Bran to drive you to the hospital."

Another round of silence. Then, "Do we have to do this out here? Because, to be honest, I'm freezing."

"I'm sure. It'd be more comfortable to do it at Bran's place. Especially since I'll need to get you out of these clothes."

What the fuck? Fletch planned to take her clothes off? Bran glared at his friend.

Fletch placed his hand in the small of Harper's back, almost on her ass. "It's warm in my truck. You can tell me what happened and how you feel." Fletch shot Bran an arch look over Harper's shoulder. "See you at your house."

"How am I supposed to get both these ATVs back?"

"Not my concern. I have a patient to look after." Fletch stopped at the front end of his rig. "Take your time. I plan on doing a thorough examination on Harper. Just to make sure I don't miss anything."

Bran wondered how Fletch's smarmy smile would look with a few teeth missing.

∞

Her boss had called a veterinarian to check her out.

The jerk.

Her head hurt. Her butt hurt. But the sting to her pride? That hurt the worst.

Did Bran really think she was a heifer?

"I really think he meant well, Harper," Fletch said gently as they bumped through the pasture.

She folded her arms across her chest and snorted.

"How long have you been working for him?"

"A week. A very long week."

Fletch chuckled. "And how long did you sign on for?"

"Too long." Harper stared out the window, watching the snow blanket everything in white. It wasn't fair to take her anger out on Fletch. Not his fault that Bran was a jerk. "So you're a veterinarian who makes house calls?"

"Yep. I don't handle cats or dogs in my practice. I'm strictly a large-animal vet, so I make lots of ranch calls."

"Terrific. Now I really feel like a heifer."

Another chuckle. "Why don't you tell me what happened?"

After she finished, she studied his face as he processed the information. The guy was . . . big. He had to be at least six foot four. And broad. It appeared his shoulders took up half the seat back. His face was classically handsome, hazel eyes, and longish hair the color of strong coffee. A dark complexion, which hinted at Native American ancestry. And when he smiled? Lord. That dazzling grin glowed brighter than the snow surrounding them.

How was it that she'd never met him? Muddy Gap was a small community. She and Celia had frequently hung out with Hank and Abe's buddies. She definitely would've remembered August Fletcher. "You live around here?"

Fletch nodded. "In Rawlins. I also work in Cheyenne, Laramie, and all spots in between. I'm gone a lot."

He parked sideways, blocking the front steps to Bran's trailer. Harper wondered if he'd done it on purpose. Seemed like Fletch wanted to poke at Bran, to pay him back for calling him all the way out here to treat a human. A human female, no less. She was all for it.

Inside, Harper started a pot of coffee and returned to the living room.

"Why don't you take off the coveralls, boots, and all that outerwear and sit on the couch?" He tossed a fleece blanket at her. "Cover up in this to stay warm."

Fletch wasn't particularly chatty, nor was he in any hurry to start the exam. Or had he planned to have Bran present for it? When the whining ATV motor sounded close to the house, Fletch's entire demeanor changed.

"Stand." Then Fletch did the oddest thing; he dropped to his knees in front of her. He poked her lower abdomen through her shirt.

He'd moved up a couple of inches to test her ribs when Bran barreled in. Lordy, lordy. Bran was mad enough he didn't take off his boots. He clomped across the carpet, leaving muddy footprints and chunks of snow.

"What the fuck do you think you're doin' with your goddamn hand up her shirt?"

Fletch didn't acknowledge Bran at all. "Does this hurt?"

"No."

Two more soft pokes under her bottom rib on the opposite side. "This?"

"No."

"I can't see . . . Maybe it would be better if you unbuttoned your shirt, Harper."

"You gonna start humming the melody from *The Stripper*?" she asked lightly.

He chuckled.

Bran wasn't laughing at all.

She bit the inside of her cheek. Bran almost seemed . . . jealous.

Ha. Wrong. She had to be misreading him. Bran Turner didn't even like her. He thought she was a bunny-saving fat cow, for crying out loud.

As Fletch watched, Harper tried to keep from blushing, tried not to notice the avid stares at her chest, tried to keep her hands from shaking as she slipped the top button free from the buttonhole.

"Enough," Bran said hoarsely. "Goddamn it. Enough. If she needs to be examined that closely, I'll take her to the damn doctor."

Fletch rolled to his feet. "Fine. I'll remind you that *you* called me, Bran. I have one more reaction to test."

"Do it quick."

He unclipped a pen from his pocket and clicked it. A tiny beam of bluish light streamed out the end. He held her jaw firmly in his big hands, with his thumb pressed into the left side of her jaw. "Just a quick concussion check." He centered the silver pen in front of her nose.

"Follow the movement of the pen with just your eyes. Not your head."

Harper did.

"Good. So, how did a beautiful woman like you end up as this guy's hired hand?"

"Fashion merchandising and marketing jobs are a little hard to come by in Muddy Gap. So I had to improvise."

"Is that what your degree is in?" He switched the pen to the other side and slowly moved the beam of light.

"I'd have to finish school to have a degree."

"Do you plan to go back to college?"

"Maybe. Probably. I hope so, but not for a few years until Bailey and I are settled someplace." She gave him a brief rundown of why she was stuck in Muddy Gap.

"If you change your mind and want to stick around, I can always use a veterinary assistant in Rawlins. But fair warning, we'd be on the road together. A lot."

Was that a snarl coming from Bran? No, it was a sarcastic bark of laughter. He said, "Yeah, Harper is a real natural with goats."

"I am a bit of a greenhorn with livestock."

"We all are at some point." Fletch winked. "Bran must have really pissed off his last girlfriend, Charlie, to have gotten those fainting goats from her as a breakup gift."

Charlie was a woman? Seemed Bran had left out that factoid. No wonder the goats' names were Pox and Hex.

"Now stare straight ahead. I'm gonna shine this in both your eyes, but I don't want you to look at the light."

The instant that light hit, her eyes watered.

"Doin' okay, Harper?"

"I guess. For you searing my retinas into ash with that light."

"You can swear at me if you want."

"Thanks, but I don't swear."

"Ever?"

"Almost never."

"Why not?"

"Because my mom and my sisters have taken cursing to a whole new level and I couldn't possibly compete with some of their more . . . clever uses of the f-word."

Fletch chuckled.

"Plus, swearing like a cowboy is frowned on in the pageant system. Even in Wyoming."

"I hear ya. Just one more. There. We're done." Fletch clicked the penlight off and ran his hand down the side of her face. "You did great. I don't see any signs of a concussion, but I imagine you've got a helluva headache."

She nodded.

"I have to head back to town. Can I drop you someplace?"

"If it's not too much trouble."

"No problem."

"I have a problem with it," Bran said tightly. "She is my responsibility. She can crash here until her head feels better. I'll get her some aspirin and make sure she's able to drive before I send her home."

"*She* is capable of answering for herself, *boss*," Harper reminded Bran with false sweetness.

"And . . . that's my cue to leave." Fletch reached inside his coat, pulled out a business card, and pressed it into her hand. "You need anything, call me. My personal cell number is on there too." He stopped in front of Bran, who was rather pointedly holding the door wideopen. "Don't even think about bitching at me when you get the bill." Then he was gone.

Harper sagged to the couch.

And Bran, the always confident, always gruff Bran, actually looked . . . nervous, remorseful, and a little scared.

Served him right. But he also looked so . . . lost she just wanted to wrap herself around him.

He jammed his hands in the front pockets of his jeans and restlessly shifted his feet. "Ah, hell, Harper. I'm sorry. It was a stupid idea, havin' Fletch show up."

"Yes, it was."

If Bran was shocked that she hadn't gone all soft and let him off the hook, he didn't show it.

"I'll . . . ah, just get you that aspirin. And a pillow." He hustled down the hallway.

She didn't want to crash on Bran's couch. She preferred to go home. But her head was pounding and chances were high that Bran would argue with her, which would make her head hurt worse.

He returned with a bottle of aspirin and brought her a glass of water. "Here."

After she downed the pills, she reluctantly stretched out, tucking the pillow beneath her cheek.

Bran covered her with a blanket.

That was sort of sweet. Until she remembered he'd called her a heifer.

"Need anything else?"

"Just for you to wake me up in two hours because I have to work at Get Nailed."

"Can't you call in sick?"

"No. I promised Bernice this job with you wouldn't interfere with my job there. I'm the only nail tech she's got."

"Then I promise I'll wake you. I'll be back in my office doin' bookwork. Just holler if you need anything."

But Bran made no move to leave. They stared at one another.

He said, "What?"

"Do you really think I'm a heifer? Meaning I'm fat, uncoordinated, and stubborn?"

Horror filled his eyes. "No. God, no. That's what you think?"

She nodded.

"Of course you do, because that's what I said. Jesus. I'm a fuckin' idiot." He stepped forward and crouched down close to her. Very close to her. "You're about as far from fat . . ." Bran's gaze swept over her blanket-covered form, as if he were imagining her naked beneath it. "You're so goddamn flawlessly built with all these curves, I can't believe you'd think I'd ever see you as anything less than perfect."

"Oh."

"As far as uncoordinated, you were doin' just fine on the ATV until your hare-raising experience."

She fought a smile.

"So next time you see a bunny? Run the damn thing over, okay?"

Harper blinked at him. Faced with the same situation again, she would do the exact same thing.

Bran bestowed that heart-stopping smile on her. "You are stubborn, I'll give you that much." His smile faded. "Harper. Are you sure you're okay?"

"Besides the headache?"

"Yeah. I mean, if this is too much for you, I'd understand . . ."

"You'd understand if I . . . what? Wanna quit?"

His stormy gray eyes stared back at her, but his mouth stayed shut.

"Because I had one little spill?" Harper rolled her eyes. "Please. I understand working as a ranch hand can be dangerous, but so can any other job."

He didn't look convinced. "Oh, really?"

"Absolutely. For instance? When I was a waitress, the dishwasher spilled soap all over the floor and I crashed into the wall and nearly broke my arm. And when I was cleaning motel rooms, the vacuum I used had a short in the cord and I almost electrocuted myself. Not to mention all the times my butt got pinched when I was slinging drinks at the sports bar. Or worse, if a guy 'accidentally' stuck his face in my boobs. That was far worse than taking a tumble off a slow-moving ATV, trust me."

A dark expression crossed his face. "I hope you got sore knuckles from clocking those motherfuckers who pinched you. You shouldn't have had to put up with that shit—"

"My point is, any type of work can be risky, Bran. No biggie. I'll be fine, okay?" Harper squeezed his upper arm. Whoa. Talk about big biceps. She should move her hand, but somehow . . . she didn't.

"Okay. But I'll be watching you a lot closer. Guaranteed."

Why did the thought of Bran watching her closely send a delicious shiver through her from head to toe?

Probably because you're cold.

In a move that was hot, seductive, and unexpected, Bran ran the back of his rough-skinned knuckles down her cheek. "Sweet dreams, sweetheart."

She closed her eyes, wishing he'd continue that gentle stroking motion until she fell asleep. But his touch disappeared and his footsteps faded down the hallway.

Her dream was anything but sweet.

A bucolic scene unfolded, golden rays of sun shining on lush green grass. A floral-scented breeze stirred her hair, blowing the loose strands across her face. She looked down and saw boots on her feet, dark denim covering her legs, and her glove-clad hands wrapped around the top rung of a metal corral.

A man-size shadow fell across her and she shivered, but not with fear. Warm lips landed on the side of her neck, tasting the skin up to her ear. His breath teased the sensitive area until she arched closer for more.

"That's my girl," he murmured in a deep, husky tone.

When she turned her head for a kiss, he denied her. He held her chin in his fingers, forcing her to face forward. "Watch," he whispered gruffly.

A big black bull entered her peripheral vision, his cock distended, his balls swaying with every lumbering step. Two cows stood side by side. Waiting. Their breath coming hard and fast. The cow on the left cranked her head, and made a bellowing *moo* before trotting off. The cow on the right just stayed in place. Waiting.

"See how she lifts her tail? Letting him know she's ready?"

Harper nodded and Bran's fingers slowly traced the curve of her neck to where her heart pulsed in her throat.

"Is this rapid heartbeat telling me you're ready?"

Yes. For anything.

Then all fifteen hundred pounds of bull was practically vertical as he mounted the willing cow. After a half dozen powerful thrusts, the bull stilled briefly and dismounted.

The cow didn't move at all. She just went back to grazing.

"Aren't you glad that with human males it's not all about speed? It's about stamina. Not how many we service, but how well we service . . . just one?"

"Bran—"

"Ssh. Watch. The other one is gonna make him work for it."

Sure enough, as soon as the bull closed in, the cow trotted away. Not across the length of the pen, but far enough that the bull had to come to her. The male snorted and bulled his way forward. The cow twitched her tail and moved ahead of him.

Bran gave her a blow by blow of the bovine foreplay, which shouldn't have been sexy, but somehow was. His husky voice rasped terms like *thrusting power* and *hard mount* in her ear, and the simple words danced across her skin like fire.

Finally the bull had run the cow into a corner. She delicately lifted her tail and the grunting bull rose on his haunches. His big body shook as he thrust. But like the first go-round, this mating was short.

Bran's hands traveled the length of her arms and followed the length of her torso down, to circle her hips. He angled his head and nuzzled the other side of her neck. "You ever been taken like that, Harper? Hard and fast and dirty?" Those thick fingers squeezed her hipbones. "When all you care about is feeling your male's raw thrusting power?"

Harper whispered, "No."

"I could show you. Drop your jeans and be inside you in thirty seconds." He latched onto her earlobe with his teeth and tugged playfully. "But I wouldn't go fast. I'd go slow. Achingly slow. I'd stay deep. I'd stay on you. In you. Prove to you I don't think you're a heifer."

Her hands tightened on the corral. Her head spun with the feel of him, the scent of him, the hard strength of his body holding her up, turning her on even as he turned her inside out.

He trailed moist kisses to her nape. "Let me show you. All you have to do is open the gate."

"Gate? What gate?"

A buzzing in her pocket brought Harper out of the dream with a gasp as she opened her eyes. Ceiling tiles wavered above her, not the endless blue sky of the pastoral scene.

Holy crap. She was at Bran's house, having a wet dream about him.

How embarrassing.

How sexy and totally ... hot.

But still, she couldn't face him, knowing he would grill her about how she was feeling ... and *horny* wasn't an answer she was prepared to share. Her worst fear? That Bran would see the look on her face and figure out what she'd been dreaming about. Them. Getting ready to have sex against the corral fence like animals.

She dug her phone out of her front pocket and read the text message from Bailey. Shoot. She had to go. Now. She listened and heard the deep, rumbling tones of Bran talking on the phone. She dressed as quietly as possible and snuck out.

Chapter Five

❧

"**W**e've got time for coffee," Bran said the next morning. He shifted his grocery bag and ambled inside.

Harper followed him into his trailer. Would he mention her leaving without a word yesterday?

Bran kept his boots on, so Harper followed suit. She ditched her winter wear and sat at the chrome and black 1950s dinette table in the kitchen. He tossed a box of powdered-sugar doughnuts on the table and handed her a napkin. "Help yourself."

"Thanks. I can't remember the last time I had a doughnut."

"I'll admit I don't normally buy them either." He offered a rueful smile. "Consider them an early apology."

"For what?"

"For you havin' to be here this morning and then havin' to come back later tonight." Bran bit into the sugary confection and white powder dusted the front of his flannel shirt. "We're gonna have a bunch of calves drop tonight."

Harper broke her doughnut into four pieces. "So do you always know when the cows will start dropping?"

"No. But after checking them last night, I fully expect we'll see lots of activity. Will that be a problem as far as your sister?" He snatched another doughnut, as his first one was already gone. "Because you'll need to be here for the next few nights."

"She'll be eighteen soon and she is very responsible. I know she doesn't party, so me being gone won't be an excuse for her to invite her friends over."

"Totally opposite kid than I was my senior year. When I was seventeen my grandparents left me overnight to go to a stock show. We had a helluva party."

"Did they find out?"

"Yep. Ain't nothin' a secret for long in Muddy Gap."

"I suppose so." Harper grabbed another doughnut before her conscience could recite fat and calorie content. "Did you get in trouble?"

"Extra chores for a month, which wasn't a big deal since I knew Grandpa planned on making me do that shitty stuff anyway. So havin' the party was definitely worth it."

The coffeemaker beeped and Harper automatically stood.

"Sit. I'll bring you some. Black, right?"

"Right." She felt ridiculous for Bran waiting on her. As his employee, shouldn't she be waiting on him?

"What about you?" he asked as he set down two cups of coffee. "Were you ever a wild party girl?"

"No. Not that my mom would've cared if I'd gone out every night and got stinking drunk."

Bran lifted his eyebrows. "Really?"

"In fact, she would've preferred it. Then we could've been drinking buddies and we would've had at least one thing in common."

"You talkin' before or after you moved here?"

"Before. Once my mom figured out I could enter pageants . . . well, then she wasn't so embarrassed about me being a straight arrow. Drunk-and-disorderly charges are not exactly beauty pageant material, are they?"

"Hell, I don't know. Sorta depends on the title you're holding. Say you were crowned Miss Hulett during the Sturgis Motorcycle Rally? Them bikers would expect you to be tough enough to throw down shots with them." His lips twitched behind his coffee mug. "And hot enough to look good wearing next to nothin' riding on the back of a bike."

Harper pointed at him with a piece of her doughnut. "Which is why I haven't entered those types of contests."

"What made you choose the ones you did enter?"

Should she hedge? Or be totally honest?

Bran backtracked. "Sorry. Ain't my business. You don't gotta tell me."

"No. It's okay. I'm just trying to figure out how to phrase this to my new boss without it coming out sounding greedy." She took a drink of coffee. "The amount of prize money was generally the biggest reason to enter any contest."

"So it wasn't the sashes and trophies, and bein' crowned the best-lookin' girl in three counties with men drooling over you with lust that drew your entry?"

Lust? She almost snorted. "No. My mom never had a stable job. We never knew when she'd wanna pack up and leave. The prize money allowed me to buy my own car. Gave me a little stability. It also paid for college classes here and there." How had they gotten off track? "So, did you go to college?"

"No." Bran pointed at her cup. "Drink up. We've gotta get a move on."

Talk about an abrupt subject change. Harper ate the

last section of her doughnut. When she stood, Bran was right there.

The man smelled good. Warm with a hint of spicy aftershave. The skin on his cheeks and jaw was smooth, any shadow of his dark whiskers having been scraped away. His eyes were a deep gray, the color of a stormy summer sky. And his lips . . . so full and soft-looking. She could lose herself in them, kissing and nibbling and tasting him for hours. She spied a tiny bit of powdered sugar on his upper lip, and she used the tips of her fingers to brush it away.

His breath caught and she met his eyes. His eyes darkened, then smoldered with liquid heat. A look she'd never seen before and certainly one never aimed in her direction. She swallowed the immediate punch of lust.

This man is your boss. No playing kissy face with him.

Somehow, even though Bran kept staring at her, she found her voice. "Umm. You had powdered sugar on your face."

"Thanks." As if he remembered he shouldn't be standing so close, he sidestepped her. "Meet you at the truck."

∞

The day sped by—albeit almost in complete silence. Harper left the ranch, changed clothes at home, and hoofed it to her second job.

Nails, gossip, and Bernice lightened her mood—until an hour before quitting time when the front door chime jangled. They both glanced over to see Bran Turner stomping in. He didn't look at Bernice, just made a beeline for Harper and got right in her face.

"What is the point of havin' a cell phone if you don't ever answer the damn thing?"

"I don't answer it when I'm working, Bran."

"No shit. I've been calling you for two hours."

"So? You knew I had another job when you hired me.

Now, what's so all-fired important that you had to bust in here like an angry bull and chew me out in front of my boss?"

That question actually took Bran aback. "Sorry. I wasn't thinkin'." He sent Bernice a sheepish smile. "Miz Watson. I apologize for my rude behavior."

"I'll excuse it this one time, but you'd better offer up an apology to Harper too."

"Sorry, Harper." He didn't look at her, focusing instead on Bernice. "Would it be possible for me to have a word with her?"

"Sure. I'll be in the back." Bernice walked between them, leaving a trail of cigarette smoke in her wake.

Bran stared at Harper with that inscrutable gaze that gave no hint of what he was thinking.

"So? What's got you running to town like a crazy man?"

"I'm sorry. It's just . . . things have gotten hectic since you left and I hoped you could come back to the ranch earlier than we'd talked about."

"I'm free after my next appointment. Then I'll have to go home and change, but I can be right out after that."

"That'll work. Thanks." Bran's gaze dropped, taking its own sweet time traveling up the span of her body, lingering on the curve of her hips, encased in a short khaki skirt, and the tight fit of her blue satin Western shirt across her breasts. Finally his eyes caught hers and his wholly masculine appreciation, "Goddamn, you look good," knocked the breath out of her lungs.

She fought a blush . . . and lost. "Thanks."

"But I gotta admit, as much as I like seeing you lookin' all soft and girly? The way I like you best is when you're wearing my dirty coveralls."

Bran granted her that irresistible cowboy grin before he sauntered out the door.

The cowboy sent off mixed signals like no man she'd ever met.

∞

At two in the morning, Bran figured they'd seen the last calf of the night. They'd had to pull three, always a pain in the ass. Luckily all the calves and mothers survived, which wasn't always the case.

Harper had learned that fact firsthand last night, seeing a stillbirth. The mama cow mourned the loss of her baby with a series of frustrated bellows, and she kept licking the dead calf, nudging it, wanting it to get up but not understanding that it never would. Harper's eyes had taken on a sad sheen and she'd walked off by herself for a few minutes. Bran hadn't said a word to her when she returned; he'd just squeezed her shoulder. It'd been good for him to see some of this day-to-day ranch life—stuff he'd gotten cynical about over the years—through Harper's eyes.

They hadn't talked in the truck as they made their way back from the herd. When they reached the last gate, Bran had to shake Harper awake to get out and open it. Muttering, she hopped out of the cab and slammed the door. She stumbled, disappearing from Bran's line of sight. When she didn't immediately reappear, he slid from the truck's warmth and found her lying by the front tire, staring up at the sky.

Shit. Had she gotten hurt again? He crouched next to her. "Harper? You all right?"

"The stars are so pretty out here in the middle of nowhere, aren't they? They look so different in the wintertime. Almost like they've shriveled up from the cold."

"Come on, sweetheart, let's get you back in the truck."

Her gaze snapped to his face. "You're kinda pretty too, Bran. And sometimes? Your eyes twinkle like the stars."

She must've whacked her head to be spewing such sweet bullshit. He stood over her and enclosed her gloved hands in his. "On the count of three I'm gonna pull you up. You'll need to help me, or else I'm liable to jerk your arms out of the sockets. You ready?"

"No. I'm tired. Just let me sleep."

"You'll freeze to death out here. Count with me. One. Two." On three, he used the weight of his body to propel hers off the ground. As well as it worked, it also brought Harper directly against his chest, and he had to wrap his arms around her to keep them both from pitching over backward into a snowdrift.

Oh, man. She was so soft, and she smelled like flowers. And why was she wrapping her arms around him and pressing her lower half against his lower half?

No. No. No. If she touched him or gave him any kind of encouragement . . . Too late. Harper did a little grinding movement against the front of his coveralls. His body might be dragging, but all of a sudden his cock was wide-awake.

She sighed and ground into him again. "That was fun. Can we do it again?"

"Nope." Rather than trying to get her to walk, Bran scooped her into his arms. He managed to get the truck door open and deposit her inside without injury. He was dead on his feet as he opened the gate. Drove through. Closed it.

What seemed like an hour later, Bran parked and shook her awake. "Harper. Wake up."

"Where are we?"

"At the trailer."

Something must've clicked because she climbed out on her own and beat him to the door. She stopped.

"Whatcha waitin' for?"

"For you to unlock it."

He snorted. "I never lock my door."

"Someone might break in."

He shut the door and turned off the porch light. "You've seen the piece of shit trailer I live in, right? I ain't got nothin' worth stealing."

"But you have all those cool fishing doohickeys in your spare bedroom. I know. I peeked."

Fishing doohickeys. He fought a laugh.

Harper yawned and swayed into the wall.

He steadied her. "Whoa there."

"Tired."

"I know. Let's get you outta these clothes before you crash."

"'Kay."

Great. Now she was down to one-syllable answers. He tugged off her hat and gloves. Then he sat her on the ottoman and pulled off her boots. He unzipped her coat and the coveralls before bringing her upright again. Harper stood statue straight, not helping, but not impeding his progress in undressing her. Once she was down to socks, jeans, and her long-sleeved shirt, Bran began to remove his outerwear.

Harper said, "Good night," clear as a bell and walked down the hallway. Straight to his bedroom.

"Oh, no. Oh, *hell*, no." If that woman went into his bedroom, he couldn't guarantee he'd ever let her out again. Bran hopped on one foot as he removed his boots, and accidentally left his sock inside the shaft. *Zip.* His coat hit the floor. He shimmied out of his coveralls and left them wadded in a ball in front of the door. He took off down the hallway. "Harper. Don't . . ." Then he came to a dead stop in his doorway.

Holy. Fucking. Shit.

Harper had stripped down to her panties and bra. She'd sprawled sideways on his bed, the side of her face pressed into his comforter, her hair sticking up all over the place like she'd shoved her finger in a light socket.

Keep looking at her head, man. Do not let your eyes wander.

His eyes wandered.

Straight to her ass. Sweet Jesus, did that woman have a mouthwatering ass. Curvy and just wide enough for a man to grab a handful as he fucked her. She wore turquoise bikini panties with bright red lace around the leg holes and the waistband. The sweetest slice of her butt cheeks hung out of each side, where her thigh connected with her bottom.

Bran was instantly awake. And instantly hard. Again.

Oh, this is bad. Very, very bad.

He clenched his hands into fists, fighting the temptation to trace the curve of her legs from her ankles up and over that amazing ass, dipping into those sexy little indents at the base of her spine, then up the feminine arc of her back, stopping only to unhook the red bra. He'd brush the hair from her nape, letting his hot breath tease her before he kissed her there first, imagining the sweet and salty taste of her skin.

Harper stirred, making a sexy, low-pitched moan. She turned her head. Lifted her shoulder.

Oh, no. Oh, hell, no. Please do not turn over.

She rolled over.

Keep looking at her head, man. Do not let your eyes wander.

His eyes wandered.

Straight to the crotch of her panties. His mouth watered, hungrily taking in the rise of her mound, the cleft subtly pointing the way to her core. He forced his gaze up, sweeping over her flat abdomen and the cute notch of her belly button, stopping when he reached those luscious tits.

Holy. Fucking. Shit.

Her nipples practically spilled out of the deeply cut bra cups. The edges of the bra dug into the pale upper swells, leaving red marks on each side. That had to be uncomfortable.

Maybe you oughta take her bra off to alleviate the pressure.

No way.

Maybe you oughta kiss it and make it better.

Jesus. What was wrong with him? He was standing there drooling and fantasizing over her like a twelve-year-old virgin faced with his first half-naked woman.

But even Bran had to admit, this half-naked woman was riding the top of the leader board with one of the best bodies he'd ever seen.

Harper made that sexy-sounding sigh again and his dick jumped against his zipper.

Enough.

Bran grabbed the extra blanket off the dresser and threw it over her, resisting the temptation to tuck it around her. Any contact with her body would destroy his good intentions.

He retreated to the bathroom and locked the door. After shedding his dirty clothes, he stepped into the shower. The initial blast of cold water didn't affect his hard-on at all. His dick slapped against his belly when he leaned over to grab the soap.

Goddamn it. He'd get no rest until he got some relief.

Hello, Jack Off, his old friend. A friend he'd known intimately the last six months.

He rested his left forearm level with his forehead on the longest side of the enclosed shower. The water spray hit his groin. Bran grabbed his cock firmly by the root and started to stroke.

Harper's face appeared. Then it was her hand working him, not his. She knew exactly how he liked to be touched—slow, slow, and then *wham!* Fast and faster.

But in this wet dream, her fingers played with his balls as she kept the steady rhythm on his shaft. She wasn't watching her hand; she was watching his face. Raptly. When he groaned and sucked in a swift breath, she swept the pad of her thumb across the sweet spot beneath the cock head. Her breath whispered across his skin, drawing the flesh into goose bumps as she brought him closer to the edge. Heart racing, hips pumping, the slapping sound of skin on skin increasing inside the steamy shower.

She was attuned to his body's every response. When she felt his balls draw up, she eased her finger back behind that sensitive section of skin and rimmed his anus.

Bran started to come. In his mind, he'd pushed Harper to her knees. He replaced her hand with his own and aimed his cock at her chest. He came with a roar. Spurts jetted out the end of his spasming dick and hit the white shower wall. The image blurred again and he saw his seed landing on Harper's pale chest. Each spot of come slipped down the slope of her tits. One heavy dot clung on the end of her nipple like a milky teardrop.

Keeping her gaze locked on his, Harper caught the drop on her fingertip. She stuck that fingertip into her mouth and sucked.

Hot as fucking hell.

Bran let go of his dick and it bounced against his belly. He opened his eyes from his mental skin flick. Getting off had taken the edge off, but it left him craving the real deal.

Harper. Naked. Nine ways 'til Sunday.

He cleaned up the shower. After he'd toweled off he realized he hadn't brought fresh clothes with him. No fucking way was he sleeping in a towel all goddamn night when he'd already given up his bed. He made as little noise as possible as he slipped into his bedroom.

Harper had kicked the covers off.

Not only was she gorgeous, but she was so damn … cute. She'd charmed him this morning with the delicate way she'd eaten her doughnut—a proper lady having high tea. She'd surprised him when she'd slipped on his old cowshit- and grease-stained Carhartt coveralls, looking far removed from the gorgeously put-together beauty queen he'd seen her as at the salon earlier.

But the capper for him in this losing battle to keep things platonic? When she'd reached up and casually brushed the sugar from his lips as if it was the most natural thing in the world. It'd taken every ounce of his control not to suck those questing fingers into his mouth. As she'd traced the arc of his lips, she looked like she wanted to do so much more than just touch him, but she had no idea what to do first.

That was when Bran first suspected that Harper Masterson wasn't as skilled in bedroom arts as he imagined. Oh, she wasn't totally innocent. A beautiful woman like her wouldn't be untouched. But hers was a different level of innocence, and that scared him because he wanted to be the man to show her the pure pleasure of giving herself over to a demanding lover. How intense, sweet, and fulfilling it'd be to lose that sheen of innocence with a lover who would unleash all sides of her sexuality and expect her to embrace them without apology.

But on the flip side, Bran knew they'd be in close quarters, especially for the next couple of weeks. He needed her focused on helping him finish calving, not focused on whether her boss was going to make a pass at her.

How long could he hold out?

Another night, for sure.

He pulled on a pair of sweatpants and a T-shirt. He snagged a pillow and his sleeping bag, then shut off all the lights before bedding down on the couch.

Any additional fantasies about Harper faded as exhaustion overtook him completely.

Chapter Six

❧

*M*mm. The blanket felt soft and fuzzy against her bare skin, but it wasn't very warm. Harper shivered and rolled over.

Wait a second. She shouldn't be able to feel the blanket against her skin, since she never slept naked. Too many years of the fear that she would run into whatever bar rat her mom had picked up the night before if she went to the bathroom or the kitchen.

She opened her eyes and jackknifed in the middle of a king-size bed. Clutching the blanket to her chest, she squinted at her surroundings. Wood-paneled walls. Two dressers against the wall with a small window. Sliding doors that hid a closet. A ginger jar lamp on the nightstand next to an alarm clock. The red numbers flashed 3:15, but that wasn't right. It felt like early morning, but not that early.

The whole space was impersonal. Bland even. She inhaled a deep, slow breath and the scent of man, of the clean tang of aftershave filled her nostrils. Harper was in Bran's bedroom.

But where was Bran?

She'd slept on top of the covers. The sheets weren't mussed. Neither were the pillows. She scooted to the edge of the bed and set her feet on the floor. Her clothes were in a pile.

Good Lord. Why couldn't she remember stripping and falling into Bran's bed?

Maybe Bran stripped you.

Shoot. That was definitely something she wouldn't want to sleep through.

Harper shoved the blanket aside and dressed quickly, wrinkling her nose at the barnyard smell wafting from her clothes. She had a blurry memory of standing in front of the trailer door, waiting for Bran to let her in. Then . . . nothing.

She ventured out of the bedroom, passing the bathroom and two closed doors before she was in the living room. There he was. Warmth flowed through her when she saw Bran sprawled on the couch, his forearm across his eyes, the stubble of his beard darkening the angular lines of his face.

Although he was mostly covered, the lower part of his leg peeked out from beneath the fleece blanket. His sweatpants had slid up to his knee, revealing the dark hair on his leg and the muscled flesh of his calf. The muscles gave way to the stoutness of his ankle and the smooth white skin covering the top of his bare foot.

She'd never seen cowboy Bran without boots, or at least socks, on his feet. Seeing that vulnerable part of him—well, she wouldn't have felt more like a Peeping Tom if she'd gotten a glimpse inside his boxers.

Don't stare at his crotch.

She purposely scrutinized his foot, from his heel to the tip of his big toe. Mighty long. Hmm. She wondered if foot size really *was* an indication of the size of his . . .

"If you're done gawking at me, I'll get up and make us a pot of coffee," he said gruffly.

"Sorry. I didn't want to disturb you."

"Were you planning on takin' off without saying good-bye again?"

That was the first time he'd mentioned her sneaking out. She honestly thought he hadn't noticed. Or cared. "No. I just . . ."

Bran moved his arm and she was staring into his eyes. Oh. Not fair. Why were his eyes more blue than gray this morning? A bottomless blue like the wide Wyoming sky? She could totally lose herself in his eyes.

"Harper. You just . . . what?"

Her cheeks flamed as she realized she'd been gazing at him like he personally hung the moon and the stars solely for her. "What? Oh, right, I'm, ah, still pretty confused. I just don't remember anything from last night."

A dark brow winged up. "Nothin'?"

She blushed harder, if that were possible. "I remember you opening the door. That's it."

He shifted until his feet hit the floor. "Not much to tell. I helped you get your outerwear off. As I was takin' mine off, you disappeared. I found you in my bedroom stripped down to your very sexy underthings and passed out on my bed." Bran locked his gaze to hers. "I threw a blanket over you. Then I came out here and crashed on the couch."

Such a gentleman.

Such a pity.

Get a grip. "I'm sorry if I was a problem."

Bran grinned the wicked cowboy grin that fired every feminine molecule she had. "The only problem I had was walking away when I had a gorgeous half-nekkid woman in my bed."

How was she supposed to respond to that?

Don't. Ignore it.

Brightly, with a totally fake smile, Harper said, "I'll make coffee."

Was it her imagination, or was Bran . . . chuckling?

The coffee supplies were still on the counter from yesterday—had it really been only one day?—so she didn't have to dig through his cupboards. She sat at the dinette table, surprised that Bran hadn't changed out of his jammies.

Right. Like big, bad, tough cowboys called them *jammies*.

Silence. Complete silence beyond the gurgling noises of the coffeemaker. She couldn't think of a blasted thing to say.

"Harper? Are you okay?"

"No. I feel like such an idiot. Not remembering what happened last night, not only after we got back here, but before that. Everything is blank after we pulled that last calf. I'm sure you're used to hired hands who are tougher, able to go days without sleep. I just hit a wall."

"Part of calving is bein' completely exhausted, and that's why I needed help. I can't do it on my own. To be honest? I don't remember a whole helluva lot from last week. It's a blur. I'm fairly sure I didn't do nothin' stupid and endanger the cattle by falling asleep at the wheel and running them over."

Harper smiled. It was really sweet of him, trying to make her feel better.

"We're in the midst of the worst of it. About two and a half weeks from now, we'll be back to regular ranch chores for the rest of the time you're working here. It'll seem kinda boring."

"I doubt that." The coffeemaker beeped. Harper made him sit while she poured them each a cup and brought it back to the table.

He leaned back in his seat and stared at her as he held the mug between his big hands. "Since you spent the night in my bed, should I be offering to make you breakfast?" he asked with a silky growl.

Her face heated to the point she probably could've fried an egg on it. "Bran."

"Damn. Woman, I love to see you blush."

Really? He did? "It's dorky. All splotchy-faced like a fourteen-year-old girl."

"It's sexy," he countered with another one of those rumbling growls. "Makes me want to find out firsthand if that pretty pink flush covers your whole body, not just your cheeks and your neck."

Harper managed to look Bran in the eye. "Do you tease Les like this? Or are you doing it to me because you think I won't fight back?"

"I give Les ten times more crap on a daily basis than I've given you." Bran shrugged and sipped his coffee. "It's just the way I am."

"Is this where you tell me you wouldn't tease me if you didn't like me?"

"Yep." He smirked. "But from what I've seen? You can hold your own. So don't be afraid to call me on my shit if you think I'm full of it."

"Bet on it." Harper grabbed her purse and fished out her cell phone to check the time. After nine. Hopefully Bailey had hauled herself out of bed and made it to the bus stop. There weren't any missed calls or text messages, so she took that as a good sign.

"Problem?" Bran asked.

She met his gaze. "No. If it won't upset your schedule too much, I'd like to be at home today when Bailey gets out of school and stay with her until after we've had supper."

"That'll work. I doubt we'll see too many births during

the day, but I'd like to check the cattle before you take off. We need to ear-tag last night's calves."

"Okay."

Both she and Bran were dragging as they split bales of hay. When ear-tagging the new calves, Harper distracted the mamas while Bran attached the tag to the baby. With some of the mamas she could walk right up to the calf and they wouldn't fuss. But others, if she got too close, they'd paw the ground like a bull and charge. So far Bran had snuck in without getting knocked around. She felt safer being on an ATV, figuring she could outrun the protective cows on a machine faster than she could on foot.

They didn't finish until noon. Harper had to leave the driver's-side window open and allow frigid air to blow on her on the way home to keep from falling asleep.

As she stumbled into the house, she realized that for the past three days her life had been a blur. Work, shower, sleep. Work, shower, sleep. She shed her clothes at the front door and made a beeline for the bathroom.

She couldn't muster enthusiasm to put on anything except her robe, which reminded her that all her casual clothes were filthy. She filled the washing machine and flopped on the couch, planning to rest her eyes until the load finished.

The front door slamming brought Harper straight up off the couch. She blinked bleary eyes at her sister. Her angry sister.

"Fuck. I hate school. I can't wait to be outta there. I'm gonna flip off every goddamn teacher right after I get my diploma and burn my goddamn uniforms." Bailey's backpack hit the floor with a thud. She threw off her coat, kicked off her snow boots, and stomped to the bedroom—a feat in stocking feet—and slammed the door.

This should be a fun afternoon.

Yawning, Harper tossed her clothes in the dryer before she took stock of the food situation. She had all the supplies to make lasagna—Bailey's favorite—and it might coax her out of her room sooner rather than later. Bailey was pretty even-keeled, but when she got mad, she stayed mad. Through trial and error, Harper had learned not to force her sister to talk it out. Some days, being a parental figure to Bailey was overwhelming, especially when Harper still felt like a lost kid herself.

Cooking soothed her because it was one of the few things in her life she could control. Mixing the right ingredients, adding her twist to traditional dishes that allowed them to be unique yet familiar.

Harper had been cooking, or at least scrounging up meals, since the year she'd turned twelve and Liberty had left the family to join the army. Their mother had spiraled into a drunken rage, spending months in deep depression, forcing Harper to become the responsible one in the household. Since Mom tended to blow all her tips on booze, cigarettes, and lottery tickets, Harper had learned to keep cheap staples on hand so she and Bailey wouldn't starve during the weeks when there wasn't money for groceries. Over the years, Harper had gotten very good at budgeting food and money and trying to make whatever crappy rental they landed in feel like a real home.

How many times had she imagined growing up a normal kid? Where home was a two-story Colonial house in the suburbs with a manicured lawn, a tire swing hung from an old oak tree in the backyard next to a playhouse, or better yet, a tree house. She'd dreamt of birthday parties with layer cake and homemade ice cream and beautifully wrapped presents. Surrounded by friends. She'd wished for a bike for herself and a baby doll for Bailey to appear under the tree on Christmas morning. She'd imagined hot summers selling lemonade on the sidewalk and swimming at the lake. Winters sledding and ice-skating and coming home to a steaming cup of hot chocolate with mini marshmallows.

Around age thirteen she'd given up on hopes for a normal life, pushing girlish dreams aside. She just wanted to survive until she turned eighteen and could take off like Liberty had.

Except that hadn't happened. With the way things always went in Harper's life, it probably never would. Some people were born lucky, or at least with a sprinkling of cosmic goodness, and things went their way once in a while. Not her. Not ever. She'd gotten so used to picking herself up, dusting herself off, she wouldn't know what to do if the universe ever smiled on her.

After sprinkling Mozzarella cheese on the top layer of sauce, Harper popped the lasagna in the oven. She washed the last of the veggies, which were looking a bit wilted, and chopped a salad, adding a sweet-and-sour dressing. She set the bread machine on the counter, dumping flour, oil, yeast, and a pinch of sugar and salt into the inner pan. Nothing in the world smelled as delicious as fresh-baked bread filling the house with a homey scent. Plus, it was a lot cheaper to bake her own.

She poured a glass of water and scowled at the postage stamp–size backyard covered in a layer of dirty snow. The hedge separating their house from the one behind it offered minimal privacy. In the summertime Harper hesitated to hang their clothes on the line, suspecting that snoopy Mrs. Johnston was peering through her blinds to see if Harper or Bailey wore stripper clothes or indecent lingerie.

And speaking of lingerie . . . could she just say a prayer to the underwear gods for being down to her last clean pair of underwear and bra yesterday? Forcing her to put on the nicest ones she owned? Thank God she hadn't worn tattered granny panties and the underwire bra that actually had a wire poking out of it.

But maybe Bran thought she wore matching lingerie all the time. That'd fit the beauty queen persona he attributed to her. So, how long had he checked her out before he'd covered her?

Her cell phone buzzed in her robe pocket. "Hello?"

"Little sister. How is the hellhole known as Muddy Gap, Wyoming?"

"Cold and snowy. How is the hellhole known as Afghanistan?"

"Cold. And shitty. So, speaking of shitty . . . Bailey tells me you've got a shitty new job—literally shoveling shit as a hired hand on some dude's ranch. What's up with that?"

Harper filled a mug with water and put it in the microwave. "I lost one of my jobs and had to find another ASAP, oh, you know, so we can eat and pay rent and trivial stuff like that."

"But a ranch hand? Harper? You? Really?"

"With the mess Mom left us in this time no one in town wants to hire me. Beggars can't be choosers."

"So why is Bailey in a piss-poor mood and hiding in her room?"

"Who knows?" She heard Liberty exhaling. Smoking like a chimney—another great habit their mother had passed on to her oldest daughter.

"Tell me about this rancher dude. Is he old? Fat? Mean? Ugly?"

"No. No. No. And definitely no."

"Spill. I've been without sex for . . . God, I don't even remember what it's like to have someone else's fingers touching me or what an orgasm is like without a vibrator."

Liberty had always been blunt to the point of rudeness. Serving in the army, surrounded by mostly men, only increased her bluntness and crudeness.

"You doing the nasty with him?" Liberty asked.

Harper dunked a mint tea bag in the cup of hot water. "No, I'm not sleeping with him. I'm working for him. And *ew*, I didn't need to know why you're always asking us to send you extra batteries in the care packages."

Liberty laughed. And coughed. And went right on smoking. "So this rancher dude is young, built, nice, and good-looking?"

"Yes. Yes. Yes. And definitely yes. Before you ask, yes, he's straight."

"Damn. I was having a *Brokeback* moment."

"You are hard up."

"You have no idea."

"How's that possible, Lib? You're surrounded by men."

"The guys in my unit are off-limits. The guys in the other units stationed here are all married, or they look twelve years old and act like it. So I ain't getting any until I finish this deployment."

Another thing Harper added to her list of worries: the danger to Liberty in her service to Uncle Sam. "When is this deployment over?"

"Who the fuck knows? Rumor is they're extending us for another three months, until the replacement units are up to speed. That's all I can say or this call will mysteriously end."

"I understand. It's just . . . I miss you." God. She sounded whiny. "It's probably stupid, but I was hoping you could be here for Bailey's graduation."

"I would if I could, Harper. You know that."

"Yeah. I do." In the background she heard a man shout, "Bert. Get your ass over here."

"Shit. I gotta go."

"Who's Bert?"

"That's me. Being called Bert is a fuckload better than the sissy-ass name Liberty that Mom saddled me with. Jesus."

"At least you didn't have kids calling you Harpy."

"True."

"Be safe."

"Always. Love you."

"Love you too." The line went dead.

Two hours later, not even the scent of tomato sauce, melted cheese, and oregano coaxed Bailey out of her room. Harper ate alone, and wrapped up a package of leftovers for Bran. She shoved the rest of the food in the fridge and headed out to the ranch, trying to shake the feelings of desolation and isolation.

∞

Ridiculous how happy Bran was to hear Harper pull up. He paced the short length of his living room, forcing himself to wait a solid minute before he opened the door.

Then he felt like a total heel because her arms were loaded with stuff. "Hey. What's all this?"

Harper didn't say anything until she'd set the plastic grocery bags on the table and started to unload containers. "I hope you don't think I overstepped my bounds as your employee, but I had food left over from our supper, so I brought you some."

Bran tried not to stare at her with distrust, but he'd become wary of women who "had a little extra food." They always had an ulterior motive, usually a night or two in his bed. But some made no bones about the fact they wouldn't mind cooking for him every night. Nothing sent him into full retreat faster than a woman thinking she could set up housekeeping with him.

Even a woman like Harper? Who is gorgeous, sweet, funny, and sexy as shit?

Before he could figure out Harper's motive, she began putting all the containers back in the bags.

"Whoa. What are you doin'?"

"Taking this back to the truck."

"Why?"

She gazed at him coolly. "You don't want it. I was stupid to assume you would. It won't happen again."

Guilt kicked him in the ass. "Look, Harper, it's nothin' personal. I just get suspicious of women who want to feed me."

"No need to explain, boss." She sidestepped him and reached the door before he stopped her.

"Goddamn it, wait just a second."

She blinked those hard, whiskey-colored eyes at him.

"It's a knee-jerk reaction, okay? I know you're not one of the local women who see a bachelor and think the way to my heart is through my stomach and I'll be so damn grateful for a home-cooked meal that I'll propose marriage. We both know that ain't the case with you. You're leavin' at the beginning of the summer."

When her eyes didn't soften at all, Bran swore. "Jesus, I'm doin' this all wrong. You did something nice for me just to be nice, and I threw it back in your face. I'm sorry. Really goddamn sorry. Been a long damn time since anyone has done anything nice for me without wanting something in return. Obviously I don't know how to act, and my grandma is probably spinning in her grave. So if it ain't too late, I'm starved, the food smells great, and . . . Thank you for thinking of me, Harper."

Her lips curled into a smile. "Apology accepted. But you lost any hope of me dishing it up for you."

"Hell, I'm such a boor I'll probably just eat it right out of the damn container."

She handed over the plastic bag. "Have at."

Bran spread everything on the table and opened the fridge. "You want a beer?"

"No." She paused. "You know what? On second thought, yeah, I could use a beer."

"Me too." He popped the tops on two bottles of Bud Light. "Ah. You want a glass or something?"

She shook her head and took a long drink.

He grabbed a fork and lifted the lids on the food. Lasagna. Some kind of veggie salad. And bread. Soft, fresh, homemade bread. He might've actually moaned a little. God knew, his mouth was watering like a busted sprinkler. He took a bite. Yep. It was as delicious as it smelled.

Neither spoke as he shoveled in every morsel. He mopped up the last of the red sauce from the lasagna with the last hunk of bread. Then he pushed his chair back and sighed. "That was amazing. Can you cook like that every night?"

"Yep."

"I've changed my mind. Will you marry me?"

Harper laughed. "No. Way. I'm getting out of Dodge, remember?" She swigged from the bottle and smirked. "And to think I didn't even make dessert."

You could be my dessert.

"You'd be putty in my hands if I whipped up a batch of my triple chocolate caramel brownies."

You'd be putty in my *hands if you let me put my hands on you.*

"Bran?"

He drained his beer. "Sorry. I got to thinking about something else. We'd better get a move on before I start to feel sleepy from that tasty supper. Thanks again."

"You're welcome. I'm glad someone appreciated it." She gathered up the containers and set the plastic bag by the front door.

"Didn't Bailey like it?"

"I don't know. She wouldn't come out of her room."

They stood in the small entryway, donning the heavy winter clothes that were such a pain in the ass to take on and off multiple times during the day. He whistled. "Harsh."

She shrugged. "Her loss."

Ask her if she and her sister had a fight.

No. Bran promised himself he'd keep it friendly with Harper. Not flirty, just friendly. Treat her like he'd treat Les . . . if Les had great big beautiful tits, the face of an angel, and an ass he'd like to take a bite out of.

Great. They were only ten days into this hired-hand business. He'd sworn last night he would cool his libido. How was he supposed to keep it businesslike?

Treat her like an employee.

Bran pulled his gloves on. "When we get back, bring me your time sheet and I'll get it ready to take to the accountant."

Harper never glanced up from zipping her coveralls. "My first paycheck or my final paycheck?"

"First. You've done a good job so far."

"Thanks, boss." She grabbed the bag with the empty food containers. "I'll take this out to the truck and find my time sheet and give it to you now. That way I won't have to come inside when we get back."

"But—" he said to the door slamming in his face.

Even when Bran swore to himself that he'd done the right thing, reminding Harper of their employer/employee relationship, her clipped reaction stung a bit.

And he suspected it'd get a whole lot colder in the weeks to come.

Chapter Seven

❧

Three weeks later . . .

The woman was driving him fucking nuts.

Keeping their interaction businesslike hadn't cooled his lust—no, just the opposite. It had increased that lust exponentially.

Harper had morphed into the chilly blonde with an icy smile. She wasn't rude, but she didn't speak beyond answering his specific questions or asking questions. She showed up on time. She knocked on the door to let Bran know she was there, but she didn't help herself to a cup of coffee. Nor did she come inside to get warmed up when they'd been working in the dead of night in the frigid cold. She climbed in the ranch truck and returned to town.

Goddamn, Bran knew it made him a hypocrite for wanting things to revert to the way they used to be—their sexy banter, the sweetness and thoughtfulness she showed him—because he was the freakin' idiot who'd initiated the reversion to a purely business relationship.

And it amazed him how quickly Harper had caught on to everything in the daily, never-ending grind that constituted ranch work. She worked as hard as he did and rarely questioned his decisions—something Les hadn't managed to do over the years.

With only about twenty calves left to drop, Harper hadn't been returning at night. She showed up at o'dark thirty, worked until three o'clock, when her sister returned from school, and then headed to her shift at Get Nailed.

Instead of experiencing the usual wave of happiness that filled him at the end of calving season, Bran had spent the last two days in a foul mood. Really foul. He hadn't snapped at Harper. Hell, he'd barely spoken to her. But he'd been watching her. Man, had he ever been watching her, consumed with jealousy.

Seemed Miss Harper had transferred the care and concern she'd briefly lavished on him to the assorted critters around the ranch. Including a hutch of bunnies that'd taken up residence under his front deck. She left scraps of lettuce and vegetable peelings scattered outside the rabbit hole, trying to coax them out so she could pet them, for chrissake.

So in his wisdom, or machismo, or whatever stick he'd had up his ass that day, he'd curtly told her to stop feeding them, tossing off the comment that the fuzzy targets were as good as dead anyway when he pulled out his twenty-gauge shotgun.

That was the only time in the past twenty-one days that Bran had caught a glimpse of the old, sassy Harper. She'd gotten in his face and told him if she wanted to feed the mama rabbit and her bunch of babies, she damn well would. And he could deal with it or fire her.

Yes, the clean-mouthed beauty queen who wouldn't

say *shit* if her life depended on it had sworn at him that day.

Fucking pathetic how much it'd turned him on.

So the wee wittle wabbits had become a point of contention between them. Harper continued to feed them; he continued to bitch about it.

Not only had the pied piper of Muddy Gap befriended bunnies, she'd made amends with the goats—by sneaking them treats. Lots of treats. Bran hadn't been happy to discover that she paid for those carrots and apples out of her own pocket. But when he'd attempted to put an end to the gourmet goat grub, once again the woman flat-out ignored him and followed her own agenda. It'd gotten to the point that the goats didn't give a shit if he ambled into view with an entire bucket of premium oats. They only had eyes for Harper.

A feeling he was beginning to understand way too well.

But despite their prickly relationship, Harper busted ass on the ranch from the moment she arrived until the moment he dismissed her. She'd cleaned out the biggest stall in the barn without complaint when Bran had brought his favorite pregnant mare in to foal. Harper had stuck around to watch the birth and cried when the colt had taken its first wobbly steps. That birth created a bond between Harper and the little guy, plus she'd paid the proud mama proper attention, so the mare and her baby were smitten with her.

Another feeling Bran understood only too well.

So she hadn't seemed happy when she'd shown up at the ranch today and discovered Bran had turned the pair out. But she hadn't questioned him, or confronted him, she'd just gone back to work. Bottle-feeding the calves. Indulging the goats. Baiting the bunnies. Goading him by ignoring him.

Bran knew a fight was imminent.

They'd gone about daily chores as usual. She cut the strings on the bales of hay after he'd scooped them up with the tractor. She dutifully jotted down notes when he spied sections of fence that needed fixing. She opened and closed gates, while humming that annoying "9 to 5" song.

The instant they pulled into the yard, she bailed out of the truck as if she couldn't stand to be in the cab with him another second.

Bran stormed after her into the barn and snapped, "What do you think you're doin'?"

She whirled around. "My job."

"Huh-uh. You jumped outta the truck before I had the chance to tell you what job I wanted you to do next."

"So sorry, boss, that I jumped the gun and took some initiative. But I'll remind you I need to finish up what I didn't get done after I got here this morning because you had to chew me out first thing for feeding the bunnies."

"I told you to stop feedin' them, Harper."

"I don't get why it's such a big deal."

He loomed over her, crowding her against the outer stall. "Ever heard the phrase 'reproducing like rabbits'? That's what happens when they have an unlimited food supply. You feed them, and suddenly I've got a bumper crop of bunnies, which I sure as hell don't want to deal with after you're gone."

"Oh, yeah? Well, I'm surprised you haven't scared them off, with the way you've been stomping around for the last couple of days, grumpy as an old bear."

"It's your fault. If you hadn't—"

Harper drilled him in the chest with her index finger. "No, sir. You are *not* pinning your crap attitude on me, Bran Turner. I've been doing everything I'm supposed to do and then some. So I don't know what else you want from me."

In a split second, Bran made his decision. He said, "I'll show you what I want." Then he lowered his mouth and kissed her.

It wasn't a hard kiss; though God knew he could've inhaled her lush lips and sweet mouth from the get-go. He forced himself to take it slow, giving her every chance to push him away.

Harper didn't even try.

But neither did she move. She just let him brush his mouth across hers, over and over. Tasting her top lip, and bottom lip. Kissing the corners of her mouth, coaxing her to kiss him back. To open her mouth and invite him inside. When Bran licked the seam of her lips, her breath caught on a soft gasp.

He swallowed that gasp, taking her invitation for an openmouthed kiss. His tongue sought hers, teasing and stroking, cranking the intensity until they were sharing the same breath. Even as they changed the angle of their heads, attempting to swallow each other whole, their lips were only apart for a fraction of a second as undeniable hunger consumed them both.

When Harper's arms slid up his chest to circle his neck, he growled a warning, pushing her hands against the wooden slats above her head. Letting her know that he was in charge.

She moaned, arching her back, forcing their bodies to touch. Despite the fact that they were dressed in thick winter clothes, that movement affected him as strongly as if they were skin to skin.

Bran kissed her harder, bumping his hips into hers. Wanting her beneath him in his bed. Wanting her bent over the edge of the couch as he took her from behind.

Wanting her straddling him as they rocked in the easy chair. Wanting her on her knees with his hands gripping her hair as his cock plunged in and out of her pliant mouth.

Would you be paying her for these services? Since she works for you?

He froze immediately and pushed back from her, staring at her kiss-swollen lips. Lust, fear, need, anticipation, and regret swam in his head, leaving him so confused he wasn't sure which emotion was the right one in this situation.

If he felt that way, what was Harper thinking?

At this point, he was too much of a chickenshit to stick around and find out.

His voice was barely a whisper when he said, "Fuck. I . . . we can't . . . I shouldn't do this." He spun on his bootheel and walked off without looking back.

∞

Put that amazing kiss out of your mind.

Confused and hurt, Harper unloaded the last of the stuff from the pickup and shut the barn door.

On the way home she cranked up the country music and sang along with the radio, tunes about lying, cheating, and drinking. She showered and changed into her favorite outfit for her shift at Get Nailed, but even that didn't improve her mood.

Bailey came home and chattered away, appearing not to notice Harper's distraction. As the middle sister, Harper had always been incredibly attuned to her family's moods. Might be petty, but it sucked that Bailey didn't care about her frame of mind. Chewing her sister out for being a teen wouldn't be fair, so Harper left for the shop early.

Friday afternoons were busy with a younger female crowd looking to get prettied up for a wild weekend. Talk

turned to bar hopping, one-night stands, and normal par-
tying stuff that people her age did. Harper didn't begrudge
anyone fun, but even if she hadn't been responsible for
raising Bailey, it wasn't her style to go out every weekend,
trying to get drunk and laid. She'd witnessed the aftermath of that attitude and lifestyle with her mother, and
she had no desire to repeat it.

"That purply pink would look kick-ass with what I'm
wearing this weekend."

Roused out of her melancholy, Harper plucked the
color from the row of pinks and held it out to her former
classmate, Tiffany DeMeter. "This one?"

"Perfect."

As she brushed the polish on, she sensed Tiffany staring and braced herself. "What?"

"Why don't you come out with us tonight? We're
whooping it up at Cactus Jack's. It'll be a blast. We can
crash at Lita's place so we don't have to drive back from
Rawlins."

"Thanks for the offer, Tiff, but I have to work bright
and early tomorrow morning. So make me jealous and
tell me what you're wearing that'll wow all the cowboys."

The instant Tiffany had the chance to talk about herself, she ran with it. Harper barely got two words in edge-
wise, which was just the way she liked it.

"Well, hello, handsome," Tiffany said with a throaty
purr.

Harper's back was to the front door, away from the
temptation of looking up whenever a new customer
strolled in. This time, however, she did turn around. Tiffany had hit the nail right on the head—the long, lean
cowboy was striking, and that was saying something.
Good-looking cowboys were a dime a dozen in this neck
of the woods.

This guy doesn't have anything on Bran Turner in the looks department.

She ground her teeth. She'd done such a great job of putting the man out of her mind. Facing Tiffany again, she switched her hands. "Do you know him?"

"No, but I'd like to."

"Maybe you should invite him to Cactus Jack's tonight."

"That's a damn good idea. Ooh, and look. Bernice is cutting his hair, so he won't be able to get away when I talk to him."

The thought of the poor man being unaware that he'd become Tiffany's captive audience caused Harper to grin.

With no other customers scheduled, Harper cleaned up her station. For the first time in weeks she didn't have to hustle to race to her other job.

"Excuse me."

Harper whirled around. The object of Tiffany's affection stood on the other side of her table. "Yes?"

"Do you have time for another manicure?"

"Sure." Harper expected he'd bring in his wife or a girlfriend, or even his mother. Never in a million years had she expected him to sit down. Her mouth dropped open. "A manicure for . . . you?"

"You sound shocked."

"I am. I've never given a man a manicure before."

He grinned. The tiny gap in his front teeth added a certain roguish charm to his almost too perfect golden good looks. "Manicures ain't all the rage for real Wyoming men?"

"No, sir."

"Maybe I'll start a trend."

Harper laughed.

"Such a melodic laugh you have," he murmured.

Blushing, she scooted her chair up to the table. She gestured for him to set his hands on the towel. Instead, he thrust his right hand at her.

"I'm Renner Jackson."

"Harper Masterson."

"Pretty name for a pretty lady."

Harper rolled her eyes. "Be careful with the compliments and pickup lines, Mr. Jackson. I might think you're overcompensating for something."

He threw back his head and laughed. Harper knew everyone in the salon was watching.

"Harper, darlin', I assure you I'm all man. And I'll admit to liking the ladies a little too much—that's probably why I've got two ex-wives." He finally set his hands on the towels.

She winced. His fingers were a real mess. The skin was red, chapped, cracked, and peeling. Two of his fingernails were completely black. He'd be losing those two nails before long. The lines under his fingernails were pure black. Too black to merely be dirt.

"Nasty, huh?" he said.

"Are you a mechanic?"

"As a hobby. My main business is a stock contractor, which means I'm outside a good chunk of the time. I wear gloves"—he turned his hands over, palms up—"but sometimes that makes it worse because the gloves get wet. Then my hands chap and freeze. It's a never-ending cycle."

"So what have your other manicurists done? I'll admit this is out of my league." She met his gaze. Wow. Up close, Renner had startling eyes. A periwinkle blue.

"Honesty. I appreciate that, Harper. Usually, they soak 'em, clean the nails, and push back the cuticles. I reckon the same treatment you give other clients."

"That's all?"

"Then they give me a wax dip, or rub heavy-duty cuticle oil into them and then put on a pair of cotton gloves and let the oil soak in."

"We don't have wax, but I've got a really good oil that penetrates fast. It'll help."

"Anything would be better than this. Tomorrow I gotta look like a businessman, not a grease monkey."

Harper found the deepest tub and he winced when she placed his hands in it.

After he relaxed, Renner focused on Harper's hands. "You don't have fancy fake nails like other nail technicians I've seen."

Was her lack of acrylic nails with designs that could be changed on a whim considered bad advertising? Heck, she never painted her nails these days. Keeping them trimmed was the extent of her nail maintenance routine.

"Is it because you're the only nail tech in town and you can't do your own nails?" Renner prompted.

"No. I swore when I finished my last official obligation as Miss Sweet Grass, I wouldn't ever wear fake nails again."

"You were Miss Sweet Grass?"

"And Miss Rawlins. And Miss Carbon County. And Miss Sweetheart of the Rodeo Stampede. And Miss Sage and Spurs. And Miss Wyoming Beef Council."

"And Miss Wyoming?" he asked.

"Nope. First runner-up. Three times." She leaned back in her chair. "Tell me, Renner Jackson. What brings you to Muddy Gap?"

"I lived with my grandparents here for a year growing up, so when their old place came up for sale again, I bought it. Plus another acreage that bordered it."

"Which place was that?"

"The last people who owned it were the Kleins."

Harper shook her finger at him. "Now I know who you are. You're the outsider who's bringing ruin to Carbon County by buying up all available land when you're not local. You'll probably only let your big-city buddies hunt. Or worse, you'll turn it into a hippie compound."

His gaze narrowed.

The man had a serious death glare. Harper leaned forward. "I was kidding. But I'll warn you, from one non-native Wyomingite to another? That's the attitude you'll run into around here."

"Tell me about it. And it doesn't help when I'm keeping my evil plans close to the vest."

"So are you going to live around here?"

"Eventually. Once I get the building under way and I—" Renner snapped his mouth shut. Then a slow, cocky grin spread across his handsome face. "You're a wily one. Sweet and curious. I like that. Maybe I oughta offer you a job."

"Aw, lookit you. Already planning to steal the help away from the local businesses—that'll go over well."

"Divide, conquer, and charm. That's my motto."

"But it won't work with me because I'm leaving this town for good in another two months."

Renner asked questions and seemed genuinely interested in listening to her answers. It was a nice change from being ignored, talked over, or conversing with the cattle. And Renner was a really nice guy. Smart. Funny. After she got his hands fixed up, he gave her a big tip.

"This is too much," she demurred, trying to hand the twenty-dollar bill back.

"Consider it a bribe."

She frowned at him. "A bribe for what?"

"When local folks ask if that outsider sissy-boy Renner Jackson really got his nails done? You've gotta lie and say you were pulling pieces of barbed wire out, or something equally manly."

Harper laughed. "Deal."

"You do have a great laugh, Harper. I'll see you around."

Bernice lounged behind the front desk. "So. Doing a man's hands. That's kinda freaky, even when he's that good-looking. Did you put . . . polish on his nails?"

Harper shook her head. "Actually, I'm not supposed to say anything. But I was pulling metal shards out of his fingers."

Bernice blew out a cloud of smoke. "Really?"

"Yes. He was welding and thought soaking them in hot water would bring the metal pieces closer to the surface. It worked." She smiled brightly. "I got most of them, so he was happy."

"We're all about happy customers here."

The door flew open.

They both turned as Celia Lawson barreled in. "Surprise!"

Harper threw her arms around her friend. "Celia! When did you sneak into town?"

"Just now. I wanted to swing by before I got stuck at the house tonight with the brothers Grimm."

She held Celia at arm's length and gave her a once-over. Celia was a cowgirl to the core. On her feet were her favorite pair of beat-up Justin boots. Her dark blue jeans were tighter than the type she normally favored. The gold and silver circuit championship belt buckle, attached to a fuchsia rhinestone belt, matched the pink-and-purple-striped Western shirt. Her heavy black duster nearly grazed her ankles. She wore her cowgirl hat, a black Stetson that accentuated her fair coloring.

Celia's once-boyish figure had filled out in the past couple of years. She wasn't curvy like Harper was, so they'd never swapped clothes in high school, another rite of passage that had passed them by.

"You look great," Harper said. "Life on the road agrees with you."

"Flattery will get you everywhere with me," she cooed. "So, I'm spending the day tomorrow with Eli. He's going over Mickey with a fine-tooth comb. But tomorrow night? You and me? We're hittin' the bar."

"Good. Harper needs to get out more," Bernice said. "I'm all for you revvin' her up, Celia."

"Corrupting the former Miss Sweet Grass is a job I take very seriously." Celia rested an elbow on the counter. "Can I steal her away, Bernice?"

"Yep. We're all done." Bernice captured Celia's swinging braid, which hung like a thick golden rope and brushed Celia's butt. "Girl, I know I've said it a hundred times, but you've got such gorgeous hair."

Celia lifted the braid and threw it back over her shoulder. "One of these days I'll surprise you and we'll cut it all off so I can donate it to Locks of Love."

Harper snagged her coat off the rack and grabbed her purse from beneath the counter. "See you next week, Bernice."

With the size of Celia's F-350 truck and her horse trailer, she'd practically parked up the entire block. Harper hoisted herself in the passenger side and had a hard time finding a place to sit.

Celia scooped up an armload of stuff—CDs, a pillow, empty food wrappers, a curling iron, and a pushup bra— and tossed it in the back of the club cab. "Sorry. I'm used to spreading out since I travel alone."

"Does that bug you?"

"Some days. I've picked up riders here and there. For a month at the end of last year I had a saddle bronc rider tagging along with me."

"Was he cute?"

She smirked, glancing in her side mirror before she pulled out. "Very. He had the nicest ass I've ever seen. Tight. Muscular."

"You never mentioned him."

"I've learned to live the rodeo cowboys and cowgirls creed—if you don't talk about what happens on the road, then it didn't happen."

Harper smiled. "That fits you."

Celia parked in front of the rental. "Short ride."

"That's why I walk."

"Is that Bran's ranch truck?"

"Yeah. He insisted I drive it since it's four-wheel drive. It's been handy to have two vehicles."

"How are things going with Bran?"

He kissed me today and blew my mind. "Good. It's slowed down. I'm not out there in the dead of night, thank God."

"There's nothin' else goin' on . . . ?"

"Besides our business relationship? No. I can't thank you enough for getting the ball rolling. Although, Bran was surprised to see me. Why didn't you tell him I was interested in the job before I showed up?"

Celia squinted at her. "Because he would've said no. I didn't give him a chance, and see how well it's worked out? For both of you." She smiled cockily. "I'll call you tomorrow, but let's plan on meeting at Buckeye Joe's around seven."

Harper slid out of the cab and stopped in front of the empty, dark house. Bernice was right. She did need to get out and have a life.

∞

Abe Lawson had whipped up a batch of his famous Wyoming jambalaya and invited their pals to the Lawson place. In addition to his girlfriend, Nancy, Hank and Lainie, Max Godfrey and his date, Nikki—who looked all of fourteen—Abe had included Eli Whirling Cloud, Kyle Gilchrist, and Ike Palmer in the bachelor contingent.

Just as they sat down to eat, Celia showed up, surprising her family. Evidently she hadn't let anyone know she'd planned on coming home.

Bran hugged her, noticing her stiff posture and her "don't fuck with me" expression—which was mainly aimed at her family. After Nancy cleared the plates and brought out more beer, talk turned to rodeo, as it so often did when Kyle was around.

"You've really gone up in the standings since the ninety-one-point ride in Tulsa," Max said to Kyle.

Kyle shrugged and sipped his brew. "Thanks. But this early in the season only a few points separate the top twenty riders."

"But if you can get an early lead and stay on top of it, you're way better off than the person sitting fiftieth," Celia pointed out.

"Where are you in the standings right now?" Kyle asked Celia coolly.

"As of last weekend she's ninth in this circuit and twenty-second overall," Lainie said.

Bran saw Celia send her sister-in-law a soft smile before she returned to picking the label off her beer bottle.

"Do you guys ever run into each other on the road?" Max asked.

Kyle and Celia didn't even look at each other.

Lainie jumped in. "When I first started in the CRA, I wondered how they decided which geographic areas needed their own circuits and how some circuits have, like, fifteen states. Despite that, I seemed to always run into the same people."

"I'd say who you see is about money, since that and points are what everything boils down to." Kyle shrugged. "But I'm probably wrong."

"Like that'd be a first," Celia grumbled.

"You know, come to think of it, I *did* see Celia a few weeks back," Kyle offered.

"Where?" she demanded.

"Pueblo. But I doubt you saw me, since you were otherwise . . . occupied."

"What were you doin', Celia?" Abe asked.

She smiled at Kyle—all teeth. "Just blowing off some steam."

Kyle choked on his beer.

What the hell? Bran looked at Eli, who shrugged. Everyone waited for the fireworks to ignite. Kyle had teased Celia mercilessly from the time they were kids, and it'd only gotten worse in the last five years.

"Play nice, you two," Abe warned, "or take it outside."

"Which is where you might be sleeping, since we had no idea you were coming home," Nancy joked lamely. "I'm afraid your old room is piled with stuff for the rescue mission in Rawlins. I'm sure your bed is under the mess someplace—it'll take some doing to clean up, but I'll help."

"Not necessary. I'll sleep in my horse trailer."

Hank got in Celia's face, forcing her to look at him. "You aren't sleepin' in the goddamn horse trailer. You'll freeze to death. You can sleep on the couch."

She wrinkled her nose. "I'll stay with Eli, since I'll be over there all day tomorrow anyway."

Eli shook his head. "Sorry. No room. Kyle is crashing at my place."

"Fucking awesome." Celia drained her beer and stood. "Supper was great, Abe. Thanks. See you guys later."

"Where are you goin'?" Hank demanded.

"Harper's." Her duster flapped and she was out the door before anyone could say a word.

Bran knew Celia wasn't going to Harper's. Stubborn girl would sleep in her horse trailer just to spite her brothers.

Girl? Celia's the same age as Harper, and you'd never call Harper a girl.

True. Harper was all woman.

"If you'll excuse me." Nancy stormed off and Abe followed.

Hank and Lainie exchanged a look. No doubt they were counting down the days until they had their own place and could steer clear of the drama.

Kyle passed out another round. "Okay, Hank, give it to me straight. Did Renner Jackson really buy the three hundred acres of shit land bordering the Kleins' old property on the north?"

"Yep. It's a done deal."

"When did this go down?"

"Before Christmas."

"Fuck." Kyle drained the beer and reached for the bottle of Jack Daniel's on the buffet. "Who's in the mood for a throwdown with Jack tonight?"

"Count me in." Lainie opened the china hutch and grabbed eight shot glasses.

Eli and Nikki passed. Kyle poured the whiskey and lifted his shot glass. "To never getting what you want, no matter how goddamn hard you try."

Lainie put her hand on Kyle's arm. "That, my friend, is a shitty toast, and I'm not drinking to it. How about this one instead: to friends who stick by you no matter how goddamn hard you try to push them away."

Kyle laughed and smooched Lainie on the forehead. "Such a little optimist. Fine. Let's drink to the optimistic bullshit Lainie said."

Glasses clinked. Bran knocked his whiskey back, shuddering at the taste, chasing the burn with a swallow of beer. Before they veered onto another topic, he focused on Kyle. "Why're you so pissed about Renner Jackson buying that land?"

"Because I wanted it." Kyle poured and consumed another shot. "But like everything in my life, I'm a day late and a million dollars short."

"Kyle. You don't want that land, trust me. It's bad luck land."

"What the fuck is that supposed to mean?" Kyle snapped.

Hank relayed the bad luck stories that'd befallen the landowners. Including the Lawsons' parents, who'd died of carbon monoxide poisoning a few years after purchasing the tract of land. "I wasn't surprised Renner bought it, bein's his grandparents lived there, but I don't get why in the hell he considers himself lucky to have it."

"And how do you know so much about him, anyway?"

"He's been around off and on for the last year or so. To be honest, I think he's a great guy and he'll be an asset as a neighbor."

"I agree. Although I would've preferred you as our neighbor," Lainie said.

Kyle rolled his eyes. "What's he gonna do with it? Ain't raising cattle. It's shit land for growing grass."

"He's a stock contractor," Ike said. "Maybe he'll have pens. Or use it as a feedlot."

"Do you know him?" Kyle asked.

"I've dealt with him. Helluva head for business. And like Hank said, he appears to be a nice guy." Ike's eyes narrowed. "Have you tangled with his stock?"

"Not recently that I can recall. I'm sure Renner is a nice guy. It just sucks. By the time I have the money to buy land around here, there ain't gonna be land to buy. I might check into land prices in South Dakota."

Silence.

"Is that Breck Christianson's idea?" Hank asked.

Kyle nodded. "He's been suggesting it for the last year. I've been too . . . set on livin' in Wyoming to take him seriously. Maybe it's time I did." He poured another shot. "So, Bran. What's this rumor that Harper Masterson is your hired hand?"

"Not a rumor. She's filling in until Les is back on his feet."

"I'll bet you're filling her too." Kyle winked. "Well done, my friend. She's hot as fire."

"You're a fuckin' pervert. Harper works for me. That's it."

"Seriously? You ain't tapping that?" Ike said with complete skepticism.

"Nope. And for havin' little ranch experience, she's turned out to be a damn good worker."

Nikki fluttered her fingers. "Harper is my manicurist. I'll be sad when she moves."

Hank broke out the cards. "Who's feelin' lucky tonight?"

For the next hour they played low-stakes blackjack and poker. Bran missed hanging out with his friends, trash talking, losing his ass to Ike the cardsharp. He hated to think their group would scatter even more if Kyle moved to South Dakota permanently.

Abe came around the corner and leaned against the

doorjamb. "Hey, can you guys keep it down? Nancy has a headache."

"So send her home," Hank suggested.

"It's eleven o'clock and time for the party to be over anyway," Abe said.

"We're in the middle of a poker game, Abe."

"I don't care. Wrap it up."

"Come on, man," Max said. "Why you actin' so old and grumpy? Sit down and play a few hands. Relax. Have a beer."

Bran caught Eli's eye and knew they were on the same page. This situation could get real ugly, real fast. Abe and Hank and Lainie needed to work this out without an audience, regardless if it happened tonight.

Eli threw his cards in the center of the table. "Actually, I'm out. I'm heading home anyway. Gotta be up early." He lightly punched Kyle in the shoulder. "Come on, *kola*, you're with me."

"Yeah, yeah." Kyle swayed to his feet.

"I'll be taking off too," Bran said.

"Well, hell, ain't no reason for us to stick around," Max said to Nikki. "Come on, angel, let's go."

"You guys all okay to drive?" Lainie asked.

"Nikki's the DD for me."

"Bran? How about you?"

"I'm fine."

Hank stood. "Tell you what. Let's meet at Buckeye Joe's tomorrow night. We can get as loud as we want and ain't no one gonna chase us off."

Abe glared at him and walked away.

Bran couldn't get out of there fast enough.

∞

The next morning Celia Lawson was leaning against the old outhouse, enjoying a smoke, when she heard footsteps crunching in the snow. She didn't move, nor did she stomp out her cigarette like a guilty teen. She knew Eli hadn't come looking for her. He didn't give a shit what she did when she wasn't on her horse. That left one other possibility.

She inhaled a lungful of smoke and blew it out before she said, "Mornin', Kyle."

"Mornin', Celia."

"How's your head?" Start out snarky, keep it snarky—that was her motto when it came to dealing with Kyle Gilchrist.

"You assume I got shit-faced last night?"

She shrugged. "Ain't my business even if you did. Just makin' conversation."

"My head's just fine, thank you for asking."

"You're welcome." *Now go away.*

"How long you been smoking?"

"Since I joined the circuit. Keeps me awake on the long stretches of road."

"It's a disgusting habit."

"Says the man who chews tobacco," she said with saccharine sweetness.

"You're in a mood."

A bad mood when I have to deal with you.

She smoked, gazing across the snow-covered hills stretching as far as the eye could see. The landscape was completely different here, at Eli's place, than on Lawson land, although only thirty miles separated the ranches.

So why did she feel so far away?

She'd come home because she was homesick. After her arrival, she felt more homesick. The place she'd driven all night to get to . . . didn't feel like her home anymore.

It'd left her unsettled. Which pretty much described her life in the last year and a half.

"You have just this week off?" Kyle asked.

Why was he being so goddamn nice to her? Usually the asshole went out of his way to embarrass her. Like last night. Bringing up Pueblo.

Speaking of . . . Celia wasn't about to let him off the hook for that. "So you walked into Breck's horse trailer when I was givin' him a blow job, huh?"

Kyle's mouth tightened. "It wasn't the first time I'd seen someone on their knees in front of Breck. I doubt it'll be the last."

"Got a high opinion of your sometime traveling partner?"

"Breck's a great guy. Great competitor. But the man is a fuckin' slut. I was surprised to see you'd gotten sucked in by him."

She laughed, inhaling one last drag of her cigarette before tossing the butt to the snow and snuffing it with her bootheel. "I was the one doin' the sucking, Kyle."

"Jesus, Celia."

"What? You can be crude but I can't? Typical macho chauvinistic behavior for you."

"That you're tryin' to be like me warms the cockles of my heart, dumpling," he said with a silken drawl. "I didn't think Breck was your type."

"He's not. I don't have a type. Breck and I hook up when we cross paths. No big deal. It ain't love. I'm not expecting a ring and a vow of devotion."

"Or a vow of chastity."

"For either of us."

"So you're not . . . falling for him?"

Celia rolled her eyes. "Not hardly. He's amazing in bed, and sometimes I just want to be with a guy who has no sexual boundaries."

Kyle pinned her with a look. "Then you know that Breck is sometimes with guys?"

"I figured. But it's not like we've talked about it.

Wouldn't be a good thing for Breck if word got around the circuit." She cocked her head. "How'd *you* find out he swings both ways?"

The muscle in Kyle's jaw jumped as he gritted his teeth. Bingo. She'd sent a question mark right to the heart of Kyle's sexuality. He deserved it for all the comments he'd made over the years about her less than feminine attributes and tomboy actions.

"I don't know from personal experience, smart-ass. I showed up at our motel room an hour early and found him fucking some dude. Breck freaked out, because he thought I'd freak out. I couldn't care less who he does as long as he ain't putting the moves on me."

"Spoken like a true homophobe."

"Wrong. I don't like people pushing their religion on me neither."

"Ditto." Celia fired up another smoke. "Why'd you follow me out here?"

"To be a complete and total dick to you, naturally. See if I can get you to punch me in the face or knee me in the 'nads."

Seeing Kyle's megawatt grin, Celia forced herself not to smile back.

"The reason I followed you out in the frigid fuckin' cold is to ask you what the hell is goin' on with your family?"

Her focus snapped back to him. "Why?"

"Because we were havin' a good time playing cards and shootin' the shit last night. Abe came out of his room and told us to pipe down because Nancy had a headache. Then Hank said Nancy should go home. Seemed Abe and Hank were about to come to blows. So that, coupled with the way you took off . . . Are Hank and Abe havin' problems?"

Celia tipped her head back and puffed out three smoke rings. "Yes. Most of the problems are her fault. Nasty Nancy. Jesus. I hate her. Why do you think I left? It'll be a long goddamn time before I come back here." She pointed at him with her cigarette. "You'd better not tattle to Hank or I *will* punch you in the face and knee you in the 'nads."

"Still the same tough girl," he muttered.

"When are you gonna get it through your thick goddamn head that I haven't been a girl for a long time?"

"I noticed, Celia. Believe me, I noticed." He shifted his stance. "You're friends with Harper. What's goin' on with her and Bran?"

She wasn't surprised he'd changed the subject. He always did when she reminded him of her age. "She's working for him."

"That's what he says too."

"You don't believe him?"

Kyle shook his head. "I've seen the way he's looked at her over the years."

"You've *all* looked at Harper like that over the years," she pointed out.

"Not like Bran has. Not by a long shot."

"You noticed it too, huh?"

"Yeah. Wonder why he's never asked her out. They both live here. Seems kind of stupid that he hasn't ever made a move."

"My guess is because he thought she'd turn him down. Bran is cautious. I love him like a brother, but he's got a chip on his shoulder about not bein' much more than the boring hometown guy."

"Really? Why?"

"Remember, you're a rodeo star. Hank was a bullfighter. Devin's a famous singer. Bran's . . . just a rancher."

"He's a successful goddamn rancher. Doesn't he know I'd give anything to have what he has? Why do you think I'm busting my ass out there on the circuit?"

Ever since Kyle had joined the CRA, he'd competed in as many rodeos as possible, trying to earn as much cash as possible. Rumor had it he'd given up his playboy ways and was totally focused on his career. She'd admire his tenacity . . . if he wasn't such a douche bag.

Keep telling yourself that.

"Well, Harper's never been impressed by the sort of men other women are." She inhaled. Let out the smoke slowly. "If anything, she secretly craves the kind of stability Bran could offer her."

"Do you think anything will happen between them?"

Celia grinned. "Oh, I'm counting on it."

It took a second, but Kyle returned her grin. "You little sneak. You set them up."

"Without apology. I saw an opportunity and ran with it. I just hope they're smart enough to take it, especially when it's been right there under their noses the whole time."

Kyle looked at her strangely.

She snapped, "Why you eyeballin' me like that, Kyle?"

"Because I'm surprised by your romantic streak, Celia. It's . . . sweet."

"Fuck off."

Kyle laughed. Hard. He even slapped his leg a couple of times. "If it works out with Bran and Harper, will you fix me up with some hot chickie? Bein's you think of me as a brother too?"

No smart-ass comment jumped into her head. She stared at him. "The last way I think of you, Kyle Gilchrist, is like a brother."

His eyes, always dancing with mischief, were suddenly deadly serious, turning a deep liquid green as he stared back at her.

Oh. This was not good. She'd definitely given too much of herself away.

"Celia," Eli yelled, "we doin' this today or what?"

Grateful for the interruption, she turned and walked off. She knew Kyle would let it go for now, but this conversation was far from over.

Chapter Eight

❧

"To good friends. Men suck. Screw 'em. Or better yet, let's *not* screw 'em."

Harper clinked her lowball glass to Celia's beer bottle. "So you're not trolling for some buckle action between the sheets?"

"To be honest, just hanging out is a nice change from life on the road. I get tired of being looked at as a piece of ass."

Harper frowned. "I thought that's what you wanted. You always complained that none of the guys around here gave you a second glance."

"Yeah, well, I was an immature idiot." Celia drained her beer. "I need another. How about you?"

"I'm good."

"Be right back."

Saturday night was hopping at Buckeye Joe's. With the slight warming trend in the weather, residents grabbed the chance to socialize, do a little dancing, and catch up with neighbors who'd literally been snowed under for months.

Harper purposely didn't allow her gaze to wander to the far side of the bar, where Bran and his buddies—including Celia's brother Hank—sat. She'd prepared herself to call it a night if they issued an invitation to join their group. But Celia made it clear that she didn't want to hang with them. Harper could tell that something major was going on with Celia and her family, but she knew better than to push her friend to spill her guts; if she did, Celia would expect Harper to follow suit.

And wow, how could she tell Celia that she lied yesterday and everything had changed since the moment Bran had kissed her?

Without thought, Harper flashed back to the sensation of Bran's lips rubbing against hers. Nibbling. Teasing. Followed by the slick feel of his tongue invading her mouth. Her belly swooped, remembering the way he tasted of coffee, and the sexy, growling groan he'd released when she didn't rebuff his advances. Her pulse had quickened immediately as he'd pressed her hands against the wall, taking charge, imprisoning her hips between his, proving how amazing it felt with the hot, hard length of his body against hers.

She'd wanted to plow her hands into his hair and trace the contours of his scalp with her fingers as she kissed him stupid. She'd wanted those nimble fingers popping the buttons on her blouse so he could put his rough-skinned hands on her bare skin.

Was it a good sign or a bad sign that they broke the kiss at the same time? Bran's muttered "Fuck, I . . . we . . . shouldn't do this" delivered the blow of how he felt about their reckless lip-lock: It was a bad, bad idea.

Yes, crossing the line had repercussions for them both, but Bran hadn't apologized.

This morning had been particularly tough. Not the physical work. When she'd arrived at the ranch, she'd bottle-fed the calves. Then she'd hopped on the ATV and checked the mama cows' usual hiding spots for calves that might've dropped overnight. She'd managed to concentrate on the job until she parked the ATV in the barn and Bran finally appeared, acting brusque. He'd barely looked at her.

As soon as she'd filled him in on the chores she'd finished, he told her to take the rest of the day off and Sunday too. For once she hadn't cared about the loss of income; she needed a chance to regroup.

So she hadn't been thrilled to see Bran at Buckeye Joe's even when she couldn't help but watch him. He danced with Hank's wife. Then some other woman she didn't know. Not that she expected he'd ask her to dance. Not that she wanted it.

Celia slid back onto her barstool. "So how many guys hit on you in the five minutes I was gone?"

"None. As soon as I finish this drink I'm heading home."

"I hear ya. Is it okay if I crash at your place tonight?"

"If you don't mind sleeping on the couch."

"It'd be better than another night in the horse trailer," Celia muttered.

Harper threw caution to the wind. "Okay, Cele. Fess up. What's going on at home that makes you not want to go home?"

"Everything. Nothing. Hell. The biggest thing is I feel like I don't have a home to go to." Celia picked at the label on her beer bottle. "Hank and Lainie are building a new house. I don't blame them for wanting their own space. And Abe is good with it too, since technically, our parents' house belongs solely to him. But that bitch Abe's been dating for a few months has practically moved in. Whenever I'm home she makes me feel like an intruder in the goddamn house I grew up in. I hate it. I hate her. Everyone thinks I'm bein' a big crybaby because I don't like change or they think I don't want Abe to be happy. But he's not happy. He's just settling for that woman and he deserves better."

Knowing Celia, she'd probably told Abe exactly what she thought of his new squeeze.

"This is why I haven't been coming home. When I'm on the road I can pretend everything back here is sunshine, roses, and rainbows. I have a loving family and they're happy to see me. Instead, about an hour into my homecoming, I sense they're counting down the hours until I leave again. Especially Nancy. I get that vibe from Abe too, and . . . Jesus, Harper, it hurts like a bitch. It was me'n him and Hank for so long. I'm seriously considering renting a place in Denver so I never have to come home again."

A gasp sounded behind them. Their heads whipped around to see the source of the gasp: Celia's sister-in-law, Lainie.

"What are you talking about, Celia? Never having to come home again?"

Celia's face went red. She turned and snapped, "We were havin' a private conversation, Lainie, so butt out."

Lainie completely invaded Celia's space. "Like hell. This is serious shit and I won't let it fester another second, since it's obviously been bugging you for quite some time. Not that you've said anything to any of us."

"So? Just forget it."

"No. Way. I'm tired of the drama. And if there's something wrong we need to fix it. Right away. When we're still sober." Lainie snagged Celia's leather coat off the extra barstool. "Come on. We're leaving right now."

"I'm not some teenager you can just order home, Lainie."

"I know." Lainie closed her eyes for a second and took

a deep breath. "Shit. Sorry. It rips me apart to think I've had any role in making you feel this way. You know in your heart that your brothers will be upset to hear this. So, please. Let's go home and talk about it."

"Will Nancy be there?" Celia asked snottily.

"No. Even if she is, I'll kick her ass out. She's not family. She has no part in the conversation. To be honest, I've had issues with her that I've let slide because I figured I'd be gone and in my own house. Now I realize that's not the way to deal with the problem either. I'm done pussyfooting around her and Abe." Lainie held out Celia's coat again. "Do you want to ride with us back to the ranch or are you okay to drive?"

"I'm fine. I'll meet you at Abe's house."

Harper knew Celia couldn't see Lainie's wince. Had Celia really stopped thinking of the Lawson ranch as home?

As soon as Lainie was gone, Celia upended her beer. "Damn it. I do not want to deal with this right now. I'd much rather stay here and get rip-roarin' drunk with you."

"Much as I want that too, Cele, you've gotta get a handle on this situation. It's been eating at you. I'm sorry I didn't push harder to get you to open up to me."

"I'm stubborn that way. I ain't gonna talk until I'm ready. So maybe it was a cosmic sign that Lainie just happened to be standing right there. She's pushy as hell, which I actually really love about her." Celia smiled and stood. "I'll call you tomorrow. Try to have some fun tonight."

Famous last words. Harper nursed her drink while listening to the band. She turned down four invitations to dance—two from Ralph, owner of the C-Mart. Creepy jerk made her skin crawl. But she'd managed to stay polite. When the band segued into slow songs, she grabbed her coat and headed to the door.

The covered entryway to the bar protected customers from the harsh Wyoming winter elements. She stopped in the empty hallway to slip her gloves on. The tap on her shoulder caught her off guard and she whirled around.

Creepy, leering Ralph stood there—way too close for her liking. "Where you goin'? You promised me a dance."

Harper ignored him and kept walking until she was outside.

But Ralph was relentless. He followed her. "Hey, I was talking to you."

She didn't respond, figuring he'd give up.

Wrong.

Ralph grabbed her and pushed her face-first against the building. "I tried to be nice to you, but you're a stuck-up bitch, ain't ya? So you must think you're better than me?"

"No. I didn't feel like dancing. I didn't dance with anyone else either." Why had she thrown that in? She owed this drunken jerk nothing.

He pressed closer. "Maybe I want a private dance from you anyway." His boozy breath burst across the side of her face like a sour dishrag. "Maybe I'll settle for a kiss instead of a dance."

"Maybe I'll give you a bloody lip if you don't let me go right now."

"Ooh. Feisty thing. Makes it more challenging."

When Ralph bumped his hips into her backside, Harper lost it. She threw her head back, connecting with his nose.

He made a sound somewhere between a shriek and a groan, immediately releasing her.

She spun and kicked him in the crotch while he was still trying to figure out if his nose was broken.

Ralph grunted and fell on the ground, curling into a ball.

Harper was in a red rage. She kicked him in the back, aiming for a kidney. She would've kept kicking him if not for the two steel bands that immobilized her flailing arms and lifted her feet off the ground.

"Let go of me right now or I swear to God I'll—"

"Harper, sweetheart, it's okay. He ain't gonna hurt you now."

She stopped fighting. "Bran? What're you—"

"I watched him follow you. I didn't like the way he was lookin' at you, so I came out to see what was goin' on."

"What's goin' on?" Ralph spit out a mouthful of blood. "This fucking psycho bitch attacked me!"

"You liar!" she shouted. "You pushed me up against the building—"

"I'm calling the sheriff," Ralph said. "Havin' you arrested for assault."

No. She couldn't go to jail. She would not end up like her mother. A sob caught in her throat and she thrashed against Bran, yelling, "You bastard," at Ralph.

But Bran didn't release her. If anything, his hold on her tightened. His mouth moved closer to her ear. "Harper. Calm down and listen to me."

For some reason Bran's voice soothed her and she stilled.

"Let me handle this."

Ralph struggled to his feet. He patted his pockets as if searching for his cell phone.

"I wouldn't call the sheriff if I were you, Ralph."

"It's a fuckin' good thing you ain't me, Turner, because I can't wait to see her handcuffed as she's getting her ass hauled off to jail where she belongs."

"Yeah? They'll be arresting you too, dumb shit."

"For what?"

"For attempted sexual assault."

"*I'm* the one bleeding," Ralph practically whined. "It'd be her word against mine."

"And mine. I saw you grab her. I saw you throw her up against the building. I saw her defending herself against a man who attacked her," Bran said tersely.

"So? She's a two-bit bar whore just like her mama. I'm a tax-paying business owner in this county. Who do you think they're gonna believe?"

Bran released her and stalked Ralph, who cringed on the ground. "I oughta bust your teeth out for sayin' that, you worthless piece of shit. Now you listen up because I've had enough of your senseless blathering. You're gonna get the fuck outta here and you ain't calling the sheriff."

"Don't threaten me."

"You really want people knowing that she kicked the crap outta you? How the fuck you think you'll hold your head up in this town? Jesus. *I'm* embarrassed for you and I knew you had it comin' to you. Imagine what other folks will think."

Ralph's bleary eyes narrowed.

"I ain't bluffing."

"Fine. If I don't call the sheriff, she keeps her stupid mouth shut too."

"Deal. But if you ever touch her again? You'll deal with me, and we both know you ain't got balls enough to cross me twice."

While Bran and Ralph exchanged dirty looks and more harsh, threat-laden words, the shame of how Ralph viewed her brought Harper's every insecurity front and center. She backed away quietly and ran the two blocks to her house without stopping.

Once she was inside, she threw the dead bolt and ditched her coat. Needing something to do with her shaking hands, she poured water in a mug and shoved it in the microwave. As she grabbed the tea, she heard banging on her front door.

Startled, she dropped the spoon on the countertop.

"Harper," he yelled. "Let me in." A pause. "It's Bran."

Bran had followed her? Why?

To see if you made it home safely.

He had an inner core of a cowboy gentleman, even though he hadn't shown it to her in recent weeks.

She walked back through the living room, pausing beside the door but keeping the locks in place. "Thanks for checking on me, but I'm fine. Really."

"Open the goddamn door, Harper."

"Bran—"

"Now."

Reluctantly, she flipped the lock and let him in. He threw off his coat and toed off his boots as if he planned to stay a while.

"By all means. Make yourself comfy." Harper spun on her heel, intending to return to the kitchen.

Bran stopped her, turned her to face him, holding her upper arms. "Why in the hell did you run off like that?"

"Wouldn't you have?"

"We ain't talkin' about me here, sweetheart."

"You sure felt entitled to speak for me when Ralph was already on the ground, didn't you? Maybe I wanted him to call the sheriff. Maybe I'm sick and tired of his harassment."

"That's not what . . ."

His look of surprise fueled her frustration with him. "You know what, Bran? Just go. I cannot deal with you right now."

"Tough shit. I ain't leaving until you talk to me."

Harper broke his hold on her. "I'm not on the clock at the Turner Ranch. I owe you nothing, including a conversation. So back off." She sidestepped him, but he followed her to the kitchen anyway. She took the mug from the microwave and dunked the tea bag in it, not offering him a cup. Maybe he'd get the hint.

She meandered back to the living room and curled up in the easy chair instead of the couch so Mr. Helpful couldn't sit next to her. Wrapping her hands around the mug, she closed her eyes and willed this day to be over.

Cupboard doors opened in the kitchen. Footsteps came closer and stopped. When Harper heard the sound of glass clinking against the glass-topped coffee table she opened her eyes.

Bran set two juice glasses and a half-empty bottle of Jameson whiskey between them. He poured the amber liquid in each glass, then held one out to her. "Trade ya."

Harper allowed the exchange—Bran would get his way no matter if she gave in now or ten minutes from now. And for some stupid reason, his high-handed behavior didn't bother her.

He lifted his glass. "To you knocking Ralph in the dirt where he belongs."

She raised her glass to his toast and tossed back the shot. A full-body shudder worked free as the alcohol seared her throat and hit her stomach.

"Ah," Bran said, after draining his whiskey. "You want another?"

"I'm good."

"Yes, you certainly are." Bran poured, drank, and studied her with a look akin to admiration. "Tell me . . . where'd you learn to defend yourself like that?"

"My sister Liberty. She's had hand-to-hand combat training in the army and she's drilled both Bailey and me on basic defense moves."

"Was tonight the first time you'd ever used it?"

Harper shook her head.

"Christ." Bran consumed another shot. "It shouldn't have happened. None of it. I should've . . ."

"What could you've done to prevent it?"

His gaze met hers and held. "If I hadn't been such a chickenshit and had asked you to dance, you would've been sitting with me, not alone. I sure as hell wouldn't have let you walk outside alone."

She permitted a small smile. "You're so sure I would've danced with you?"

A rare vulnerability flashed in his face. "I figured maybe I could guilt you into it, bein's I'm your boss and all."

Silence.

His gaze flitted around the living room. "This is a nice place."

Harper choked back a laugh. "Right. It's a rental."

"You fixed it up nice. Looks a lot better in here than my trailer." He pointed to the colorful display on the top of the bookshelf. "Are those antique perfume bottles?"

"Yes."

"They look cool lined up like that."

"You aren't here to praise my decorating skills, Bran."

"True."

"Why are you here?"

"Because I needed to make sure you were okay."

"Thank you, but as you can see, I'm perfectly fine. You shouldn't feel obligated to stay."

"Obligated." Bran laughed, a little bitterly. "You have no fuckin' clue what I feel." He reached for the whiskey bottle, thought better of it, and dropped his hand.

"So tell me what you feel."

"You sure you wanna do this, Harper?"

"You brought it up."

Then those amazing silvery gray eyes locked on hers. "When I say this, understand that I ain't speaking as your boss. I'm speaking as a man."

Gulp. "Okay."

"That kiss knocked me for a loop. Mostly because I've been fantasizing about kissing you since the day you showed up at my place."

Harper's pulse spiked.

"I probably ought not be telling you this because I'd never want you to compare me to that piece of shit Ralph." Bran squinted at her. "He offered you a job at the C-Mart, didn't he?"

She nodded. "Last fall after the Tumbleweed Motel closed for the season. But there were . . . conditions."

"What kind of conditions?"

"He said he'd give me the prime morning shift if I promised to be in his bed thirty minutes after my shift ended. I declined. He was honestly surprised I didn't jump at the chance to jump him. And since I turned him down? He goes out of his way to say nasty things to me. Like tonight. Calling me stupid. A two-bit bar whore. Telling me I'm exactly like my mother. He makes me feel . . . dirty."

Bran's hand tightened into a fist on his thigh. "Am I making you feel that way?"

"No. God, no. I know if I said, 'Bran, leave,' you'd do it. Maybe not happily. But you'd respect my choice. Ralph makes me feel like he's doing me a favor coming on to me. Like I'm somehow beneath him, but he'd love nothing better than to literally have me beneath him. It's screwed up and I'm sorry you got dragged into it tonight."

Instantly Bran was out of his chair, looming over her. "The only thing I'm sorry about is that you had to deal with that slimy fucker at all and I didn't get to beat him to a bloody pulp first."

Harper stared at him. Specifically at his mouth. God. Bran was just so . . . powerfully male. But even as close as he was and as angry as he was, he didn't scare her.

"The last time you looked at me like that I kissed you," he warned, his voice a deep rasp.

"I know."

"Damn it, Harper. Tell me to stop."

"I can't."

He swore softly before he pressed his mouth to hers, gently at first, and then inhaled her in a raw, consuming kiss. He dragged her out of the chair so their bodies met—hardness to softness.

She melted even as she burned. This time as they kissed, Bran didn't restrict her hands, allowing her to touch him wherever she pleased. She traced the angles of his face, fanning her palms down the column of his throat. Over his wide shoulders and hard chest, then back up to wreathe her arms around his neck.

His hands gripped her hips. When the kiss intensified, he squeezed her hipbones. When it slowed, his thumbs stroked the bared section of skin above her waistband. He changed the angle and the timbre of the kiss. Gentling it. Sweetening it. Making her want so much more than just kissing.

Bran broke the seal of their mouths and nuzzled her cheek. "Sometimes I can't think straight for wantin' you. But neither of us is in the frame of mind to do anything about it tonight."

There was his gentlemanly side again.

Pity.

Harper wouldn't have denied him anything. But the last thing she wanted to feel when they acted on this attraction was regret.

"Do you want me to stay here tonight?" he murmured against her temple. "I could crash on the couch."

She laughed softly. "And just how long do you think that'll last?"

Bran nipped her earlobe. "It was worth a shot."

"Really, Bran. I'll be fine. Ralph won't come after me."

"You sure?"

"Yep. He's lazy. And the fun is gone for him now that you know he's been harassing me."

Bran's hands framed her face. He kissed her forehead. Her cheeks. Her chin. Her mouth. "Come over tomorrow."

A little dizzy from his tender ministrations, she blurted, "I thought I had tomorrow off."

"You do. This invite ain't about work. There's a lot between us that don't have anything to do with you bein' my ranch hand. And we need to talk about it, instead of ignoring it." He kissed her with surety and seduction. Then he released her.

Bran slipped on his boots, his coat. His gloves. His black cowboy hat. He gave her one last smoldering look that would keep her warm the whole night through. He said, "Lock the door after me," and then he was gone.

Chapter Nine

❧

After spending hours tossing and turning in her bed, Harper decided to do something impulsive for once in her life: She'd throw herself into a sexual fling with Bran because there was an end date. No chance she'd fall for him or that he'd want more from her than sex.

Wasn't that a man's ideal relationship? All sex and no commitment? If that was what she offered, wouldn't he jump at it?

Harper knocked on Bran's door at ten o'clock the next morning.

He immediately opened it, looking sexy and yummy—and that was before he gifted her with a sweet smile. "Harper."

"Ah. Hi."

"Hi, yourself. Come on in."

She went through the ritual of removing her outer-wear, like she'd done so many times at this very spot. But this time was different. This time she felt Bran's eyes on her as she undressed. And when their gazes collided, he didn't bother to bank the desire burning in his.

Silence stretched. They didn't move closer. They weren't really even looking at each other.

Awkward.

Just as she was ready to chalk this up to a dumb idea, Bran towered over her and cupped her face in his hands.

He murmured, "Finally," and snared her mouth in a kiss. A chaste kiss, as he kept their lips connected, sliding, gliding, a teasing test of how long they could maintain the soft, sweet, innocent smooches.

Harper slid her hands up, leaving her palms flat on his chest. His heart beat as fast as hers. She thrust her tongue between his lips, not wanting careful kisses and measured touches. Wanting heat and fire.

And did the kiss ever catch fire. Frantic, hungry, breath-stealing, a hot never-want-to-put-it-out kind of inferno.

When the kiss was no longer enough for either of them, Bran ripped his mouth free. "Tell me to stop or I'm takin' you right now."

She arched her neck, moaning as his damp lips trailed across her throat. "Don't stop."

The last barrier between them shattered.

Bran kept kissing her as he herded her down the hallway to his bedroom.

As soon as they were in the room, he yanked the comforter and sheets to the end of the bed. He worked the buttons on her blouse free, stringing kisses as each button revealed another inch of her feverish skin.

Once her shirt hung open, Bran peeled it off and let it flutter to the floor. A primal heat darkened his eyes as his fingertips traced the swells of her breasts. "You're beautiful." He bent his head, using his tongue to follow the path his finger had taken.

Straight down. He dropped to his knees.

Her skin tightened, raising goose bumps. She shuddered at the delicious sensation of his hot mouth on her body. How long would he tease her before removing her remaining clothes? Hopefully he'd take his time, not rush into the naked, thrusting part of sex. As much as she liked that body-to-body intimacy and the sensation of that ultimate physical connection, in her limited sexual experience once the goal of getting inside her was achieved, it ended quickly. And she always got the short end of the stick.

"Harper? You still with me?"

"Uh-huh."

His fingers popped the button on her jeans. He lowered the zipper and placed his warm mouth below the waistband of her bikini panties. He tugged the denim until it stopped at her knees. "Sit on the bed so I can get these off."

She complied. Jeans gone, socks gone, Harper wore just her bra and panties while Bran was fully clothed.

He placed his hands on her knees and gently pushed. "Make room for me." He scooted close enough that his belt buckle dug into her crotch. Those rough-skinned hands slid up the tops of her thighs, around her hips, and up her back to the clasp of her bra. One quick tug and the cups loosened. The straps started to fall down her arms and then Bran's hands were right there, impatiently removing them.

The look of hunger on his face when he saw her naked breasts for the first time soaked her panties and increased her hopes that all her fantasies about the kind of amazing lover Bran would be would come true.

Bran palmed her breasts, placed his mouth around her right nipple, and sucked.

Yes. This was what she wanted. Harper arched and let her head fall back.

Then he switched to the left nipple, giving it an open-mouthed kiss as his hands kneaded the mounds of flesh.

Then his mouth was gone, and so was his body as he stood.

She opened her eyes.

He yanked his T-shirt over his head.

Harper's mouth went dry. Oh, wow. He had a really great chest. Well-defined muscles. A smattering of dark hair. A line of hair she followed down to where it disappeared into the waistband of his jeans. She watched, her heart racing madly, as he unhooked the belt buckle. Unfastened the button. Unzipped. The jeans hit the carpet with a muffled thump. The tip of his penis poked out of the top of his navy blue boxer briefs. Then the entire length was staring her in the face, rising from between muscular thighs and more of that same dark hair.

Okay. So Bran wasn't huge, but he was bigger than either of the men she'd been with. Way bigger. Heat burned in her cheeks and she swallowed hard, an equal mix of anticipation and anxiety.

Bran walked to the nightstand. He rustled in the drawer and she heard the sound of crinkling plastic. When he turned around he wore a condom.

That was fast.

He grinned. "Scoot up in the middle of the bed and spread out."

Harper moved and Bran was right there, fusing his mouth to hers. Kissing her with more eagerness than finesse. She wrapped her arms around his neck, threading her fingers through his hair, sinking into the kiss.

But the kiss didn't last long. His lips followed the line of her jaw up to her ear and he whispered, "I'm dyin' to be inside you."

At that moment, she froze. Surely there was more than . . . this?

Bran's hips and chest met hers. His hand slipped between their bodies and he placed the blunt cock head at her entrance. He buried his lips in her neck and pushed inside her channel. Slowly. So slowly she felt every inch filling her until he was all the way in.

"You okay?" he murmured.

She nodded.

He pulled out and pushed in.

By the sixth thrust, she'd wrapped her legs around his waist and rolled her pelvis to meet his thrusts. This was getting better. After each withdrawal she held her breath, wanting that deep plunge again. Wanting that delicious fullness. That wet friction.

Then Bran's hips moved faster. Short, shallow strokes that really did nothing to increase her enjoyment but seemed to do a whole lot to increase his.

He arched his back and slammed into her fully. And stopped, softly groaning as his climax overtook him.

Nothing she did, squeezing her interior muscles, canting her pelvis to more fully connect with his, brought her release.

Bran slumped against her, his body still quivering with aftershocks.

Must be nice.

In her fantasies, she'd built up sex with Bran Turner to a multi-orgasmic fulfillment of all her long-held sexual desires. Once again, she was disappointed. More than she'd ever been.

The reality never lived up to the hype.

∞

Breathing hard, Bran rolled off Harper and stared at the ceiling above his bed. That hadn't taken long. At all. So much for wowing her with his staying power. Or sexpertise. Once he'd gotten his dick inside her warm, snug pussy, he'd lasted about two minutes before he'd shot his load.

He could claim that it'd just felt too damn good, or

it'd been too damn long for him, or he was afraid he'd scare her with his sexual demands, or he'd intended the first time to be over fast so he could take more time with round two. Those were all valid reasons for being so quick on the trigger.

You gonna lie to her too? Or just to yourself?

The truth was, he was out of practice. And he wasn't sure if she'd even come.

Some red-hot lover you are, stud. Making sure you got yours first.

Harper pushed up, keeping the sheet covering her breasts as her feet hit the floor on the opposite side of the bed.

Bran placed his hand in the center of her bare back and she jumped. "Goin' someplace?"

"I—I should get dressed."

"What's your hurry?"

"We're done, right?"

That cinched it. She definitely hadn't come. Wasn't happy about it either.

Not that Bran blamed her.

"Besides, now that we've got that out of our systems—"

"Harper," he said sharply. "Look at me."

She peered over her shoulder at him. "What?"

"Did I say we were done?"

"No. But it's obvious—what are you . . . eep!"

He'd grabbed her around the waist and pinned her to the mattress, straddling her hips, holding her arms above her head. "What's obvious to me is that you didn't come. And I owe you an apology for the wham-bam way this ended up. It wasn't what I wanted or intended. But damn, woman, you're so sexy and hot and I've wanted you for so long that I sorta lost my head."

The skepticism stayed in her eyes.

"Okay. I see you don't believe me. I can prove it and make it up to you."

She relaxed slightly.

"But first we need to set a couple of things straight. We should've talked about these things before we hit the mattress today. As much as I hate the word, I am your boss. I write your paychecks."

"Well, technically *you* aren't writing the paycheck. Your accountant is."

"Do you really see it that black and white, Harper?"

Silence descended between them. Her gaze skittered away briefly before her eyes met his again. "No. I know how much you ranchers hate rules, but if we are going to start this . . . we need to set a simple . . . guideline and both agree to abide by it."

"Such as?"

"Keeping this strictly a working relationship during working hours."

"That's it?"

"Yes. Then what we do together when I'm off the clock shouldn't matter, should it?"

"No messing around at all while we work together?"

"None."

He whistled. "That's a hard stance."

"But a simple solution."

"True." Bran smooched her nose. "You are such a smart woman. So you're all right with us starting this? Because once we start, Harper, you're mine until you leave town."

"Same goes, Bran."

He liked the possessive note in her voice. "Then it's settled. Now if I have the accountant cut you a perfor-mance-based bonus check, you won't have to worry that it was because you gave me a spectacularly good blow job."

Harper's face flushed and she let loose an awkward laugh.

Holy hell. She blushed and tittered like a schoolgirl at the mere mention of the words *blow job*? Bran leaned closer. "How much sexual experience do you have?"

"Umm. More than my limited amount of ranch experience, but not much." She debated for a split second and blurted, "I've only been with two guys before you and neither were long-term."

With deliberate care, he moved to the edge of the bed and scrubbed his hands over his face.

"Bran? What's wrong?"

"I don't . . . You don't . . ." Hell, he couldn't form coherent sentences. He'd suspected her innocence, but hearing her admit it? An unfamiliar instinct surfaced— one he couldn't voice because he didn't understand it.

"My lack of sexual experience bothers you?" she prompted.

How was he supposed to answer that?

"So, you're saying you'd want me more if I'd been with a million guys instead of just two?"

Bran whirled around. "No. Jesus, that's not what—"

"Then what? You thought I'd be as indiscriminate with men as my mother was?"

"Wrong answer, sweetheart. I would never compare you to your mother. Never."

"Or are you into kinky stuff? Stuff that I haven't done in my limited experience?"

He tried to stay calm even as she seemed to be baiting him. "I guess it depends on what you consider kinky."

Frustrated, Harper jammed a hand through her hair. "I know even less about kinky than I do about cows. I've had plain sex. That's it. I don't know if I look like a woman who'd automatically say no to the kinkier stuff or if the guys I was with were into the basics."

He frowned. "Explain what you mean by the basics."

"Missionary position. Me on top. Oral."

Bran's gaze dropped to her mouth. He'd couldn't freakin' wait to see those luscious lips wrapped around the base of his cock. Feel her cheeks suctioned tight as he pumped his seed down her throat.

"I've gotten oral too," she said, breaking his wayward train of thought, "but not as often as I'd like."

He chuckled. "Fond of that?"

"Mmm-hmm."

He slid his hand up her leg. Her skin broke out in chill bumps. "Well, I'll have no problem showing you new things."

Her whiskey-colored eyes were so serious. The cute little wrinkle between her eyebrows indicated she was deep in thought.

"What?"

"Since I've been honest with you, be honest with me. How much experience do you have?"

"Plenty." He crawled back up her body, trapping her hips between his knees and pinning her hands above her head. "I ain't into kinky shit like golden showers, or hard-core pain games like using a crop or a cat-o'-nine-tails on you, or havin' you sit on a pallet at my feet like a slave girl and service me like an unpaid whore. I'd never do anything to you that you didn't want, Harper. That said, I plan to be very demanding in bed. That'll especially hold true with you."

"Why?"

Because it'll give me a chance to explore my raunchy side, something I've never had the guts to ask a woman to let me try.

"Because you're inexperienced and I'm not. I prefer doin' things my way." Bran kissed the surprised O of her mouth. "And it ain't gonna be one-sided pleasure, like earlier. I plan to use my hands, my mouth, and my cock to fuck that basic vanilla sex right outta you."

Her breath caught.

He felt the increased pounding of her heart where his fingers circled her wrists. "Tell me you want this," he growled, scenting her excitement. "Tell me with a word, that for the next two months, your body, your pleasure, your sexual will belongs to me."

"Yes."

Rather than roar like a beast that had procured its next meal, Bran placed his lips on her ear. "Let your legs dangle over the edge of the bed." He released her and rolled to his feet.

Harper kicked aside the sheet and maneuvered herself into position. Each sliding scoot of her ass made her tits bounce. Nice. Bran planned on spending a lot of time getting acquainted with them. Later.

He snagged two pillows. "Put these under your head so you can see what I'm doin'." As soon as she was settled, he fell to his knees.

There was her sweet, surprised intake of breath again.

And he hadn't even put his mouth on her yet.

Bran's hands tracked her long, shapely legs from her ankles up her shins to her knees. His fingers inched up the outside curves of her thighs until he reached her hips. Man. Her waist was so tiny his hands nearly spanned its width. He followed the feminine arc of her body to grab a handful of her ass cheeks.

"Bran—"

"Put your feet on my shoulders."

She bit her lip, hesitating for a second. Then her toes brushed his biceps and her heels settled into the cups of his shoulders.

"Keep your hands by your sides and watch me." Bran bent his head and lifted her sex to his mouth, swiping his tongue up the glistening pink folds. God. She was so tangy. So sweet. His mouth watered for another taste of her, so he took a leisurely lick. And another. He closed his eyes and savored her. Since he'd blown it before with sex, he doubled his determination to make this first intimate kiss memorable.

Her body began to shake. The muscles in her thighs tightened, as she attempted to keep them from trembling. He smiled against the crease where her thigh met her hip, pressing kisses on the closely trimmed blond curls covering the rise of her mound. Again his tongue delved into that creamy slit, pushing deep into her opening. He dragged his tongue back up to her pussy lips, sucking them into his mouth.

Harper moaned.

Bran flicked the tip of his tongue over her clitoris and met her eyes as he looked across the plane of her body. He expected her to ask him to send her over the edge. Maybe even plead. But she just stared at him with such a yearning need that he knew he was a goner for this woman. He'd take her any way he could get her, even for a short time.

Needing to prove to her that he was the man who could satisfy the need in her eyes, Bran settled his lips around that throbbing bit of flesh, alternating sucking with butterfly licks.

"Oh. Yes. I like that."

He applied more suction, lost in the taste and feel of her sweet syrup coating his tongue and flowing down his throat.

"Bran. I'm . . . almost." Her legs and her belly quivered and her breathing quickened.

Then boom, her orgasm was right there. And so were her hands, gripping his head as she bowed into his mouth, her pussy pulsing against his lips as she gasped, "Oh God, oh God, oh God."

He loved her uninhibited reaction and gave her everything he had, keeping a steady rhythm until the last orgasmic pulse faded.

She slumped back into the pillows with a very satisfied, very feminine sigh.

One down, more to go, because he wasn't nearly done with her. With his dick as hard as a fence post, he would've liked to plow into her, sate his obsessive need, but instead he explored. Kissing her hipbones, letting his tongue lead the way up all those luscious curves. His hands squeezed her ass, then moved to her belly, smoothing up to the underswell of her full breasts.

Bran's thumb lazily traced the dusky pink areola. The tip puckered and he latched onto it with his mouth. He groaned. A man could lose his mind in the sensation of her flesh soft against his face and her nipple diamond hard against his tongue. Her quick bursts of breath stirring his hair.

Harper made another mewling whimper.

He sucked and teased, lightly scraping his teeth across the peak, testing how much pressure she could take, testing that line between pleasure and pain. While his mouth worshipped one breast, the center of his palm gently stroked the other, the contrast between his explicit attention and casual treatment letting her know that he planned to mix it up.

Her hips shifted restlessly and her hands were back on his head, urging him forward, urging him to take all of her breast in his mouth.

Bran lifted his mouth from her kiss-swollen nipple. "You don't get to direct how I do this, Harper. Understand?"

"Uh-huh."

He kissed her for a good long time. Pleasing himself but also enjoying her impatience. The proof of his impatience poked her in the belly. He pushed up and rolled on his back beside her.

Harper looked at him with total confusion. "Did I do something wrong?"

"No." Bran brushed the wild, staticky blond strands behind her ear. "Ride me, sweetheart."

Pink tinged her cheeks as she rose to her knees and threw one leg over his thighs. The uncertainty on her beautiful face almost had him taking control again. But he forced himself to be patient. She scooted up, circling her fingers around his condom-covered cock as she aligned their bodies and impaled herself. She began to bounce on his pole as if there was a race and she intended to get first place. Her hands landed on his chest and her head fell back as she bounced.

Slap slap slap echoed as their flesh connected. As good—okay, as amazing—as it felt, what was her rush? He curled his hands around her hips, stopping her frantic movements.

Harper opened her eyes.

"Are you tryin' to get this over with as soon as possible?"

"No! It's just . . . you got me so worked up, I want to come again." Her chin fell to her chest. "You probably think I'm really selfish."

"Not at all. Harper, look at me." She lifted her head and those wonderfully expressive eyes locked on his. "I think bein' greedy is good and I can't deny you a damn thing. Tell me what you want." Bran let his hands drift up her torso. Such smooth skin. He cupped her abundant breasts in his hands and feathered his thumbs across her nipples. "Do you want my hands here?" His finger traced the valley of her cleavage down, over her belly button, past her bikini line, right to where the heart of her joined the heart of him. "Or here?"

"There. Definitely there."

He chuckled. "Put your hands on my legs, sweetheart, so I can touch you. Let me make you fly."

When Harper placed her palms behind her on his thighs, the beautiful arch of her back changed the angle of her body, allowing him total access. Oh, hell, yeah. Now he could even see all her soft, wet, pink parts perfectly.

Bran anchored her hip with his left hand while his fingers stroked that sweet cleft. She jumped and gasped when he made direct contact with her clit. "You like that?"

"Uh-huh." She bumped her hips. "That's almost as good as your mouth."

He growled.

"But after this you could use your mouth again, you know, just to refresh my memory."

Cheeky thing. "Oh, someone's gonna be usin' their mouth, but it ain't gonna be me."

Harper peered at him from beneath lowered lashes and smirked. "So the quicker you get me off . . ."

The quicker he could have his cock buried in her sweet mouth. With a grin bordering on evil, Bran increased the up-and-down movement.

She stilled completely, her grip increased on his thighs, and she moaned.

Bran flicked just the tip of his finger over that swollen bud, faster and faster. With her hips bumping crazily and her body writhing above him, he pinched her nipple. Hard.

Harper shrieked as she came undone.

She was absolutely breathtaking. Bran just stared at her.

When she blinked those sated, caramel-colored eyes at him, he brought her mouth to his for a ravenous kiss. He rolled until she was on her back. He pulled out and grabbed her hand, hopping to his feet. "Come on, sweetheart. Time to pay up."

"Pay up for what?" she asked as he dragged her into the bathroom.

"For making you come fast." He ditched the condom and turned on the shower. When Bran looked at her again, she wore the oddest expression. "What?"

"We're having shower sex?"

"Yeah. Why? Don't you like it?"

"I've never tried it. Always wanted to, though."

He traced the curve of her jaw, once again touched by her surprising innocence. "Then this is your lucky day."

"In more ways than one."

"Meaning?"

"I've never swallowed before, but I'm betting that'll change too." Harper's gaze swept him head to toe and she licked her lips before she stepped into the tub. "Coming, cowboy?"

"Not yet. But soon. Very, very soon."

She laughed, a throaty, sexy, very . . . confident laugh, and Bran wondered if he'd been had.

Chapter Ten

✦

The next morning was remarkably free of sexual tension. Almost to the point that Harper wondered if she'd imagined them lolling around in bed, in the shower, and then back in bed before she'd gone home.

The workday on the ranch started normally as once again they were back to sharing coffee and small talk. The bouts of silence in the truck cab weren't weighted with awkwardness. So the fact that they'd both stuck to the "no messing around during working hours" rule was a relief.

Rather than head home after she finished chores, Harper tracked down all the empty feed buckets and stacked them outside the tack room in the big barn. She gathered the insulated coffee mugs she'd found scattered in various places. Sometimes Bran was seriously disorganized. He'd complained that all his coffee mugs had grown legs and run away. Washing dishes wasn't part of her job, but she carried the armful into his kitchen and dropped them in the sink.

She'd poured herself a glass of water when the door opened and Bran sauntered into the trailer. He must not have expected to see her because he froze.

Her mouth had gone completely dry. She carefully set the glass on the counter behind her, never taking her eyes off him.

While they stared at one another, Bran removed his leather work gloves, finger by finger, and tossed them on the table. He unzipped his Carhartt coat and hung it on the peg by the door, never taking his eyes off her.

He epitomized sexy and commanding, standing before her in a frayed flannel shirt, faded Wranglers, and dirty work boots. Under those ratty clothes was a body that screamed perfection. A body forged from physical labor. Sinewy muscles. Rock-hard abs. Strong shoulders. Ripped chest. Delineated muscles earned the hard way. She'd mapped his masculine form with her hands. With her mouth.

Imagining her tongue tracing the dips and hollows of his naked form caused a puddle of drool to form on her tongue. She swallowed loudly and met his molten gaze again.

His big, rough hands were clenched into fists at his sides.

"Harper."

One word.

That was all he said.

That was all he needed to say.

The next thing she knew, they'd collided in the middle of the room, just like in the movies. Kissing crazily. Hands roaming, bodies straining to get closer, fingers fumbling with buttons and zippers. Feet shuffling to remove boots.

Never had she felt this intense burning need. Her heart threatened to beat out of her chest. A low hum overtook rational thought processes in her brain as the words *more, more, more* competed with *now, now, now*. Every part of her being that should've warned *slow down*, screamed *speed up!*

Her coat hit the floor.

Bran started backing her toward his bedroom. He broke their tongue-tangling kiss to lift her arms over her head and yank off her long johns shirt. Then his lips were back on hers in a sensual caress as he cupped her breasts over the white satin material of her bra. His fingers found the front clasp and popped it open. He muttered, "God-damn, I love your tits," against the corner of her mouth.

Her back connected with the wall at the start of the hallway. Bran's tongue followed the slope of her breast straight to her left nipple. Then to her right. His lips, his teeth, his tongue all worked together, driving her higher until she restlessly rubbed her thighs together, craving relief from the wet ache he'd created. Relief that only he could give her.

"Bran—"

His mouth ended her protest and his fingers made quick work of the snap and zipper on her jeans.

Harper followed his lead, reaching between them to undo his buckle. His hands got in the way of her hands and he pushed back away from her with a frustrated growl.

"You do yours, I'll do mine."

She shimmied out of her jeans in record time, but she didn't beat him in the race to get naked. His fully erect cock bounced against his abdomen, leaving a slick spot on the trail of dark hair. She looked up at him and the stark need reflecting back at her caused another spike in her pulse. She'd never had a man look at her like that. Ever. Not even all the times she'd paraded across the stage in a skimpy swimsuit.

Bran slammed his mouth to hers, stoking the fire inside her with breath-stealing kisses. His rough-skinned hands cupped her butt cheeks and he lifted her, using his body weight to hoist her against the paneled wall.

Her legs automatically circled his hips. She felt his cock trapped between their bodies, hard and thick and eager. She reached down and guided the head, canting her pelvis, giving him easier access, giving herself over to him completely.

With one quick snap of his hips, Bran was buried to the root inside her.

Oh, that felt good. Full. Amazing.

"Hold on to me," he rasped.

Harper wreathed her arms around his neck. Hard thrust after hard thrust should've sent her back slamming into the wall, but Bran held her protectively as he plunged in and out.

"You're so wet," he murmured against her temple. "So tight. So perfect."

Her body trembled. The deep rumble of his voice seemed to be vibrating inside her skin.

He licked the shell of her ear, sending a strong shudder through her again. His rapid breathing teased the damp spot. "I could fuck you for hours." His teeth tugged her earlobe, his warm mouth brushed the sensitive hollow below her ear. "And I will. But I'm too far gone to make it happen now."

The tiny part of her brain not lost in foggy pleasure wondered if he'd get his orgasm first, then worry about hers.

"Widen your legs a little," he urged thickly against her throat.

She arched slightly, allowing her thighs to spread.

Then Bran rearranged his stance. The top of her pubic bone connected with his groin in the exact spot that rubbed her clit.

Harper gasped.

He chuckled and let his open mouth slide down the tendon straining on the side of her neck. "Like that, do you?"

"Yes. God. Yes."

Bran stopped thrusting and left his cock buried deep, shifting his hips side to side, keeping constant contact with her clit. He scattered firm-lipped kisses across the slope of her shoulder, while his fingers squeezed her butt cheeks to the same rhythm as his hip movements.

Sweet Lord. Who knew the man could move like that standing up?

She dug her nails into the back of his neck. Her head fell against the wall as she let his heat, his hardness, and his expertise push her closer to that elusive point of throbbing orgasmic goodness.

"Fly apart for me," he whispered as he nuzzled the tops of her breasts. "I'm right behind you."

"No. You're right in front of me."

"Smart-ass. Next time I'm takin' you from behind," he half growled.

Harper angled her head to kiss him, but Bran zeroed in on the spot at the base of her throat guaranteed to make her come. He merely opened his hot mouth on that section of skin and sucked.

Tingles chased after goose bumps, sensitizing every inch of flesh on her body. Her clit pulsed, contracting her pussy muscles around Bran's nearly motionless cock. She cried out, each spasm built on the last until she hit the pinnacle. Then the pulses decreased in intensity and faded away.

As soon as she could remember how to breathe, she opened her eyes.

Bran's whole body shook. He lifted his head from where it'd rested in the curve of her neck.

She caressed the side of his damp face, humbled that he'd seen to her needs at the expense of his own. She murmured, "Your turn to fly, cowboy," and kicked him in the curve of his butt with her bare heels, spurring him on.

He began pumping into her with enough force that her spine connected with the wall. But she didn't mind. She was lost in the look of bliss on Bran's face when he threw his head back and shouted hoarsely as he came.

Harper felt his cock jerking inside her. With each burst of warm seed she tightened her pussy muscles, earning another low growl of male approval.

His hips quit moving. He leaned forward and kissed her, switching to a better grip on her ass as he tugged her away from the wall. He caught her surprised gasp in his hungry mouth as he carried her down the hall to his bedroom.

It was heady stuff, Bran laying her on the center of his bed, feeling his cock still embedded inside her. Feeling his cock hardening as he pressed his body to hers. He broke the kiss and said, "Again. Right now."

Those three little words uncoiled her desire like a long, silken ribbon.

He rested on his haunches, bringing her with him at an angle across his bent knees. He pushed her legs apart until she was almost in straddle splits.

"Bran—"

"Keep your legs like that and grab the headboard."

She curled her fingers beneath the brass rails and held on.

His thumb distracted her as it slid up and down her creamy slit, from her clitoris down to where they were joined. His passion-glazed eyes didn't stray from watching his cock tunnel in and out of her body.

With her legs spread so wide, her pussy felt fuller. With Bran's dick buried deep, the tickling brush of his balls teased the pucker of her ass. She moaned at the surprising eroticism.

He'd managed to tear his gaze from where their sexes joined to watch the bounce of her breasts with his every hard thrust.

The sucking sound of the plunge and retreat of his cock, the squeak of the bed as he rocked into her, his harsh breathing, the blood whooshing in her ears, all mixed together, created a sensual, sexual stupor.

Harper never would've believed she'd come again on the heels of such an outstanding orgasm against the wall. But with Bran's every plunge into her slick channel, coupled with the masterful caresses on her clit, the climax caught her completely off guard. She arched higher and moaned louder as the blood pulsed in her clit, pulling her pussy muscles tight around his cock.

As the tail end of her orgasm washed over her, Bran swore and rammed into her, grunting as once again hot bursts of semen bathed her still spasming vaginal walls.

Neither moved until the sound of the heater kicking on broke the silence.

Finally, Bran whispered, "Harper."

She opened her eyes to see his smirking mouth lower to hers for one of those drugging kisses he excelled at.

He pulled back and stared into her eyes. "You okay?"

"I'm great. Better than great. Kind of sticky, though."

Comprehension dawned on both their faces simultaneously.

"Goddamn it. I forgot a condom. Shit, I forgot a condom both times. I never forget—"

She put her fingers over his lips. "It's okay. I'm on the pill."

"You are? Even when you're not . . ."

"I prefer to have a regular cycle. Plus, my mother had not one, not two, but three unintended pregnancies. I won't make the same mistakes." Harper didn't admit she'd put Bailey on birth control pills at sixteen, just like Liberty had done for her when she'd turned sixteen. Some families threw a Sweet Sixteen party to mark the rite of passage. The Masterson girls were thrown a packet of birth control pills.

"I hardly think you're a mistake, gorgeous, but I do understand what you meant." Bran kissed her again. "I'm glad, damn glad we're covered. I ain't anywhere close to ready to start a family." He eased out of her and grabbed tissues to clean up. Then he tugged the covers over them and wrapped his arms around her.

She laid her head on his chest, lulled by a feeling of contentment. "So, since you're not ready to have a family of your own, tell me about your family, Bran Turner."

Chapter Eleven

❧

*H*is family story would be short, if he had his way. He caressed the curve of her spine. "What would you like to know?"

"The sign above the entrance says 'Turner Ranch—Established 1907,' which is a long time to be in the ranching business."

"We're one of the oldest ranches in the county still in existence. Though according to my grandparents, it was touch and go there for a few years for my great-grandparents during the dirty thirties when their neighbors lost their places."

"Did they buy up more land?"

"Couldn't afford to. When things started to look up, they bought a couple of sections that'd been foreclosed on and the government wanted to recoup their losses. But it's been the same size since the start of World War II."

"So you've always known what you'd end up doing with your life?"

That was tricky to answer. As a teen he'd lashed out

at his grandparents, threatening to sell the whole shooting match after they died. A pang of sadness punched him in the gut when he recalled the shock on his grandmother's face after he'd issued that selfish statement. Pearl Turner had just looked at him and said quietly, "Land is the only thing that's forever."

"Sorry. I don't mean to pry."

Bran swept his hand down Harper's back and absentmindedly kissed the top of her head. "It's okay. I was just thinking that like most ranch kids, part of me wanted to rebel. Do something—anything—other than be tied to this land until the day I died. But the bigger part of me couldn't imagine doin' anything else."

"Did your parents feel the same way?"

His body stiffened.

Harper felt it and lifted her head to look at him. "What?"

Normally he breezed over this part of his family backstory, because it wasn't exactly a secret. But the scandal about his birth had happened so long ago, and his grandparents had been so well respected in the community, that the only part of his lineage that mattered now was his last name.

"You think I'm snoopy, don't you?"

"Yep." He kissed her nose. "But it's okay. The truth is, I don't have a fuckin' clue who my dad was. My mom ran away from here the week after she turned eighteen. My grandparents never heard from her until she returned to Wyoming five years later carting a six-month-old baby with her. She told them my father was out of the picture and she'd named me Branford after her favorite bar in San Francisco."

"Your real name is Branford?"

"Weird as it is, at least it could be shortened into something more normal, like Bran. I tell myself it could've been much worse, given that my mother had turned into a total hippie."

"I hear ya. My mom claims she came up with our names because of where we were conceived. But I suspect we were all named after the booze she was drinking when she got knocked up."

Bran laughed softly. "I doubt my grandparents were happy that she'd given her out-of-wedlock child their last name."

"But you grew on them, didn't you?"

"It wasn't like they had a choice. Evidently my mother stuck around for two weeks before she told her parents they were animal murderers, since she'd become a vegetarian. So she dumped me with them. My mother was an only child, and I suspect she'd been breaking my grandparents' hearts since the day she was born."

Harper squeezed his arm in a show of sympathy. "Did she ever come back?"

"Once. When I was about four, I guess. Didn't stay more than two days. She died of a drug overdose a couple of years later. And without sounding crass, I can say my grandparents were relieved. There was always the fear that she'd try to take me away from them. I don't remember her at all."

"Did your grandparents adopt you?"

"No need to after she died. In fact, it would've put the ranch in some kind of weird legal limbo, as far as estate taxes. So as the sole heir, I inherited everything."

"How old were you when they died?"

"Grandpa died when I was eighteen. Grandma didn't last quite a year after he passed on. I know she died of a broken heart."

Harper kissed his chest. "I'm sorry. Although it's sad, it is sort of beautiful too. To love someone that much that you'd rather die than be without them."

"Worst year of my life when they both passed. I couldn't stand to be in their house without them in it. So I did the mature thing. Boarded it up and bought a trailer."

Again Harper sweetly kissed the area above his heart, and it warmed something inside him he'd suspected was long dead.

"Do you have any intention of ever living there again? Or would it cost too much money to fix up?"

Money. That was one thing Bran had plenty of.

After the lawyer had read the will, he'd spent the next week in a stupor. He'd had no idea his grandparents had squirreled away that much cash. He'd had no clue what the ranch he'd inherited was worth. It'd boggled his mind. He was rich.

At first he'd been tempted to *buy buy buy*. A brand-new truck with all the bells and whistles. A fast foreign sports car. Fancy new duds. He'd imagined how differently all the women in Muddy Gap would look at him. The pretty ones who'd never given him the time of day, preferring to flirt with Hank, Kyle, Fletch, Devin, Ike, or Braxton. Hell, even bashful Eli had more chicks hitting on him than Bran Turner did. As a guy aware of his level of attractiveness to the opposite sex, Bran knew he wasn't butt ugly, yet he also knew he hadn't been blessed with the same head-turning good looks as his buddies. So his way of thinking upon learning about his cash windfall? Money was the great equalizer in the dating arena and everywhere else.

But a funny thing happened with his intent to become a rich braggart flashing a wad of bills—he'd realized he'd done nothing to earn the money. His inheritance had been entrusted to him; he would be a fool to blow the legacy on unimportant stuff like custom-made boots and attempts to buy a girlfriend.

Not even Bran's closest friends knew what he was worth. He'd taken a chunk of the money and invested it in the stock market and bought more livestock. Even now he spent only the money he paid to himself as a salary and he lived way below his means.

Way below. And if his low-key lifestyle didn't scare the ladies off, the fact that he resided in a cheap, cramped trailer usually did the trick. The assumptions made about him were amusing and he hadn't bothered to try to change them.

In five years, he'd doubled his profit from his expanded cattle operation—despite Les's continual arguments that Bran was always doing something wrong. Now Bran was once again at a crossroads, wondering if he should increase the size of the herd or let it ride another couple of years.

"Are you okay?"

Bran snapped back to the present with the beautiful Harper draped across his chest. Naked. "I don't know why we're talkin' when you ain't wearing any clothes." He rolled, pinning her beneath him, grinning at her surprised "Eep!"

She snaked her arms around his lower back and squeezed his butt as they kissed. And kissed. His libido, which had dropped to idle, roared back to life.

His cock slapped his belly when he retreated to sit in the middle of the bed, legs outstretched, facing the headboard. He held out his hand. "C'mere."

Harper crawled toward him like a jungle cat.

"Sit on my lap."

A curious expression appeared on her face as she placed a knee on each side of his hips. "Like this?"

"Perfect. Now offer me those beautiful tits, Harper."

Her cheeks flushed a deep shade of pink. She slid her

hands up her torso and cupped the pale flesh, pushing the mounds together before selecting the right one.

Bran groaned, leaning forward to lick the proffered tip. The nipple wasn't completely hard and he lapped a wide circle around it. With each swipe of his wet tongue, the circle became smaller and smaller until his tongue constantly flickered across the tight peak.

He glanced up to see Harper peering at him, her teeth digging into her bottom lip.

"You like that?"

She nodded.

"Then offer me the other one."

The little vixen turned it into a tease, dropping her hands to drag her fingers sensuously back up her flat belly. She rubbed the centers of her palms over her nipples. Then she cupped her left breast, angling her shoulders to offer it to him.

Two could tease. Bran licked, sucked, and bit every inch of her tits until she whimpered. Until he felt her thighs clenching against his. Until he smelled the sweet cream drifting from between her trembling legs.

Enough.

Bran rolled and Harper was on her back. Then he rolled her again and she was on her belly. He hiked her hips up, primal need beating in his chest as he held her, spread her, and impaled her.

Harper gasped into the mattress, turned her head and said, "Do it again."

He plowed into her, so insanely hot by the sight of her gorgeous ass clutched in his hands and his cock disappearing into her pussy that he might actually lose his mind with lust.

Her arms were stretched out above her head. She pushed her hips back, meeting his rhythm, emitting a soft groan every time he filled her. So he filled her as fast as he could, as many times as he could, over and over, pulling out completely but never pausing between thrusts.

Shit. He was gonna blow. On his next withdrawal, he grabbed the base of his shaft and slid it along her slit, letting the rim of the cock head glide over her clit.

"Bran!"

"I've gotcha, baby. Can you come for me like this?"

"If you go faster, but with shorter strokes right— omigod! Right there. Just like that. Don't stop—oh, please, don't stop."

He gritted his teeth and kept rubbing the tip of his dick up the rise of her pubic mound, over that pulsing hot spot. When Harper wailed, he felt the contraction against his cock head like little sucking kisses.

Hold on. Sweet fucking Jesus. Don't stop before she's done.

When Harper's pelvis sagged, he slid back to the mouth of her sex and unleashed his need for release.

Six. Seven. Eight. Nine. By the tenth stroke, he was balls deep, coming inside her—body rigid, head spinning, eyes crossed and toes curled kind of coming. When the last pulse blasted out of his dick, he felt so fucking exhilarated that he laughed. Then he layered his sweat-covered chest over her sweat-covered back and scattered kisses across her shoulders, tasting the salt on her skin. "You all right?"

She mumbled, "Mmm-hmm. Never done it that way before."

He flexed his hips and his dick moved. "Did you like it?"

"What do you think?" Harper clenched her cunt muscles around his cock and he hissed.

After a few more openmouthed kisses up the side of her neck and down her spine, Bran eased out of her.

Her lower body sank to the mattress and she sighed.

Bran lay beside her, letting his fingers roam.

She opened her eyes and looked at him. Smiled. "That. Was. Awesome."

"For me too, sweetheart. For me too."

Harper turned her head toward the dresser and squinted at the clock. "Is that the time?"

"Uh-huh."

"Crap!" She shot up from the bed. "I'm gonna be late for work!"

Bran bit back his automatic "So?" response.

When she ran from the room, he followed her, leaning against the wall to watch her dress. Because damn, she jiggled in all the right places as she put on her clothes. Seemed a shame she had to wear clothing at all.

Her eyes narrowed at him. "I know that look, Bran."

He blinked with total innocence. "What look?"

"The one that's questioning why I'm still putting in hours at Get Nailed when I'm making more money working for you."

Whew, he'd dodged a bullet there. He'd totally been eyeballing her ass. "The thought did cross my mind. But I'm guessing you like painting fingernails and all that girly sh—stuff?"

Harper gave an annoyed huff. "I like my customers. But the reason I won't leave Bernice high and dry is because she is the only one who would hire me after my mom ran off. Everyone else in this town pointed and whispered, acting like Bailey and I were a personal affront to them. Wanting us to pay for our mother's sins. So my loyalty to Bernice doesn't have any bearing on me liking to do 'girly' fingernail stuff—getting covered in cow poop, horse poop, goat poop, and mud on a daily basis should be proof enough for you."

Man, he'd really stepped in it. He crossed to her as she slipped on her coat. "I'm sorry. I'm an idiot."

"Yes, you are."

Bran smiled, wanting so badly to lay a big, wet kiss on her, but he held back. "Drive safe."

"See you tomorrow, boss."

He really was starting to hate that word.

Chapter Twelve

One week later . . .

*B*ran was out in the big barn when he heard a vehicle pull in. Too big an engine to be Harper's ranch truck.

Huh. Les had driven that old ranch truck for the last five years. When had he stopped thinking of it as Les's and started thinking of it as Harper's?

Since you're thinking of Harper all the goddamn time, dumb ass.

He shoveled horseshit into the wheelbarrow and waited to see who'd shown up.

"Hello?" echoed to Bran at the back of the barn. "Is anyone here?"

"In the last stall," he shouted. He didn't recognize the voice.

A guy close to his age and his build meandered into view. Bran couldn't tell the color of his hair beneath the custom-made beige felt cowboy hat covering his head. He wore standard rancher clothes: a tan duster, jeans, a long-sleeved shirt, a modest silver belt buckle, and battered, shit-covered boots. The guy looked familiar, but Bran couldn't place him. "Can I help ya?"

"Probably. I'm not sure if you remember me." Soon as the man was close enough, he took off a stained leather glove and thrust out his hand. "Renner Jackson."

Ah. The guy who'd bought the Kleins' place and the land surrounding it. Since Hank and Abe had talked about him and seemed to think he was a decent sort, Bran relaxed. He smiled and said, "Bran Turner. Good to finally meet you, Renner."

"You too, Bran."

His visitor relaxed and hung over the wooden stall partition, allowing Bran a closer look at him. Renner's dark blond hair and pale blue eyes brought back a fuzzy memory. "Hey, now I remember you. Mrs. Tata's class, right? Hank reminded me you'd lived here for a year when we were kids."

Renner grinned. "Yep. Did he tell you I was the projectile vomit kid? What a thing to be known for, eh?"

"Better that than the nickname we gave Lewis Vargas. Poor sucker is still stuck with it."

"What was it?"

"Skid. And no, we didn't give him that nickname because he was really great at sliding into bases."

A low chuckle. "I suppose that is worse."

"So, Renner, why are you stopping by my place?"

"Well, technically, we're neighbors. I'm hopin' that still means something around here."

"Why wouldn't it?"

"Seems I started out on the wrong boot since I set foot in Muddy Gap. I've pulled a helluva lot of imaginary knives out of my back in the last couple of months," Renner admitted.

Bran pushed his hat up higher on his forehead with

the tip of his gloved thumb. "We're a skeptical lot. Especially since no one who's ever bought that chunk of land has stayed here more than a few years. Don't pay to get to know them—know what I mean?"

"Yeah, I guess I can understand that."

"You livin' here full-time now?"

"Not yet. Still traveling between here and Kansas, bein's I'm handling stock contracts for the CRA Midwest circuit. I don't gotta hit all the rodeos anymore—luckily I've got a great crew to take care of most of it. But I believe in prevention instead of intervention. I wanna make sure nothin' becomes a problem, so I keep my eye on things, which means hands-on work."

"I hear ya there."

"Since I don't have enough shit to do in my life, I got it in my head to buy up my grandparents' place when I saw it went back on the market. Plus I added some of the other surrounding land . . ." Renner spit a stream of tobacco juice on the ground. "Don't know why in the hell I'm telling you all this. You probably already know it."

Bran shrugged. "Some. I'll admit bein' a little confused by the other parcels of land you bought up. It ain't good for nothin' in cattle country. You know that, right?"

"True. I had my accountant do a cost analysis and give me a breakdown on how long it'd take for me to earn back the initial investment." Renner offered a rueful smile. "Made me wonder if the twelfth of never was an actual legal time frame."

Bran smiled. Mostly because it sounded like something his accountant would say.

"Anyway, no matter what advice she warned me off with, I went with my gut and bought it anyway."

"No offense, but that still don't tell me what your plans are."

"No offense, but I ain't sharin' that info with anyone

yet," Renner shot back with a quick grin, "including the gloom-and-doom accountant. Or your buddy Hank, who's nagged me every goddamn time I've seen him."

"Can you blame us for our curiosity? Rumor is you're putting in some kind of big building."

A beat passed and Renner sighed. "There's some truth to that one. I'll tell you this much, there's gonna be more than one building."

Interesting. Bran decided to drop the subject for now. "Can I offer you a beer?"

"I never turn down a beer."

Bran ducked into the tack room, which held an ancient refrigerator they'd used for storing milk, vaccines, and beer. He took out two bottles of Bud Light and returned to the main part of the barn. He passed a bottle to Renner.

"Thanks." Renner looked up at the roof joists. "They just don't build stuff like this anymore, do they?"

"Nope. While I'll admit I liked the price of the metal barn and the fact that it went up start to finish in two weeks, there ain't anything like this structure left around these parts. Most've fallen into ruins."

"Why hasn't this one?"

"Solid foundation. I follow my granddad's advice and have it thoroughly checked by a qualified carpenter every couple of years." Bran pointed with his beer bottle to the far back corner. "We were startin' to get some natural settling, which put extra pressure on the joists, so he shored it up."

"Whoever he was, he did a damn fine job."

"His name is Holt Andrews."

"Is he from around here?"

"Yep. And if you're looking to build, Holt's the one you want. Especially if you're wanting some of the old-school touches like this in your multiple buildings."

Renner ignored Bran's *multiple buildings* remark. "If you're serious, I'd sure appreciate his number. I've got a crew coming next week, but I'd like to get locals involved too."

Smart plan. Bran was dead certain this guy didn't miss a trick.

They wandered outside. The temperature gauge read thirty-one degrees, which was damn near balmy for this time of year. Renner seemed interested in all aspects of the operation, including the family history of the ranch, and Bran wasn't shy to talk about what worked and what didn't. Renner got a huge chuckle out of the fainting goats, and it brought Harper back into Bran's mind, front and center. Right. Like he needed goats to remind him of Harper. Everything reminded him of her.

Muddy Gap was a small town. Had Harper been subjected to Renner Jackson's charms?

Nah. She was either out here working for him, or filing and painting fingernails, or home with her sister.

Still, Bran was damn glad he'd sent his beauty queen home early today. After he'd had his way with her. Twice. Once on the couch because the bed was too far away. And once on the living room floor because the bed was still too far away.

After chatting about calving, Bran extended an offer for Renner to come over and help out during branding. Not only could he use the help, but with most of his other neighbors there lending a hand, maybe Renner would be more forthcoming about his plans for the property.

"Anyone else you specifically remember from our school days?" he asked.

Renner sipped his beer. "Besides you, Hank, and Abe? Well, you and Hank were always hanging out with an

Indian kid. He had a biblical name?" He looked at Bran expectantly.

"That'd be Eli Whirling Cloud. You won't find another person who knows more about horses than Eli."

"I'll keep that in mind." He squinted across the horizon. "Also a scrawny kid who charmed his way out of detention at least once a week."

"That was Devin. Bastard still has that smooth-talkin' way about him." Bran didn't share the info that the country crooner used his silver tongue to talk groupies and buckle bunnies into the back of his tour bus and out of their skimpy clothes.

"Another kid had a side business selling candy on the playground to poor suckers who lived out of town."

"Ike Palmer. These days he's a cattle broker."

Renner shook his head. "Figures he'd be in the sales game. I do remember Ike palled around with a big kid. Quiet."

"Reese Davidson. He joined the army right outta high school. His folks still live on the other side of Rawlins. But none of us hear from him very often."

"He still in the army?"

"Far as I know. Last I heard he was in Afghanistan." Bran took a drink. "Do you remember Braxton Meckling? He was a real daredevil. He'd do damn near anything we dared him to."

"Vaguely. What's he up to?"

"Became a bronc rider, but got busted up when he was nineteen and almost died. He quit rodeo cold turkey. Went back to Vo-Tech and learned to weld. Spent some time traveling the world doing high-risk jobs on oil platforms and cell towers. Made a shit ton of cash in a short amount of time, enough that now he's doin' metal sculpting full-time."

"He's an artist?"

"Yeah. Normally I don't like much of what's called 'art,' but Braxton finds stuff in junkyards and turns it into Western sculptures. It's actually really cool stuff and really popular."

Renner said, "Does he do commissions?"

"No idea."

"I'd love to talk to him."

"I'll give you his number."

"Thanks. One person from Muddy Gap I have crossed paths with a couple of times in the last month is Kyle Gilchrist. Hank mentioned he's a good buddy of yours."

Bran wasn't sure if wariness was what weighted Renner's tone, so he kept it impersonal because Kyle was notorious for pissing people off. "Kyle didn't mention tangling with your stock last time we spoke."

"Bastard is the only guy who's ever ridden my bull, Satan's Spawn, which was a contender for CRA Bull of the Year last year," Renner complained good-naturedly.

"Kyle's done well for himself since switching from the Extreme Bull Showcase to the CRA. He's here whenever he gets a break from the circuit." Maybe by the time branding rolled around, Kyle would be over his snit about Renner's buying up the land he'd been eyeballing.

"I find it amazing that you're still friends with the same guys you met in grade school. Seems no one forges those kind of lifelong connections anymore. Mostly because no one stays in one place for very long."

"I suppose we might've all gone our own ways—and some of us have. But it was the damnedest thing, all this . . . tragedy hit a bunch of us at once. Hank and Abe's folks died in a freak accident. My grandparents died of old age. Braxton's folks split up and moved away. Eli's dad went to jail. Ike's mom got breast cancer and was dead within two months. The only ones left with both their parents alive are Devin and Reese. Kyle's mom was always single, as was our buddy Fletch's dad. After all that bad shit happened, it was like we became our own family—including our friends' brothers and sisters. Folks in town called us 'the orphans' for a while. We still look out for each other. Probably out of habit."

"It sucks that you all went through that shit at an early age, but I envy you the friendships. Since my dad was in the air force, we constantly moved. That's probably why I have such great memories of this place. Wyoming always seemed like home to me." Renner finished his beer. "Didn't mean to blather on and get sentimental."

"It's okay. Come on up to the house and I'll get you those numbers."

After they traded contact info, Renner left.

Rather than sitting around and brood about missing Harper, Bran retreated to his trailer and tied flies until he couldn't see straight.

Chapter Thirteen

⁓

They'd been lovers a couple of weeks.

A couple of very incredible weeks that'd flowed from day to night and back to day. Every moment with Harper was filled with passion that threatened to rob him of sanity.

This lust should've cooled.

But it hadn't. Not even fucking close.

Today seemed particularly bad. Every time Bran thought he had a handle on the urge to bend her over the tailgate and fuck her senseless, she'd make a sexy noise or look at him from beneath those incredibly long eyelashes, blowing his good intentions.

It'd gotten to the point he didn't dare look at her, because if she licked her lips one more time he wouldn't be responsible for his actions. In the last hour, his overpowering need for her had shattered his focus and he hadn't heard a single word tumbling out of her mouth. He couldn't see beyond his mental image of her wrapping those lush, wet, pink lips around the base of his aching cock and sucking him dry.

And it was barely noon. The workday wasn't over. Which meant hands off until the proverbial whistle blew.

He backed the truck up to the big barn door and practically threw himself out. He blew into the barn, bypassing the stalls and the tack room until he hit the back section with its stockpile of miscellaneous machine parts. He had to do something to make himself look busy. A complicated, manly, mechanical something. He unzipped his Carhartt coat and tossed it to the ground. Since when had it gotten so goddamn hot in here?

"Bran?" Her melodic voice echoed from the doorway.

Screw it. Literally. He had coffee cans of screws to sort. A mindless activity with no purpose—but Harper wouldn't know that. He dumped the screws on the wooden bench. For the first time ever, he thanked his grandfather for hoarding useless shit.

When he got a whiff of her perfume, or whatever the hell that damnably appealing scented part of her was, he withheld a snarl. And his directive for her to go away or get on her knees.

Either way would relieve him. But he certainly preferred one way over the other.

"Why are you mad at me?" she asked.

He glowered. "I'm not mad."

"Okay. Then what did I do wrong?"

"Nothin'."

"Then why are you being—"

"I'm not bein' anything. Go home, Harper. We're done."

"Since when? You told me we had a pile to do today and you're sending me home?"

"Yep."

"I don't want to go home."

"Tough shit. You're off the clock."

Yeah. Be an asshole to her. That'll get her to leave.

Harper shifted her stance. Her feet scuffled against the dirt floor. The sounds should've indicated she'd left. But Bran knew she was still there. Waiting. Why in the hell was he attuned to her every breath? He squeezed his eyes shut, gritted his teeth, and counted to twenty as he sorted screws.

He was so busy counting and ignoring his goddamn erection that he didn't feel her tugging on his sleeve until she was right in front of him.

Sweet Jesus. She was fucking breathtaking. Those brandy-colored eyes set in an angelic face. Her blond hair looked like hell, though, and that only increased her appeal.

Any continued resistance fled.

Bran grabbed the lapels of her coat and hauled her to her toes for a ravenous kiss. A wet, hot, tongue-thrusting explosion of passion as he inhaled her. Losing his mind in her softness, her sweetness, her fire. He kept changing the slant of his mouth over hers, taking the kiss deeper, giving her every ounce of himself as he took every bit of her he could get.

Harper slid her damp lips down and lightly sank her teeth into his chin. Bran peered at her with his heavy-lidded gaze. "What?"

"Am I really off the clock, boss?"

He hated it when she called him *boss*. She knew that. He growled, "I said you were, didn't I?"

"Good. Then I know you're not paying me to do this." Harper grabbed the coat he'd whipped onto the ground and fell to her knees on it. "Unbuckle your belt and drop your pants, Bran."

Didn't have to ask him twice.

He kept his eyes trained on her face as she watched his movements. Avidly. When she licked her full lips as he lowered the zipper, he couldn't withhold a ripple of anticipation.

Harper helped him tug his jeans and boxers down to his knees.

"What—"

She smacked him on the thigh. Hard. "No talking."

Fuck. That little bit of bossiness and tiny spark of pain was a turn-on.

She connected her gaze to his and placed her hands on his bared thighs, slowly sliding the leather gloves up. The closer her mouth got to his cock, the more it jerked for her attention. She released a throaty chuckle and let her hot breath drift over the cock head. She rubbed the side of her face on his shaft, and he hissed in a breath at the coolness of her cheek on the hottest, most swollen part of him. Her hands circled his hips and she licked straight up the bulging vein from the root to the tip.

Bran's mouth went desert dry. The woman intended to torture him.

Would he let her? Since he'd made no bones about the fact that he preferred to be in charge?

Yes. He'd let her do whatever the hell she wanted. Although she was always up for any fun and games he suggested, this was the first time she'd taken the initiative.

When her warm, wet mouth enclosed his cock, he lost any rational thought at all.

She chuckled again and the vibration zipped up his spine, increasing that buzz of need building inside his groin.

Bran loved the scrape of her teeth against his shaft. He loved how the long strands of her baby-soft hair tickled his thighs as her head bobbed. He loved the velvety sensation of her tongue lapping every inch. He loved the power of her cheek muscles as she sucked lightly, then forcefully. He loved how she pulled back to flick just the very tip of her tongue beneath the cock head. He really loved the little humming moans she made as she blew him to heaven.

It took every ounce of his control not to clamp his hands on her head and fuck that sassy mouth hard and deep to reach the tipping point.

Harper's hands went from gripping his hipbones back down the tops of his thighs. Her left hand rested on his right quad, which was almost as rigid as his dick. Then her right hand slipped down the inside of his left thigh to his balls.

The coarse material of her glove rubbing on that sensitive area startled him. "Holy fuckin' shit."

She didn't react beyond keeping the rhythm maddeningly precise.

Slow, fast, fast. Slow, fast, fast.

The contrast of the rough leather stroking his sac and the smooth, wet heat of her mouth sliding up and down his length zapped every nerve receptor in his body with pure pleasure. He groaned. The need for release was equally balanced against his desire for her to never ever stop. He managed a hoarse "Jesus. You're killin' me here."

No verbal response, just another amused chuckle. She stroked and fondled his balls, allowing her finger to slide back to circle his anus as she suckled the head of his cock.

His body was strung tight. Fists and jaw clenched. His balls were drawn up, ready to blow.

Harper kept a solid hold on the reins, knowing the exact moment to let go. She sucked harder and moved faster, bringing her right hand to the root and stroking up his shaft as her slippery, suctioning mouth slid down to meet her fingers.

No fucking way could he hold back.

With a sound akin to a roar, Bran wrapped his fingers around her jaw, forcing her mouth to open wider. He pumped his hips twice and stilled as each hot shot jetted out of his dick.

Her throat muscles contracted as she swallowed in almost the same cadence as the pulses blowing his mind.

Bran's hands kept her in place. He eased out of her mouth, savoring the sensation of her slick warmth releasing his shaft inch by inch into the colder air. He fell back against the bench and Harper nuzzled his lower belly, stringing sweet kisses from hipbone to hipbone. She looked up at him with a pleased grin.

"I'm the one who oughta be smilin' like that," he murmured.

"You are now. You were sort of crabby before."

"I do like this mood improvement technique of yours, Harper."

"My pleasure." She stood and smooched the corners of his mouth. "See you tomorrow." She turned and quickly walked off. Hell, she practically *ran* off.

He scrambled to yank his underwear and jeans back in place. "Hey. Wait." But by the time he'd gotten dressed, including grabbing his coat, Harper was in the truck, driving away.

What the hell was wrong with her? Why would she just bail like that?

Because you gave her the rest of the day off.

She hadn't touched him until he verified she was off the clock.

Stupid rules. Well, tomorrow he was breaking all the rules—hers and the self-imposed ones. He just hoped he could hold off until after chores were done.

∞

Harper wasn't sure how to take Bran's chipper mood the next morning.

She'd purposely raced away yesterday, hoping he would chase her. In her fantasy, he'd caught her and taken her up against the pickup in a fast, dirty, hard coupling. Warning her in that sexy, gruff, gravelly voice never to give him head and head out again.

Truth was, she had been teasing him all morning. Building the tension. Whenever he'd glanced her way, she'd purposely licked her lips, figuring that given his obsession with her mouth, he'd crack. His lust would transform him into the take-charge lover he'd promised her he would be. She hadn't banked on the man becoming moody because she'd made him so horny.

Yet there was power in his reaction. She'd gloried in it.

But it didn't change the fact that Bran, for all his talk about liking his sex kinky, hadn't followed through. Granted, they had sex every day. Sometimes twice a day, after working hours ended. It was great sex, better sex than she'd ever had. But it wasn't all she wanted. Harper sensed that Bran held back in bed. She'd counted on him being an animal. Going all caveman on her ass. She'd given him free rein . . . and he'd reined himself in? So that's why she'd goaded him. And if she had the chance today she'd push him even further.

They'd spent the morning turning the cattle out into another pasture, looking for five missing cow/calf pairs. Bran was concerned that the cattle had discovered a break in the fence line and escaped for greener pastures. Which was a better alternative than his fear that rustlers were showing up with a semi or a horse trailer to load the cattle in the dead of night. Cattle rustling hadn't gone by the wayside the same time as frontier justice. Cattle theft still happened frequently in the modern-day Wild West—the thieves had just gotten more high-tech.

So right before noon Bran had become preoccupied. They'd finished the remaining chores quickly and in complete silence. Hadn't been uncomfortable. Just there.

Bran told her to feed the goats and come back to the trailer before she called it a day. She'd dragged out the feeding because she got such a kick out of the critters. Mama Pox was both protective and proud of her new baby, nudging little Nina toward Harper so she could coo and pile on admiration and alternately kicking the crap out of the fence if Harper got too close. Daddy Hex just watched everything with a bored goat expression as he ate. Sometimes Harper scared him, just to see his angry air after he came to. Their little faces were so expressive that Harper was totally smitten.

She was half tempted just to climb in the truck and hit the road for home. But Bran hadn't officially called it a day, and she needed to find out if he had something else for her to do. She bounded up the steps and slipped inside the trailer. After toeing off her muddy boots, she looked up and stilled.

Bran sat in the middle of the couch.

"Ah. Hey. I didn't see you there."

"You all finished with feeding?"

"Yeah. Why? Is there something else I need to do?"

"No. You're officially off the clock."

She stared at him because he wore the strangest expression. Almost . . . dangerous. And he'd made it very clear she was done for the day. "Oh. Okay, I'll just—"

"You'll just stand there and tell me what the hell is goin' on. Not that I didn't love the way you sucked me off yesterday, but why'd you do it and then leave?"

"I thought maybe you'd chase me down."

His eyebrows lifted with complete surprise. "You did, did you? And what, pray tell, would I've done when I caught you?"

Holy crap. Thinking about her fantasies was one thing. But admitting them out loud to Bran? Embarrassing.

Maybe she wasn't as free-spirited as she imagined.

"Answer the question," he said curtly.

"I thought you'd . . . discipline me. With sex. Which as we both know isn't a punishment, but I thought you'd take sex to another level. A darker level. Less . . ."

"Vanilla," he finished.

Harper nodded. She waited, resisting the urge to twist her fingers or bite her lip. Or look away. Bran's stare was as mesmerizing as it was disconcerting.

Then his panty-soaking, I'm-the-big-bad-wolf grin appeared and she wondered why she'd baited the wild beast inside him.

"Well, it just so happens that I planned on changing our usual fuck-and-suck encounters to something a little . . ." He laughed. "I guess you'll just have to wait and see, won't you, sweetheart? Lock the door and strip."

He hadn't mentioned her performing a sexy striptease. By the time she'd stripped down to her birthday suit, her entire body shook and her nipples were pebble-hard.

"Cold?" he said with amusement.

"A little."

"Come here. I'll warm you."

She sauntered forward and stood between his legs so her knees brushed the couch cushions. That was when she noticed the red fabric he held in his hand. Her heart took off at a full gallop.

Before she could ask his intentions, he said, "On your knees." After she knelt before him, he dangled the red neckerchief in front of her face. "Close your eyes while I blindfold you."

Harper felt his every exhalation on the top of her head as he wrapped the folded cloth over her eyes and secured it at the back of her head with a knot.

"Can you see anything?"

"No."

"Good." Rough hands cradled her face and Bran's lips connected with hers. This wasn't the no-holds-barred kiss she'd expected but a leisurely exploration of her mouth. It also served as a subtle warning; this would be the last gentleness she'd see from him for a while.

A tremor of impatience rolled through her. She couldn't wait to find out what he would come up with.

Bran's hands gripped her shoulders as he urged her to stand. More caresses. More distracting kisses. More disorientation as he pushed her backward into the kitchen.

"Bran?"

"Right here. I want you to hold on tight once I get you in place."

In place? What place?

Her hips brushed a solid object and Bran's hand guided her forward until she was lying flat on a cold surface. The cold jarred her body into a mass of goose bumps, from her cheek, to her nipples, to her belly.

"Stretch your arms above your head and grab the edge of the table."

Harper complied, although now her feet were completely off the floor. Questions bounced around inside her brain, but she was having trouble giving voice to any of them.

"Do you have a good grip?" he asked.

"Uh-huh." Her fingers tightened just in case she wasn't prepared for whatever he had in store for her.

When the first crack landed across her buttocks, she knew. Spanking.

Two more sharp whacks brought her up off the table.

Bran's hand in the middle of her back pushed her down. His lips were on her ear. "Stay still. Every time you rise up I'll add to the punishment."

"How many are you giving me?"

Whack. Whack. "As many as it takes."

Then Bran really went to work, peppering swats over every inch of her buttocks until both cheeks were sunburn hot. He wasn't using his hand, but a flat object that made a loud crack every time it connected with her flesh.

He didn't speak. He just spanked her. Repeatedly. In total silence.

A fluttery feeling had taken wing in her belly. She'd begun to anticipate each blow. And after every connection of the flat object against her skin, she experienced a momentary sense of relief. Then she'd tense up again, waiting for the next strike, until the expectation became a sort of sexual déjà vu.

"You like getting your ass smacked," Bran murmured in her ear. "You should see how pretty it looks, red stripes across the white. Like flower petals." Then Bran traced the crack of her butt down to the mouth of her sex and pushed a finger inside. "You're wet."

She tried to shake her head in denial. She was utterly shocked when Bran painted her lips with the slickness of her juices. "Now do you believe me?"

"Yes."

"Taste yourself. Lick your lips like you were teasing me yesterday."

Her tongue darted out and she brought her musky essence into her mouth and swallowed.

"Again," he said gruffly, applying more proof of her arousal to her lips. When her mouth opened he snuck his finger inside. "Suck it clean. Suck it like it was my cock."

She did. She even used her teeth.

He emitted the animalistic sound that turned her on beyond measure.

Harper lifted her head, switching to her other cheek. Her chest seemed glued to the table from her sweat.

How she could be sweating when she was stark naked in the kitchen in the middle of March boggled her mind.

A rattling noise caught her attention. Again she raised her upper torso and again Bran pushed her back to her belly. The two hard swats that landed on her butt, courtesy of Bran's strong hands, made her breath stall in her lungs. But her gasp became a scream when her flaming-hot ass was bathed in ice.

"Omigod! Bran! What are you doing?"

He laughed. "Cooling you down after heating you up. This sweet piece of ass is lookin' a little tender. I'm afraid I might've gotten carried away with your punishment, 'cause I was havin' such a damn good time." He paused, drawing cold, wet circles on her swollen skin.

The fiery sensation gave way to numbness, except for the icy water dripping everywhere—down her hips, over the roundest section of her cheeks, into the creases of her thighs, down her butt crack, and straight to her pussy. The *drip drip drip* tickled, and she squirmed to get it to stop, which earned her another crack on the butt.

"Stay still. We ain't done."

A hum of excitement zipped through her body because this was what she wanted—Bran unleashed.

"Lift up."

She pushed upright and he shoved a towel under her hips, which angled her lower body higher.

Bran's cold hands spanned the top of her hips and he slowly moved the rough-skinned palms up, his thumbs digging into her spine. Warm kisses started from her left shoulder and arced across her upper back to her right shoulder.

He nuzzled her hair, kissing the skin below the blindfold, drugging her with his lips, soothing breath, and unintelligible mutters whispered behind the hollow of her ear.

So Harper was completely relaxed, floating in that sea of bliss, when a slick finger prodded her anus. She tensed a little, even though Bran had teased her with anal play before.

"Relax, sweetheart, and let me in."

That thick finger slipped all the way inside her anal passage. The intrusive burning sensation increased and she was just about to tell him to get it out when he whispered, "Oh, don't be getting all vanilla on me now, Harper. Soon as you're used to this finger, I'm gonna add another." He slipped the finger in and out as he spoke. "And as soon as you're stretched with two fingers, I'm gonna shove my dick in here as far as it'll go. It probably won't be a long fuck, since this virgin channel will test my stamina."

She couldn't speak. She couldn't move. She couldn't believe she was turned on by Bran's chest-thumping declaration. Any part of her feminist side bowed to the primitive part of her makeup that wanted to be taken by this man—in every way imaginable.

When Bran slipped the second finger in, she sucked in a surprised breath as he scissored the digits open and closed. He moved his slick fingers in and out of her passage, not gently, not harshly, but with firm authority.

Harper's grip on the table ledge tightened when those fingers disappeared. Even over the thundering beat of her heart she heard the sounds of him slicking up his cock. He wiped lube on her anus and used the head of his cock to smear it in.

The man gave her no warning. He just pulled her butt cheeks wide apart and forced his way into her ass with a single unending thrust.

A stronger, deeper burning pain made her buck her hips, trying to get him out. "Oh. That hurts."

"Stop clenching. Relax those muscles and it won't hurt as bad."

"You sure?"

"No." He laughed. "But goddamn, it feels fine to me." His hands landed beside her rib cage. "Really fine. You're so fuckin' tight. It makes me want to ream you, so you'll remember I'm the first."

While he'd been talking, his hips kept bumping her pelvis into the nubby towel bunched beneath her, abrading her clit. The prickly sensation rode the line between pleasure and pain. Her entire body throbbed.

Plop plop plop hit the middle of her back and the droplets slithered down her spine. Given the angle of Bran looming above her, the liquid had to be his sweat. He was still holding back, even when he admitted he didn't want to.

Harper clamped down hard on his cock with her anal muscles and he got the hint.

He started fucking her ass with the intensity she expected. Withdrawing fully, ramming in fully.

Every time the head of his cock forged through the rigid ring of muscle, she gasped at the sharp pain. But after a few thrusts, she anticipated the long glide, craving that pleasure/pain of his hardness buried in her bowels. She didn't push back to meet his thrusts, leaving him in control.

And he took it as if it were his due. Relentlessly. Powerfully. Loudly. Bran enjoyed her body with gusto. In his carnal enjoyment, Harper let the power of his need consume her.

"Shit. I can't hold back." Two more fast strokes and he stilled. A drawn-out groan accompanied ejaculate that coated her anal passage in a blast of liquid heat.

His broken breaths filled the air.

She waited for him to regain his balance, even when she was ready to climb out of her skin.

Bran eased out of her and said, "Let go of the table."

As soon as Harper released her death grip, Bran rolled her on her back, clamped his hands over her thighs, and yanked her to the opposite end of the table. "Bran? What are you—"

"Put your feet on my shoulders."

Still blindfolded, she had no idea where his face was in position to her and she didn't want to accidentally kick the man.

He made a disgruntled sound and his strong fingers circled her ankle. The instant her feet connected with his hot flesh she squeaked.

Then his mouth was on her sex, sucking and slurping and more sucking right on that little pearl. She'd become so dizzy from his unyielding attentions that her orgasm didn't build. It blindsided her.

Ironic, given the fact that she was blindfolded.

Bran ate into her soft tissues as if looking for another climax hidden within her feminine folds. And he found one, driving her to the pinnacle again and pushing her over. After he'd brought her down to earth, he kissed a path over her damp mound, up her pelvis to rest his forehead on her belly.

She loved this intimacy. The way he smelled of sex and sweat and leather. She removed her blindfold and tossed it to the floor, needing to look in his eyes as she raked her fingers through his hair. They stayed locked together for the longest time. Finally she said, "That was . . ." *Stupendous*. She couldn't even get the word out.

"First time I've seen you speechless," he murmured.

She yawned and admitted, "I'm absolutely whupped. You wore me out. I cannot keep my eyes open, Bran."

He scooped her up and held her to his chest.

"What are you—"

"Ssh. It's all right. I've got you."

He carried her to his bedroom and set her on his bed. She sighed as he pulled the comforter under her chin and kissed her brow.

"Rest. Need anything before I hit the shower?"

A sitz bath. He probably wouldn't know what that was. If he did, mentioning it would make him feel guilty, so she merely said, "No."

She drooled over his perfectly muscled butt as he walked to the door. He stopped and sent a smoldering look over his shoulder. "Still think I'm gonna keep this vanilla?"

Harper managed a laugh. "Definitely not." Then she closed her eyes and drifted off.

Chapter Fourteen

❧

*O*ver the next couple of weeks, Bran proved to Harper just how far from vanilla sex he could steer her.

She flashed back to the night he'd bound her arms behind her back with rope and propped up her lower torso, keeping her feet flat on the mattress. He'd sucked her nipples and fingered her clit until she came. Twice. Then he'd just . . . taken her. Repeatedly. His way. With no thought to her pleasure, just to his own. Bran had become wild, not unlike a male animal in rut. He'd wedged himself between her knees. His fingers clutched her with such tenacity as he'd hammered into her that he left finger-shaped bruises on her thighs. At the moment he reached release, he'd pulled out and ejaculated all over her breasts.

Harper loved that he'd marked her in such a primitive manner. Then he used his seed as a lubricant and slid his dick in the valley of her cleavage. He held her breasts so close together that her nipples nearly touched. His rapt face as he watched his cock disappearing between her fleshy globes was heady stuff. It turned her on listening to his labored breaths as he took his pleasure. Made her crazy with lust to see the sweat trickling down the corded muscles in his neck. A tiny orgasm throbbed when he pumped his hips faster and looked into her eyes with such admiration. A sense of power built. She could make this gruff man lose complete control. But she knew he'd never take her past the point where he compromised her trust.

That's when she'd known this wasn't just sex. She could love this multifaceted man. Love him with everything she had. And she ached because she would have him for only a little while longer.

Over the next few days they'd gorged themselves, eager to experience every kinky fantasy.

One afternoon he'd shown her the carnal delights of sixty-nine, with her head hanging off the edge of the bed and her legs in straddle splits. In that position he could shove his cock so far down her throat she couldn't taste him when he came. Also in that particular position, he could burrow his lightning-fast tongue so deep into her pussy that she swore she felt the tip of it tickling her uterus.

Then there was the morning he tied her spread-eagle to his brass bed headboard and footboard, taking a full hour to pound into her ass, while he used vibrating objects on her clit. Who knew the stem portion of an old electric toothbrush, the backside of his electric shaver, and the mini massager he claimed he actually used for sore leg muscles could be turned into impromptu sex toys? He'd made her come five times.

Although she loved every kinky, fun, raunchy sexual scenario Bran suggested, or enforced, she equally loved hanging out with him after they put their clothes back on. He hadn't balked when she'd cooked for him a few times. She'd watched him tie flies—funky ones, ugly ones, beautiful ones. He truly had a gift.

When she asked him about it, he clammed up. At her assurance that she didn't consider him a dork, he relaxed and almost shyly shared that artistic part of himself. He'd even promised to take her fishing—after they laughed about him being such a jerk the first time they'd met at the fishing hole. His sheepish confession that his rude behavior was because she'd intimidated him came as such a sweet surprise from the always confident cattleman that she'd almost melted into a puddle right then and there.

His honesty allowed Harper to open up as well. Telling him her fears about never getting a chance to pursue her dream career. How being the responsible one in her family had made her feel and act much older than her twenty-four years. He didn't offer advice. He just listened. Listened and held her, made love to her, treated her like she mattered.

From that point on, their relationship changed, evolving into something . . . more than either of them expected. But Harper wasn't entirely convinced that the short-term nature of it didn't inflate the significance of these feelings.

Or maybe she was just lying to herself so it'd be easier to bear the separation from Bran when she left.

∾

They finished chores early the following Friday so Bran could attend an auction outside of Rawlins. When Harper confessed that she'd never been to an auction, he convinced her to come along. They loaded up the trailer and took off.

Thankfully this wasn't a liquidation auction used to pay off a banker's debt while the poor family stood around in misery, watching as their worldly possessions sold for pennies on the dollar. The descendants of this estate were eager to unload equipment and household goods, as well as the small acreage. Bran toyed with the idea of buying the land and holding it for Kyle, since it was close by and it was the type of place Kyle had been searching for. But Kyle's curiosity was second only to his pride, and he would demand to know how Bran had scrounged up that kind of cash on such short notice. So Bran discarded the idea. At this point, admitting to his friends that he could write a check for the entire amount and it wouldn't affect his financial situation at all would likely piss them off. After all the years of friendship, they'd think he didn't trust them.

Isn't that the truth? You don't trust anyone?

No. Being a braggart was a worse sin than nondisclosure, in his opinion.

After he registered to bid, they walked along the tables piled with stuff. Junk, mostly. Some dishes and housewares, but Bran was distracted, searching for what he'd driven all this way for. Fishing supplies.

The catalog hadn't given a detailed description of what was for sale beyond the generic wording "fishing items." But Bran had done some research, and apparently the old man who'd died had spent his life tying flies. So Bran was highly curious about the supplies he'd collected over the years.

Harper wandered off and Bran hit the mother lode about two tables in. Bags and boxes of every supply imaginable. He slapped on his poker face and kept walking, stopping at the next table over to scour the boxes of *Boys' Life* from the 1950s. Not that he gave a shit about crusty old magazines, but he wanted to keep an eye on other auction patrons who might be interested in the fishing supplies.

A few browsed. No one very closely. He focused on the auctioneer and the next set of items up for bid. A box of glassware, including antique perfume bottles.

Harper had a few of those scattered around her place. If he bid on that lot, in the guise of buying her a gift, it wouldn't appear that he was waiting around to bid on the rare fly-tying supplies.

The goal at auctions was to hide your interest in the items you wanted to buy. If you didn't, some bastards would bid against you and drive the price higher just because they could.

He wandered to the auction stand. Not a big crowd, which could be a bad thing. Knowing the order of the auction meant some people didn't show up until right before their coveted item went up on the auction block.

The bidding started low and stayed low. The entire thing lasted around two minutes. For twenty-five bucks he picked up the entire box of Depression-era glassware.

Bran bid on a scythe and lost. He waited a couple of items and bid on an ugly coffee table and lost.

Since he hadn't seen Harper for a while, he went looking for her. He froze, watching her leave the concession wagon with an ice cream cone. A vanilla cone.

Was she trying to make a point?

He'd toned down the kink the last couple of days, preferring to take her to his bed and make love to her body to body, face to face. Having sex with her multiple times a day in the past month had allowed him to build his stamina—now he could fuck her for an hour, wringing at least three orgasms from her before finding his own release.

His mouth went dry as her lips enclosed the swirled creamy curlicue in the cone and sucked. Then she licked along one side, turned the cone, and licked again. Another couple of swipes with her hot little tongue and her lips were coated with the sticky whiteness.

Jesus. His cock jerked, trying to get out of his pants.

Harper took enjoyment of her ice cream cone to a

whole other plane. When she lapped around the base with the flat of her tongue and then jammed the stubby ice cream entirely into her mouth, keeping her lips stretched around the cone as she sucked, he almost came. Right then.

The woman had no idea she was torturing him.

But she would.

As soon as she finished her treat and wiped her mouth, Bran approached her. She smiled. "Hey. I wondered what happened to you."

"I bought these. I need to put them in the trailer."

Just as he expected, she fell into step beside him. "See anything else you want?"

Hell, yeah.

Bran dug out his keys and unlocked the trailer doors. He gestured for her to go in first and he followed a beat later, closing the doors behind them.

"Holy cow, it's dark in here."

He set the box on the floor and clicked on the flashlight hanging from a rope on the ceiling.

"Oh. That's better. What are we—"

Bran's mouth cut off her question. He kissed her hungrily, her mouth cold and sweet from the ice cream. He broke the kiss and said, "On your knees, Harper."

She blinked at him with confusion. "What?"

"I saw you licking that *vanilla* ice cream cone and it got me so fuckin' hard I can't see straight. Since you caused the problem, you get to be the solution. Now. On your knees." He undid his belt, pushed his zipper down and yanked at his clothing until his jeans and boxers were around the tops of his boots. He spread his legs as wide as his jeans allowed.

Wordlessly, Harper slid down the wall until she was on her knees.

Without preamble, Bran fisted his cock in his right

hand and painted her lips with the wet tip. "You've got me so worked up this ain't gonna be slow and easy."

She opened her mouth to speak and Bran shoved his cock fully inside.

When she gagged he waited until the reflex passed.

"Put your hands on me, 'cause you'll need something to hold on to."

As soon as her cool fingers gripped his hips, he braced his forearm on the wall and curled his left hand around the right side of her face, holding her head in place against the wall.

He rocked into her mouth, over and over. Wetness, heat, darkness, suction. So goddamn good. His responses were primal grunts and groans as he fucked that hot, sassy mouth like he owned it.

He thrust into her so deeply he felt the bite of her teeth at the base of his cock. That familiar static charge began at the top of his head and zipped down his spine to his groin, pulling his sac up. He was done. His shaft contracted, sending out a wave of ecstasy with every surge of seed.

Harper didn't move beyond sucking and swallowing. But she couldn't, since he'd pinned her head against the wall.

Bran was easing out, fully intending to return the favor by burying his mouth between her thighs, when he heard the blare of the auction speaker.

"Now up. Lot number twenty-seven."

"Goddamn it! That's the lot I've been waiting for." He jerked his jeans up so fast he almost caught the tip of his cock in the zipper. He tucked his shirt in and buckled his belt as he strode to the doors.

Not cool to leave her on her knees without so much as a good-bye.

Shit. Yeah. He was one classy guy. Bran looked at her.

"I'll be right back. Umm. Thanks." He made sure to shut the door behind him but not lock it.

Bidding for the fishing supplies was changed to lot number twenty-nine, but Bran was paranoid that he'd miss it, so he stuck close to the auction block. His cell phone buzzed and he ignored it. By the time they'd started the bidding on lot number twenty-nine, he'd forgotten about his unread text message. He won the lot, but paid plenty—to the tune of twelve hundred bucks. Struggling to carry the three boxes to the trailer, he set them on the ground and opened the doors. No sign of Harper.

Did you really expect her to be here waiting for you in the dark? Especially after the rude way you used her and left her?

Scowling, he dragged the boxes inside. He started to wander around, then figured it'd be easier just to call her. His finger skated across the screen and he noticed he had a text message. From Harper.

Harper? She never texted him. He touched the icon and the message appeared.

Ran into Alice & she offered me an early ride home. Need 2 talk 2 Bailey 2-nite. C U ltr.

He didn't know what he'd expected, but it wasn't that.

Chapter Fifteen

～

$\mathcal{W}$ith all the hours Harper spent with Bran, and Bailey's school schedule, she and Bailey hadn't spoken in person for over a week. But Harper had a sneaking suspicion Bailey was avoiding her for some reason. Tricking her sister seemed childish, but it was her only option to get Bailey to talk to her.

The front door opened. Harper knew Bailey couldn't see her lounging in the chair in the living room, since she'd turned off all the lights. She didn't want to scare her either, but again, no choice. She said, "Bailey."

The girl screamed like a horror movie queen.

Harper clicked on the table lamp. "Sorry."

"What the fuck are you doing, lurking in the damn dark, Harper?"

"Waiting for you."

"Holy crap. I thought you forgot to pay the electric bill."

"No. I figured you were avoiding me, so I chose a sneak attack. Liberty would be proud."

"Awesome." Bailey shifted from foot to foot, as if debating whether to make a break for it.

"Sit down. We need to talk."

"Where's Bran's truck?"

"Around. You wouldn't have come inside if you'd thought I was here. Have a seat."

"I only came home for a second. I have to go—"

"Wrong." Harper pointed at the couch. "Park it. Now."

"Fine." Bailey flopped down, arms crossed over her chest, a belligerent set to her mouth. "What's so damn important?"

"First, I wondered if you wanted to have a graduation party here and invite your friends."

A look of horror crossed Bailey's face. "No fucking way."

Was Bailey's vehement denial due to the fact that most of her classmates attending the small private high school outside Rawlins had money? Was she embarrassed about living in a dumpy rental?

"Look, Sis, that's sweet of you to offer. But most the kids I'm graduating with are total douche bags. I'd rather celebrate the fact I'll never have to see any of their stupid faces again . . . without them."

No party. Not that she was surprised. Check that off the to-do list. "Fine."

"So *that's* what was so damn important that you had to hide in the dark and scare the shit out of me? To talk about a freakin' graduation party?"

"No. I want to know where you are on the college decision process. I recall a couple of the colleges have housing application deadlines soon, so you're going to need to make a decision on where—"

"I said I'd handle it. Stop nagging me. Jeez, I'm under enough pressure with finals and all the other stuff. I don't need you adding to it."

"Tough. I'll remind you that your decision affects me too. I'll need to look for a job. And a place to live nearby."

Bailey scowled. "Why don't you just forget about me and figure out where *you* want to move?"

That jarred her. "What?"

"I'm eighteen. You don't have to babysit me. You're off the hook, Harper. You can do whatever you want with your life. Go anywhere. Don't base your decision on where you want to live on mine."

Annoyed by Bailey's blasé attitude, Harper snapped. "What's really going on, Bailey? You afraid your older sister will cramp your style at college? That I'll be tagging along all the time, wearing my toga, screaming, 'Where's the frat party?'"

She rolled her eyes. "Maybe you should enroll in drama classes. You've got a knack for comedic timing."

"Don't be flip. This is serious."

"I know. But as you've pointed out, this is *my* decision. You've got to let me make it." *Even if you don't like it* was implied.

An impasse. Big surprise.

After the day she'd had, she wasn't in the mood to let her baby sister run roughshod over her. Harper stood. "Just when I think we've both escaped Mom's influence . . . you're acting exactly like her." She walked briskly to her bedroom and slammed the door.

Mature, Harper.

She fell back on the bed and gazed at the ceiling. Trying to stay one step ahead to keep her stress level down was a losing battle. She couldn't give their landlord notice until she knew they wouldn't be living in their car.

Oh, really? Or is there another reason why you've been dragging your feet about finalizing your intent to move?

No. Being in limbo had nothing to do with Bran and everything to do with her sister.

Maybe the crack about Bailey acting like their mother had been unfair. But Harper had watched Dawn, the master manipulator, at work for years, and she recognized the signs. Putting Harper on the defensive was the first indication that Bailey was hiding something. But what?

The outer door slammed. Since her eighteenth birthday, Bailey had stopped telling Harper where she was going or who she was going with. Harper didn't want to spend another night alone, dissecting the deteriorating situation with her sister. Nor did she want to brood about Bran Turner and that intense interlude in the trailer at the auction today.

Not that she had a clue what had caused his uncharacteristic behavior.

Wasn't like she had anyone to talk to about relationship stuff, especially since what was going on between her and Bran wasn't really a relationship, just sex. Liberty had a ton of experience with sex, but access to her was limited—plus her older, wiser sister wasn't known for her warm fuzziness. Celia was on the road and winning. Like many athletes on a winning streak, Celia held on to certain superstitions. She started and ended each day the same way. Ate the same food. Listened to the same music. Talked to the same people. She even wore the same clothes until the streak ended. Since Harper hadn't been on Celia's daily call list when the streak started, even if Harper left a message, Celia wouldn't return her call, in case that one change would jinx her winning streak.

So, yeah, maybe she was just a tad annoyed with everyone—friends, family, her lover. It was Friday night. Maybe it was time to make new friends. Drinking friends. Because all of a sudden, Harper was in the mood to drink.

She rifled through her closet. She chose a stretchy button-up Western shirt, swirled with patterns of gold, brown, and rust. She paired the dress shirt with a gold lace camisole and pulled on her slim-fitting Levi's, threading a brown rhinestone belt through the belt loops, centering the modest rhinestone buckle between her hips. Needing further proof that she could still look like a girl, not a ranch hand, Harper fixed her hair to fall in loose curls around her shoulders. She applied enough makeup that it didn't appear she was wearing any makeup at all. The final touch was slipping on her dancing boots just before she scooted out the door.

Buckeye Joe's wasn't swamped. She wasn't sure if that was a good sign or not.

Susan glared at her, as usual, when Harper ordered a whiskey Coke. But also as usual, Susan had no problem taking Harper's money.

She almost headed to her usual table hidden in the back, but she realized that sitting alone, avoiding people, defeated her purpose tonight, so she grabbed the first barstool at the closest empty table.

And what is your reason for being here?

To have fun. To win friends and influence people. For some reason that cheesy *rah-rah* Dale Carnegie phrase made her laugh out loud.

"I'll have what you're having, since it appears to have the effect I'm looking for."

Harper spun on her barstool.

A petite woman, no bigger than a minute, leaned against the wall. She had short black hair, cut pixie style, which reinforced her elfin image. In this light, her enormous eyes looked purple. Her smile nearly spanned the distance from her left cheek to her right cheek, and that darling smile was offset on both sides with deep dimples. Good Lord, she was cute as a button. Everything about her was delicate, feminine, and tiny, making Harper feel like an overblown, bubble-headed, busty blonde in comparison.

Harper realized that not only was she staring but she hadn't answered the question. "Umm. It's a whiskey Coke. And the only reason I laughed is because I don't normally drink alone. So you're welcome to join me."

The invite seemed to shock the pixie chick, but she grinned. "I'd love to join you." She hoisted herself onto the barstool and thrust out her hand. "Janie Fitzhugh."

"Harper Masterson. I take it you're not from around here?"

"Used to be. A long time ago. A lifetime ago, actually." Her eyes clouded briefly and then she offered another deeply dimpled grin. "Anyway. Everything comes full circle, doesn't it? I'm back here to do a job."

Harper knew firsthand that jobs were few and far between. "Is this a temporary job?"

Janie shrugged. "We'll see how it plays out."

The waitress stopped by their table and Harper ordered two drinks for herself. Janie followed suit.

"So, Harper, please don't take this the wrong way, but why is a beautiful woman such as yourself sitting alone in this dive?"

"Take a guess."

"Man trouble?"

"Partially." She slurped her drink. "Don't think I'm some kind of unload-my-problems-on-a-stranger freak, but everyone in my life disappointed me today. I thought I'd see if Jack Daniel's would improve my attitude."

"Me'n Jack go way back."

After the waitress dropped off their drinks, Janie held up her lowball glass. "To Jack Daniel's. The only man you can count on."

"Amen to that, sister." They clinked their glasses.

"What're *you* doing out alone?" Harper asked.

"Probably tempting fate," Janie muttered.

Weird answer.

"Seriously, I don't know. I just wanted to see if anything had changed in Muddy Gap."

"Has it?"

"Not really. Except . . ." Janie pointed to the bar. "Mac used to bartend instead of Susan. I wonder what happened to him."

Harper snickered.

"What? You know the gossip, don't you?"

"I sure do."

"Come on, we're drinking buddies now. You have to tell me."

"Mac ran off with my mother, who used to be a cocktail waitress here."

Janie choked on her drink. "Are you freakin' kidding me?"

"I wish." Harper related the sordid tale, including coming back to Muddy Gap to take over as Bailey's legal guardian and their recent issues.

"You are one selfless woman, Harper, to get saddled with that responsibility and not complain."

"I'm not selfless. I thought I was keeping our family together and keeping us from becoming another statistic, but now I wonder if I haven't forced the sister bond." Harper drained her drink and started on the next one. "Do you have siblings?"

Janie scowled. "Two half sisters and one half brother that are young enough to be my kids."

"Do you have children?"

"No. Thank God I dodged that bullet. Though, at the time, that's all I wanted. I believed a baby would fix everything in our marriage."

"I take it you're divorced."

"For eight years."

Harper's eyes widened. "Wow. You were a child bride or something?"

"Sort of. I'm thirty-three. How old did you think I was?"

"My age. Twenty-four."

"I appreciate the compliment." Janie sipped her drink. "So tell me about this man problem."

From an early age Harper had learned to keep her private business private, mostly because Social Services was always sniffing around. But it wasn't like she was eight years old anymore. And hadn't she just been lamenting the fact she didn't have anyone to talk to?

"Sorry. I'm nosy," Janie said.

"No, it's not that. Just trying to decide if by telling you that I'm sleeping with my boss, you'll automatically assume I'm like my mother."

"I'm the last person to pass judgment on anyone."

So over the next half hour, Harper told Janie about Bran, the work she'd been doing on his ranch, and their intense sexual relationship, all without divulging his name. Because if Janie had lived here, even years ago, chances were good she knew Bran.

Immediately after she finished sharing her story, Janie demanded, "Are you in love with him?"

Yes. "I don't know. But it doesn't matter anyway, because I'm leaving."

"You sure about that?"

Harper shrugged.

The band started tuning. More people wandered through the doors, shaking off the cold. Both she and Janie kept an eye on the arriving patrons. "See anyone you know?"

"I recognize a few. It's probably a good thing the lighting in here is bad and no one will recognize me."

"Why? Did you leave town in the dead of night with the townsfolk's money earmarked for the orphanage? And they sent a hanging posse after you?"

Janie laughed. But her mirth vanished suddenly and she muttered, "Shit," then ducked behind Harper.

"See someone you know?"

"My ex-husband. Damn it. I knew this was a bad idea."

"Where is he?" Harper asked, craning her neck, without it seeming like she was trying to get a gander at who might be Janie's ex.

"Ladies. May I join you?"

Harper stopped trying to block Janie with her body and turned to face the male voice. "Renner? What're you doing here?"

"You know him?" Janie said.

She wasn't sure if Renner wanted it to be common knowledge that he'd come into Get Nailed for a manicure. She deflected the question and asked Janie, "How do *you* know him?"

"He's my boss."

"Boss?" Harper repeated.

"I'm the interior designer and all-around slave for his hunting lodge and spa project."

Renner rolled his eyes. "I haven't even started to slave you yet, Janie dear. Anyway, I'm glad to see you two have met." He yanked an extra chair from the table next to theirs.

The band launched into a peppy cover version of Faith Hill's "This Kiss."

Janie grabbed Renner's hand, held it between her hands prayerlike, and begged, "Please, please, please, you have to dance with me. Right now."

"Why?"

"Because he's here."

"No shit. Where?"

"Right over there. To your left."

"Oh. Okay. I see him." Renner appeared to regroup. "Lemme get my coat off." As soon as he hung it on the back of the bar chair, Janie was dragging him away.

Over his shoulder, Renner tossed out, "Order us another round of whatever you're drinking, Harper, and make mine a double."

Harper nonchalantly looked over to see who had sent Janie scurrying to the dance floor. She recognized the hat right off.

Bran.

Holy crap. Her vision dimmed. Blood roared in her head so loud it drowned out the band. What if the ex-husband Janie had been talking about was . . . Bran? Stupidly, Harper had assumed Bran had never been married, but she'd never thought to ask.

She saw Bran's eyes scanning the dance floor and knew the instant he recognized Janie. His eyes narrowed to tiny slits. He cocked his head, as if he couldn't quite believe who he was seeing. Then he herded his group— Abe, Nancy, and Ike—toward a table in the back. But Nancy wrinkled her nose and chose a table right up front. Close to the dance floor.

Was that panic in Bran's eyes? If he didn't want to run into his ex, why didn't he just leave?

What if he still had feelings for her?

Harper slammed her drink, knowing she had no right to be jealous. She had no claim on him. She fumed, deciding it was typical behavior for closemouthed Bran not to tell her something important, oh, like, he'd been *married* before, for crap sake.

Fortunately, Bran hadn't seen her. But Harper could see him. She signaled the cocktail waitress for another round, times three, and settled back to watch the show, hoping it wouldn't be one of those tearjerkers where she cried at the end.

∞

This was not good. Not good at all.

Bran should've stayed home instead of letting Abe badger him into coming to Buckeye Joe's. The idiot was still trying to prove to his friends that Nancy wasn't so bad—by forcing them to spend time with her. Wisely, Hank and Lainie had declined to participate in this farce. Hell, Bran had to bribe Ike to get him to show up. Even Abe's best friend, Max, had refused to come. So far, no one in their group had given Nancy the stamp of approval, no matter how hard Abe tried to push it.

He didn't like Nancy any better than anyone else in their group did. But Abe had always stood up for Bran, same as he had for Hank, so Bran had slapped on a smile and said, "Sure," to a night out with Nasty Nancy.

Didn't it just fucking figure that Janie had picked tonight, of all nights, to make an appearance in Muddy Gap? After eight years? Abe would blow a freakin' gasket when he saw her.

Jesus. He needed a goddamn drink. The cocktail waitress took their order: a glass of white wine for Nancy, after she'd demanded to look at a wine list—in Buckeye Joe's, for chrissake—and three Bud Lights for him, Abe, and Ike. Bran was half tempted to order a couple of shots. As close as they were to the dance floor, he figured he'd need the whiskey sooner rather than later.

Ike leaned forward and spoke to Abe. "Did you buy any of them extra calves from Olson's?"

"About a dozen."

"Can we please can the cow talk?" Nancy complained.

Bran bit back his response that she'd better get used to it if she was involved with a cattleman. "What would you like to talk about, Nancy?"

"I'm so glad you asked. I saw this fascinating documentary on . . ."

As soon as she uttered the word *documentary*, Bran tuned her out. As did Ike. And if he wasn't mistaken, Abe's eyes glazed over as he greedily gulped his beer.

The band segued into a slow song and Bran expected Nancy would nag Abe to dance. But she kept yammering on.

And on.

All of a sudden Abe's body stiffened.

Shit.

Nancy nattered on, oblivious to the change in Abe's demeanor.

However, Ike noticed and exchanged a concerned look with Bran because he also had seen Janie on the dance floor.

Now everyone witnessed Janie and Renner Jackson doing a country version of dirty dancing, with zero discretion.

The next thing he knew, Abe was out of his chair and stomping toward the grinding couple.

Damn it. Not good. Bran chased after him.

Abe latched onto Janie's upper arm and wrenched her away from Renner. "What in the hell are you doin' here, Janie?"

"Darning socks. What the hell does it look like I'm doing, Abe?"

Her response took Abe aback. He wasn't used to the woman he used to call "sweet plain Jane" snapping at him. He loomed over her, since she didn't even reach his shoulder. "You're actin' like you want him to fuck you right here on the dance floor."

Janie drilled him in the sternum with her index finger. "Maybe I do. What business is it of yours?"

"Don't you fuckin' push me, cupcake. You ain't gonna like the results."

She did just that. She placed her hands flat on his chest and pushed him.

Abe wasn't expecting it and he stumbled back a step.

"Cupcake?" she repeated. "You haven't changed a bit."

The other dancers had stopped moving and a crowd gathered.

Including Nancy. Her petulant "What is going on?" was largely ignored.

"And it looks like you have changed, cupcake." Abe flashed his teeth. "And not necessarily for the better."

"Why don't we all just take this down a notch?" Renner suggested, stepping between the warring couple, using his body to block Janie from Abe.

Abe got right in Renner's face. "What the fuck do you think you're doin' with my wife?"

The air went absolutely still.

Janie sidestepped Renner and poked Abe in the chest again. "Wife? I haven't been your wife for a long damn time, Abe Lawson, so you can just back off."

Bran caught movement out of the corner of his eye and turned to see Harper—his Harper—whispering in Renner's ear.

Renner smiled at whatever Harper had said and turned his head, so their mouths were a kiss apart. They stared at each other for a beat or two, as if sharing some secret, and then grinned.

First of all, what was Harper doing here? Second of all, when the hell had she gotten so freakin' chummy with that smooth-talking bastard? Bran had an overwhelming urge to punch Renner right in the kisser.

Then Renner wrapped his arms around Janie's middle, picked her up, and carted her off the dance floor. Harper followed, laughing, ducking Janie's legs and arms.

Abe emitted a primitive growl that Bran had never

heard before, which matched the possessive yowl in Bran's head. When Abe started after Renner, both Bran and Ike held him back.

"Let me fuckin' go, right now. He has no right—"

"No, *you* have no right. You need to chill out," Ike said.

"I agree," Bran said. "I think it's time to call it a night."

"Fuck that," Abe snapped. "We just got here."

Bran stood nose to nose with Abe. "Sit your ass down and forget about her."

Abe moved his head and stared over Bran's shoulder with such a look of longing that Bran felt it as surely as a punch in the gut. No need for Abe to say, "I can't," because Bran knew. He'd always known that Abe had never gotten over Janie.

Christ. What a fucking mess.

Ike clapped Abe on the back. "Come on. Let's sit down and get another drink, if we're stayin'."

Finally Abe nodded and sauntered off the dance floor, his death glare focused on the table where Janie and Harper were cozied up to Renner.

Before they sat, Nancy grabbed Abe's arm. "I said I'm ready to go home, Abe."

"So go," Abe shot back.

"What is wrong with you?" Nancy demanded. "You're acting like a complete idiot. In public, no less. And what's that garbage about you calling that woman your wife?"

"She's my ex-wife."

That seemed to further incense Nancy. "I want to leave right now."

"So leave. I ain't stoppin' you."

Yeah, Hank was gonna be damn sorry he missed this. Too bad the bar didn't serve popcorn.

Nancy's mouth tightened. "I rode here with you, remember?"

"Then I guess you're stayin' if you're waiting on me for a ride home, aren't you?"

"No. I will not stand here and watch you make a fool of yourself and make a fool of me."

"Your choice. But I *am* sitting down. And I *am* staying." Abe sat, which he never did when Nancy was still standing.

"I mean it, Abe. This is not a joke to me. If you don't take me home right now, we're done. For good."

Abe shrugged, almost absentmindedly. "I understand. To be honest, I'm tired of fighting with everybody in my life that matters about . . ." *You* went unsaid. "It's probably best we call it quits anyway."

The pinched look left her face and her mouth dropped open in shock. "What? You're serious. After all I did—"

"To try to destroy his family relationships?" Bran supplied. "Yeah, he's serious."

"I wasn't speaking to you," Nancy snapped.

Ike grabbed his coat. "Enough. I'll take you home, Nancy, but we're leaving right now."

"Fine." She took her time buttoning her coat, glaring at Abe, who was too busy glaring at Janie's table to notice.

When Nancy realized Abe really didn't give a shit if she left or not, she whirled around and stomped away.

Ike drained his beer before he followed her.

The waitress brought a fresh round. Abe contemplated his bottle for a long time.

"What's up?" Bran asked.

"Besides havin' my head up my ass?" He snorted. "Was Nancy always such a manipulative bitch?"

"Yes. And I can safely speak for all of us when I say I'm glad you finally saw the light. I ain't gonna claim she's not your type, but we never understood what you saw in her."

Abe sighed. "Eight years I've been divorced from Janie. Eight years I've been fucked up by it. I was happy to find a willing woman and get laid a couple of times a year, until Hank and Lainie . . ." He sighed again. "I don't begrudge Hank his happiness and I love Lainie like a sister. Seein' them happy reminded me that I want that happiness for myself. A wife and kids. A woman wasn't gonna fall in my lap, so I started looking for one."

"And you found Nancy."

"She really is different when it's just the two of us. Anyway, I was gonna ask Nancy to move in with me. Then I see Janie for the first time in two years . . . and it's like . . . what are the fucking odds? The night I decide to carve out a new life for myself, my ex-wife shows up. Talk about a cosmic clusterfuck."

Bran frowned. "I figured it'd been a lot longer than two years since you'd seen Janie."

"At first. I didn't talk to her for years after the divorce was final. She called me outta the blue about two years ago, wanting to meet, and like an idiot I agreed to . . . Never mind."

Before Bran could ask Abe what the meeting had been about, he saw Harper flit past, laughing, holding hands with that son of a bitch Renner Jackson as he led them onto the dance floor.

Did that smarmy fucker have every single goddamn woman in the county falling all over themselves?

Abe saw the opportunity to corner Janie and was across the room before Bran could stop him. Which left Bran in a shitty situation. Either stay here and watch Renner plaster himself against Harper, or cut in so he could plaster himself against Harper, and let Abe twist in the wind.

Grinding his teeth, Bran watched another man putting his paws all over his woman. They laughed . . . after whispering to each other. Renner spun them into the middle of the crowd, so Bran lost track of their grinding bodies. When they danced back into view, Renner had slipped his leg between Harper's, so it appeared she was riding his thigh.

Enough. As soon as this song ended he was getting Harper the hell out of here and away from Renner Jackson.

"Bran?"

He spun toward the voice and saw Janie crouching down by the table. "Janie, what the hell are you—"

"I'm avoiding Abe. Here are Harper's coat and purse. Can you make sure she gets home okay? She's had a few drinks and I have to get out of here right now."

"Not a problem."

Janie patted his leg. "Good to see you, Bran. Thanks for keeping Abe somewhat calm. We'll talk more later." And she scooted out, ducking into a crowd.

Bran was on his feet when the last chord twanged. He didn't even look at Renner. He just held out Harper's coat.

"What do you want?" she demanded.

"I'm taking you home."

She swayed as she invaded his personal space. "You're not my boss right now, so I don't gotta go anywhere with you."

"You're drunk."

"Says who?" Almost on cue, she hiccuped.

Bran grinned. "Says me. Now be a good girl and get your coat on."

Her eyes narrowed at his choice of the word *girl*.

Renner put his hand on Bran's back and spoke to Harper. "That's my cue to leave, now that I see you're in good hands."

"You're abandoning me?" she complained to Renner.

"Yep. Thanks for the dance, doll." He walked off.

Smart man.

Harper snatched her coat from Bran's hands and wouldn't let him help her put it on. She spun around, whapping him in the face with her hair as she sauntered off.

He followed her outside, ignoring the pointed stares of the other bar customers.

When it appeared that she intended to stumble the two blocks home on her own, Bran stepped in front of her and hoisted her over his shoulder. He'd come back for his truck later.

They were going to have this out right now.

Chapter Sixteen

❧

"*You* cannot hang me upside down like I'm a slab of meat, Bran Turner!" Her head bounced with Bran's every confident footstep.

"Sweetheart, your indignity would mean a helluva lot more if I could understand what you're sayin', but bein's your words are muffled against my ass, I can't."

Irritated, Harper smacked the backs of his thighs like she was playing the bongos. "Let me down, you big mean jerk!"

"Sure thing. Right after I dump you in your house so I know you ain't gonna fall on your butt and lay out here and freeze to death."

"I am not that drunk." And so what if she was? She was an adult. Making new friends meant buying a few rounds. And maybe she had had a celebratory shot after she'd found out that Bran hadn't been married to Janie. In all the years that she'd listened to Celia complain about Abe's whiny ex-wife it'd surprised Harper that Janie didn't fit that description at all. Maybe Janie had changed, grown up, whatever. Harper really liked Janie, another reason she was glad the woman hadn't worn Bran's ring and slept in his bed.

"Didja pass out back there, Harper?"

She smacked his buttocks in response.

Bran laughed. "Careful. I kinda like that."

"So you'll let me turn you over my knee like you did to me?"

That answer earned her a sharp crack on the ass and she yelped. "Don't be telling tales outta school where anyone can hear you."

"You're not making any sense. Maybe *you're* drunk."

"Not hardly. You had a head start on me." He shifted her slightly.

She tried not to worry that she weighed too much. But she'd seen him haul a hundred-and-fifty-pound calf on his back, and if he got a crick in his neck, well, good. She hadn't asked to be lugged around in the cold like a helpless heifer anyway.

"Is your sister home?" he asked.

"No. She's mad at me and she's probably not coming home." Shoot. Maybe she shouldn't have admitted that.

"Good. Because you and I need to get some things straight."

"I wouldn't think you'd care about setting things straight, being's you think I'm so drunk and all—which, FYI, I'm not."

His amused "I know" was followed by another male chuckle. A cocky one, in her opinion.

Bran whistled while he crossed the next block. *Whistled.* Like he was having a jolly old time.

She whacked his butt just for that.

He laughed again.

"Almost there." He turned up the sidewalk and didn't set her down until he'd reached the top step. "Keys."

Harper shouldered him aside, giving him her back. "I didn't lock it."

He sighed.

"What? You don't lock your door either, hypocrite. So just go. I'm home in one piece. Mission accomplished. Good night."

She opened the door only far enough to let herself in and attempted to shut it in Bran's face.

His laugh wasn't amused this time. He pushed the door open and followed her inside.

Harper tossed her purse and her coat on the chair. She didn't bother to kick off her boots but just headed for her bedroom. She didn't get far.

Bran spun her to face him, trapping her face in his hands as he fastened his mouth to hers.

She wanted to kiss him back. She craved these sweet, needy kisses from him because they were so rare. But she also knew why Bran was kissing her like this. He felt guilty. And he should.

So she turned her head away, breaking her lips free from his, keeping her eyes closed, waiting for him to let her go.

He did.

Without looking at him, she started toward her room.

But Bran was determined. He wrapped his arms around her middle, holding her lightly but firmly, nestling his chin into the curve where her neck met her shoulder. "Talk to me. Please. I know you're upset."

Harper allowed herself to lean against him, wanting his closeness, but he needed to apologize without her having to ask for it. She disentangled from his embrace and faced him, keeping her arms folded across her midsection. "Do you know why I'm upset, Bran?"

"Yes."

"Tell me."

"Why? We both know why you were upset. You were there."

"Not good enough. Tell me with words."

He took a step back and dry-washed his face. Then ran his palm along the top of his head and down to his neck. "I was outta line today."

"Meaning what?"

"Too demanding."

"Wrong. The word you're looking for is *demeaning*."

His face turned red, and the muscle at the base of his jaw jumped as he clenched his teeth hard.

"I can handle your demanding side. I've never felt ashamed of liking that part of you. You've never made me feel like I'm some kind of whore whose job is to service your sexual needs at your whim." Harper stared at Bran until he met her gaze. "Until today. You made me feel that way at the auction today."

"I'm sorry."

"I know. But it doesn't change anything."

"It changes everything, Harper, don't you see? I don't ever want to do that to you again." He stepped forward and gently gripped her upper arms. "Tell me what will fix this. What can I do to make it better? I'll do anything, sweetheart. Anything."

As she studied him, she knew Bran wasn't just saying that; he really meant it. Still. What she had in mind . . . might actually shock him.

"I know that look. You know what you want. Tell me."

She raised her chin a notch and gave him a haughty look. "I want to be in control."

"Okay. In control of what?"

"You."

He balked a little. "What?"

"I want you to know what it feels like to have someone else calling the shots, because I'll bet you've never tried it, have you, Mr. Large-and-I'm-Always-in-Charge?"

Bran shook his head.

"Do you trust me?"

His eyes searched hers. After a beat or two he nodded. Not exactly confidently. For some reason that boosted Harper's confidence and her determination.

"Good. Then I know what I want that'll fix this." She shrugged out of his hold and looked at his crotch, then back in his eyes. "I want to spank you while you're jacking off."

His face paled. "What?"

"You heard me." Harper walked straight to her room. Would he follow her? Probably. Would he try to change her mind? Probably. Would he be successful?

No way. She had to stand her ground or the man would run her into the ground every chance he got.

Plus, it sounded like fun.

She stopped at the window and double-checked that the blinds were closed. She heard his boots scuffing on the carpet. His footsteps stopped.

The door clicked shut. The lock engaged.

Harper slowly turned to see Bran resting his shoulders against the door, staring at her.

He said, "You look surprised."

"I am."

"I told you I'd do anything to fix this. So here I am." He spread his arms wide. "Ready to take my punishment like a man."

Since Harper had zero experience with this sort of thing, she dug deep inside herself, grasping the tiny dominant nature she usually let lie dormant, and let it fill her. She gave him a cool once-over. "Strip. Completely."

While he got naked, so did she.

"Now, face the wall and brace your left arm at eye level. Keep the other arm by your side."

As soon as he complied, she moved in behind him. The man smelled good, like Zest soap, hard work, and Bran. What a sense of power to feel his big body jump when she smoothed her hands down his tight, muscular buns. He stayed tense as she touched and rubbed and petted him. Gently. Tenderly. Softly.

So her first hard smack across those perfectly round white cheeks surprised him. He hissed in a sharp breath. Then she went back to stroking him. Not just his butt. From his lower back up to his broad shoulders. And back down, her thumb tracing the long indent of his spine from his nape to his tailbone.

Harper let her nipples graze his bare skin and he shuddered. She realized she wasn't making this about punishment for him, but about trust. He'd abused her trust today and she needed to show him, to remind him, what true trust entailed, especially why it was so important in a sexual relationship when one partner held the reins.

She reached between his legs and fondled his balls, pleased to find them already hard and tight. Then she stroked his shaft. She tortured him slowly, with feather-light butterfly touches, more fleeting than solid, never staying in the one place he most wanted her caresses.

Bran's whole body rippled and he groaned.

She stopped touching him.

He groaned louder.

Grabbing his hand, she curled it around his cock. "You do this. But don't make yourself come. In fact, you don't get to come at all until I say so. Understood?"

"Ah. Yeah. Sure."

Harper let her hand stay on top of Bran's while he pleasured himself. Such power and surety in his strokes.

He tugged much harder on the rigid shaft than she would've attempted. Using her thumb, she swiped away the bead of moisture gathered on the cock head.

He made a growling noise and his fingers tightened.

She slid her hand up his flat belly, stopping to tweak his nipple, smiling when he sucked in a quick breath. She sank her teeth below the skin of his left shoulder blade while her hand connected with his right butt cheek.

He jerked upright and went still. But he didn't protest or falter in the pace or movement of his hand on his cock.

She peppered him with swats until his firm butt cheeks turned a soft shade of red and were hot to the touch. Harper let her tongue follow the curve of his spine. When her mouth connected with his heated buns, he groaned. She rubbed her cheek against the warmth on either side, placing gentle kisses on the redness.

An unintelligible word rumbled from his chest.

He kept stroking.

She kept torturing him.

And she knew he was into it. His heavy breathing made his whole body heave. Sweat trickled down his back. She could smell his arousal, a special scent his body released that was pure musky male essence.

This power of pleasure was heady stuff. No wonder Bran liked it so much.

Harper alternated between kissing his back and leaving bite marks. She rubbed her nipples on his arm as she spanked him and he spanked himself.

It was unbelievably hot. Her pussy was drenched. Her skin felt too tight. Her heart raced. Her hands smarted from connecting with Bran's flesh. She felt his movements slowing as he tried to keep himself from coming.

She stood on tiptoe and whispered in his ear. "Turn around. I wanna watch you come. I wanna see you spray all over your belly. Like you did when you marked me with your seed. Mark yourself for me, Bran, since I can't mark you."

Bran flipped around, resting his upper back against the wall. His hand jerked his shaft hard and fast, a constant slapping of skin meeting skin. He let his head fall back and a low curse rasped from his lips. His jaw went tight, then slack. He groaned as he pulled his cock closer to his abdomen. Jets of come splashed at the top of his ridged abs. He kept pumping his hips and his dick until he'd milked himself dry.

Harper watched as the thick liquid ran down his belly, mixing with the sheen of sweat covering his quivering skin.

Finally he looked at her, male satisfaction riding high on his handsome face. His fist stayed around his cock and he awaited her further instruction.

"My turn," she said in a husky bedroom voice. She backed up until she sat on the edge of the bed. Splaying her knees open, she slid her hands down her stomach. When she reached her swollen pussy lips, she spread them apart, revealing every inch of her hidden folds, the mouth of her sex, and her engorged clit. "See how wet I am?"

Bran growled.

"Put your mouth on me. Now. Make me come."

He hit the carpet between her legs so fast he probably got rug burns on his knees. He layered his hands over hers, keeping her cunt wide-open so his tongue could plunge into her. He licked the cream coating her sex, flicking the very tip of his tongue over her clit. He sucked, making possessive male sounds that vibrated against her intimate flesh.

"Yes. Like that."

Two fingers pushed inside her channel. He rubbed the tips against the sensitive spot on her inner wall as he suctioned his mouth to her clitoris, catching the rhythm of her blood pulsing through her veins, sucking in tandem.

Each rhythmic pull of her clit into the heat of his mouth sent her closer to the edge. She bumped her hips up, grinding her sex into his face, desperate for release.

Then Bran backed off. He blew a stream of air over her engorged flesh. Her skin tightened from her pussy to her nipples to her scalp. He rapidly flicked his tongue across her clit, barely there wet lashes that intensified with each stuttered heartbeat.

Harper's legs shook. She teetered on the brink, needing . . . wanting . . . "Please. I—"

He reached up and pinched her right nipple hard at the same time his teeth nipped her clit.

That did it. She sailed headlong into dark pleasure as Bran fastened his oh so clever mouth to her throbbing clit and sucked.

And sucked. And dear God, he sucked some more, doing some exquisite maneuver with his tongue until she felt she'd had three orgasms instead of one. Until her insides trembled as strongly as her thighs, arms, and belly. Until a haze of bliss settled over her. A gratifying hum that streamed across the surface of her skin as she was totally submerged in unadulterated pleasure.

But Bran didn't give her long to bask in the afterglow of a triple-play orgasm. He pushed her back flat against the mattress, hiked her hips up, and plunged inside her pussy to the hilt. The ferocity of the thrust caught her off guard, but not the fact Bran had retaken control.

Harper let his body propel hers into the middle of the bed so she could wrap her legs around his waist. She put her arms above her head, because she knew how much that sign of surrender affected him. She loved this position. The feel of his strong body pressing into hers, chest to chest, belly to belly.

Then his hungry mouth sought hers, nearly burning her lips with a blistering kiss. She tasted herself on his tongue. Bran rocked into her hard enough that she worried their teeth might clack together. He must've sensed it at the same time she did, because he slid his lips to her ear.

"You make me crazy. Only you, Harper. What you do to me." He left a string of sucking kisses down one side of her neck and then back up the other side to her ear. "I wanna fuck you until we both pass out."

"Anything you want, Bran. You know I won't say no. I never have." *God help me, but I fear I'll never deny you anything.*

His very approving, very male groan exploded in her ear. "Smack my ass again while I'm fucking you."

When his cock was buried in her body completely, she brought her hands down, simultaneously slapping both his butt cheeks.

He shuddered.

She did it again.

And again, until Bran circled her wrists and pinned them above her head, grinding his mouth onto hers in a frantic kiss. His hips pistoned faster. Then he stilled completely. He ripped his mouth free and roared like a beast as he came.

Harper felt every pulse as his cock gave up its seed, bathing her inner walls with slick heat as she contracted the muscles around it, trying to prolong his orgasm.

He gasped, "Enough. Stop. You're killin' me."

She traced his skin with her hands, loving the rippling movements in the muscles of his damp back.

As he started to move off her, she whispered, "Stay with me tonight," hoping he wouldn't deny her the chance to have him in her bed until dawn.

Bran sweetly nuzzled her jawline. "I need to clean up first—"

"No. I like you sticky."

He lifted his head and looked at her strangely. "Why?"

"Because we always clean up and then I go home. Just for once I'd like to stay like this, a sweaty, sticky, tangled mess. All night."

His eyes took on a softer sheen and he said, "Anything you want."

Chapter Seventeen

❧

*B*randing day started as early as everything else in the cattle business. Helpers on horses, on ATVs, and in pickups headed for the pastures to round up the cattle. Anxious mama cows weren't happy to be separated from their babies, and by the corrals the din of moos was deafening.

Harper was relieved to stay at the house and coordinate the food. She'd seen enough of the cows and calves up close and personal, and it appeared Bran had plenty of help. Given the rainy weather the last few days, she'd been happy to see sunshine for the branding and for the feast afterward.

Bran's neighbors had shown up, as well as his friends and even their family members. He'd explained that other nearby ranches staggered branding days, spreading them out over a few weeks so they could help one another. The long-held tradition in the community was one they all took seriously.

He'd also assured her that other women would come bearing food. So after Harper set up the tables under the big white canopies and organized everything she could possibly organize, she found herself at loose ends.

She had just decided to take a quick drive up to the corrals to see where they were in the branding/vaccination process when Lainie Lawson's Dodge Durango pulled up to the trailer. She ambled over and saw Lainie unloading a huge box. "Hey, Lainie. Let me help you with that."

"I've got this one, thanks, but there's another one in the back."

Harper caught a whiff of something sweet and tangy. "Is this all food? My God. You baked, like ... half a dozen pies. From scratch."

"They're just rhubarb pies. No big deal."

They carried the two flat boxes over to the tables. Harper's mouth watered at seeing the perfectly browned crusts and the pink liquid that had bubbled up through the precisely made slits in the center of the top crusts. "Lainie. These look wonderful. I'm afraid if we don't leave right now I might just sit down and have myself a pie-eatin' contest."

Lainie laughed. "I'll admit I've been bribed to share my grandma Elsa's famous recipe because it's so darn good."

"Can I get you something to drink? There's lemonade and iced tea. And beer. Lots of beer."

"Cowboys and beer? Say it ain't so."

Harper smiled. "Since I'm not much of a beer drinker, Bran bought me 'bitch beer,' also known as Mike's Hard Lemonade and Jack Daniel's berry-flavored mixers."

"I've never been fond of that term," Lainie said. "So I'll take a real man's beer—Bud Light."

"Coming right up."

After they'd cracked the tops and wandered under the tent, Harper caught Lainie giving her a subtle inspection. Paranoid that she'd broken an obscure rancher's rule, she said, "Is there something wrong with what I'm wearing?"

"God, no. You look fantastic, as usual. It pisses me off a little, to be real honest. Anyone else would look like a total wannabe cowgirl, wearing that super-girly floral dress and boots to a branding. But it's a natural look on you." Lainie swigged her beer. "I'm jealous. Wish I could pull it off."

She waved off Lainie's compliment. "Sure you can."

"I don't have any fashion sense whatsoever, since I spend most my time in scrubs at the hospital." She grinned. "Or naked, if Hank has his way."

Harper almost said, "Bran is of the same mind-set," but she bit back the comment and changed the subject. "How goes the house-building project?"

"Slow. I can't freakin' wait to have our own home. Sounds like we'll be able to move in two weeks."

"How are things between Abe and Hank?"

"Better. Us having our own space will help. Sometimes I think Hank has mixed feelings about moving out of the house he grew up in. It's the only place he's ever lived."

"I've never had that kind of permanence in my life." Harper pointed to Bran's abandoned ancestral home. "So I don't understand why Bran doesn't live there. I know he still considers that his grandparents' house, but it's a shame to let it fall to ruin."

"I agree. When I asked Hank why Bran lives in a trailer, he looked at me as if I'd lost my mind. But it does remind me of my grandma's house. I loved that place and was really sad I couldn't afford to keep it after she passed on." Lainie took another sip of beer. "Have you ever been inside?"

"Nope. You?"

"Nope." Lainie looked at Harper with challenge in her eyes. "What do you say we take ourselves a little sneak peek?"

Harper started to refuse, wondering if Bran would consider that a breach of privacy, but he'd never exactly come right out and said she *couldn't* explore it. Curiosity won out over propriety. "Let's do it."

She wasn't surprised the front door opened without a key, since Bran never remembered to lock his own door. Dust motes danced in shafts of watery sunlight streaming through the dirty windows.

They stepped into a large entryway with a wide staircase stretching along the back wall.

"Left or right?" Lainie asked.

"Umm, left?"

Their footsteps sounded hollow on the wooden floor as they entered what must've been the dining room. Big windows faced the shelterbelt, and Harper could imagine sitting at a long table, gazing out those windows, watching the seasons change.

"Look at the woodwork in here," Lainie said, running her hand down the mahogany-colored trim around the doorframe.

"It's gorgeous." Dark trim also ran the length of the floor, and the ceiling boasted elaborate crown molding. Harper walked through an arched doorway to the kitchen. No appliances had been left behind. The countertops were dated and chipped, as were the cupboards and the linoleum covering the floor, but the space was large for the time frame in which it'd been built.

"It's weird that the kitchen is in the back of the house. Almost every house I've seen from this era has the kitchen in the front. And you enter the house more formally through the back."

"You mean like this?" Harper asked. An enclosed porch spanned the breadth of the back of the house.

"Oh, wow. This is seriously cool. We're putting one of these three-season porches off our kitchen too. This house was seriously ahead of its time, although it does appear to have been constructed backward."

Harper wandered through another arched doorway into the living room. It also had a door that opened onto the porch. More windows. More gorgeous woodwork. More feelings of sadness that Bran could just ignore this beautiful home that was so much a part of his personal history and should be part of his future.

She wound through the L-shaped room, discovering a small bathroom with limited headspace that had been constructed beneath the stairs as an afterthought when they'd added indoor plumbing. "I'm going upstairs," she said to Lainie.

The handrail and the balustrades were made of that same mahogany-colored wood. The instant she cleared the last step at the top of the stairs, she smiled. The floor was wider than a hallway, with a sunny landing. She imagined Bran as a little boy playing with trucks and Legos under the watchful eye of his grandmother.

Five doors were spread at random intervals. Behind the first door she found a full bathroom. The next two doors she opened led to small bedrooms. She knew that neither of these rooms had held Bran's childhood dreams and memories. The biggest room appeared to be the master bedroom, but it was small in comparison to modern-day master bedrooms and master suites.

The room directly across the hall, she knew without a doubt, had belonged to Bran. No faded marks from posters marred the walls. But there was one obvious sign of his residency: fishhooks embedded in the woodwork surrounding the window. Probably some fancy hand-tied lures, which made her wonder why he'd taken everything out of the house but left those.

"Harper? I think I hear the guys coming back. We'd better get going."

She gave the barren room one last, lingering look and returned downstairs.

ATVs, pickups, and horses trickled in from the field. Around that same time, wives and kids, girlfriends, and others showed up with heaping bowls of side dishes. Harper knew almost everyone, and if they were surprised to see her acting the part of hostess at Bran Turner's branding, they didn't mention it—an achievement itself in their small community.

After the guys washed up, they dug in like they'd never seen food. Harper had secretly suspected Bran was crazy for having her order a hundred pounds of shredded beef and fifty pounds of shredded pork, but now she wondered if there'd be enough.

The weather was beautiful, the food delicious, the beer cold. Everyone was having a great time. Even Bailey had driven out with her friend Amy. They hadn't stayed long, despite the urging of the younger single cowboys for them to stick around for the bonfire.

Both she and Bran mingled, separately. But she sensed his gaze on her several times. Okay, all the time. It gave her a secret thrill that no one had a clue about his rapt attention because his eyes were hidden beneath dark sunglasses and his ever-present cowboy hat.

Harper knew, though. Her skin prickled with awareness in anticipation of what he'd do to her when they were finally alone.

Food consumption dwindled as people lounged beneath the canopy and chatted. Harper gathered the temperature-sensitive condiments and took them to the trailer. She'd just shoved the mayonnaise into Bran's refrigerator when the screen banged open. She looked over the fridge door and saw Bran stalking toward her. All male, muscled sweaty goodness. Wearing the dark, sexy—God, hungry—look in his eyes that let her know he'd tracked her down for one reason and one reason only.

And he wasn't taking no for an answer.

Her blood raced. Her body heated and softened. He could do this to her. Without a word. Without a touch. With just a single look.

Bran shut the refrigerator and pressed her up against it. His mouth greedy on hers, his hands roving down her sides to grip her butt. His tongue invaded and conquered. He tasted like beer and sunshine and need.

Need. How could she need him this much?

He'd plastered his body to hers. Harper latched onto the denim covering his hips. One of his hands slid up to her scalp. He threaded his fingers through the loose strands of her hair and tugged her neck to the side, giving himself total access to the flesh of her throat. His lips followed the curve of her jaw to her ear. "Fuckin' sexy little goddamn sundress. Been drivin' me nuts all day."

A shiver washed over her, his hot words searing her skin like a brand.

"Want you, Harper. Now."

"Yes."

Bran stepped back, grabbed her hand, and dragged her into his office. As soon as they were inside, she was between a hard cowboy and a hard door.

She let his passion consume her, drive her higher. She ripped open his pearl-snap shirt and raked her nails down his chest, eliciting his full-body shudder. When she stroked and pinched his nipples, he groaned in her mouth.

The kiss grew more and more frantic until she couldn't breathe without breathing him in.

He buried his face in her throat. "Can't stop. Sweet Jesus I don't even want to slow down."

"So don't."

"Remember you said that." He nipped her neck and pushed back, giving her a head-to-toe inspection. Without taking his eyes off her, he rolled the chair away from the desk. "Bend over the chair."

She didn't hesitate. She brushed past him and placed her palms flat on the foam armrests of the chair, her pulse pounding from her nipples to her groin as she awaited his instructions.

Strong, impatient hands landed on her hips. Battered Tony Lamas appeared between her boots and kicked her feet apart. "Widen your stance."

Her heels slid out a couple of inches.

"Wider."

Her position must've pleased him, because he growled. His thumb traced the arc of her spine up to the nape of her neck. A hand tangled in her hair. Instead of urging her head up, he pushed it down so she could see between her legs. "Watch me."

Cool air teased the backs of her thighs as Bran flipped her sundress up. His fingers hooked in the elastic band of her panties. He tugged them past her kneecaps and stopped. "I'm hobbling you."

She bit her lip. He had no reason to hobble her; she had no intention to try to get away from him.

"Better yet, I'm taking them all the way off." *Yank. Rip.* "Oops. Looks like you're goin' commando the rest of the day. It'll be handy for later."

"Later?"

"Uh-huh. This is just an appetizer. Later, I'm gonna want a full meal of you." He gathered the dress material and tucked it out of his way. When he dropped to his knees, every inch of her body seemed to catch fire.

But even her flaming skin couldn't match the desire burning in Bran's eyes. Those strong, callused hands clamped onto the outsides of her thighs. He licked the crease of her left knee and swept that naughty wet tongue up the sensitive skin of her inner thigh.

Gooseflesh broke out, tightening her already taut skin.

He opened his mouth directly below the curve of her butt cheek and sucked. Hard. Hard enough to leave a hickey.

"Bran!"

"Hush." Then he nibbled up, across her behind, letting his tongue follow her butt crack until the tip reached her tailbone. And back up went that meandering tongue and wandering mouth. He sank his mouth and teeth into her flesh, gifting her with the same sucking love bites on the opposite side.

"Oh, God."

Before she'd recovered from his intimate mark, Bran licked her slit. Twice. Three times, never quite reaching the top of her sex. His frustrated rumble vibrated across it. "Bend your knees and cant your hips so I can taste you."

It was one of the sexiest sights she'd seen, peering between her spread legs, watching Bran's hungry mouth working her—lips, teeth, and that amazing tongue. She imagined his eyes were closed in ecstasy as he ate and sucked at her soft, wet folds.

His hands moved from the outsides of her legs to the insides, his fingers holding her pussy open so she could feel every bit of his sensual blitz.

Liquid excitement poured from her core. She caught a whiff of her own arousal and heard wet sucking sounds as Bran pleasured her. All those sensations, combined with the fierceness of his grip, increased her body's urgency to hit that point where she flew apart.

The spiral toward orgasm didn't begin slowly; it spun inside her as fast and furious as a tornado. "Oh, God, Bran, please."

Somehow, despite the unusual angle of his head, Bran's mouth fastened to her clit. When he sucked—*ding ding ding!* game over. She came hard and fast, digging her nails into the arms of the chair, throwing her head back, gasping his name. The man knew just how to send her soaring, and he did it without hesitation.

She was still experiencing buzzing aftershocks when he released her throbbing clitoris and scrambled to his feet.

His belt buckle rattled, the tines of his zipper made a quiet rasp, and his clothes rustled. The head of his cock prodded her entrance once and then he slammed inside fully, with enough force to move both her and the chair forward.

"You feel so good, Harper. Every goddamn time."

Instead of holding her hips, Bran curled his hands around her shoulders, giving him the depth he needed with every powerful stroke. His pelvis pistoned lightning fast, matching the thundering in her pulse and his harsh, labored breaths. Each relentless thrust built on the next until he shoved deep and stayed there, grunting while hot spurts heated her channel as his cock jerked inside her. She squeezed those muscles and he swore a blue streak even as he groaned her name.

He slumped across her back, exhaling into her hair, placing kisses across her shoulders where his fingers had dug in. She loved that Bran was so affectionate in the aftermath of explosive sex. She remained quiet, not wanting to ruin the moment.

"Now I don't wanna go back out there." His breath teased the damp skin below her ear. "I wanna take you into my bedroom and lock the damn door for the rest of the day and all of the night. And all day and all night tomorrow too."

Harper turned to nuzzle the side of his head, trying not to read too much into his declaration. "How long does this shindig last?"

"Usually the guys stick around the bonfire until the wee small hours. But I'm thinking tonight ... I might hurry them along a bit."

"Mmm. I like the sound of that."

Pause. Then he murmured, "Harper, I — "

The hallway creaked and the bathroom door slammed shut.

Immediately Bran pulled out with a muttered curse as if he just realized they were screwing in his office where any partygoers could hear them. They hadn't exactly been discreet. Or quiet.

Normally she'd be the one worrying if people were standing outside listening, gossiping about her reckless behavior or comparing her to her mother. But right now, sated from an intense sexual encounter with a smokin'-hot man who couldn't keep his hands off her, she had a hard time caring what anyone thought.

The jangle of his belt broke the silence between them as he yanked up his jeans.

While she was dissecting the situation, Bran helped her stand and straightened her dress. He kissed the back of her head, twice, with infinite sweetness.

She could give her heart to this man. So easily.

"Can you stay tonight after everyone leaves?" he whispered hotly against her throat. "Just you and me, Harper. Sitting by the fire, lookin' at the stars." His lips brushed her ear. "I'll even make you s'mores, since I remember how much you used to love them."

Maybe it was too late. Maybe she hadn't been careful enough. Because what she felt for him felt like a whole lot more than great sex.

It felt like love.

"What do you say?" he prompted with another sweet kiss.

"I say yes."

∞

Bran was pretty sure he had an extra swagger in his step when he returned to the party. Harper continually surprised him. He'd expected that she would kiss him crazily and play a little grab-ass before shooing him outside. But she'd given in to his demands. No, better yet—she'd given all of herself to him. Without boundaries. Without conditions. Without hesitation.

He just wished they didn't have to pretend that theirs was an employer/employee relationship. Oh, sure, he understood the reasons they were keeping their off-hours relationship on the down low, given Harper's mother's reputation in Muddy Gap and how hard she'd tried to rise above it. Sleeping with her boss—and, face it, no matter how they tried to spin it, Bran *was* Harper's boss. But he would do anything to protect her. Everything about the woman kicked his protective instincts into overdrive.

Still . . . he would love to exit the trailer holding her hand, hearing catcalls from his friends, seeing the knowing looks from the people in his life who mattered, who would know exactly what he and Harper had been doing for the last fifteen minutes. Instead, he had to settle for the secret knowledge of why her hair no longer looked so damn perfect while her taste lingered on his tongue.

She fit in. She fit *him*. She was the first woman who ever had. Maybe the only woman who ever would. And wasn't it just a kick in the nuts that she was leaving in three short weeks?

Before that panicked feeling took hold and he did something stupid, he saw a big rig that he recognized as Renner Jackson's pulling in, redirecting his attention.

As soon as Renner ambled toward him, he couldn't help but razz the man. "Typical stock contractor. Shows up when the work is done."

Renner thrust out his hand. "Sorry. Last-minute schedule change and the only one who could handle it was me, unfortunately. So—didja get 'em all branded?"

"Yep. Had a great crew this year."

"Looks like it."

Strange. Renner almost seemed nervous. "Come on over. I'll introduce you and find you a beer."

Once they were under the canopy, introductions done, and polite chitchat exchanged, Bran asked the question that was on everyone's mind. "So, whatcha building up there, Renner? I ain't the only one who's wondering what your plans are."

Renner groaned. "This is why you invited me, wasn't it? Ply me with beer and food and make me stare into the faces of all your neighbors and explain myself."

"Yep."

Laughter.

"I'm sure that most of you noticed I put in a road and poured the concrete footings last fall for four separate structures. I had planned on spending all winter up here getting the framing done."

"What happened?"

He sipped his beer. "Honestly? I ran out of money. As some of you know, I'm a stock contractor. We had a shit year, and the income I'd counted on from the livestock business, to start my building project, wasn't there. So I had to suspend all construction until I found an investment partner. Which I have, thank God."

"What exactly are you building?" Fletch asked.

"I'll bet it's a huntin' lodge," Ike said.

"Of sorts. It'll be more like a . . . resort."

A chorus of male groans caused Renner to grin. "Hey, I'm lookin' beyond just a hunting lodge. I want men to come and bring their women. So it'll also have a spa." He looked at Fletch. "Plus I'm hoping to move part of my stock operation up here and give the customers a taste of working on a ranch, in addition to hunting."

"I'm always ready for more work," Fletch said.

"How many locals are you hiring?" Abe asked.

Renner got a funny look on his face. "A few. So go ahead and spread the word that I'm looking to hire locally, especially experts in the areas where I'm no expert."

"Which would be in what areas?"

"All of 'em," Renner said dryly.

More laughter.

Talk turned to whether he'd try to stock the area with wildlife for hunting parties. The downturn in the economy.

Bran didn't envy Renner the work he had cut out for him to get the place up and running, but he admired the guy for his honesty. He could've kept hedging until the building process was under way.

"So, do you and your employees plan on living in Muddy Gap full-time?" Abe asked.

Bran almost snorted. Yeah, right. Abe was interested in exactly one of Renner's employees—Janie.

"For the most part. I'll still be traveling the rodeo circuit with the stock contracts I've lined up for the next few years. When I'm not on the road, I'll be living here. As will a couple of my key employees."

Beer was consumed. Stories told. Bullshit shared. Bran was having a great time, but that didn't keep him from looking for Harper every time the trailer's screen door banged.

Such a sucker. You are so totally whipped over that woman.

No lie. He had it bad.

Dusk fell and the guys headed home, complaining of aches and pains. Comparing bruises. Branding was hard physical work. Not the branding part, but wrestling the calves to the ground and holding them for the branding iron. Bran had his fair share of bruises.

With no hot young cowgirls, the younger guys had taken off, as had the families and Hank and Lainie. The last stragglers were Fletch, Abe, Eli, Ike, and Harper. Bran lit a bonfire anyway.

But Harper wasn't cuddled by his side. She'd taken it upon herself to put away all the leftover food and clean up. It wasn't something a hired hand would do; it was what a wife would do.

Wife. Right. Sex and beer were clouding his brain. Or maybe he'd taken a hoof to the head wrestling calves today.

"That Renner guy seemed a decent sort," Ike commented.

"You're just sayin' that because you're lookin' to pick him up as a client," Bran pointed out.

"That is true. Hey, it's a shitty economy all around—gotta search out new opportunities."

"No lie," Fletch said. "I'll be dropping my business card off as soon as I'm sure he ain't gonna run outta cash again."

"You know, I was surprised he offered that up," Abe said.

"I wonder who he got to ante up for this resort."

"He did get a sour look on his face, like he wasn't too keen on his new partner."

"I doubt it's someone local. Probably some bigwig who'll bring his buddies out here for hunting as an extra perk for bein' the moneylender."

"Nothin' worse than a bad partner, as I know first-hand," Eli said. "I'm glad to be out of that situation. However, I too will be letting him know I can provide him with horses he might need for trail rides."

Silence fell. More beer was passed around. Insects buzzed on the periphery of the crackling fire. The spring chill set in.

"Too bad Devin ain't around. He could sing us a tune or two."

"Bastard would probably charge for entertaining us these days," Abe grumbled.

Much to everyone's relief, Abe hadn't reconciled with Nancy. He was almost back to being the old Abe, but oddly, he did have a harsher edge than before, and that worried Bran, but he wasn't about to bring it up.

"Well, guys, I'm whupped." Fletch stood.

"Me too." Eli pushed to his feet.

"I ain't ready to go home," Abe said. He looked at Ike. "You wanna hit Buckeye Joe's and see if anything's goin' on?"

"Sure. Ain't like I gotta get up early and go to church."

More laughter.

Bran wondered if Abe's new fascination with Buckeye Joe's had anything to do with his ex-wife's interest in the place. According to Harper, Janie had become a regular—and she'd regularly called Harper to drink with her.

Harper strolled out of the house after the guys left. Wrapped in a blanket, she stopped on the opposite side of the bonfire from where he sat.

"Hey," he said.

"Hey."

"Thanks for cleaning up." He finished his beer. "It was a ton of work. I appreciate it. You can put the hours on your time sheet, if you want."

Her eyes narrowed. "I didn't show up today as your hired hand, Bran. I'm here as your . . ."

Silence.

"As my what?" he prompted.

She sauntered forward. "As the woman who wants you to keep her warm."

Bran opened his arms. "Come here, my woman, and snuggle up on my lap."

A wide grin split her beautiful face and she practically ran to him. She sat facing the fire, nestling the back of her head into his neck and draping her legs outside his.

He tucked the blanket around her. "Better?"

"Mmm-hmm."

They watched the orange and yellow flames dancing up the long chunks of wood as the embers glowed red.

After a bit, she sighed. "There's just something mesmerizing about a bonfire, isn't there?"

There's something mesmerizing about you.

"Bran, I have a confession to make."

"Okay."

"I broke into your grandparents' house today. Well, technically I didn't *break* in because the door wasn't locked, but Lainie and I got to talking, and we were both curious, so we just sort of . . . went in."

Any anger he expected didn't surface. He didn't say anything because he didn't know what to say.

"Are you mad?"

He brushed his lips over her temple. "No. I guess I'm figuring you're gonna chew me out for letting it sit empty."

"It is a cool house. Much bigger on the inside than I imagined. It would take a lot of money to get it updated, so I do understand why the repairs might seem daunting."

"But?"

"But. It's where you grew up. It just seems to be waiting for you."

"Waiting for me . . . how?"

"Waiting for you to settle down and decide to make it your home again. Most people never have that kind of chance."

Such a sweet, romantic notion from a woman who defined practical. It made his heart ache to hear Harper's sentimental side and realize how she longed for a home of her own. Once again he was at a loss for words. He couldn't tell her about the strange mixed emotions she aroused in him, but he could show her. He kissed her temple and said, "Can you get up for a second?"

"Oh, sorry. I'm probably giving you a cramp, sitting on your lap." She scrambled off and almost planted her face in the bonfire.

He snatched her back by grabbing her hips. "Steady, sweetheart."

"I think my legs fell asleep."

"I'll wake 'em back up." Bran quickly unbuckled his belt and dropped his jeans and his boxers to his knees. Then he sat again, grateful that he'd chosen a chair with lower arms. He slapped his bare thighs. "Okay. Now you can sit on my lap."

Harper whirled around, her eyes immediately zeroing in on his erection. "My, my. What a hard, hot poker you have there, Mr. Turner."

"All the better to stoke your fire with, baby." He used the edges of the blanket to tug her closer. "Straddle me. I want to see your face bathed in firelight as I'm inside you."

Her eyes softened. She lowered herself onto his legs carefully.

Bran lifted her dress out of the way and shifted his hips, sliding her forward. The head of his cock brushed the warm wetness at her center.

Harper pressed into him, taking him inch by inch. Once his cock was buried fully, she closed her eyes and her head fell back.

He hooked his finger into the front of her dress and tugged the material until her bra appeared. Another tug and her nipples poked out. His mouth opened over the pale peach tip and he sucked, loving the way the bud responded. Loving her surprised gasp and the not so subtle way she attempted to get him to take more of her delicious nipple into his mouth by arching her back.

She pulled herself closer. With her hands on his shoulders, Harper gained extra leverage and did a twisty roll with her hips.

"Keep doin' that, sweetheart." He returned his focus to her luscious tits. Man, he could not get enough of them. In his mouth. In his hands. Gliding his cock between them. Nuzzling this softest part of her drove them both crazy.

"I thought you wanted to see my face by firelight," she said softly. "Because you seem to be focused on my chest. Again."

Bran's gaze snapped up and her nipple slipped from his mouth with a soft *pop*. "But I am looking at you. You're beautiful, Harper. Just like I knew you'd be." His fingertips stroked the delicate line of her collarbone. "Much too pretty for the likes of me."

She crushed her lips to his. Sucking his sanity right into her hungry mouth with a scorching yet playful kiss.

The sweet, slow lovemaking didn't vanish in a fresh burst of passion, but stayed on course as they moved together. Or in opposition. He couldn't touch her enough. His hands shook as they trailed from her jaw to her neck to her shoulders to cup the heavy weight of her breasts in his palms.

Harper curled her hands around his face and muttered, "And you're much too smart for the likes of me."

He laughed.

"I love to hear you laugh, Bran. You don't do it often enough."

"You make me laugh. Maybe I should keep you around as comic relief."

She gave his forehead a slight head butt, which strangely enough reminded him of the way his goats showed affection to each other. "Maybe you should."

"Mmm. Grind your clit into me. Make yourself come. I wanna watch."

"I can make myself come a lot faster if I use my fingers."

"Show me."

She traced her index and middle finger across the seam of his lips. "Open. Get them wet."

He did.

Then she slipped her hand between their bodies and stroked in time to the bumping of his hips.

"That's sexy as hell, Harper. Everything you do is sexy." He latched his mouth onto the sweep of skin where her neck flowed into her chest and left little nibbling kisses.

"More. God. More, please. I'm so . . . almost . . ."

Wet, juicy ripples seemed to draw his cock deeper into her cunt during her orgasm. Holding off was pointless. After he shot his load, he rested his head back and stared at the profusion of stars above them.

But nothing beat the glow on Harper's face after she'd floated back to earth.

"Why the big smile, sweetheart?"

"Because this was definitely better than s'mores."

Chapter Eighteen

✎

"**I** just don't know what I'm going to do when you leave town, Harper," Rose Smith confided.

"I'm sure Bernice will find someone to take good care of her nail clients." At least she hoped so. Max's girlfriend, Nikki, had applied. She seemed a sweet girl—if a bit flaky—but she was genuinely interested in doing nails.

"But anytime there's a change, the prices go up."

Telling Rose everything would stay the same was a big fat lie, so Harper kept her mouth shut.

"Getting my nails done is a luxury and I'd hate to give it up."

"After working your fingers to the bone on the ranch the last fifty years, I don't know anyone who deserves pampering more than you, Rose."

"You're such a sweet girl."

Harper braced herself for Rose's gentle chiding. "Why aren't you married?" But for once Rose didn't voice her concern for Harper's lack of marital happiness. She went off on another tangent about the perils of loving the wrong man.

For some reason Harper thought of Bran.

Which should serve as a warning—if Bran's name was the first one that popped up when she thought of the perils of love. If she wasn't careful, if she looked too deeply or read too much into his change in demeanor around her since the branding, she might believe he'd started to have feelings for her too.

Too.

Face it. You're already past the point of no return with the sweet and raunchy cowboy.

". . . such a shame, really."

Harper refocused on her client. "Sorry, Rose. I missed what you said. Such a shame about what?"

Rose went into a long-winded explanation about the marital woes of the youngest Benton girl, who'd recently turned forty. When Harper heard stories of infidelity and heartbreak, she wondered why anyone was so hot to get married. Especially when most unions ended in divorce. Not that she advocated her mother's lifestyle or her screwed-up view of the world, but at least Dawn Masterson hadn't compounded her mistakes by marrying any of the men who'd impregnated her.

After Rose left and Harper was cleaning up her station she looked up when the doorbell chimed. Her heart did that swoop-flip-roll thing at seeing Bran just inside the door.

He seemed ill at ease amid all the "girly" stuff, so she met him halfway. "Hey. What brings you by? Need a manicure?"

He snorted with disdain. "Like that'll ever happen. I was on my way to get some stuff in Rawlins and wondered if you wanted to ride along."

"Stuff?" she repeated. "What kind of stuff?"

"Ah, the usual . . . ranch stuff."

Silence.

She couldn't figure out if this impromptu trip was business or a personal errand. Part of her didn't want to press him to define it, because she was happy to see him. Might make her a lovesick fool, but she missed the rugged cowboy during the hours she wasn't working with him on the ranch. If his expression was any indication, questioning his motives would put him on the defensive. She smiled. "Sure. I could use a change of pace. You've got great timing—I just finished up and was about to close down."

"Need any help?"

"No. But I do have to lock the back door." Harper cut through the salon, first checking to make sure all the appliances were shut off in the back room. She slid the dead bolt and clicked the lock on the heavy steel door. When she turned around, Bran was right there.

"I didn't want to do this in full view of the windows, in case someone was peeking in."

"Do what?" she breathed.

"This." Bran sealed his mouth to hers.

The kiss was warm and sweet. Thoroughly mind-blowing in a way that belied its tenderness. He didn't touch her anywhere besides where their lips met, but Harper felt the kiss from head to toe, as if they were body to body, soul to soul, and completely naked. Lord have mercy— she'd fallen hard for this man.

He eased back, gifting her with his devilish grin. "If we don't go now, I'll be mighty tempted to lock the front door and test out one of them spinning chairs."

Harper reached up and caressed his smooth face, ridiculously pleased that he'd shaved. Like this was a real

date. "Your kisses make me dizzy enough that I don't
need a spinning chair."

"You tryin' to charm me so you can get into my pants
later?"

"A girl can hope." She smooched his smirking mouth.
"Let's go. I expect you'll feed me in Rawlins so I can
keep up my strength to seduce you."

"I'll buy you the biggest steak in town."

Despite wearing a skirt, Harper slid next to Bran in
his truck when he'd patted the empty middle space. Since
she hadn't dated much, and rarely cowboys even then,
she'd never been the girl who'd scooted close to her
honey in his big ol' pickup truck and straddled the gearshift. At first she'd felt silly, but the hard muscle of Bran's
right leg pressing into hers and his strong arm across the
back of the seat changed her mind. Everything about
being with him, being this close to him, felt right.

As soon as they hit the outskirts of Rawlins, Bran
said, "We've got to stop at Runnings."

"What for?"

"I need some new gloves."

So this *had* been an excuse to spend time with her off
the ranch. She knew the man didn't need gloves; he
owned, like, twenty pairs. But she nodded and said, "I
could use a new pair myself."

The ranch supply store's parking lot was empty. Harper
turned to ask Bran if it was closed, and again, he was
right in her face, lips on lips, his mouth controlling hers.
His hand slid up her leg beneath her skirt and he teased
her sex through her satin panties. He kept kissing her,
kept stroking her, until she forgot about everything but
the taste, the touch, and the scent of this man.

Bran pulled away. The look in his eyes was serious
and seriously hot. "Harper, do you trust me?"

"Umm. Why are you asking me that now?"

"Just answer the question. Yes or no."

"Yes. I guess."

His answering grin was decidedly wicked. "Good. Let's go shoppin'."

The inside of the store was as deserted as the parking lot. An oblivious teenage girl leaned against the register partition, texting.

Bran approached her. "Excuse me. Is anyone around tonight to load corrals if I buy some?"

She shook her head. "We close in an hour. Just me and Reggie here and he's in the back."

"Thanks. Next time I'll have to come earlier in the day." Bran placed his hand in the small of Harper's back and directed her to the glove aisle.

She snagged the first pair she saw, while Bran debated on styles, thickness, and new brands until she couldn't stand it. She wandered over to the clothing section.

Ranch-supply stores had everything from baby chickens and corrals to industrial tools and livestock feed to food and clothing. Harper had a serious thing for Western clothes.

At first she'd worn the traditional floral patterns and flannel to make herself feel more like a Wyoming native, but along the way she'd fallen in love with Western styles. The slim cut of the women's dress and casual shirts. The rhinestones on everything. The sheer variety of jeans that fit every shape and size of woman under the sun. And the boots. If she had the money, she could spend every last dime on cowgirl boots. She loved to browse, trying to figure out funky ways to put together cool outfits with limited cash. She let her fingers follow the ruffled pattern on the bottom of a denim miniskirt.

"You should try that on," Bran said behind her. "I bet it makes your ass look fantastic."

What a flatterer. But she wasn't immune to it. "Really?"

"No foolin'. Go on. Try it. The dressing rooms are straight back there." He pointed.

Harper peered over his shoulder at the girl employee still engrossed in poking buttons on her cell phone. "Do you think I should ask her first?"

"No need. We're the only ones in here."

Okay, then. Harper picked the biggest dressing room, in the corner. She slipped off her skirt, leaving on her knee-high heeled boots. Just as she was about to shimmy the skirt up her legs, two brisk knocks sounded on the door.

Crap. She knew she should've checked with that girl first. Holding the skirt across her lower half, she cracked open the door. "Yes?"

Not the employee standing on the other side, but Bran.

He bulled his way inside and locked the door.

"What are you doing?"

He snatched the skirt out of her hands and tossed it on the bench. He stalked her until her spine hit the mirror. His fingers pinched the fabric of her shirt beneath her collar, and the metal snap buttons went *pop, pop, pop, pop, pop* until her shirt hung open. Then Bran's mouth was hungry on hers, his fingers twisting the front clasp of her bra. The little chunk of plastic was no match for his determination, and her breasts tumbled free.

She considered protesting for five seconds until Bran's wonderfully rough hands were on her breasts, rasping across her nipples. Her heart kicked into double time when he shoved his thigh between hers and began to slide it up and down, creating delicious friction across her damp slit.

He kissed a line from her mouth straight down her

neck to gift her cleavage with sucking kisses. "I want to fuck you. Right now. Facing the mirror."

"But—"

Then he was nose to nose with her again, all hot, hard, single-minded male. "You drive me wild. I can't get enough of you." He nuzzled her cheeks with his, rubbing back and forth as if he was marking her. "You're a drug," he whispered huskily. "Feed my addiction, Harper. Right now. No one will know what we're doin' in here besides us."

She lost control of her will when he blew in her ear. His magical hands spanned her hips, and his thumbs hooked the edges of her panties as he whispered hot, sweet, sexy words against her throat.

"Be adventurous, darlin'. Say yes."

Harper wanted this. To be wanton. To be fun. To be sexually spontaneous. To have a man want her so desperately that he'd take her hard and fast in a dressing room of a Western store on a Monday night. "Yes."

Bran smashed his mouth to hers and roughly pulled her to him. He tore at her clothes. Her shirt hit the floor. Then her bra. He tugged her panties until they pooled between her feet. He broke the kiss and turned her around. "Bend over and put your hands on the mirror," he said while unbuckling his belt.

She watched the play of emotions on his face in the mirror as she placed her palms at waist level. Lust. Eagerness. Mostly she sensed his impatience as he threw off his duster and shucked his jeans down to his knees.

He inserted his booted foot between hers, gently kicking her feet apart. "Wider." He kept his focus on her sex as he fed just the tip of his cock into her wet channel. Then he ran his rough-skinned hands up her naked back, curling one hand over her shoulder and twining her long tresses around the thick fingers of his other hand. He pulled her hair hard enough to get her attention. "Keep your head up. I wanna see your face while I'm fucking you." He snapped his hips and filled her in one endless stroke.

Yes. He knew just how she liked it. Hard. Fast. Deep. Harper arched her neck and let her eyes flutter closed.

Another sharp tug on her hair and her eyes flew open. "Watch," he demanded.

His next couple of thrusts were powerful enough that Harper was thankful she'd braced herself against the mirror. The warm friction of his cock was familiar and yet foreign as he drove into her without pause.

Bran's eyes were no longer on her face but on her breasts, which swayed and bounced with his every jackhammering thrust. He licked his lips and growled before catching her gaze in the mirror. Then he stopped moving. Keeping their gazes locked, he angled forward and placed a surprisingly tender kiss on her left shoulder. "Sweet Jesus, look at you. So goddamn lush and sexy and beautiful." He kissed the hollow below her shoulder blade. "I love takin' you from behind, but this is so much better because I can look at you. I can watch your eyes. I can see how you react to what I'm doin' to you."

The fact that he'd practically snarled the words only increased their impact. Harper felt like the sexiest woman on the planet, with Bran's possessive touch on her body, his fiery eyes locked to hers, his hard cock impaling her. She tilted her hips, bringing him deeper inside her. "See my reaction, Bran, when you make me come."

A smug expression of satisfaction entered his eyes, and he returned to fucking her with absolute gusto. He kept one hand tangled in her hair, forcing her head up, while the other smoothed the outside curve of her body, over her swaying breast and the slope of her belly, stopping at the rise of her mound.

Keeping the base of his hand anchored on her pubic

bone, his middle finger followed her slit to where his cock joined their bodies. He dragged his finger back up, separating the pussy lips hiding her clitoris. After a few teasing circles, he began to stroke that pouting bit of flesh in a countermotion to his pumping hips. But since his strokes were getting faster, his attention to her clit was constant. And accurate. Holy cow, was it accurate. The man knew—had memorized—all her hot buttons.

That drone of need began to build. Harper's fingers slid on the mirror as she tried to squeeze the glass. She looked at herself, bent over, spread wide, sex drunk, seeking that point of pleasure that only Bran could provide her.

He slightly changed the angle of her head. Without missing a single stroke, he opened his mouth over the vulnerable slice of skin next to her nape and sank his teeth in.

The sexy love bite sent Harper sailing into the chasm of bliss. She gasped loudly, forgetting they were in public, as each orgasmic wave throbbed through her body. She gasped again when the clenching pull of her interior muscles clasped Bran's cock, bringing it to that magical spot inside her that caused another set of strong ripples.

Then Bran swore and started to come.

How much time passed, Harper didn't know. Her world had been pared down to this small space filled with heat, the scents of sweat and sex and Bran. Just Bran. Nothing else existed. Nothing else mattered.

Keep telling yourself that and you'll end up like your mother.

Whoa. Talk about a random thought to take the shine off the afterglow.

Bran was slumped across her back, pressing his sweaty forehead between her shoulder blades, his breath stuttering and his body shuddering from his climax. His cock was still buried inside her when three insistent raps sounded on the door.

"Hello? Are you all right? I heard noises in here."

Noises? Had they really been that loud?

"Hello?" Then, "Shit, I'll have to get the key."

That spurred Harper to answer, "Ah, no, it's okay. I'm fine. Just having a devil of a time getting this"—she pushed her hips back into Bran's pelvis—"*thing* off me. It's a tight fit."

Bran murmured, "It *is* a tight fit," and bumped his hips forward into her again. "Really tight. Perfectly tight."

"Did you say something?" the girl demanded.

"No. I'll be out in a second." Using the mirror, Harper pushed herself upright, intending to dislodge Bran from her body.

But he held her in place and let his hands skate up her torso, cupping her breasts. She watched his slow, sensual movements reflecting back to her. He acted as if he had all the time in the world to touch her, which spoke volumes about the type of man he was. He would not be rushed. He would not be bullied. His breath was hot in her ear. "I wanna fuck you like this again."

"Now?" she whispered.

"Would you say yes?"

She nodded her head yes even as she mouthed, *No*.

He laughed softly.

When she turned, he kissed her in an openmouthed duel of sliding tongues and lips.

As he pressed a moist kiss to the cup of her shoulder, he pulled out. Although he'd only untucked his shirt and dropped his pants for their encounter, he helped her put her clothes back on. Bran's idea of help was stealing kisses, copping a feel, generally making a nuisance of himself. But Harper didn't mind a bit.

Once she was as presentable as she could make herself, she was half tempted to tell Bran to sneak out first.

Why? You aren't ashamed, are you?

No. Heck, Harper was proud that she'd brought out such a primitive need in a man like Bran Turner, who prided himself on total control. She opened the door and walked out of the dressing room in front of him.

The salesgirl looked at them. Suspiciously. Knowingly.

Harper smiled and handed the girl the skirt. "You know, I don't believe I need this today. Thank you."

She looped her arm through Bran's and they didn't stop laughing until they reached his truck.

Chapter Nineteen

❦

"**Y**ou promised you'd feed me. Steak, if I recall."

Bran started his truck and looked at her. Damn. He liked that Harper sat right next to him on the bench seat. He really liked the shine in her eyes and the soft set of her mouth. He fastened his lips to hers, taking the lazy, slow kiss he wanted. When she started to inch her hand up his leg, he broke the kiss with a smile. "Food first. How about the Cattleman's Club?"

"Sure. I've driven by a bunch of times, but I've never eaten there."

"They've got decent steaks. Cheap beer. Good music."

"Sounds like my kind of place."

After Bran parked and helped her out of the truck, he kept hold of her hand as he led her inside. The joint was hopping, but he didn't recognize anybody—mostly because he couldn't look away from his beautiful date. The hostess showed them to a booth up front by the stage and dance floor. When Harper tried to sit across from him, he nudged her into the booth and scooted right next to her.

"What can I getcha to drink?" the waitress asked.

"She'll have a Jack and Coke, and I'll have a Bud Light."

Harper turned toward him after the server left. "You've got a funny look on your face. What are you thinking about?"

"Miniskirts. Specifically, about the time you and Celia came along with us to Cactus Jack's. You wore that faded-jeans skirt that made your legs look a mile long. Did you hear the collective male groans every time you angled across the pool table to take a shot?"

Harper blushed. "No. I don't know what possessed me to wear that skirt. I've not worn anything that short since."

"I know. Why do you think I was so gung ho for you to try on that miniskirt in Runnings?"

"Because you wanted to nail me in front of a three-way mirror and see if you could make me scream?"

He grinned. "That too. But damn, I really love the way your ass and legs look in them short skirts."

She blushed harder, if possible. "I didn't think you noticed."

"I would have had to've been blind and dead from the waist down not to've noticed you." *Not to have wanted you. Fantasized about flipping up that sassy little skirt and bending you right over the pool table.*

"Such a sweet talker."

He focused on the menu. "Any idea what you're havin'?"

"The petite sirloin, hash browns, and a salad with blue cheese dressing."

"Sounds good. Except a small sirloin is just gonna piss me off."

She laughed.

The waitress dropped off their drinks and took their

order. Bran lifted his bottle to Harper's glass. "To mini-skirts."

"And your sudden need for leather gloves." She clinked her glass to his and drank.

Silence descended. And lingered.

Why?

Because this felt like a date.

Shit. Was he supposed to exhibit datelike behavior? Ask about her interests? Movies she'd seen? Places she'd been?

No. This was Harper. *His* Harper. They were beyond typical date behavior. He'd seen her covered in manure. He'd seen her wearing nothing at all. He'd seen her angry and aroused and determined and exhausted. He knew her, damn it. Straight down to the bone. They were beyond this trivial stuff.

Yes—he knew her because he was head over heels in love with her.

Almost as if she sensed his realization, she pushed him to move, scooted out of the booth as soon as he stood, and sat across from him.

"Was it something I said? I did put deodorant on before I left the house."

"Don't go getting your boxers in a twist, Bran. I'd like to look at your face when I talk to you."

"We don't seem to be doin' a lot of talkin'."

Harper cocked her head. "Why is that? We never run out of things to talk about on the ranch."

"We're mostly talkin' about work stuff." He grinned. "Or we're getting nekkid."

"Since we've already done that, are we just going to sit here and stare at each other?"

Bran reached out and touched her cheek. "That ain't such a hardship for me, bein's you're so beautiful you take my damn breath away."

Her eyes softened. "I like this side of you."

"Which side is that?"

"Sweet. Romantic."

It was Bran's turn to blush. "So is it considered romantic if I ask you to spend the night with me before we even get our food?"

"Only if your offer includes breakfast."

"Done."

The waitress served their salads and they tucked in. However, Harper's gaze kept straying off to the right.

"What's captured your interest over there?"

"I thought I saw someone I knew."

Speakers crackled and the feedback from a microphone reverberated loudly. They both winced. "Ladies and gentlemen, welcome to Monday night karaoke at the Cattleman's Club. I'm Bob Carlson and I'll be your host. So if you've got a burning desire to sing for these fine folks, come up and see me and we'll get you on the list."

Bran groaned and felt Harper's gaze burning into him.

"Not a karaoke fan? Or are you worried someone is going to pick your song first?"

He shook his head. "First, I don't sing. In public. *Ever.* Second, what song do you think is my favorite?"

She smirked. "Honky-tonk Badonkadonk."

"Not hardly. What about you?"

"Do I sing? Or do I like 'Honky-tonk Badonkadonk'?"

"Do you sing?"

"Singing was my talent in the various beauty contests I competed in, but that doesn't mean I do it well."

"Oh, I'm sure your voice is as sweet as a songbird's," Bran said silkily. "What was your signature song?"

Harper speared lettuce with her fork and stuffed it in her mouth.

"Come on. Tell me."

She shook her head and chewed.

"Or maybe you want to show me?"

She swallowed. "Huh-uh. I retired."

"From singing?"

She nodded.

"But I've heard you humming all the damn time while you're workin'."

Harper pointed her fork at him, a little angrily. "Not the same as getting up on a stage and belting out a tune, Bran—not even close."

Distortion from the microphone filled the room again. "Folks, I've been prompted by management to ask you to fill out your forms for the contest at the back hostess stand and not to bother your servers."

Someone yelled, "What contest?"

Bob fussed with the microphone stand. "Anyone who gets up here and sings tonight is eligible for the hundred-dollar prize."

Bran pointed his fork right back at Harper. "Now you've gotta enter."

"No. Way."

A woman passed by their table close enough that the ends of her shirt nearly dragged through Harper's salad. The woman stopped. Walked backward. Keeping her back to Bran, she said, "Harper?"

"Becca? Hey. How are you?"

"Good. I'm surprised to see you in Rawlins. Didja have enough of that shithole Muddy Gap?"

Bran studied the way Harper's smile froze and her facial muscles tightened. He'd never seen her react to anyone that way.

"No. I'm in town having dinner."

"Alone? Darlin', that's just plain pathetic, with the way men used to fall at your feet."

"She's not alone."

Becca whirled, nearly whapping Harper in the face with the jagged beaded ends of her silk shirt. Her eyes narrowed as she took Bran's measure. Evidently she didn't find him lacking because she smiled coyly. "Well, aren't you a handsome one? I never knew Harper had such good taste."

He saw Harper stab her fork into her greens. Repeatedly.

The woman held out her hand. "Becca Vincente."

"Bran Turner. How do you know my . . . Harper?"

The stout woman actually flipped her hair over her shoulder. "We used to compete in beauty pageants together. I was first runner-up in the Miss Sweet Grass contest." She shot Harper a haughty look. "And I did win the talent competition in that one, didn't I, Harper?"

Harper blinked slowly. A cute wrinkle appeared between her eyebrows as if she was deep in thought. "Honestly, I've been in so many beauty pageants and contests, Becca, I'm afraid I don't remember them all."

First time he'd ever seen Harper acting cocky.

Becca's lips flattened. "I remember, and so will everyone else when they hear me sing. I thought that's why you'd shown up here."

"To hear you sing? No. I came for the steak."

"I meant, you came to enter the contest. Tonight's winner not only gets the cash but advances to the next round." Becca flashed her teeth at Bran, then at Harper. "It doesn't appear as if you need the money like you used to."

Hell, the woman could've just called him a sugar daddy to his face and Harper a whore. "You've got it all wrong, lady."

Harper grabbed his hand and squeezed. "Now, Bran, honey, there's no use trying to pull one over on Becca. She just knows me too well."

Her eyes begged him to play along, so he did. "How's that, sugar pie?"

Becca crossed her arms over her chest and waited.

"Like I know that winning a contest without any real competition isn't much of a challenge."

Goddamn. He liked seeing this nasty side of his nice beauty queen.

"So, yes, I'm here to win some cash." Harper smiled so prettily, so earnestly, that if Bran hadn't known better, he would've believed her smile was completely genuine, instead of totally bogus. "You don't mind, do you, Becca?"

"Why would I mind? It's a free country. I welcome the competition."

Harper's smile widened. "Oh, good. Then you won't mind showing me where the hostess stand is so I can fill out my request sheet?"

"I'd be happy to do it for you, if you'd rather."

"That's so sweet of you to offer, but I'd probably better make sure they've even got the song." Harper slid out of the booth and cooed, "Be right back, dumplin'."

"Nice meeting you, Brad," Becca said.

Brad. Right. His night wouldn't have been complete without a backhanded compliment from this chubby bitch. He smiled. "Nice meetin' you too, Bertha."

Becca scowled at him and said, "Come on," to Harper before she stomped off.

Harper followed, her eyes searing holes in the back of Becca's head.

By the time she returned, the steaks were on the table. Harper didn't sit on her side of the booth, she slid in right next to him and snagged her plate. "This looks delicious."

He sliced off a piece of meat and studied it. "So you wouldn't get up onstage if I asked you, but you'll get up onstage and sing to spite a woman you hate?"

"Yep. She shouldn't have taunted me. I would've been perfectly fine, sitting here having a lovely dinner with you, but she had to go and ruin it. So I'm gonna return the favor and snatch that hundred bucks right out of her sausage fingers."

Bran brushed his lips across her ear and filled his lungs with her addicting floral scent. "Your mean streak is a serious fuckin' turn-on, Miss Sweet Ass."

She angled her head, allowing their mouths to connect, and she delicately swiped her tongue across his bottom lip. "Does that mean you'll let me spank you again later tonight?"

"Hell, no."

Harper smooched his mouth before focusing her attention on her steak.

After the waitress cleared their plates, they each ordered another drink. Harper drained half hers in one swallow.

Bran stretched his arm along the back of the booth and toyed with her hair. "Nervous?"

"Very."

The fact that she'd admitted her nerves brought out his protective instincts, and he wanted to reassure her. "You'll do great. What song are you singing?"

"It's a surprise."

"Does Becca know what song you're performing?"

Harper's lips curled into a secretive smile. "She thinks she does, but she'll be surprised when I literally change my tune."

"Are you on before her?"

"After. I'm second to last. They capped it at twenty-five contestants."

She snuggled into him as they watched the karaoke performances. Having Harper acting so publicly affectionate thrilled him. A couple of the singers were good, but most were awful. When Becca took the stage, Harper immediately stiffened up. Becca had chosen Patsy Cline's "Crazy" as her song.

Applause echoed, but Bran wasn't impressed with her performance. He said as much.

Harper didn't respond.

He sensed her mentally pulling away. He continued to run his fingers over the ball of her shoulder in what he hoped was a calming manner.

When the host called Harper's name, she turned toward him for a quick kiss and slipped out of the booth. She spoke to the guy manning the sound system and he frowned.

Bob, the host, said, "Give us just a second, we've had a last-minute change in song selection."

The guy nodded to Harper and she took center stage. She closed her eyes and curled her hands around the microphone as the background music started.

The instant she opened her mouth, Bran fell under her spell. Her voice was sultry, but it held a hint of sweetness as she hit the higher notes of "Don't It Make My Brown Eyes Blue." The crowd, fairly sedate up to this point, went sort of crazy when she held the last note. Wild applause broke out.

She seemed ready to leap off the stage and hide in the shadows, which made no sense to him, given the fact that she'd just knocked it out of the park.

As soon as he'd cleared the booth, Harper launched herself at him and he caught her in a deep hug. This woman felt so right, so perfect, in his arms that he wanted to burst out in song himself.

"You were amazing, Harper. Flat-out amazing."

"Really?"

"A winner for sure. And you can tell Becca to bite you, but darlin', that's my job."

"I like the way you bite me. Makes me all tingly."

"I live to make you tingly."

Harper won the karaoke contest.

Bran wasn't surprised. He wasn't surprised either that she didn't want to stick around after she grabbed the cash. She insisted on paying for dinner, which was a new experience for him, and then she practically dragged him out to his truck.

Back at his place, the constant physical need for each other consumed them both once again. He stripped her where she stood and took her to bed. This wasn't a frenzied mating—he made love to her with deliberate leisure, eking out every ounce of pleasure he could muster. Caressing her everywhere. Feasting on her everywhere. Allowing her the same luxury. They rolled across his mattress, giving and taking. Lost in passion tinged with sweetness.

As he floated into contentment with Harper draped across his chest sleeping peacefully, he knew he wanted this—her—for the rest of his life.

How could he convince her to stay in Muddy Gap with him instead of leaving with her sister?

Especially when he didn't understand why Harper felt she had to go where Bailey went. Bailey wasn't a child. Granted, Bran didn't have siblings, but wasn't this the ideal time for Harper to let Bailey go? Make her sister stand on her own, just like Harper had been forced to do for years?

Somehow he knew pointing that out would have the opposite reaction than he intended, no matter how tactfully he phrased it. So he was back to square one: how to convince Harper to stay with him in Muddy Gap.

Tell her you love her.

Right.

Tell her you have a boatload of money and you can take care of her so she won't need to worry about finding another job.

Somehow he didn't think that would matter to her either. She was stubborn and independent and determined to do things her own way.

Well, he could be stubborn too. They would have a serious talk about their future. Tomorrow. Whether she liked it or not.

Chapter Twenty

*H*arper kissed Bran's sternum. Then his nipples. She rubbed her cheek against the hair on his chest, loving the musky, warm, sexy way he smelled in the morning.

His hand absentmindedly stroked her bare back. "Is it mornin' already?"

"Uh-huh. And we need to get started on chores."

He groaned.

"You should be used to getting up at the crack of nothin', cattleman."

"I could get used to havin' you in my bed," he said silkily. "Let's blow off chores for a bit. In fact, speaking of blowing ..."

Did he really mean he could get used to having her around on a permanent basis?

No. The thought of her mouth on his cock always brought out his sweet side. She kept it light. "I need to borrow clothes, since the only ones I've got aren't appropriate for working cattle."

"Mmm. Or you could go nekkid." His palm connected with her ass. "I like you nekkid. A lot."

She pushed away from him. "I noticed."

"Is that a complaint?"

"Not hardly. Where might I find clothes?"

"There's sweatpants on the dresser. T-shirts and socks in the top drawer. They'll be big on you, so you sure you don't wanna go nekkid?"

"Positive." Harper gave him a smacking kiss on the mouth. "Thanks. I need to track down my bra and underwear."

"Follow the trail of clothes."

She didn't bother wrapping the sheet around her before exiting the bedroom with the sweat clothes. After all they'd done, not only last night, but for the last two months, modesty seemed . . . ridiculous.

"Such a sweet ass, sweet Harper. Why don't you come back here after you find your unmentionables and I'll help you put them on?"

"Nice try," she yelled down the hallway.

He laughed. The bed squeaked.

Aha. She found her bra by the couch. Her underwear was on the coffee table. Lord. She had no recollection of how they got there beyond his frantic stripping of her the instant they'd cleared the threshold. She folded her skirt and blouse. Before she shoved them in her big bag, she dug for a hair clip and secured her hair away from her face. She picked up Bran's shirt and held it to her nose, inhaling deeply. She loved the way he smelled. She loved everything about him—inside the bedroom and out. But confessing the whole "I love you" thing after a night of spectacularly rocking sex was something her mother would do, so that's precisely why Harper wouldn't do it.

Yawning, she started coffee. She heard the shower kick on. She needed to brush her teeth, but if she went into the bathroom while Bran was standing there naked and wet . . . chances were slim she'd be able to keep her hands off him.

She tidied up the kitchen. This was her last week of work as Bran's ranch hand. Next week she'd be packing up and getting ready for Bailey's graduation. Since Bailey hadn't said a word about her post–high school plans, Harper assumed they'd be moving to Laramie. She'd already located a cheap motel to rent by the week until they found permanent residence. Neither of them had much in the way of material goods, so packing shouldn't take more than a day.

Yippee.

Her enthusiasm for moving away from Muddy Gap had waned considerably.

The door banged open and a little man with a cane shuffled inside. The balding redhead wore a plaid flannel shirt in a hideous shade of kelly green, black pants, and black work boots. Holy crap. His resemblance to a leprechaun was uncanny. Harper blinked, but he didn't disappear, nor did she see a pot of gold anywhere near him. Dang.

He didn't smile. In fact, he scowled. "You must be Harper."

"Who are you and why did you just barge into Bran's house? You're lucky I didn't attack you."

The man harrumphed. "I'm Les. Bran's full-time ranch hand." His gaze zipped over her, almost with contempt. "You don't look like you could hurt a fly, although you don't look much like a beauty queen neither."

Was she supposed to be flattered or insulted by that comment?

He didn't wait for a retort. He glanced at the coffee-maker. "Havin' coffee made is one of the benefits of hiring a woman, I guess. Bran never could get me to make coffee."

It would be wrong to kick his cane out from under him since he was recovering from a broken hip.

Play nice, Harper.

"Another benefit of hiring Harper? She ain't nearly as crotchety in the mornin' as you are, Les."

Les plopped in the closest kitchen chair with a grunt. "She also ain't had her hip replaced after getting stomped by one of your pissed-off bulls."

Bran ambled by her, smelling of soap and toothpaste. She wanted to jam her fingers into his damp hair and breathe in his clean scent and taste his minty mouth.

"Didn't know you'd planned on coming back to work this week," Bran said. "A phone call would've been nice. Especially since you felt the need to call me a couple of times a day, every day, during your recovery."

She'd watched Bran's face as he'd listened to Les's complaints whenever he called. The conversations were very one-sided as far as she knew. Then again, Bran and Les had been friends for years, so maybe Bran had confided in him about all aspects of his life when she wasn't around. That thought made her nervous.

Bran set three cups on the counter and poured. He nudged one cup in her direction and carried two cups to the table, sliding one in front of Les before sitting across from the man.

Les gave off negative vibes, so Harper opted not to join them at the table.

"The doc cleared me yesterday," Les said. "Besides, I'm sick of sitting on my ass at home. Another day and I'd like ta gag that sister of mine."

"I'm sure she's thinking the same thing. In fact, I'll bet it was Betty who encouraged you to get back in the saddle, wasn't it?"

Les scowled and slurped his coffee. "So where's the ranch truck?"

"At Harper's."

"Why?"

"It's been havin' some issues," Bran lied.

Smooth, Bran.

"She's out here awful damn early." Les squinted at her with blatant accusation.

Harper fought the urge to bristle, but she couldn't offer the crabby man a fake smile either. "I'm an early riser."

Les didn't acknowledge her. "So what're we doin' today?"

"Moving the bulls into the north pasture. We've gotta double-check that the fences and gates are secure."

"Why?" Harper asked Bran.

But Les jumped in to answer before Bran could. "Because we don't want our bulls getting out and impregnating Henderson's cows. Don't make the Hendersons none too happy neither, since half the herd in their south pasture, which borders ours, is full of purebreds. They lose a whole shit pile of money if the calves ain't purebred, but were sired by one of our mongrel bulls."

"My bulls ain't all mongrels, but they ain't the caliber that the Hendersons are known for."

"But they are your neighbors, right? Wouldn't they know better than to put such valuable purebred stock in a pasture where their cows might be sullied by your horny low-class bulls?"

Bran laughed. He gazed at her with the pure warmth that caused a funny tickle under her breastbone. "You have such a unique way of seeing things, Harper."

She smiled behind her cup.

"That said, if the bulls do get out? The financial responsibility falls on Bran's shoulders. Some neighbors wouldn't push it, but the Hendersons do."

"Meaning what?" she asked Bran, but naturally Les answered.

"Meaning the Hendersons require us to buy the contaminated purebred stock. To the tune of a grand a calf."

Harper looked at Bran. "Seriously?"

Bran shrugged. "Ain't nothin' I can do except try to keep the bulls penned up and hope the Hendersons have already bred their cows." He grinned. "Or hope they've put the heifers in that section. Nothin' more skittish than a heifer goin' through her first mating cycle. Some of the bulls just give up."

The dream she'd had about Bran standing behind her while they watched the bovine mating dance floated into her mind and she fought a blush.

"'Cept it cost you fifteen thousand last summer. And you sure didn't get that back when we sent them to market."

Fifteen thousand dollars? For what was basically an honest mistake? Just when Harper thought she'd gotten a handle on some of this ranch stuff, she realized she'd only seen the tip of the iceberg. She said as much.

"Well, there ain't no sense in you stickin' around and learnin' the rest of it now that I'm back. I imagine you'd like to go home and get back to your real life."

Any humor fled Bran's face. "I oughta send you home, since you're here a week early. Harper is workin' this week. Period. If you've got a problem with that, Les, best say so now."

Les drained his coffee. "I don't. But we don't normally sit around shootin' the shit when there's work to be done. Let's get to it."

Did Bran always let Les boss him around? Given Bran's bossy nature, and the fact that Bran was, oh, Les's *boss*, she was surprised he put up with it.

The trio separated outside the big barn. Harper fed the goats while Les and Bran discussed whatever Les figured she didn't need to know. By the time she returned, Les was waiting impatiently by the ATVs and chewed her out for lollygagging, which she hadn't been. Apparently Bran had already gone to start moving the bulls. Les raced off, not waiting while Harper readied her ATV. And by the time she'd gotten through the first gate and closed it, she could barely see him. Since she'd been left with the oldest ATV, the one that frequently crapped out, she knew if she didn't keep up, he'd lose her. That was probably Les's intent anyway.

Since this was her virgin voyage on bull relocation duty, she wasn't certain where Bran planned to move them. The morning air hung damp and sticky from last night's rain, turning the fields into a mud bog.

It took all morning to drive the bulls to the far corner of the selected pasture. None of the bulls charged, which Bran warned her could happen. She hung back, yelling, "Yaw!" at the stragglers, getting them to mosey along. Another thing she learned? Bulls were never in a hurry.

Les ordered her to check along the upper fence line for breaks. She automatically looked to Bran to verify Les's directive, but Bran was on the phone, gesturing wildly, while trying to round up the last bull.

With no alternative, she headed north, scrutinizing the barbed wire fence for any compromised sections. She kept up as quick a pace as she dared in an effort to prevent the ATV from getting mired in the muck, but she didn't want to drive too fast lest she miss a broken segment of fence line.

The borrowed sweatpants stuck to her skin. Her fingers were curled so tightly around the ATV's black rubber handle grips that her knuckles were pasty white. The whine of the engine and the concentration needed to perform three tasks at once took its toll on her. A screaming headache stabbed the inside of her brain about the same time the visibility dropped to nothing. Banks of fog played peekaboo between the fence posts. Harper stopped and squinted at the sky, wondering when the sun would appear and burn off the billows of mist.

It took a while.

By the time she could see more than six inches in front of her face, she realized she didn't know where she was. She couldn't hear the low hum of ATVs in the distance, nor the huffs she associated with livestock. Rather than panic, she whipped a U-turn and started back down the rolling hill, keeping to the fence line.

Nothing looked remotely familiar. But she kept plugging along, unsure how much time had passed, cursing herself for forgetting her cell phone.

Cursing Les for sending her off on a wild-fence chase.

The sun glinted off metal in the distance and she recognized a stock tank. As she sped toward it, she heard distinctive mechanical whines. Bran and Les crested the rise below the stock tank and waited until she reached them.

"Are you all right?" Bran demanded. "What happened?"

Harper inhaled, ready to spew ire at Les, but she snapped her mouth shut at the last second. The fog wasn't Les's fault. He'd probably only told her to do what Bran had passed down. Plus, how could she admit she hadn't been paying the closest attention to the fence line when she'd been looking for the route back to the ranch? She couldn't. She would come across as incompetent, and the last thing she needed was to furnish Les with more ammunition. She straightened her shoulders. "I was checking the fence and the fog rolled in. I couldn't see anything, so I waited it out. Somehow I got turned around."

Bran gazed at her skeptically. But he didn't grill her further. They drove back to the ranch.

Quiet didn't last long with Les around. Lord, the man loved to hear the sound of his own voice. He jabbered while they cleaned the mud off the ATVs. He kept up a running dialogue regardless if she or Bran answered him.

No wonder people questioned whether Bran ever talked. Why would he have to? Les said everything. Les knew everything. And Les acted as if Bran wouldn't have his successful ranching operation if not for Les's insight and expertise. It made her mad. If ranching was so easy, why didn't Les take his expertise and start his own operation? But again, she said nothing.

By three o'clock, Bran had had his fill of his chatty ranch hand and sent him home. In fact, Bran insisted on calling Betty personally to come and fetch her brother.

Les fumed. As soon as he'd shuffled out to his sister's Mercury Grand Marquis, Bran's truck keys were in his hand and they were out the door and on the road to town.

Harper didn't slide next to him. Neither did Bran reach for her hand or stretch his arm across the back of the seat to toy with her hair. Was he pulling away? Now that Les was back in the picture and the end was in sight?

Bran pulled up to the curb in front of her house and let his pickup idle, which meant he didn't intend to come in. Bailey wasn't home, and the notion of being alone in that crappy rental made her sadder yet. But she wouldn't show it. She managed a smile. "Thanks for . . . last night."

"I'd hoped to hear a thank-you for this mornin' too. It sucks that Les popped in."

"He was just anxious to get back at it after being laid up for so long. Lucky thing he believed I'd shown up early, not that I'd spent the night with you."

Bran frowned. "I don't care—"

"Oh, so you don't care if I take tomorrow off so I can squeeze in a couple of nail clients?"

He stared at her with a strange, almost regretful look, but said, "Sure."

"Thanks."

"No problem. Have a good night, sweetheart."

Sweetheart. He only called her that when he was frustrated with her.

She said, "You have a good night too, boss," and bailed out of the truck.

∞

In the last three months Bran had gotten used to the rhythm of working with Harper. He preferred her sporadic humming to Les's tendency to fill the day up with busywork and nonstop yammering.

Damn it. He missed her like his right hand. Which made him smile, knowing she'd get a chuckle out of his rare play on words.

"Got everything?" Les asked for the tenth time.

"I guess. Let's go."

The ride to Hank's new place was silent, and to be honest, that unnerved Bran more than Les's tendency to chatter like a magpie. It meant the man was thinking, and Les had no problem whatsoever sharing his thoughts.

They'd started down the driveway when Les finally spoke. "She's trouble, you know."

Bran didn't have to ask who was trouble.

"How long you been fucking her?"

His head snapped toward his hired man. "What the hell business is it of yours?"

"It's my business if you're thinking of keeping her on to replace me. I know you, Branford. You're wondering if you can have your cake and eat it too. Pay her to work for you, pay her to be in your bed. And as much as I need this job? I ain't gonna suck your dick to keep it like she will."

Bran slammed on the brakes just short of parking. "You watch your goddamn mouth. You're talkin' out your ass, like usual. You don't know a thing about Harper. Not a fuckin' thing."

"Yeah? I think *you* don't know a fucking thing about her. She's just like her mama, though I'll admit she a helluva lot prettier. Which means that pretty face will allow her to fuck her way to the top of the pile—the top of the money pile, and we both know around Muddy Gap, that's probably you."

Les didn't know Bran's financial situation and it pissed him off whenever Les acted as if he did. "She ain't like that."

"No? Weren't you the one who told me she'd been sniffing around your grandparents' house during the branding? Telling you what a shame it is that it's sitting there abandoned? I'll bet she's got it all decorated in her mind." Les's eyes narrowed. "I'll bet you let her cook supper for you, too."

Several times. And it'd been more than Harper feeding his belly. It was as if she'd fed his soul. "So?" He hit the gas and pulled up next to an electrician's van.

"So she's been setting you up from the start. Working for you, cooking for you, sleeping with you."

"Did it ever occur to you that maybe I like havin' a

woman wanting to do those things for me? Or with me? Maybe I'm tired of bein' alone?"

"Ask yourself why she picked you. She's a damn beauty queen. She could have any man in Wyoming or anywhere else that she wanted. We both know you ain't exactly Brad Pitt."

Jesus. Les could undermine his confidence in a heartbeat. How had he forgotten that?

Bran exited his truck, angry about the conversation. Over the years, Les had overstepped his bounds plenty of times, and not always when it came to ranch work. He'd chalked it up to a generation gap, since Les was old enough to be his father. Now he wondered if the bouts of hostility weren't something else.

Footsteps sounded behind him.

Les wasn't going to let it go. "Mark my words, boy. She'll get herself knocked up and you'll marry her outta a sense of duty. She'll drop a couple more kids, ensuring she has plenty of guilt and blood money for years to come. Then she'll take you for everything you're worth and divorce your ass. You'll end up alone anyway."

With that comment, Les went too far.

Bran whirled on him and pushed him back, snarling, "Shut your fucking mouth or I will."

Les caught himself on the grille of Bran's truck and winced.

Shit. In his fury, Bran had forgotten the man was recovering from an injury. "Goddamn it, Les, I didn't mean—"

"See? She's already tied you up in knots and you ain't thinkin' straight. I'll bet she's questioned why you even need me around. When I've been a constant in your life since your grandparents died. *Me*. I've been the only one who's cared about you for a long damn time. You remember that."

"What the hell is goin' on?" Hank demanded.

"Ask him," Les huffed and stomped away.

"Bran?"

He refocused on Hank and not on Les's stiff gait as he disappeared around the side of the house. "Les was a serious dick to Harper when he came back to work yesterday. Talkin' trash about her to me just now. Damn fool don't know when to keep his mouth shut."

Hank crossed his arms over his chest. "It's obvious you have something goin' on with her."

"Obvious to who?"

"Don't know if it's obvious only to me since I've known you forever, but I saw you two at the branding, tryin' so damn hard not to notice each other's every move."

The branding. When Harper and Lainie had hung out. "She didn't blab to Lainie or nothin' about us bein' involved?"

Hank shrugged. "She might have, but if so, my wife didn't talk to me about it, so maybe *you* oughta talk to me about it."

"Ain't much to say. Harper's leaving next week after Bailey graduates from high school. I knew that when I hired her." Bran could claim he hadn't intended to fall for sweet, sexy Harper, but from the moment she opened up to him, he'd been a goner.

Regardless what Les thought, Harper hadn't insinuated herself into Bran's life because she was trying to hook a husband. She needed the job. Neither of them had anticipated that things would grow and change between them so quickly. As much as he'd enjoyed getting naked with her, he'd enjoyed just being with her every day a helluva lot more.

"You're just gonna let her leave?"

"It's what she wants."

"What about what you want?"

"That's the thing, Hank. I don't know what I want."
He clapped his friend on the shoulder. "Thankfully, I do
know what *you* want. Me to get my ass busy so you and
the lovely Lainie can move into your own place as soon
as possible."

Chapter Twenty-one

❧

*H*arper was up with the sunrise. Because of the situation with Bran and Bailey's continual avoidance of her, she hadn't slept worth beans the last two nights anyway. She showered and scribbled a packing list as well as a to-do list as she waited for the brew cycle on the coffeemaker to end.

"Hey."

She jumped, startled by Bailey's appearance in the dining room. "Whoa. You're up early. Or are you still up from pulling an all-nighter for finals?"

Bailey shook her head. "I got up at the butt crack of dawn to talk to you about some stuff."

Finally. It'd been hard, waiting for Bailey to come to her, but Harper needed to ease up control now that Bailey was of legal age. The coffeemaker in the kitchen beeped. She stood, but Bailey grabbed her arm, stopping her. "Wait."

"What's up?"

But Bailey didn't rattle off the litany of problems that

plagued her teenage life for a change. She said, "I joined the army."

Harper squinted, turning her head to hear better. "You're joining Amy to do what?"

"I said I joined the army. I leave for basic training in Mississippi a few days after I graduate."

A surreal stillness surrounded Harper. Maybe it was the sound of her world crashing around her. "You're serious."

"Completely. I, ah, have the official paperwork in my room if you want to see it."

Coffee forgotten, Harper folded her arms over her chest. "When did you do this?"

"The day after I turned eighteen I drove to the army recruiter's office in Cheyenne."

"So it wasn't a spur-of-the-moment thing?"

Bailey shook her head.

"Why didn't you talk to me about it?"

"Because I knew you'd try to talk me out of it."

No kidding. This was a nightmare. Another sister going off to God-knew-where, risking life and limb. Bailey was a baby. Too young to go to war. Didn't she realize that?

"Look, Harper, I didn't—"

"Think it through? That is obvious. When did you plan on telling me?"

Bailey threw up her arms. "I tried!"

"When?" she demanded. "Because I definitely would've remembered that conversation."

"When I told you to do what you wanted with your life and not to plan your future around mine."

Harper's eyebrows rose, as did her temper. "*That's* what I was supposed to glean from that discussion, Bailey? That you wanted to blow off all the college scholarship opportunities you've worked so hard for ... to become a soldier? Wrong. You could've told me and you didn't."

"I'm an adult now. I don't answer to you," Bailey shot back with typical teenage snark. "And besides, is this really about me going to college? Or are you living through me because you didn't finish school?"

Anger and shame bubbled inside her from Bailey's low blow.

"Shit, Harper. I'm sorry. That came out wrong. I didn't mean—"

"You never mean it, but it never stops you from saying mean things, does it?"

Bailey broke eye contact.

"Did Liberty put you up to this? Tell you what an adventure it'd be to live in the barracks, shoot stuff, and see the world from the inside of a Humvee while you're wearing full body armor?"

"No! And it pisses me off that you think I can't make up my own mind about what I want to do with my life."

The girl couldn't make up her mind what shoes to wear most days. And she'd decided to wear combat boots in perpetuity? "Okay. What inspired this adult decision?"

Bailey paced. "The army is paying to put me through school. And while I'm in school learning a trade, I'll earn a paycheck. How is that not a good deal all around? I'll have a place to live, training, health care, and education. This is the perfect solution. One that I hadn't considered until the recruiter came to school and talked to us."

"Does Liberty know you joined the army?" When Bailey looked away, Harper knew. A sick sensation invaded her stomach. She lived with Bailey, took care of her, worried about her, and none of that mattered? Her sister didn't think enough of her to share with her how drastically her future plans had changed?

Or have you been so wrapped up in Bran that you hadn't noticed?

No. Even if Harper hadn't spent a large chunk of her time working like a dog, working to ensure that Bailey had the bright future she deserved, Bailey should've made the time to talk to her, no matter if they'd had to hold the conversation in Bran's barn.

"I know you don't understand, Harper."

"You're right. I don't." She managed a short laugh. "And to think I've listened to you bitch for the last two years about how you hated wearing a school uniform. Now you'll be wearing a uniform every day for . . ." She met Bailey's eyes. "How long did you sign up for?"

"Six years."

Don't cry. Don't accuse and say something you can't take back. Don't be like your mother.

Harper bit the inside of her cheek so hard, she tasted the tang of blood in her mouth. She kept her composure as she retreated to the kitchen. She reached in the back of the cupboard for the metal cylinder with "Sweet Dreams Tea" emblazoned across the front and dumped out the tea bags—and a roll of bills. She'd skimmed a hundred bucks out of her paychecks from the Turner Ranch as an emergency stash. Maybe this didn't qualify as an emergency, but Harper knew sticking around in her frame of mind wasn't an option.

As she passed through the living room, Bailey called out, "Can we please talk about this?"

"No."

"Please, Harper, I'm begging you."

"I said no." Then Harper shut her bedroom door in her sister's face. Grabbing the small overnight bag from the closet, she shoved in a few changes of clothes. Then she took the bag into the bathroom and loaded up toiletries. Now she was good to go.

But where?

It didn't matter. She just had to get out of here.

Bailey leaped up from the couch when Harper returned to the living room. "Look, I know you're upset and I don't blame you—"

"I'm glad that *you* don't blame *me* for being upset, Bailey, because God knows, I couldn't go on if I didn't take the goddamn blame for every shitty thing that happens in this family."

Her sister gasped. "You're really pissed. You actually swore."

Harper slipped on her trench coat. She shouldered her overnight bag and plucked her purse off the coffee table.

"Where are you going?" Bailey asked in a very small voice.

Don't fall for the distressed-sister act. She's not the wounded party here, you are. "I don't know."

"When are you coming back?"

"I don't know."

"Why are you doing this? As some sort of punishment for me?"

Harper looked at her sister with absolute incredulity. "You know, I'm just now starting to understand how wrong it's been for me to do everything for you. And you're right, maybe I should've worried more about myself, because God knows you don't waste any energy worrying about *me*."

Bailey's face flushed with guilt.

Good. Harper snatched the car keys from the hook and opened the door.

"Wait. Are you taking the car?"

"Yep."

"But why can't you take the truck?"

"Because it's not mine."

"But . . . what am I supposed to do?" Pure panic filled Bailey's voice. "How am I supposed to get anywhere?"

"You're an adult, remember? You'll figure it out." She didn't turn around as she slammed the door, climbed in the car, and drove off.

Harper made it four miles outside of Muddy Gap before she pulled over. Tears poured out as she finally let loose the grief, frustration, and disappointment that moved through her body like a slow-acting poison.

What would she do now? She'd saved enough money for cheap living expenses for about two months. She'd counted on Bailey taking the full-ride scholarship to the University of Wyoming. Harper figured she had a better chance of getting a job in Laramie in the summer months when the college students were gone. By the time school started in August, she'd be established in a new job and Bailey would be ready to move into the dorms.

She'd had it all planned out, except for one thing: That wasn't what Bailey wanted.

Had it ever been something that Bailey had wanted?

Yes. They'd talked for hours over the last year and a half about what they'd do once they finally got out of Muddy Gap. Harper hadn't imagined those conversations. She'd happily given up any semblance of free time to help Bailey fill out college applications. Watching Bailey's excitement as she realized that the opportunities available to her had been worth the effort of concentrating solely on her academics.

Now it felt like wasted effort.

No. It just hurts.

Harper leaned her neck into the headrest. Spring wind blew through the open car window, cooling her burning cheeks. The morning rays were a fiery gold spread across the empty fields, shining on patches of green grass sprouting in a ring around the mud puddles. Clusters of purple barnyard lilacs dotted the hillside along with the tan stalks of last year's grass. Yellow clover lined the ditch. If she listened closely, she could hear birdsong trilling on the breeze and the buzz of insects. With nature's splendor surrounding her, why did she notice that the sky was the same gray as Bran's eyes?

Bran. Just another situation she had no idea how to handle. She loved him. But she suspected he'd thrown himself into their affair because she was leaving. Although he hadn't admitted it, she suspected he'd never gotten up the courage to show his raunchy side to past lovers. To make the kind of sexual demands of them that he'd made of her. She'd loved every minute, especially when Bran had no issue showing her his sweet side ... Good Lord, the man could be so incredibly sweet it made her heart ache.

So how could she spring it on him that she had no-where to go? The last thing she wanted was Bran's pity. Neither did she want him to feel obligated to help her out. The job she'd signed on for was temporary. So was their relationship.

But they'd become friends as well as lovers. And if Harper just happened to show up at his place ... and if he just happened to ask her what was wrong ... there'd be no harm in telling him, would there?

No.

Mind made up, she pulled back onto the highway. Her cell phone vibrated and she ignored it. The turnoff to the Lawson ranch loomed ahead. Harper missed Celia. But her friend was dealing with her own issues, which strengthened Harper's determination not to unburden herself. Janie Fitzhugh's voice popped into her head: "Anytime you need anything, call me." Harper doubted Janie had been serious.

The fish-shaped mailbox signifying the turnoff to

297 SADDLED AND SPURRED

Bran's place didn't bring the sense of relief it usually did. She putted down the rutted muddy tracks, wishing she'd driven the truck. This time of year reminded her why this part of the county had been christened "Muddy Gap."

When she reached the house, she noticed Bran's truck wasn't around. Les meandered over from the big barn. Brusquely, he said, "I was hoping you'd be bringing my pickup back."

She offered him a fake smile. "I can't very well drive both vehicles at once, now, can I? Where is Bran? I need to talk to him."

Les's eyes gleamed. "You don't wanna mess with him today, Harper. Maybe you oughta run on home."

Whatever territorial instinct she had about Bran pushed front and center. "Where is he?"

"How about if you tell me what you want to talk to him about and I'll pass along the message?"

Miserable little man. *Yeah, why don't you go ahead and break the news to Bran that I love him. And even if my sister wouldn't have joined the army without telling me, and we were moving according to my plan, I'd still feel like I was leaving a piece of myself—a big piece— with him.*

When she didn't answer right away, Les snapped his fingers. "Sorry. I'll bet you're here to ask about your paycheck."

Paycheck? Wow. Les really thought she was a money-grubbing bitch, didn't he?

Her contemplation of Les's motives for putting her in her place vanished when she heard the familiar sound of Bran's truck barreling up the drive.

He parked in his usual spot and hopped out, skirting the front end.

Harper's heart turned over. The man looked good. He always looked good. But he didn't grant his usual I'm-imagining-you-naked grin. Nor did his eyes soften. In fact, his eyes went hard and cold. He glanced at her car, then at her.

"Where's the truck?"

"At my house. I was ..." *Desperate to talk to you.* "Bran? What's wrong?"

"I'll tell you what's wrong." Les barged right between them. "You didn't do your job checking fences. The bulls got out. All of them. Me'n Bran spent all yesterday trying to get our bulls outta the Hendersons' pasture. And we've gotta head back there today to finish up."

All the blood drained from her face.

"I can't believe you were so stupid—"

"Les, that's enough," Bran snapped.

Bran was boiling mad. Livid like she'd never seen him. And the truth of it was, she couldn't blame him. She hadn't paid attention. A whole section of fencing could've been down when she was trying to find her way in the fog. It'd been an honest mistake. Didn't he see that?

No. She doubted he could see anything through the red haze surrounding him.

Harper studied Bran's face. Upon closer examination, he didn't look like a million bucks. Dark circles discolored the skin beneath his eyes. His mouth and jaw were set in a grim line. His posture was one hundred percent closed off.

Closed off from her. Probably for good.

She'd screwed up big-time. He'd given her a job when she needed it and how had she repaid him? By making a stupid mistake and costing him tens of thousands of dollars.

No way could Harper tell him how the world she'd known had crumbled. With Les around to remind Bran what an idiot she was, she doubted he would ever forgive her. She whispered, "I'm sorry."

"You should be," Les sneered.

Bran didn't defend her this time.

Les said, "She was askin' about her last check."

Again, Bran just gave her that inscrutable cowboy stare. *Don't cry.*

Would it salvage her pride if she kept this business-like? No. But it was all she had. "If you could just tell me when I can pick it up? At the accountant's—"

"I'll drop the damn check off at your house, Harper."

"And what the hell are you gonna do with it when I'm not there?" *Stay calm.* "Just send the damn thing to my address. The post office will forward it to me."

"Fine." He rubbed his temple. "When are you leavin'?"

"I'm not sure. So you'll be wanting these. Here"—she tossed him the keys and he caught them with one hand—"your truck is parked in front of the house."

He gave her a cool appraisal before he pushed off from where he'd been leaning against his pickup. He spoke to Les. "Come on. We've gotta get a move on and fix this mess with the Hendersons."

No good-bye. No anything. On wooden legs, Harper climbed in her car and drove off, without any idea where she was going.

∞

Had she really come just for her check?

Jesus, that pissed him off.

He waited until her piece-of-shit car was on the high-way before he stomped to the barn.

"Where you goin'?" Les demanded.

Away from you so I can think.

Bran didn't respond. Livid, and more flustered than he cared to admit, he spun around and headed back the way he'd just come—straight to his truck. Ignoring Les's shouts, he tore out of there, spewing gravel and curse words.

Goddamn it. Contrary to Les's opinion, Bran hadn't blamed her for the bulls' getting out. It'd been an ongoing problem and he hadn't dealt with it because for too long he'd played the part of the laid-back rancher. No more would he let his clueless, less than neighborly neighbors dictate a stupid policy that no one else in their right mind would've agreed to.

No more. He would pin Stan Henderson's ass to the wall, but not when he was in such a piss-poor mood.

He parked and got back to work digging post holes for a new fence. Hard physical labor that exhausted his body and drained his brain had always helped him deal with difficult situations in the past.

That's all Harper is to you? Another difficult situation to handle?

No. Harper was everything to him. Everything. He was absolutely sick about what had just happened. The minute he'd seen her car go by as he'd been working in the pasture closest to the house, he'd hauled ass back to the ranch. He'd intended to wrap her in his arms, then drop to his knees, right in the mud, and tell her he loved her. Beg her not to go. Ask her to marry him and stay with him forever.

But that confession wasn't something he wanted to do in front of Les. Not because he was embarrassed to admit how he felt about her, but because Harper deserved better.

Yeah? Then how is it that you ended up on your worst behavior?

Infuriated with himself, he jammed the shovel into the ground with force, leaning into the work until he was almost horizontal, spraying soil everywhere as the metal tip clanged into a solid object. Damn it. He must've hit a rock. He dropped to his knees and reached in the hole. Definitely a rock, but what the hell . . . ?

His fingers plucked the object out of the hole and the metal glinted in the sun.

For chrissake. He'd been so focused on moving that rock he hadn't noticed his cell phone had fallen into the hole. And he'd pulverized the damn thing.

Fucking awesome.

Now how was he supposed to get in touch with Harper? With her leaving, a phone call was the only way he could contact her.

Get in your damn truck and go after her. Fix this. Right now.

No. As much as he needed to cool off before he talked to the Hendersons, that went double for how he needed to present himself when he tracked Harper down. He had to get a handle on what he was going to say to her. For once in his life, he wasn't running off half-cocked. This was too damn important.

Bran swore and threw the mangled phone in the bed of his pickup. He pounded the shovel into the ground until he was coated with sweat and his back and arms ached, but the damn stubborn rock wouldn't budge.

Hopefully, that wasn't a sign of things to come.

Chapter Twenty-two

∞

*T*he drive into Casper was a blur.

Harper found cheap lodging at the Super 8. She picked up the classifieds and checked out the job situation. As long as she didn't mind working in the food industry she'd have no problem finding employment. Rent for a single-bedroom apartment was fairly reasonable, even if higher than her house in Muddy Gap.

But it didn't make sense to drive back and forth just to save a hundred bucks on housing, especially if she ended up getting two jobs. She'd work, save as much money as possible, and figure out what she wanted to do with her life.

Her cell phone buzzed. Bailey texted her. Again. And once again, Harper didn't answer. She wasn't being petty; she'd said everything she'd intended to say at this point.

She flopped on the bed and turned on the TV. Cable was a luxury and watching mindless entertainment might take her mind off the feeling that her life had completely fallen apart.

As she snacked on pizza she'd had delivered to her

room, and the two packages of M&M's from the vending machine, her phone buzzed. Fifteen calls. Ten calls were from Bailey. One call was from Bailey's friend Amy's cell phone. Two calls from an unlisted number she assumed were from Liberty. One call was from Celia. One call was from Janie.

No calls from Bran.

That made her incredibly weepy and she ripped into another bag of candy. Sadly, even the best chocolate in the world would never compare to the way Bran made her feel.

She was considering turning her phone off completely when it buzzed a sixteenth time. The caller ID read: *Bernice Watson*. Harper had to answer, even if her wily sister had tricked her boss into calling on her behalf. "Hello?"

"Hey, sugar."

"Hey, Bernice. What's up?"

"My curiosity, I suppose." Bernice coughed. "Bailey's called me, oh, four or five times, wondering if I'd heard from you. I don't think she believed me when I said I didn't know where you were. She seemed pretty upset." A whoosh of air echoed as Bernice exhaled. "Look, it probably ain't my business, but did you two have a fight or something?"

"Or something," Harper said dryly. "To be honest, I'm avoiding her until I get a better handle on the situation."

"I understand completely. Anything I can do?"

"No. Real sweet of you to ask, Bernice. I appreciate it."

"Well, I ain't made no secret of the fact I worry about you, Harper. Care about you as if you were my own kid."

Harper's eyes watered and she managed a hoarse "Thanks."

"Anyway, I am callin' for my own reasons. I've gotta take Bob to the doctor in Cheyenne tomorrow and I'm scheduled to have the Beauty Barn open. I've canceled my clients, but I'm expecting a big shipment from a beauty supply store in Colorado in the afternoon and someone's gotta be here to sign for it or else they won't deliver. Since I paid the damn rush shipping charges . . ."

"Say no more. I'll be back in town to open at noon."

A pause. "*Back* in town? Where are you?"

"Casper."

"You're not at Bran Turner's place?"

I wish. "No. Since Les is all healed up, I'm done working for Bran, so I'm looking for a full-time job."

"I'll be back around five tomorrow, with a bottle of whiskey and two glasses so you can tell me just what the hell is goin' on in your life that's sent you running."

Tears surfaced again. "I'd like that."

"Good. Thanks, Harper." Bernice hung up.

Harper set aside the classified ads. So much for filling out job applications first thing in the morning. She clicked off the TV and the light. She stared at the patterns in the acoustic ceiling tiles, listening to the clacking of the heater register for the longest time before she finally drifted off.

And she dreamt of him anyway. Foolish, girlish dreams that had no basis in reality—in her life or in the life of anyone she'd ever known. Sappy Disney dramas that always turned out perfectly in the end. The fact was, Bran wouldn't barrel up to her crappy rental house in his dirty pickup, confess his undying love for her, and they'd drive off into the sunset together.

Another thing her silly dreams got wrong—she wasn't looking for a man to rescue her. Or to take care of her. She wanted a man to love her for her. For who she was on the inside, not the outside. She'd hoped Bran was that man. He still might be. But she was too emotionally raw right now to find out.

So maybe it was childish the next day that she hid her

car behind the Beauty Barn so neither Bailey nor Bran would see it.

Since Bernice had rescheduled her hair appointments, there wasn't much for Harper to do, which drove her crazy. She'd never been the type to sit around. So she dusted. Vacuumed. Cleaned the smoky haze off the mirrors. Washed a load of towels. Cleaned the bathroom and the break room. When the inventory boxes arrived via the UPS man, she logged them in, but she didn't unpack anything because Bernice preferred to do it.

She'd settled behind the front counter with her pen and the classified ads, waiting for Bernice to return, when the door chimed. Harper glanced up as Janie Fitzhugh sailed into the beauty shop.

"Please tell me Bernice is working," Janie pleaded. She pointed at her own head of hair. "It's awful, isn't it? Looks like I brushed it with a currycomb."

"I'm sorry—Bernice is gone. She'll be here tomorrow."

"But I can't wait that long. I have business meetings, and I don't know what to do with this stupid stuff besides shave it off."

"Ack. Don't do that. Do what I do."

"What's that?"

"Disguise it."

"How?"

"Wear a hat or a scarf or a headband. Then people will believe you're chic and classy or whimsical, not that you're overdue for a haircut."

Janie snapped her fingers. "That's a great idea. Got any suggestions on how to help this mop of hair look chic?"

Harper considered Janie. From the accessories counter she selected a wide leather and metal headband with funky copper stars threaded through the elastic straps. "Try this." She slid the ends of the headband behind Janie's elfin ears, pushing the thickest part up her forehead. The headband tamed hanks of hair hanging in Janie's eyes. "See how you like that."

Janie angled the mirror to see Harper's handiwork. Her mouth dropped open. "That looks fantastic. Wow. Totally fixed the problem. I could probably avoid a haircut for another month."

"Which is why that's not a trick I usually share with Bernice's customers," Harper said dryly. "Then again, Bernice's Beauty Barn clients aren't always open to something new."

"Pity your talents are being wasted here, Harper." Janie fussed with the hair behind the headband.

"Wasted. Right."

"I'm serious. How much is this headband?"

"Fifteen bucks."

"But I can only wear it with brown. So if I needed one to wear with a black outfit . . . ?"

Harper plucked another headband from the rack, one that was crafted of twisted metal, but lacked embellishments. "This one is simple and you can dress it up or down. For a casual look, twine a ribbon or a piece of fabric through the open metal if you want to match a specific outfit. For formal, you could clip earrings or other pieces of rhinestone jewelry across the top. Then it almost looks like a crown."

"Says the beauty queen used to wearing crowns."

"You're hilarious."

"See? Now you've sold me two headbands, which is more than I would've spent on the haircut." Janie turned and gave Harper's clothes a critical once-over. "My God. Do you always look so amazingly put together? You have such a fantastic fashion sense. Is that something they teach you at pageants?"

Harper laughed. Maybe a bit wildly.

"What?" Janie asked suspiciously.

"Without seeming like a sympathy seeker, I will just say that financial necessity has forced me to get creative with my clothes. Most are purchased at secondhand stores. Although it's much hipper to call them *vintage*." Harper pointed to her cream-colored button-up shirt. "I bought this dress shirt in the men's section for, like, two bucks."

"And the rest of the outfit?"

"I've picked up pieces here and there, but I didn't pay more than ten bucks for anything I've got on, including my boots." That morning she'd paired the fitted shirt with a dark brown tank top decorated with tan leather fringe. She'd tucked the tank top into the khaki-colored mini-skirt and knotted the ends of the shirt through her front belt loops, creating her own belt. She'd slipped on her tan cowgirl boots with the suede fringe running down the back seam. In fleeing from home, she'd purposely chosen pieces that she could mix and match for several days because she hadn't known how long she'd be gone.

Janie fiddled with the button on her maroon suit jacket and tugged at the hem of her matching skirt. "I'm ashamed to tell you I paid over two hundred bucks for this outfit—and that doesn't include the shoes."

"You shouldn't be embarrassed. You look great."

"I sense a but," Janie said.

"But if it were me, and I was wearing such a severe business suit? I'd add a feminine touch, like a softer fabric shirt with a slight pattern or better yet, a high-cut lace camisole." When Janie frowned, Harper felt ridiculous for offering her advice. Obviously a successful professional woman such as Janie knew how to dress herself.

She stepped behind the register. "Is there anything else?"

"Yes."

Harper looked up at the emphatic *yes*.

Janie angled over the counter—how the tiny woman's feet were still on the floor, quite frankly, completely mystified Harper—and said, "Are you still working for Bran Turner?"

"No."

"Are you still taking off for parts unknown after your sister graduates?"

"Umm. Not exactly."

Janie's shrewd eyes zoomed to the Help Wanted section folded on the counter. "So you're looking for work in Casper?"

Nosy little thing. "Yes. Jobs are limited in Muddy Gap and a girl's gotta make a living if she wants to get out of Wyoming." Or even if she plans to stay in Wyoming.

Where had that thought come from?

"Can you do me a favor before you drop off your résumé with any of those places you've circled?"

Harper nearly laughed. Résumé? Applebee's didn't need a résumé, just a completed job application. "What?"

"Meet me at Buckeye Joe's tonight. Around seven?"

"I don't think getting drunk is going to help my iffy job situation, Janie."

Janie grinned. "Oh, I wouldn't be too sure about that. However, that's not why I'm asking." Her face became pure business. "Please. And wear what you've got on, okay?"

It wasn't like she had anything else to do besides fight with Bailey. She'd intended on driving back to Casper after she finished talking to Bernice, but she really didn't want to shell out another sixty bucks for a motel room. "Fine. I'll be there."

Chapter Twenty-three

*T*he scented steam wafted up as Harper poured herself a cup of tea. It'd be easy to knock back more whiskey to take the edge off, but her mother had always looked for answers in the bottom of a bottle and Harper knew firsthand it didn't work.

Given the state of the house, she assumed her sister had spent the night elsewhere. Maybe she wouldn't drag herself back here tonight either.

Not nice, Harper.

She wasn't feeling very nice.

Her cell phone rang and she glanced at the number over the rim of her teacup. Celia. Her finger hovered on the answer button because she missed talking to her friend. Yet she didn't feel like rehashing the past twenty-four hours. She let the call kick over to voice mail, knowing Celia wouldn't leave a message.

Story of her life. No one had left a message. Well, that wasn't entirely true. Liberty had. Surprisingly she hadn't blustered with her usual piss-off-and-deal-with-it response. She'd very calmly and emphatically informed

Harper that she'd had no hand in suggesting that Bailey opt for military service instead of college.

Bran hadn't attempted to call either. She wasn't sure how to feel about that. But being just plain numb about everything had an upside. She drained the remainder of her tea and stood. Time to see why Janie had been so insistent on meeting her tonight.

One good thing about living in Muddy Gap? She could walk everywhere.

There's more than one good thing, isn't there?

Shoot. The heart-to-heart she'd had with Bernice—as well as the slug of whiskey—had made her melancholy.

The sun still shone, although the rays had dimmed to a muted gold, allowing shadows to play hopscotch on the sidewalk. Trees were finally leafing out. Spikes of grass were green. Dandelions popped up here and there in yards not meticulously manicured. Spring came late in the mountains.

Buckeye Joe's wasn't packed to the rafters, but close. She said hi to several people, stopped to talk to several more, so by the time she spied Janie in the far back booth, ten minutes had passed since she'd entered the bar.

"Sorry." She slid across from Janie.

"No problem. I'm glad I got here early. I've never seen this place so consistently busy. Maybe it's a good thing that Mac took off." She nudged a lowball glass at Harper. "Whiskey Coke, right?"

"Right."

"Happy hour. Drink up."

"I'll probably only have one, since I ..." *Refuse to end up like my mother.* She smiled. "Thanks. I had a slug before I got here."

"Not for the liquid courage to talk to us, I hope?"

"Us?" she repeated.

"Yes, ma'am." Renner Jackson pulled a chair to the end of the table, flipped it around, and straddled it. He set his forearms on the table and smiled at her. "Heya, Harper." He focused on Janie and smirked. "Heya, indentured servant."

Janie whapped his arm. "Be serious. Do you want to go first?"

"Nope. This is your show. Pretend I'm not here."

"Let's get right to it." Janie focused on Harper. "Why were you circling Help Wanted ads in Casper?"

Harper sucked down a big gulp of her drink before she launched into the story. After she finished, Janie and Renner exchanged a look. "What?"

"As much as I suspect you're hurtin' from what happened with your sister, and fretting about where you'll end up, I hope you'll hear us out before you take off outta Muddy Gap like your boots are on fire," Renner said.

"Hear you out? About what?"

"About comin' to work for me. For us. At the Split Rock Ranch and Resort."

Harper didn't say a word. Her gaze moved from Janie's face to Renner's face and back to Janie's face again. Were they drunk?

"You know Renner is building a hunting-lodge type of dude ranch vacation getaway on the land he bought?" Janie asked.

She nodded.

"The property won't be geared toward men. We're aiming to attract couples. The guys can fish and hunt or ride a bull or spend the day as a ranch hand, while their wives or girlfriends enjoy the benefits of a relaxing spa. Or they can go horseback riding or hang out at the lodge. Or shop."

"I'll admit that sounds like a great idea, but I don't see

where I come in. You need someone to clean rooms or something?"

Janie scowled. "No."

"I guarantee you don't want to hire me as a ranch hand, as Bran Turner can attest to the fact that I suck." Oh, crap. That hadn't come out right at all.

Before Harper could clarify that statement, Janie said, "For chrissake, I'm not looking to hire you to do nails either."

Testy.

Renner set his hand over Janie's, which immediately calmed her. "What Janie means is, in addition to the main ranch house, which will contain eight large bedroom suites, a great room, a game room, and a bar, there will be two other structures. One for the spa. The other will house a dining room, an art gallery, and a retail area."

Now, that piqued Harper's interest.

Janie sensed it right away and jumped back in. "Up until this morning, we'd planned to have a high-end women's Western clothing store."

"Because the woman who can afford to fly into nowhere Wyoming for a week can afford to spend eight hundred bucks on a pair of cowboy boots?" Harper asked.

"Exactly. But our conversation at the beauty shop this afternoon struck a chord with me. We've spent all day rehashing our original direction. And we'd really like your help in the initial planning stages to implement the changes."

"Okay . . . but I don't have any idea what that means."

"Stand up."

Harper blinked. "Excuse me?"

"Stand up and show Renner your outfit."

Of all the strange requests. Harper slid out of the

booth and felt absurd as Renner Jackson eyed her from head to toe.

"See what I mean?" Janie prompted.

"Yep. She's got it. No one else has thought of doin' this, Janie. I'm damn impressed."

"That's why you pay me the big bucks, Ren."

He snorted.

"Can I sit now?" Or maybe she should run.

Janie gestured distractedly and ordered another round when the cocktail waitress swung by. Then she leaned across the table and gave Harper an impish grin. "So? What do you think about coming to work for us?"

"Doing what?"

"You'd be in charge of merchandising for the retail store, specifically finding, ordering, and setting up merchandise. New and vintage."

Harper's jaw nearly dropped to the table. "Is this some sort of joke?"

"Not hardly," Renner drawled. "We're dead-ass serious."

"Why me?"

"Because like Renner said, you've got it."

"What's *it*?"

"That elusive fashionability and sense of style that makes you look totally put together whether you're dressed to the nines or wearing flannel. And you're approachable."

She lifted her eyebrows. "Approachable? As opposed to what?"

"Darlin', you're a stunning woman. But I'll be honest. Most women who look like you?" Renner shook his head. "They tend to be first-class bitches instead of first-class ladies."

Another blush arose. They were really slathering on the flattery. But they seemed sincere. She fought her excitement because chances like this never came her way. Never.

"Today when you showed me your outfit and told me how much you paid for it? It occurred to me that mixing vintage clothes, shoes, and accessories, with new clothes, shoes, and accessories would be a unique angle for our retail store."

"And I concurred," Renner said.

"You've got my vote. But again . . . why me? I don't have a degree in marketing or business management. I'm not qualified."

Renner tipped his head, studying her from beneath the brim of his black Stetson. "There's more to runnin' a business than havin' a piece of paper framed on your wall that says you passed some classes. I ain't sayin' this because I'm some freaky kind of stalker, but I've watched you. When I came into the nail salon, you went out of your way to make me feel comfortable. Here in the bar, you know everyone. Everyone likes you. I've heard there was some nasty family business you've had to overcome in this small town, and it appears to me you have. It ain't easy dealin' with people from all walks of life, and from what I've seen, you excel at it. When Janie told me you've got mad sales skills and experience working in Western retail? In my mind you're more than qualified. You're perfect. I'd love to have you part of my team."

Breathe. Don't forget to breathe.

"Plus, I know you're a hard worker. You'd be surprised how many people with fancy degrees aren't willin' to get their hands dirty. You are. I admire that."

"Ah. Thank you."

"Renner has final approval over every aspect of the resort," Janie pointed out, "but you'd be working directly with me for the retail division."

She couldn't have been more shocked than if she'd won the lottery. "If you're serious . . . what's the catch?"

Janie and Renner exchanged another look. Which meant there was a catch. "Tell me."

"First, what we've talked about here tonight is top secret. I don't want anyone to hear what we've planned until I'm sure we can pull it off."

"You mean everything about the resort? Or just the retail end?"

"Just the retail side."

"I can keep a secret."

"Good." Renner made wet rings with the bottom of his beer bottle on the table and gestured for Janie to steer the conversation.

"The other thing—and this is imperative, a nonnegotiable point of employment. I'll need you to live on-site in the temporary housing and be available twenty-four hours a day while we're under construction."

Harper looked at Janie. "Is that where you're living?"

"Yes. Renner set up six different trailers for the various crew members. I have my own trailer, but if you accept the job, we'd be roomies, since we're the only women. For now." She sent a quick look at Renner when he scowled. "Tierney will take over general oversight responsibilities once we're up and running."

"Who's Tierney?"

"Tierney Pratt is my business partner's daughter. She's a little spy and problem child, who'll report everything back to Daddy Dearest. Tierney also holds four or five of them worthless degrees I spoke of."

"Tierney isn't our problem. Time is." Janie sank back in the booth and drained her drink. "We are targeting our opening date for hunting season. October first."

"Opening what part?"

"Everything. The lodge. The stores. The bunkhouses."

Her eyes widened. "That's only five months away. Won't it be impossible to build a luxury lodge, a spa, and retail space in such a short amount of time?"

Renner met her gaze. "Yes. But that's our deadline. If I don't get it done, I forfeit the land, the buildings—everything—to my business partner. That was the devil's bargain I signed."

Harper noticed the exhaustion etched on his face. She glanced at his hands. They were in the same raw shape as a few months back.

"It'll be damn tight to finish, even with crews workin' around the clock. So it's crucial that my staff is on hand for any major or minor issues, at all times of the day and night."

"Are they all sworn to a vow of silence too?"

Janie nodded. "The construction guys are a traveling crew. They're not real social, but we didn't hire them for their people skills. Not like the reason we're offering you a job."

Harper blinked in total disbelief. "I don't know what to say. In the last day, my life, and whatever plans I had, have fallen apart. And now? To be offered a chance at a real career, not just a job?" Harper squinted at the empty lowball glass and muttered, "I'm afraid I'm passed out in my bed dreaming."

"You're not." Janie squeezed Harper's arm. "Believe it or not, I've been in the same position you are right now. Surprised. Confused. Excited. Worried. Renner saw something in me ten minutes after we met that my ex-husband hadn't seen after being married to me for years. And also like me, I suspect you've been doing everything for everyone else in your family at the expense of fulfilling goals in your life. Here's your chance, Harper. We believe you'd be a big asset to our team. We want you to believe it too."

For the first time in her life, Harper thought things might be looking up. As much as she'd expected to be shaking the mud off her shoes and leaving this town for good, in the last month she'd begun to have mixed feelings. Seemed ironic that staying in Muddy Gap would allow her to forge her dream career. Janie had been right about something else too: It was past time she started living her own life.

"So? What do you say?"

"I say yes. I'd really love to be part of Split Rock Ranch and Resort."

Janie clapped.

Renner's phone rang. He pulled it out of his inside jacket pocket. A deep scowl knitted his dark eyebrows together. "Fuckin' awesome."

"Who is it?" Janie asked.

"The tyrant." Absentmindedly, he said, "Excuse me. I have to take this," and left the table.

"Okay, now that he's gone, and we've got you on tap for the job, what's going on with you and Bran Turner?"

"Nothing. Les is back at work. Les doesn't like me, I don't like him, and he's willing to say nasty stuff in front of me, behind my back, and to Bran's face to keep me out of the picture. And it seems like Bran believes Les over me, so it doesn't matter that I'm . . ."

"In love with him?" Janie supplied softly.

"Yeah, but I don't know if he feels the same."

"So find out."

Harper shook her head. "He thinks I'm leaving. I can't just say, *Surprise!* I'm sticking around. Part of me thinks the relationship had the intensity because of the expiration date."

"You're wrong. Sex can be intense, but it's not half as intense as love. Here's my advice. If he loves you, he'll come after you. He'll fight for you. He won't let you go."

"That's what happened between you and Abe? He let you go without a fight?"

Janie rubbed the skin between her eyes. "He didn't know me well enough to understand that's what I wanted."

"You saying he didn't love you?"

"No. Abe loved me and that covered all his bases. He talked the talk, but didn't walk the walk, know what I mean?"

"He said the words because he thought you wanted to hear them."

"Precisely. Don't let that happen, Harper. If you and Bran truly love each other, then you should know exactly why you feel that way, and he should be able to put it into words. He should know how to act on it." Then Janie was all business again. "Now, here's what we need to accomplish this week."

For the next hour, Harper's head spun. So when Janie suggested they continue the discussion in her trailer at Split Rock, Harper was so amped up she doubted she'd get a wink of sleep tonight, no matter where she laid her head.

∞

Bran missed Harper.

Missed working with her. Laughing with her. Talking to her. Teasing her. Just sitting in silence with her.

Touching her. God. Did he ever miss touching the supreme softness of her skin. Feeling her arch and purr beneath his hands as he caressed her. Watching her eyes change from the soft sheen of impending pleasure to the fiery heat of immediate need.

You're acting like it's been months. It's only been two days.

It felt one helluva lot longer than that.

"You sure you're all right?" Hank asked.

"Yeah." Except he wasn't. Here he sat, in front of Harper's house, pining for her like a heartbroken teenage boy, wishing he'd catch even the tiniest glimpse of her. Chances were good she wasn't home, since her car wasn't in the drive, but he couldn't dim that tiny flare of hope.

"Need me to stick around to see if the truck starts?" Hank prompted.

"Nah. Thanks for the ride. Go spend the night with your wife in your new house."

Hank grinned like a fool. "I intend to."

After Hank drove off, Bran crossed the lawn to the ranch truck. A creak echoed—a recognizable creak—and his gaze flew to Harper's front door as it opened.

His heart raced in anticipation.

But it wasn't Harper bounding down the steps, just Bailey.

Disappointment had him slumping against the passenger door. It'd be rude if he sped off now, so he studied Bailey as she approached him cautiously.

"Hey, Bran."

"Bailey." Bran never would've guessed Harper and Bailey were sisters—their physical appearances were almost polar opposites. Bailey was short but a bit gangly, and her face held a hint of youthful pudginess. Her dark hair, dark clothes, and dark expression fit her less than sunny personality. Whereas Harper was tall, but softly rounded in all the right places, except for the sharp angles of her face. Harper was light and grace, and her beautiful smile lit up the entire world.

You're a pathetic poet, Turner.

"Came by to get the truck?"

"Yep. Les needs it."

"Les? Oh. Right. Your hired hand. The guy Harper replaced." She hunched her shoulders. "I'm surprised Harper didn't give you a ride into town."

"Why? Harper doesn't work for me anymore."

"Oh. She's not staying with you out at the ranch?"

What the hell? Why would she think that? "No."

Bailey had yet to meet his eyes as she picked at her cuticles. "Huh. So you haven't seen her either?"

Either?

"Not since the day before yesterday." An uneasy feeling slithered up his spine. "When was the last time *you* saw her?"

"Same."

It took a second for that to settle in. "What's goin' on?"

She shrugged and studied the toe of her sneaker.

Bran fought the urge to shake her. "Tell me what you did."

Her gaze finally connected with his—as defiant as he expected. "Why do you assume it was something *I* did?"

"Because Harper would do anything for you—hell, she has done everything for you, so if you two had a fight, I'm putting the blame squarely on you."

"You don't even know me," Bailey retorted.

"Exactly. But I *do* know Harper. So why don't you tell me what happened."

Bailey's bravado fled and she deflated like a balloon. "Harper was really upset when I told her I joined the army."

"When?"

"I leave for basic training in five days."

"No. When did you tell her?"

"The last morning I saw her."

"I take it Harper didn't want you to join the army?"

"Umm . . . She didn't know I joined."

Bran felt Bailey's words like a hoof to the belly. If he had that reaction . . . how must Harper feel?

Like everything she'd done for Bailey hadn't mattered. Like *she* didn't matter.

Goddamn it. He glared at the self-centered teen, wondering if she had any idea how deeply she'd cut her sister. "You didn't think enough of her . . ."

"I screwed up. I get that, okay? I can't . . . God. I have no freakin' clue where she is."

Bran blew out an impatient breath. "You haven't heard from her at all?"

"No. I've called everyone—Bernice, Celia. I even had our sister, Liberty, try to get in touch with her, but Harper is not answering her phone."

"Can you blame her?"

"No. Have you tried to call her?"

"My phone ended up busted about two hours after the last time I saw her. So I have no idea if she tried to get in touch with me or not." His heart nearly stopped. What if Harper couldn't answer her phone? What if, right now, she was lying in a ditch somewhere? Alone and hurt? Or worse? He exploded, as much from anger as from fear. "I swear to God, if anything has happened to her because you can't be bothered to pick up the goddamn phone to check—"

"I'm not an idiot," she snapped back. "I've called around, and no woman fitting her description has been admitted to the hospital or any clinic in Rawlins or Laramie or Cheyenne or Casper."

"Well, that's a fuckin' relief." Bran paced to the sidewalk and back. "What does she normally do when she gets upset like this?"

"I don't know!" Bailey practically wailed. "It's so surreal. I've never seen her act like that. She never just leaves like our mom did."

Hopefully Bailey hadn't voiced that maternal comparison to Harper, because that definitely would've set her off. "So what did Harper do after you talked to her?"

"She packed a bag and took off with the car."

"That's it? She didn't say anything else?"

"Well, she swore at me and slammed the door."

Come to think of it, she'd sworn at him too. He muttered, "I should've seen this coming. I should've known...."

"Why? What did she say to you when you last saw her?"

Nothing. I stood by and let Les run roughshod over her. Then I watched her drive away and thought biding my time was the mature thing to do.

Jesus. He was a fucking moron.

"What did *you* do to her?" Bailey stomped over, invading his personal space.

Bran clenched his hands into fists and kept his mouth closed—sadly, that was something he was very good at.

"Omigod. Harper's disappearing act is as much your fault as it is mine. She probably drove out to talk to you about me being such an ungrateful brat and joining the army and then you ... what? Told her to turn in her time sheet and her truck keys because her time with you was done?"

He winced.

"Or did you just blow her off since your precious Les was back?"

Phrased that way ... Fuck. This was a nightmare.

But Bailey kept going, her voice cracking. "How could you do that to her?"

"Do what?"

"I'm not blind, Bran. I know it's been more than just a working relationship between you two. Harper . . . she's always so careful with guys. She never falls like this. . . . Never. I saw how you looked at her at the branding and it sure as hell wasn't the way an employer would."

That smart comment put Bran on the defensive. "Just exactly how would you know anything about employer/employee relations? Bein's I ain't heard about *you* ever holdin' down a job, just your sister. And she usually holds down two or three to support you, don't she?"

Silence.

Damn it. "Sorry. Sniping at each other ain't gonna help."

Bailey ran a hand through her dark hair and sighed. "Look, I'm sorry too. I'm just worried."

"That makes two of us."

"We both fucked up. Big-time."

"Yep."

"So what do we do now?"

"We wait." And hope. And pray. And learn to grovel.

With nothing left to say, Bailey trudged to the house.

Bran climbed in the ranch truck. He jammed the gearshift into first and smoked the tires getting away. But not even the smell of burning rubber could mask the scent of Harper's perfume still lingering in the truck cab.

Waiting would drive him crazy, but it was his only option.

∞

Harper's overnight stay at the Split Rock compound had stretched into two nights. Her phone had stopped ringing the second day and she wasn't sure if that was a good sign or not.

Her stomach tightened at seeing the ranch truck gone from the driveway. So Bran had been here. Had he spoken to Bailey? Or had he just driven off without a word?

The lights were on in the living room, which meant Bailey had returned home. Taking a deep breath, she opened the door.

Instead of Bailey remaining aloof, or acting surly, she launched herself at Harper and sobbed, "I'm sorry. So, so sorry. I've been so worried and I know you're mad at me and if I had it to do all over again . . ."

She squeezed her little sister once before she disentangled from her death grip. "It's all right."

"You've never taken off like that before. Like Mom."

Harper ignored the barb. "I needed to work some things out." She tossed her purse on the chair, kicked off her boots, and walked to the kitchen.

Bailey followed. "Where have you been?"

"Honestly? That's none of your business." Harper busied herself fixing a cup of tea. Going through the motions calmed her, even if she didn't drink the results.

"That's not fair," Bailey complained.

"No, it's not. But you'll quickly learn that life isn't fair." She pressed her backside to the edge of the counter. "We have to talk about packing your stuff for storage."

"Storage? Why can't you keep it?"

"Because I won't be in a position to take care of it for you. I'll be contacting Liberty about what she wants done with her boxes. Since neither of you owns much, you should be able to find a small storage facility in Rawlins and split the cost. I'll front the first month's rent from what I saved for your college expenses, but after that, you and Liberty will have to figure out how to make payments."

"What about your stuff?"

She shrugged. "What I need I'll take with me. Anything else, I'll throw away or give away."

"What has gotten into you, Harper?"

"A reality check. You were right to point out that I

need to start living for myself. I'm starting a new chapter of my life."

"Doing what?" Bailey demanded.

"I can't talk about it."

Bailey gaped at her. "I look at you and see my sister, but I feel like I don't know you."

Harper cocked her head and studied her sister, trying to picture her in a helmet and combat fatigues. "I know the feeling. Now, I'm assuming the army reps gave you a list of all you need to accomplish before you head to basic training?"

"I've got a lot of lists."

"Make sure I get the information on where you fly out of and when."

"But I thought . . ."

She braced herself for Bailey's guilt trip. "What?"

"I thought you'd help me get ready."

"Sorry. I've got plenty to take care of. And I'm thinking if you're old enough to die for your country, you're old enough to pack your own socks and underwear."

Bailey looked away. "Are you still coming to my graduation?"

"Of course I am." Harper set down the tea and hugged her little sister, trying to keep her tears in check. "I wouldn't miss it for the world. I'm really proud of you."

"Then why are you doing this now? When I'm leaving in a few days?"

"Because as proud as I am of you, I need to do something that makes me proud of myself."

∞

The day after Bailey left for basic training, Harper was counting the hours until her shift at Get Nailed ended. There'd been zero traffic into Bernice's Beauty Barn, and if Bernice hadn't promised Maybelle that Harper would do her nails one last time, she would've been tempted to close up shop.

While she was fretting about how Bailey was faring in Mississippi, the oddest thing happened: Susan Williams, Buckeye Joe's owner, marched in. Susan was a no-frills kind of woman. Stout-bodied, shrewd-eyed, not exactly the type to indulge in a weekly French manicure. Susan's mannish hairdo indicated that she cut her own hair— apparently with a pair of hedge clippers.

Had Susan timed the confrontation so there weren't customers around? Harper braced herself for a conversation that'd been a long time in the making.

"Hi, Susan. Something I can help you with?"

Without preamble, Susan looked her square in the eye and said, "I didn't like your mama, Harper. Wasn't my idea to hire her. We all know how that played out. But I've heard talk about Bailey joining the army and leaving you holding the bag, just like your mama done. It ain't fair. I just wanted to say if you intend to stick around Muddy Gap and you're needin' work, I'll hire ya at Buckeye Joe's."

"Really?" popped out before she could stop it. "But why?"

"You've got grit, girl. Like a true Wyomingite."

Harper couldn't have been more floored. "Thank you, Susan. That's the best compliment an outsider like me could ever hope to receive."

She snorted. "Outsider? You're part of this community whether you like it or not."

"The truth is . . . I like it."

"Good. So you're joining the ranks of the rest of us who are too stubborn or too dumb to leave?"

"Yep. And I appreciate the job offer, but I'll be working for Renner Jackson up at the Split Rock Ranch and Resort."

"You don't say? Well, good enough. Don't be a stranger to the Buckeye." Susan hustled out.

Harper stared after her for the longest time. She hadn't misread Susan's hostility over the last couple of years, yet the job offer and peace offering gave Harper a sense of closure.

The back door banged open and Bernice yelled, "Harper? I need your help for a sec."

Outside, Bernice was digging in the trunk of her car. "Bernice?"

"Can you come here and check this out?"

"Ah. Sure." She skirted the back end of the Chrysler Imperial.

"Do you think I need to get this spare tire pumped up? It's lookin' a little ratty."

She peered into the trunk. The black blob, which probably had been a tire at some point, was totally deflated. "Uh. Yeah. Maybe Bob oughta take a look at that." She turned to go, but Bernice snagged her arm.

"Between us? I think the man's gone senile. The other day he made me a tuna fish sandwich and put Cool Whip in it instead of Miracle Whip. Cool Whip! Can you imagine?"

"That does sound gross."

"And then he found these god-awful plaid parachute pants from the 1980s in his closet. He tried to put them on over his chubby butt and accused me of shrinking them in the wash when they didn't fit! Of all the nerve. Never mind the man hasn't weighed a hundred and thirty pounds since Ronald Reagan was president."

What was she supposed to say? She started toward the door. But once again, Bernice stopped her.

"Did I ever tell you about the time my granny, who had Alzheimer's, although we called it 'old-timers' back then, got up in the middle of a church service? She never did come back in and hear Reverend Billy Jack's warning about the wages of sin. When we went outside, there was Granny, perched nekkid as a jaybird on the hood of my grandpa's Impala. Grandpa tried to hustle her into the backseat and cover her with a horse blanket, but she insisted she didn't know him. Told him to take his hands off her." Her voice dropped to a whisper. "Come to find out, Granny believed she was Rita Hayworth and she was auditioning for a movie part. How bizarre is that?"

Harper wondered if Bernice had been inhaling exhaust fumes because this conversation was beyond bizarre. "Thanks for telling me, Bernice, but I heard the door chimes." She managed to duck Bernice's grabbing hands and sprinted into the shop, skidding to a stop when she heard, "Surprise!"

Ten of her regular ladies, who'd been pillars of support, a source of laughter, who'd given her a sense of belonging—even if she'd only recently realized it—stood by the windows grinning at her. They'd tied "good luck" balloons to her chair and set up a refreshment station at the counter, complete with a frosted cake—homemade, of course—and a pitcher of pink lemonade, plus they'd coordinated the fancy matching floral napkins with the paper plates and plastic cups. All the goodies Harper had never had at any birthday party. Or a party of any sort.

If she'd been floored by Susan Williams's visit, this absolutely knocked her to her knees.

Cake was cut. Lemonade poured. She chatted and shed a tear when she opened Bernice's parting gift—her very own elk antler coatrack.

As the party wound down, Maybelle stepped forward. "We'll miss you, Harper, even when you won't be going far. We wanted to let you know how much we appreciated having you here. You could've found work in Rawlins, making more money, working with a younger clientele, so we're pleased as punch you're now a permanent part of our town."

"Thank you. Good Lord, you all are so sweet, I'm gonna bawl."

When she started to cry, eleven ladies patted her arms, her back, her shoulders. Murmuring reassurances, soothing her, so Harper felt she was being held in the arms of the entire community.

How ironic that she'd been looking for a place to call home . . . when she'd already found it.

Chapter Twenty-four

~

One day later...

They'd cleared the first gate when Les tossed out, "I hear Harper is livin' up at Renner Jackson's compound."

Bran hit the brakes so hard they both lurched into the dash. His head whipped toward Les. "What the hell did you just say?"

"That your temporary 'hired hand'"—Les made quotes in the air that matched his sarcastic intonation—"is livin' with Renner Jackson."

Getting hooked with a bull's horn couldn't have ripped a bigger hole in his gut. "How the fuck do you know that?"

Les shrugged. "Heard it from Betty. Guess it ain't a big deal. Ain't like Harper's hiding it neither."

It was a big deal as far as Bran was concerned. He looked out the window and his hands tightened on the steering wheel in pure frustration.

Hell, he'd had no freaking clue Harper was still living

in Muddy Gap. He'd gone by her house and seen a For Rent sign in the yard. He'd quietly been going crazy for the week since he'd last seen her. Bernice's Beauty Barn had been closed every time he'd driven by. He'd planned to ask Les today to cover for him so he could track her down as soon as he convinced Celia to tell him where she'd gone.

And now to find out that Harper had been under his nose the entire time?

Unfuckingbelievable.

Why hadn't she told him she planned to stick around? *Because she probably thinks you don't care.*

"Goddamn it. I'm a fucking idiot."

"Told ya. She wanted one thing from you and when you didn't offer it, she hooked up with the next rich guy she could find. You're better off forgetting all about her."

"I'm better off?" Bran repeated. "What? So I can end up like you? Alone and bitter? Spending my life tying flies and fishing by myself? You've said some stupid things to me over the years, Les, but that one has got to take the cake."

"What the hell's that supposed to mean?"

"You know nothin' about Harper and yet you've felt entitled to pass judgment on her at every opportunity. If I didn't know better, I'd say you were jealous of her."

Les's face turned bright red. "Like hell."

"You know, Harper was a great hired hand. She took direction better than you ever thought of doing." When a mean glint entered Les's eyes, Bran warned, "You even think of spewing some smart-ass remark about how well she directed herself into my bedroom and I will pop you one in the mouth, old man."

His hired hand said not a word for a change.

Bran hit the gas and spun a cookie. When he reached the last gate, he got out and opened it, ignoring the temptation just to run the damn thing over. He pulled up alongside Les's ranch truck, looking at his hired man in a whole new way, mostly with gratitude for the wake-up call. "Go on and finish chores. I don't know when I'll be back."

"You ain't firing me?"

Bran scowled at him. "Why would I fire you?"

"Because you're probably bringing Harper back here and you won't need me no more."

"Les, if I can convince Harper to give me another chance, she sure as hell ain't gonna be around as my hired hand." If he had his way, Harper would be his wife.

Bran burned rubber getting to the Split Rock Ranch and Resort. Two gigantic stone pillars had been erected beside the access road since the last time he'd been by. And between those stone pillars? A heavy chain with signs every foot warning NO TRESPASSING. He snorted. Like that'd stop him.

He hopped out and unhooked the chain. He crested the rise of the big hill that hid the building from view. Once he hit the top of the hill, his mouth dropped open.

Holy shit. It was like some kind of cult compound. Close to thirty vehicles were parked in front of four buildings in various stages of construction. Half a dozen trailers were lined up off to the left. A backhoe, a grader, and a paving machine were sitting idle by a gigantic pile of steel fence posts and rolls of chain-link fencing. Two flatbed trucks stacked with lumber and Sheetrock were backed up to two structures. Even through the closed window Bran heard the loud construction noises— hammering, sawing, and the mechanical whine of generators.

He proceeded down the steep angle of the hill, surprised that Renner had chosen to build this fancy resort in a bowl-shaped canyon. Passage in the winter would be damn difficult, given the amount of snow this area received. His wheels left pavement and his truck skidded across red dirt that resembled a mud bog rather than a road.

As soon as his vehicle stopped and he'd climbed out of his rig, two burly guys approached him. They weren't local and they didn't look friendly. "Is there a reason you're trespassing when the sign on the road clearly said *keep out*?"

Bran shrugged. "I thought it was a suggestion. I'm here to talk to Harper Masterson."

The guys exchanged a look, which made Bran bristle. "What?"

"How do we know you ain't some freaky stalker dude?"

"For chrissake, I'm not a freaky stalker dude. I'm her . . ." He realized he didn't know who the hell he was to her. Boss? Lover?

Try the idiot who let her get away.

"She's here, isn't she?"

One guy glanced at the bank of trailers.

Bingo.

"How about if you give us your name and we'll see if she wants to talk to you?"

Like hell.

Bran walked toward the trailers he assumed were living quarters. Either the guards were slow or their authority hadn't been challenged before now, because neither guy tried to stop him.

Heart racing, he stopped in front of the third trailer in and yelled, "Harper. I want to talk to you."

No answer.

"I know you're here and I'm not leavin' until you come out."

No answer.

"If you want me to start banging on doors until I find you, I will."

The metal click of a screen door opening echoed back to him. Three seconds later Harper came around the front end of the fourth trailer.

His heart soared. Sweet Jesus. It was as if his world brightened. He took a step forward and stopped when he noticed Renner Jackson behind Harper. Directly behind her. His eyes narrowed. Had Les been right? Was Harper living with him?

"I'll, ah . . . just go check on some things," Renner said.

"You do that," Bran snapped.

Renner gave him a wide berth.

"Why are you here, Bran?" Harper asked.

"Because I heard a rumor you were still in Muddy Gap."

"It wasn't a rumor, as you can plainly see."

He crossed his arms over his chest. "There's a second part to that rumor."

"Which is?"

"That you're livin' with Renner Jackson. Is that true?"

She tossed her hair—a clear sign that she was nervous. But she didn't respond.

"I'll wait all goddamn day for your answer if I have to."

"Fine. I am living here."

"Why?"

"Renner offered me something you didn't."

In less than a heartbeat Bran stood over her, fuming, his whole being raw from fear that he was too late. "What is it that he can offer you? Money?"

Her jaw dropped.

"Let me tell you something, sweetheart. I've got more money than he does. A shit ton more. I can buy and sell him twice over. I just don't advertise it."

Harper continued to gape at him as if he'd lost his mind. Maybe he had—he couldn't seem to stop his damn mouth from running unchecked.

"Jesus, Harper. If you're lookin' for a man to take care of you, why ain't you lookin' at me?"

Goaded beyond her control, Harper placed her palms on Bran's chest and shoved him as hard as she could. "You pompous . . . ass! I'm not looking for a man to take care of me. I'm looking for someone to believe in me. I'm looking for someone to give me a chance and see me beyond Harper Masterson, beauty queen. Or Harper the college dropout. Or Harper the nail technician. Or Harper the hired hand."

He shook his finger at her. "I never put those labels on you and you damn well know that. You did it all by yourself. So tell me, what can Jackson give you that I can't?"

"A permanent job."

Guilt punched his already aching gut. "What?"

"I'm living here with Janie Fitzhugh. Renner hired me to work at the resort. But he and Janie are giving me more than just a job. They're giving me a chance to have my dream."

"Which is what, exactly?"

Oh shit. Harper got that look in her eye that indicated he'd said exactly the wrong thing.

Before he could backtrack, she said, "You don't have a clue what this opportunity means to me."

"Don't put words in my mouth, Harper," he warned.

"Then tell me in your own words."

"Fine. You're excited about a new job."

"This is not just any job!"

"Don't you think I know that?"

"No." She backed away from him. "I think you don't know me at all, do you, Bran?"

"I do too know you," he replied, trying damn hard not to explode.

"Name one thing that's important to me."

"Having a job is important to you."

"Name one thing you like about me that doesn't have to do with my job working for you or sex."

Bran's mouth opened. Closed.

Her eyes clouded with hurt.

Damn it. This was killing him.

Go on the offensive.

"Same question back atcha. Name one thing you like about me that doesn't have to do with your job working for me or sex."

"I can name a hundred. I like the way you laugh. I like the way you smile at me when you don't know I can see you. I like how in tune you are with everything that goes on around your ranch. I like the care and concern you show your animals. I liked the care and concern you showed for me, when I was just your employee and then when we became so much more. I think it's cool that you like to tie flies and you love to fish. I'm glad you're not addicted to sports twenty-four/seven."

Damn. He wasn't expecting that.

"Here's a news flash: I absolutely do not care, one way or another, if you have money. But I do care that you didn't tell me. And it really makes me mad that you think throwing that fact out there now would somehow make a difference in how I feel about you."

Instead of demanding to know exactly how she felt about him, he said, "Why do you think I didn't tell you?"

She tapped her chin. "Hmm. Let me think. Because I might have designs on your money?"

"Wrong again, sweetheart. I don't believe you're some kind of damn gold digger. I haven't told *anyone* about my inheritance from my grandparents. None of my friends have a freakin' clue."

"That is even sadder yet, Bran."

"And why is that?"

"They've been your best buddies for how long? Your whole life, right? And if you can't trust them . . . how did I ever hope that you could trust me?"

"It's not the same thing, Harper."

She shook her head in disagreement. "Yes, it is. Although I could understand why you didn't tell Les. You have serious trust issues, cowboy."

"So do you," he fired back.

Indignant, she retorted, "I do not. I gave you every bit of my trust. And I'm not just talking about in the bedroom."

"But you didn't trust me enough to tell me about Bailey joining the army and breakin' your heart?"

"Why do you think I drove out there that morning? To talk to you. But Les . . ."

Now they were getting somewhere. "Les said some things he shouldn't have. And I *didn't* say the things I should have. But I want to know why you didn't tell me the one thing that mattered. That you'd decided to stay in Muddy Gap."

"Because I didn't know it at the time."

"And when you figured it out? Why didn't you share that information with me?"

"Because I hadn't heard one word from you, Bran. No phone call. Nothing. The job was over. I didn't think you cared."

Bran loomed over her. "Bullshit. You know I care. My damn cell phone met the business end of a shovel. I told Bailey about it when I . . ." His eyes searched hers. "She didn't tell you I stopped by, did she?"

"No. But it doesn't matter now."

"Yes, it does. You are more to me than a damn employee. You knew that as soon as I found out you were hiding up here, I'd come for you. I'd chase you down, like you were always hoping I'd do, and then I'd bring you back where you belong."

"Which is where?"

"With me. And here's a news flash for you. I didn't get a chance to talk to you about this stuff the morning after your karaoke win because Les showed up. Then you were gone for damn near three days. When you finally came out to the ranch, you let me believe you only cared about your paycheck."

Understanding dawned in her eyes. "But—"

"Goddamn it, Harper, I wanted to tell you how I felt about you, but you deserved to hear it in private—not in front of Les."

Harper mumbled something about excuses.

Bran curled one hand over her hip, one hand around the side of her beautiful face, and took the biggest chance of his life. "No more excuses. I love you, Harper Masterson. I love everything about you."

Did she throw herself into his arms and sob that she loved him too? Did she kiss him with the fire and sweetness he craved?

No.

The damn woman stepped back and said, "Prove it."

His body stiffened. "What? I just told you I love you and now you want me to prove it?"

"Yes."

"Well, I'm here, aren't I?"

Those golden brown eyes spit fire. "Is that it, Bran? You've decided you love me because I'm conveniently nearby? What would you've done if I'd moved to Laramie? Would you've tracked me down and dragged me *back where I belong*?"

"How the devil am I supposed to answer that?"

"Let me know when you figure it out." She flounced off.

Flounced. Like a damn beauty queen in a snit.

Which she was.

Damn it.

He'd done this all wrong.

Big surprise.

He shouted, "I'll be back, Harper. Mark my words. I. Will. Be. Back."

Bran seethed even as he was half giddy from the knowledge he hadn't lost her.

Didn't know her, my ass.

He knew her. Backward, forward, inside out, upside down and sideways.

He loved her.

And, yes, he had every intention of tracking her down.

He'd prove it to her. Might take him a day or two to sort the wheat from the chaff, but he couldn't wait to make that woman eat crow.

And then he wasn't ever going to let her go.

∞

"How much longer are you going to make the poor man suffer, Harper?" Janie asked.

Bran wasn't the only one suffering.

She'd wondered how Bran would react when he learned she hadn't moved out of state, just up the road. Happy? Indifferent? Angry?

Yeah, he'd been angry.

She missed him. Three months didn't seem like enough time to figure out if you liked someone, let alone if you loved them. But she loved Bran. She knew him, heart and soul, straight down to the bone. And like Janie had reminded her, she deserved to know if that depth of feeling, of commitment, was reciprocated.

When she'd told him to prove it, she'd half expected that he would scoop her into his arms and drag her off, keeping her captive until she admitted she loved him too. It was the sort of Neanderthal tactics she'd expected.

So why was she disappointed that he hadn't reacted that way?

Two days after he'd left Split Rock in a huff, she'd feared he'd given up. She wondered if she'd been too hasty, too haughty.

On the dawn of day three, when Harper convinced herself she'd ruined everything by pushing Bran into a corner, a van arrived in front of her trailer—a van filled with lilacs. Every color of lilac imaginable; deep amethyst, vivid purple, lavender, pale pink, and creamy white. And every bouquet was in a different-colored jewel-toned vase.

Bran remembering her favorite flower earned serious brownie points.

Yesterday morning, the same van delivered a dozen doughnuts—crème-filled Bavarian, croissants covered in chocolate glaze, cake doughnuts with pink icing, long johns with rainbow-colored sprinkles—and a pot of strong coffee. At noon the van dropped off lunch—crab salad, fruit, sweet tea, and key lime cheesecake. She hadn't known what to expect when the van returned at suppertime. Steak? Lobster? Veal? Pasta?

Lifting the silver-domed plate warmer revealed ... pepperoni pizza. And in the champagne bucket? Wine coolers. The afternoon they'd stayed naked in bed just talking, laughing, feeding each other pizza and drinking "bitch beer" ranked as one of the best times she'd had with him.

His insight brought tears to her eyes. He'd turned the tables and used food as a way to her heart in such a thoughtful gesture, especially poignant because he'd sworn the food trick would never work with him.

At that point Harper was willing to admit he was taking her challenge seriously.

But Bran wasn't done offering her proof.

This morning a gigantic package wrapped in gold foil had appeared on her doorstep. Inside the box was a glass bottle, in a beautiful shade of blue, topped with a silver filigree. As touched as she was that he remembered her fondness for antique perfume bottles, the item at the bottom of the box sealed the deal and her fate.

And then she'd understood. Bran did know her. Better than anyone ever had. Better than anyone ever would. If he hadn't come to her tonight, she would've gone to him.

But Bran had shown up. With a karaoke machine, of all things. He'd unloaded the speakers and had been serenading her for the last twenty minutes.

If you could call the sounds coming out of his mouth . . . music. Good Lord. He truly was an awful singer. But his willingness to put himself out there, in front of her, and in front of the dozens of male workers in the compound, as proof of his love . . . Well, it was time she offered him proof too.

"Harper. Seriously. Go out and talk to him. Or gag him. My ears are starting to bleed," Janie whined.

Harper laughed and exited the trailer.

The instant Bran saw her, the music stopped.

Thank God.

"Hey," he said.

"Hey," she said back. "Nice tune selection. I particularly enjoyed your version of Conway Twitty's 'I'd Love to Lay You Down.'"

His eyes lit up. "Really?"

"No, not really."

"So did you come out here to make a request? I've got a big playlist. I can go all night."

She murmured, "You certainly can."

Bran seemed a little shocked by her innuendo. So shocked that he didn't make a single move toward her.

So she ambled closer to him. "Now you can say, *I told you so*, because you did prove, beyond a shadow of a doubt, that you know me."

"Huh-uh. I ain't done. There's something else. You asked me to name something I liked about you that didn't have to do with you workin' for me or sex."

"Bran—"

He put his fingers over her lips. "Let me finish. I don't know if you've figured it out yet, but I ain't exactly clever with words, especially not off the cuff. But that don't mean I can't do it—it just means I need to take my time to get the words right."

She felt her chest constrict as he inhaled a deep breath.

"So here goes. I love that you're always humming. I love how you grin when you've figured something out on your own. I love how you round up my coffee cups since I'm forever losing them or leavin' them in the barn. I love it when you take off your hat and your hair sticks up all over the place and you don't even notice. I love that you speak your mind.

"I love how you've taken to the calves, the cows, the goats and horses. Hell, I even like how determined you are to feed them damn rabbits."

"Really?"

He shook his head. "No. Not really."

"Shoot."

Bran smiled. "I love your unconditional love for your

family. I love your devotion to the old gals who depend on you to do their nails. I love that you can be all girly one second and elbow-deep in manure the next. I love watching you eat doughnuts with impeccable manners, and then I love how fast that ladylike behavior disappears when you're chowing down on a plate of ribs."

When she opened her mouth to protest, Bran placed his fingers over her lips again.

"I know this list isn't supposed to be about sex. But I love the glazed look in your eyes when I'm inside you. I love your passion and how you don't hold anything back from me. I love how snuggly you are as we're falling asleep. I love the smell of your hair and the scent of your skin. I love how whenever you pick up one of my shirts, you sniff it and smile that secret little sexy smile. I love the way you kiss me. I love the way you touch me, not only physically, but here." He flattened her palm over his heart. "I love the way you accept every weird, kinky, dorky, plain, simple, and annoying thing about me. I love that you forced me to think about all the things I know about you, because, darlin', there are a whole bunch more I don't know and I think I'll need a lifetime with you to figure them all out."

Harper couldn't speak around the lump in her throat.

"Come on. Say something."

"I never knew my cowboy had such a silver tongue." She leaned forward and kissed him. Twice. "But I'll take it. I'll take you. I love you, Bran."

Then she was in his arms, being squeezed so tightly she couldn't breathe. But she didn't mind. She'd probably never get used to the breathless way he made her feel anyway.

"I love you so damn much, Harper. Now will you please come home with me and let me prove it without words?"

"I can't."

He eased back to study her. "Come again?"

"When I took this job, I promised Renner I'd live in the compound until the resort opened. We're keeping some odd hours because we have such a tight deadline."

"How tight?"

"Five months."

"I sure as hell am not gonna be without you for five months."

Harper kissed his scowling mouth. "That's sweet, but—"

"No buts." A contemplative look entered his eyes. "How about if I move my trailer here? Then you can sneak off and spend time with me when you've got a break."

"Think Renner will go for that?"

"I ain't giving him a choice." He swept a lock of hair behind her ear. "Besides, I won't be needing the trailer at the ranch much longer anyway."

She stared at him, confused.

"Seeing Hank and Lainie so happy in their own place made me want the same for us." Bran dug in his pocket and pulled out an old-fashioned skeleton key, a key identical to the one he'd sent her earlier. "I'm finally ready to fix up my grandparents' house and move into it. But only if you'll live there with me, and help me make it a home—our home."

She swallowed, trying hard not to cry, because he was giving her everything she'd ever wanted. "And here I thought you were offering me the key to your heart."

"You've already got that. You've had it for a while now. I just had to trust you enough to let you use it. Every day. Forever."

It was no use. Her tears fell unimpeded.

"Hey, now, what's with the tears?" His face took on a

slightly horrified, comical look. "You don't think . . . You know that I'm not asking you to be my ranch hand, right? I'm asking you to be my wife."

"Well, you weren't exactly clear on the job description, Bran." She sniffed. "And being your ranch hand has been a good gig so far."

He framed her face in his hands and gently wiped her tears. "You've been a great ranch hand, but you'll make an even better wife. Say you'll marry me, Harper."

"Yes, I'll marry you, just as long as you can wait a few months for us to tie the knot."

Bran's smile was a thing of beauty. "I've waited my whole life for a woman like you. A few more months ain't gonna matter."

Epilogue

❧

Five months later . . .

From the *Muddy Gap Gazette*—Maybelle's Musings

The much-anticipated unveiling of the Split Rock Ranch and Resort took place last Saturday night after the wedding of Miss Harper Masterson to Mister Branford Turner.

Although I'm new to the *Muddy Gap Gazette* as the society reporter, as a lifelong resident of Muddy Gap, I've attended many weddings. But this wedding was truly special. The surprise addition of Harper's sisters, Sergeant Liberty Masterson and Specialist Bailey Masterson, to the wedding party, wearing their United States Army uniforms as they escorted Harper down the aisle, will resonate throughout this community for years to come. There wasn't a dry eye in the house—including mine. Harper looked lovely in a traditional ivory mermaid-style gown, while her intended, Bran, epitomized dashing in a Western-cut black tuxedo. The bride's attendant was Celia Lawson. On the groom's side was Hank Lawson.

The happy couple stuck around following the short ceremony for toasts and to cut cake, but left directly after for their honeymoon at an undisclosed location. Rumor has it they've gone fishing in the Caribbean.

Speaking of rumors . . . a couple of spats arose during the wedding reception, luckily after the bride and groom's departure, leaving many locals wondering if all is as it seems with the Split Rock Ranch and Resort. Stay tuned for further reports.

Don't miss the new book in the
Blacktop Cowboys® series,

Hillbilly Rockstar

Available in trade paperback in
August 2014 from Signet Eclipse.

*D*evin studied the outside of his new tour bus. No gigantic image of his grinning face, no signage at all about who was on board. But there was no doubt this still looked like a rock star's bus. The inside was even better. He had a big master bedroom and a decent-sized master bathroom. The promotion company had even found a bus with only two bunks instead of the standard four. This one had a second bathroom as well as a small alcove, where the bunks would've been. Even the main living area had a half-wall on both sides, which allowed for separation from the kitchen. The driver's area was enclosed like the cab of a semitruck. The only access was through a sliding-glass window.

His roadies had unloaded his bags in his bedroom and stashed his favorite guitars in the closet. He didn't give a damn if his clothes got wrinkled; he cared that his guitars were protected and accessible.

Crash wandered over with an update. "We're loaded. The equipment trucks are gone. The roadies' bus is following. We're waiting on Tay, but the rest of the band is ready to roll." He peered over the tops of his sunglasses. "Where's your new personal assistant?"

"Who knows? I haven't heard from her. If she ain't here in ten minutes . . . we're still leaving."

"Nope, sorry. I got my orders, Dev. We're waiting on her."

"Goddammit. This is so fucking stupid. I don't need—"

As he spoke two arms circled his waist and he jerked away violently.

Yeah, maybe he was a little on edge.

He whirled around and saw the shocked face of his string player and songwriting partner, Odette.

"Geez, Devin, jumpy much?"

"Sorry, darlin'." He hugged her. "You all set?"

"Yes. Thanks for scoring us a new bus too. It's sweet. Steve and I will be breaking in that king-sized bed very soon."

"TMI, little O. And if you tell me that my drummer's got the right rhythm, I will put you two lovebirds in a single bunk and rotate Tay, Gage, Leon, and Jase into the bedroom."

She whopped him on the chest. "That's just plain mean. Sounds like someone needs to get laid."

"You have no idea." Although he had groupies lined up for him before and after shows, in the past eighteen months, after all this shit had started going down, he hadn't fucked any of the women he'd invited into his ready room. He'd kept sexual contact to blow jobs and hand jobs. If those women lied and bragged he'd banged them, well, he didn't give a damn. He couldn't go back and change the manwhore reputation he'd built over the years—most of which had been exaggerated anyway.

A jacked-up Ford truck screeched into the parking lot and the driver slammed on the brakes. A scrawny, bearded guy leapt out of the cab and climbed onto the back bumper, lifting suitcases out of the truck bed and tossing them to the ground.

Just then Tay came around the back end of the truck, yelling obscenities at the man.

"You have got to be fucking kiddin' me," Devin said. "Is Tay an asshole magnet?"

"Yep. This dude followed her to Denver from Kansas City. They were going at it like rabbits. We were in the room next to theirs."

Then Tay took a swing at him with her laptop bag.

The guy ducked, jumped back into the truck and sped off, tires spitting gravel.

"Looks like another breakup to me," Crash muttered. "Can't wait for her and Jase to start fucking and fighting again ... *Not*."

Jase, the laid-back lead guitar player, and Tay, his keyboard player and backup singer, had an on-again, off-again relationship. Their fights—and subsequent makeups—were loud and obnoxious and the main reason Devin never got involved with a woman he worked with.

"Is Jase here?" he asked, watching Tay head toward the band's bus, Odette hot on her heels.

"He left with the equipment truck," Gage said behind him.

"Wise choice."

"A hundred bucks says they're back together by Friday."

"Whose turn is it to run the pool?" Steve asked.

"Gage did it last time," Crash said. "I reckon it's Devin's turn."

"Get your bets and money to me by showtime."

"Who're we waiting for?" Gage asked.

Just then a gorgeous baby blue Mustang pulled up. The driver's-side door opened and a pair of boots hit the concrete. He only saw a flip of the woman's hair and her jean-clad backside—and sweet baby Jesus, what a sweet backside it was—before she was hidden, rooting around in the open trunk.

Even as his suspicions surfaced, his head was telling him *no*, that couldn't possibly be her.

The trunk shut and she started toward him. Wind tousling her shoulder-length auburn hair, her hips swaying in jeans that hugged her every curve. With a duffel bag slung over her shoulder and another one clutched in her other hand, her well-defined arm muscles flexed. Her cherry red lips curved into a smirk as she fastened her gaze on him.

Holy mother of God. It was a miracle that he managed to keep from drooling. Or from cursing at the sky because the fucking universe had a sick sense of humor.

Or maybe this is karma beating you with the stupid stick for boldly proclaiming that you didn't find Liberty Masterson attractive. And for challenging her to look the part of your groupie entourage.

What a cruel joke—his groupies never looked that goddamn good.

Devin had about ten seconds to prepare himself before she reached him. Good thing he had his sunglasses on—maybe they'd keep his eyes from popping out of his head.

That's when his gaze landed on not one, but two bruisers behind her. One guy carried two suitcases; the other guy hefted an enormous cooler. Given the sheer size of the first guy, he could've been a linebacker or a WWE wrestler. The second guy was a mirror image of the first.

Liberty offered a quick smile. "Sorry I'm late. I had to grab a few last-minute things." She set down her duffel bags. "Which bus is ours?"

Devin pointed to the forward bus.

"Sweet upgrade. Guys . . . do you mind?"

Immediately Hulk #1 and Hulk #2 carted the suitcases and cooler aboard the bus. Then they were back, awaiting Liberty's instructions.

She stood on tiptoe to get in Hulk #1's face. "You'll make sure she's protected? No matter what?"

"Baby girl, don't worry. I promise I'll take as good of care of her as you do, okay?"

"Okay." She smiled and pressed something into his hand.

Then the guy picked her up off the ground and spun her around, giving everyone his massive back so no one could see if he was laying a big steamy kiss good-bye on her or copping a feel or what. Then he tossed her to Hulk #2, where she received the same treatment, except Hulk #2 slapped her ass and whispered in her ear before he set her down and lumbered back to the car.

It was surprising the King Kong twins fit into the front seats.

She didn't turn around until the car was out of view. "Sorry. I have separation anxiety."

"From bein' away from them?" Devin asked sharply.

Liberty gave him a *you're an idiot* look. "No. From my car."

"That's *your* car?"

Another *you're stupid, Captain Obvious* look from GI Jane.

Crash said, "Happy to have you with us, Liberty."

Odette rejoined them. "And who *are* you exactly?"

"Liberty Masterson. I'm Devin's personal assistant."

A beat passed, and then she laughed in Liberty's face. "Right. So how long have you been *personally* assisting him? Since you met him in the bar last night?"

Liberty didn't respond. She merely stared at Odette until she backed down.

Devin stepped forward, taking his life in his hands

when he draped an arm over Liberty's shoulder. Not only did she look good—she smelled good. "Liberty is handling the venue logistics, my promotional appearances, and all that stuff I hate doin' and Crash is too busy to deal with since I'm headlining this time. So to keep everything streamlined, she's traveling on my bus."

Looks were exchanged. Eyebrows were lifted. Odette nudged Tay and muttered, "Personal assistant, my ass."

Then Devin introduced Liberty to his band.

"Nice to meet all of you. But if you'll excuse me, I have to get the rest of my shit on the bus so we have an on-time departure. Since keeping Devin on schedule is part of my job."

Her bright smile was totally fake; Devin choked back a snort.

Liberty reached for the straps on her bags, and Devin moved to help her. The damn woman was so stubborn that they played tug-of-war until he shouldered her aside. "Now, sweetheart," he said from gritted teeth, "what kind of a man would I be if stood by and watched you struggle with your luggage by yourself?"

She smiled—the devious one that made his stomach drop. "You'd be like every other man on the planet." She picked up the smaller bag and hoofed it to the bus.

Devin was so focused on the mesmerizing way her butt jiggled that he didn't budge until Crash elbowed him.

"Quit standing there and move it."

He snagged the handles and let out a grunt. Had she packed cannonballs in there? He trailed behind her, trying like hell—and failing miserably—to keep his eyes off her ass. So he nearly plowed into her when they entered the bus.

"Holy friggin' hell." Liberty had stopped in the living area and was gawking.

"Keep movin'. I've gotta get these bricks unloaded," he grumbled.

"Funny. Which bunk is mine?"

"Both. Since you're the only other passenger."

"Sweet. I wondered where I'd put everything."

Devin dragged the duffel bag the last few feet. "I figured you'd be the type to pack light, not drag four bags along."

"Guns and ammo take up a lot of room."

She had to be joking.

But the look on her face said she wasn't.

Devin pointed to the area below the first bunk. "There are locking drawers for all your firepower."

"Thanks." Liberty didn't ask for help hoisting her bags.

"All right, see you guys in Salt Lake because I don't plan on stopping," Crash said.

Liberty looked at Crash. "You're on the other bus?"

"I'm driving the other bus." He grinned. "How do you think I got my name?"

"I'm thanking the universe I'm not riding with you."

After Crash departed, Devin stood there like a dumbass, staring at her.

Of course she caught him staring. "What?"

"You look . . . different."

Her gaze sharpened. "You told me to look different, remember?"

"Yes, but I didn't think you'd look like this." His admiring, borderline-lustful gaze swept her body from head to toe and back up.

"Seriously? I get the slack-jawed response that Sandra Bullock got in *Miss Congeniality* after her makeover and there's no one around to see it?"

"And that's where the comparison ends, because there ain't nothin' congenial about you."

She blushed, but kept her stubborn chin lifted.

Feeling ornery, he didn't let it go. "I find the section of blue hair . . . interesting. Why'd you do it?"

"I swear a blue streak and thought my new, improved look should reflect that."

Devin laughed. "It worked. You look"—*fucking fantastic*—"incredible."

Her silvery eyes turned a dark, stormy gray. "It's a damn good thing you're not 'attracted to me in the least,' don't you agree?"

Now he looked away. That'd been an asshole thing to say. And the fact she'd overheard it? Now he knew why she'd given him the cold shoulder at the GSC offices. "Takes two to two-step, darlin'. You swore I'm not your type either."

Her startled expression indicated she'd forgotten that.

"Now we done with this who's-hot-and-who's-not sniping so I can show you the rest of the bus?"

"We're done."

"Come on."

Liberty was properly awed by their luxury traveling coach. "I spent so many years riding in the back of transport trucks and in Humvees, I doubt I'll get used to this. This place is way nicer than my apartment. It's a little surreal."

"For me too," he confessed. "Even after a dozen years in this business, I keep expecting I'll wake up and find it's all been a dream." Why had he told her something so personal? Now she probably thought he was even more of a pussy.

Yeah, you hauling her luggage proved you're one badass dude.

Three knocks sounded outside the door. "Just wanted to let you know we're taking off."

Liberty moved and offered her hand. "I'm Liberty, Devin's personal assistant."

"I'm Reg." The rotund guy in his midfifties shook her hand with much enthusiasm. "Happy to meet you, ma'am. If either of you needs something, hit the intercom switch. It'll turn on the light on my dashboard. Since I wear headphones, it's best that you approach me that way and not through the beer window. Better not to scare the dickens out of me and I end up wrecking the bus."

"Good point."

Devin watched as Liberty put away her groceries—every bit of it labeled. "You don't have to do that," he said when she added a big L to the side of the milk. "I ain't gonna steal your food."

"Sorry. Habit left over from military life."

"Why'd you bring your own food anyway?"

"Because when we're out, I have to eat where and when you do. But because we're in public, I'll be so busy watching the perimeter, I'll forget to eat. I make sure to have decent food available for when I have uninterrupted time." Then she pulled out her own one-cup coffeemaker.

Devin didn't know why that annoyed him.

Yes, you do. That means she won't be making coffee for you.

"Once you get settled we need to go over a few things," she said.

"I'm settled now. What's on your mind?"

"This job is unlike a normal job where I work twelve hours and then I'm off shift for twelve hours. I won't have a partner to relieve me. And it'd be unhealthy and unwise for me not to have any downtime. I certainly hope you don't expect me to work twenty-four hours a day for the next three months without a break."

"Of course not," he scoffed. "Don't forget I'm used to bein' alone on my bus, doin' what I want, when I want, with no distractions and no one to answer to."

"You're most protected when we're traveling, so I'll take my downtime when we're on the road. That'll give you the quiet time you need to work. I'll just hang out in my bunk, or I'll stay in the part of the bus that gives you the most privacy."

Devin nodded. "That'll actually work really well for me."

Relief crossed her face. "Good. But as soon as the bus stops, I'm with you at all times. No exceptions unless I'm handing you off to an event security team."

"Then what will you be doin'?"

"Limiting access to you."

He snagged a Red Bull from the refrigerator and kept his temper in check. "*Limiting access* meaning . . . keeping groupies away from me? Because we already discussed my conditions on that."

Liberty studied him. "And I said I didn't give a fuck who you fucked as long as they passed my safety parameters. Which are: none of the ladies can bring purses, handbags, or backpacks into your ready room; no more than two women at a time in your ready room. I will be stationed outside the door the entire time you're entertaining your . . . fans."

Was she fucking serious? She'd be listening outside the goddamn door?

She shook her finger at him. "I'm not a pervert, nor will I get off hearing you getting off with your groupies. But this is a nonnegotiable point, Devin."

"Fine. Whatever. Let's practice havin' separate downtime starting now. I'll be in my room. See you in Salt Lake."

FROM *NEW YORK TIMES*
BESTSELLING AUTHOR

LORELEI JAMES

THE BLACKTOP COWBOYS SERIES

Corralled
Saddled and Spurred
Wrangled and Tangled
One Night Rodeo
Turn and Burn

Praise for the series:

"Her sexy cowboys are to die for!"
—*New York Times* bestselling author Maya Banks

"Lorelei James knows how to write
one hot, sexy cowboy."
—*New York Times* bestselling author Jaci Burton

Available wherever books are sold or at
penguin.com

facebook.com/LoveAlwaysBooks

LORELEI JAMES

TURN AND BURN

A Blacktop Cowboys Novel

Tanna Barker is a world champion barrel racer.
But now, a rodeo injury has left the restless spitfire holed
up in Muddy Gap, unsure what her next move should be.

Veterinarian August Fletcher has always put his job first.
He's never found a woman who could handle his
on-the-road lifestyle. But when sassy, sexy Tanna blows
into town, he finally finds the woman of his fantasies.
How can Fletch prove that he's in it for the long haul...
and that their sizzling relationship is better than winning
any rodeo medal?

"[James's] sexy cowboys are to die for!"
—*New York Times* bestselling author Maya Banks

S0495